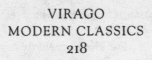

VIRAGO
MODERN CLASSICS
218

Edith Wharton

Edith Wharton was born in 1862, daughter of a distinguished and prosperous New York family. In 1885 she married a Boston socialite, Edward Robbins Wharton, and lived in Newport, Rhode Island. She became friendly with Henry James on her frequent trips to Europe. The Whartons' marriage was far from happy and she turned to writing, publishing her first novel, *The Valley of Decision*, in 1902. She was divorced in 1913 after she had moved to France permanently. By now, and for the rest of her life, she was publishing at least one book a year, her first popular success being *The House of Mirth* (1905). Her busy cosmopolitan and creative life was interrupted by energetic work during the 1914–18 war, for which she was awarded the Cross of the Legion d'Honneur and the Order of Leopold. In 1920 *The Age of Innocence* won the Pulitzer Prize; she was the first woman to receive a Doctorate of Letters from Yale University and in 1930 she became a member of the American Academy of Arts and letters. She died in France at the age of seventy-five.

Novels and short stories by Edith Wharton published by Virago

HUDSON RIVER BRACKETED

Edith
Wharton

With an Afterword by Marilyn French

All things make me glad, and sorry too
Charles Auchester

Published by VIRAGO PRESS 1986
20 Vauxhall Bridge Road, London SW1V 2SA

Reprinted 1995

First published in New York by D Appleton and Company 1929

Afterword copyright © Belles Lettres Inc 1986

The right of Edith Wharton to be identified as the author of this
work has been asserted in accordance with the Copyright
Designs and Patents Act 1988

A CIP catalogue record for this book is available from the British Library

Printed and bound in Great Britain by
Cox & Wyman Ltd, Reading, Berkshire

To

A. J. H. S.

A. J. Downing, the American landscape architect, in his book on Landscape Gardening (published in 1842) divides the architectural styles into the Grecian, Chinese, Gothic, the Tuscan, or Italian villa, style, and the Hudson River Bracketed.

BOOK I

✄ I ✄

By the time he was nineteen Vance Weston had graduated from the College of Euphoria, Illinois, where his parents then lived, had spent a week in Chicago, invented a new religion, and edited for a few months a college magazine called *Getting There,* to which he had contributed several love poems and a series of iconoclastic essays. He had also been engaged for a whole week to the inspirer of the poems, a girl several years older than himself called Floss Delaney, who was the somewhat blown-upon daughter of an unsuccessful real estate man living in a dejected outskirt of the town.

Having soared to these heights, and plumbed these depths, it now remained to young Weston to fix upon the uses to which his varied aptitudes and experiences could most advantageously be put.

Of all the events so far befalling him, none seemed to Vance Weston as important as having invented a new religion. He had been born into a world in which everything had been, or was being, renovated, and it struck him as an anomaly that all the religions he had heard of had been in existence ever since he could remember; that is, at least sixteen years. This seemed to him the more unaccountable because religion, of one sort or another, seemed to play a considerable, if rather spasmodic or intermittent, part in the lives of most of the people he knew, and because, from the first dawn of consciousness, he had heard everybody adjuring everybody else not to get into a rut, but to go ahead with the times, as behoved all good Americans.

The evolution of his own family was in its main lines that of most of the families he had known. Since the time of Mrs. Weston's marriage, when Grandma was teaching school at Pruneville, Nebraska, and the whole family depended on her earnings, till now, when she and Grandfather took their ease in an eight-room Colonial cottage in a suburb of Euphoria, and people came from as far as Chicago to consult Mr. Weston about real estate matters, the family curve had been continually upward. Lorin Weston, who had wandered out to Pruneville to try and pick up a job on the local newspaper, had immediately seen the real estate possibilities of that lamentable community, had put his last penny into a bit of swampy land near the future railway station, got out at a big rise when the railway came, and again plumped his all on another lot of land near where his mother-in-law had found out that the new high school was to be built. Then there had come a stagnant period in the development of Pruneville, and Mr. Weston had moved his wife and young family to Hallelujah, Mo., where he had repeated the same experiment with increasing profit. While he was there, a real estate man from Advance came over to take a look round, talked to Weston about Advance, and awakened his curiosity. To Advance the family went, compensated by a bigger and better house for the expense of having to leave Hallelujah. At Advance the Weston son and heir was born, and named after his birthplace, which had deserved well of Mr. Weston, since he was able, when Vance was nine or ten, to leave there for Euphoria, buy up nearly the whole of the Pig Lane side of the town, turn it into the Mapledale suburb, and build himself a house with lawn, garage, sleeping porch and sun parlour, which was photographed for the architectural papers, and made Mrs. Weston the envy of the Alsop Avenue church sewing circle. Even Grandma Scrimser, who had never been much of a hand at making or keeping money, and was what the minister of the Alsop Avenue church called "idealistic," did not question the importance of material prosperity, or the value of Mr. Weston's business "brightness," and somewhere in the big lumber room of her mind had found a point where otherworldliness and "pep" lay down together in amity.

This being so—and such phrases as "back number," "down and out," "out of the running," and the like having never been used in young Vance's hearing save in a pejorative sense—he wondered how it was that the enlightened millions, with whom it was a sign of "pep" and prosperity to go in for almost annual turnovers in real estate, stocks, automobiles, wives and husbands, were content to put up year after year with the same religion, or religions rather, since nearly everybody he knew had a different one.

Vance Weston, in truth, could not dissociate stability from stagnation, any more in religion than in business. All the people he had heard of who hadn't got a move on at the right minute, in whatever direction, were down and out. Even the most high-minded among the ministers admitted this, and emphasized religion as the greatest known shortcut to Success. (If you'd come and join their Sunday evening classes for young men, and subscribe to *Zion's Spotlight,* you'd find out why.) Yet, in spite of this, nobody had managed, in Vance Weston's lifetime, to evolve a new religion, and they were all still trying to catch a new generation with the old bait.

Thinking about religion ran in Vance's family—at least on his mother's side. Grandma Scrimser had always cared about it more than about anything else. At sixty-five she was still a magnificent-looking woman, rather like pictures of a German prima donna made up as a Walkyrie; with stormy black eyebrows, short yellowish-white hair (years before

the young ones began to be bobbed), and a broad uncertain
frame which reminded Vance (after he had acquired lights
on modern art) of a figure by an artist who had genius but
didn't know how to draw.

As a girl Grandma was said to have been gloriously
beautiful; and Vance could well believe it. Indeed, she
made no secret of it herself—why should she, when she regarded it only as an inconvenient accident, a troublesome
singularity, and (she had been known to admit in confidential moments) an obstacle to Grandpa Scrimser's advance to
Perfection? Perfection was Grandma's passion—ladies were
Grandpa's. While his wife was young her beauty might have
served to circumscribe his yearnings if only she had chosen
to make use of it. But the idea of beauty as a gift to be used,
trained, exercised, and directed was to her not so much im-
moral as unintelligible. She regarded herself as afflicted with
a Greek nose, masses of wavy amber hair, and a richly glowing dusky complexion, as other women might have borne
the cross of a birthmark or a crooked spine. She could not
understand "what people saw in it," or in the joys to which
it was the golden gateway. As to these joys she professed a
contemptuous incredulity. What she wanted was to reform
the world; and beauty and passion were but hindrances to
her purpose. She wanted to reform everything—it didn't
particularly matter what: cooking, marriage, religion (of
course religion), dentistry, saloons, corsets—even Grandpa.
Grandpa used to complain that in cooking she had never
got very far on the way to Perfection—only just far enough
to give him dyspepsia. But since she would not indulge his
conjugal sentiments unduly he was grateful that at least the
pursuit of Perfection left her little time to investigate his
private affairs; so that, on the whole, the marriage was ac-
counted a happy one, and the four children born of it were
taught to revere both parents, though for different reasons.
Grandma, of course, was revered for being a mother in Is-

rael; Grandpa for having once made a successful real estate
deal, and for being the best Fourth of July orator anywhere
in Drake County. They were a magnificent-looking couple,
too, and when Old Home Weeks began to be inaugurated
throughout the land, Mr. and Mrs. Scrimser were in great
demand in tableaux representing The Old Folks at Home,
Mrs. Scrimser spinning by the kitchen hearth, and Grandpa
(with his new set removed, to bring out his likeness to
George Washington) leaning on a silver-headed crutch
stick, his nutcracker chin reposing on a spotless stock. But
Grandma liked better figuring as the Pioneer Wife in a log
cabin, with Grandpa (the new set in place again) garbed in
a cowpuncher's rig, aiming his shotgun through a crack in
the shutters, and the children doing Indian war whoops behind the scenes. "I couldn't ever have sat still long enough
to spin the house linen, like the woman in that Lady Washington picture; but I guess I'd have been a real good pioneer's wife," she explained, not unboastfully.

"You've always kept house as if you was one," Grandpa
would grumble, pushing away his tepid coffee and shrivelled bacon; and Mrs. Scrimser would answer: "I'm sorry
your breakfast don't just suit you today, father; but I guess
it won't set you back much on the path to Eternity. I had to
let the hired girl go to that camp meeting last night, and
they always come back from their meetings as limp as rags,
so I had her cook your bacon before she went."

"Oh, Christ," Grandpa ejaculated; and his daughter,
Mrs. Lorin Weston, shook her head severely at little Vance,
as much as to say that he was not to listen when Grandpa
talked like that, or, alternatively, that Grandpa hadn't really
said what little Vance thought he had.

Grandma Scrimser was of course more interested than
anyone in the idea of Vance's new religion. In the first
place, she agreed with him that a new one was needed,
though she still thought the Rock of Ages was the best foun-

dation any religion could have, and hoped Vance wouldn't make them give up singing old hymns. It took some time to make her understand that perhaps there wouldn't be any more hymns, or any sort of formal worship, but just a mystical communion between souls to whom the same revelation had been vouchsafed. "You be careful now, Vance, how you're mystical," she chid him; "time and again I've known that to end in a baby." But as Vance developed his theory he had the sense that she could understand what he was talking about. Her education had not prepared her to follow him beyond the simply phase of pious ejaculation and contrition.

Vance's parents were totally unaffected by old Mrs. Scrimser's transcendental yearnings. When Grandpa Scrimser's digestion gave out, or he needed a change, he always packed his grip and moved in from the suburb where he and Grandma now lived to spend a week with the Westons. His other daughter, who had inherited her mother's neglected beauty, inherited also her scorn of comfort and her zeal for reform, and in the cause of temperance and high thinking dragged after her from one lecture platform to another a dyspeptic husband who was dying of a continual diet of soda biscuits and canned food. But Mrs. Lorin Weston, a small round-faced woman with a resolute mouth, had always stayed at home, looked after her children, fed her husband well, and, whenever he made a "turnover," bought a picture or a piano cover to embellish one or the other of their successive dwellings. She took a wholesome interest in dress, had herself manicured once a week after they moved to Euphoria, and by the time they had built their new house on Mapledale Avenue had saved up enough to have a sun parlour with palms and a pink gramophone, which was the envy of the neighbourhood.

As for Lorin Weston, a dry smallish man, no taller than his wife, he was like one of the shrivelled Japanese flowers which suddenly expand into bloom when put in water. Mr. Weston's natural element was buying and selling real estate; and he could not understand how any normal human being could exist in any other, or talk about anything else. If pressed, he would probably have admitted that an organized society necessitated the existence of policemen, professors, lawyers, judges, dentists, and even ministers of religion (to occupy the women: he had read Ingersoll, and his own views were Voltairean). But though he might have conceded as much theoretically, he could not conceive how, in practice, any sane man could be in anything but real estate. As in the case of all geniuses, the exercise of his gift came to him so naturally that he could no more imagine anyone earning money in other ways than he could imagine living without breathing. He did indeed take a subordinate interest in house building, because people who intended to build houses had first to buy land, and also because if you have the nerve to run up a likely-looking little house on an unpromising lot of land, you may be able to sell the house and lot together for a considerably bigger sum than they cost you, and even to start a real estate boom in soil where nothing of the sort has ever grown. Inspired by such considerations, he developed a pretty taste in suburban architecture, and was often consulted by builders and decorators as to some fancy touch in hall or sleeping porch, while Mrs. Weston's advice was invaluable in regard to kitchen and linen closet. Between them they served their trade like a religion, Mrs. Weston putting into it her mother's zeal for souls and Mr. Weston making clients come to the suburbs as his mother-in-law made them come to Jesus.

The Mapledale suburb, which was entirely Mr. Weston's creation, was Euphoria's chief source of pride, and always the first thing shown to distinguished visitors after the Alsop Building, the Dental College, and the Cedarcrest cemetery; and as success was the only criterion of beauty known to young Vance he took it for granted that whatever his father said was beautiful must be so. Nevertheless, there were moments when he felt the need to escape from the completeness of the Mapledale house, and go out to Crampton where Grandpa and Grandma Scrimser had settled down in a house lent to them rent-free by their son-in-law in the hope that they might help to "open up" Crampton. So far this hope had not been realized, and Crampton remained a bedraggled village, imperfectly joined up with the expanding Euphoria; but Lorin Weston could afford to wait, and was glad to do his parents-in-law a good turn.

Mrs. Weston did not often go to Crampton; especially did she avoid doing so when her sister Saidie Toler was there. The road to Crampton was so bad that it knocked the Chevrolet all to pieces, and besides Mrs. Weston really could not bear to see a good eight-room house, that people might have been so comfortable in, going all to pieces because Grandma would choose her help for their religious convictions and their plainness (she didn't trust Grandpa), and because she and Saidie were always rushing about to religious meetings, or to lectures on Sanitation (if she'd only looked at her own drains!), or on Diet (when you'd eaten Grandma's food!), or whatever the newest religious, moral, or medical fad was. Generally, too, there would be some long-haired fanatic there, holding forth about the last "new" something or other in religion or morals, as eloquently as Mrs. Weston herself discoursed on refrigerators and electric cookers. These prophets got on Mrs. Weston's nerves, and so did Saidie, with her slovenly blonde beauty, already bedraggled as if she left it out overnight, the way careless people do their cars. Mrs. Weston admired her mother, and felt, in a somewhat resentful way, the domination of her powerful presence; but she hated the confusion that Grandma lived in, and preferred to invite the Scrimsers and Saidie to Sunday dinner in Mapledale Avenue, and feel they were being impressed by her orderly establishment, and the authority of Mr. Weston's conversation.

Vance Weston did not much fancy his grandmother's house, or her food either; the whole place, compared with his own home, was retrograde and uncomfortable. Yet he had an unaccountable liking for the rutty lanes of Crampton, its broken-down fences, and the maple-shaded meadow by the river. He liked the way the trees overhung the Scrimser yard, the straggling lilacs, and the neglected white rose over the porch. And he was always stimulated, sometimes amused, and sometimes a little awed and excited, by Grandma Scrimser's soaring talk and Grandpa's racy commentaries. The prophets did not impress him, and his aunt Saidie he positively disliked; but he loved the old couple, and did not wonder that Euphoria still called on them to figure at national celebrations. The town had nothing else as grand to show.

≫ II ≪

CRAMPTON, unfinished, sulky, and indifferent, continued to languish outside the circle of success. The trolley ran out there now, but few settlers had followed it. Yet Lorin Weston, who was by common consent the brightest realtor in Drake County, still believed in Crampton, and kept up the hopes of the investors he had lured there. On the strength of his belief, a row of cheap cottages was springing up along the road to Euphoria, and already the realtor's eye saw garages and lawn mowers in the offing.

One warm spring day, Vance Weston strode along between the ruts, past squares of Swedish market-gardening and raw pastures waiting for the boom. These were the days when he liked the expectancy of Crampton better than the completeness of Euphoria—days of the sudden prairie spring, when the lilacs in his grandmother's dooryard were bursting, and the maples by the river fringing themselves with rosy keys, when the earth throbbed with renewal and the heavy white clouds moved across the sky like flocks of teeming ewes. In a clump of trees near the road a bird began over and over its low tentative song, and in the ditches a glossy-leaved weed, nameless to Vance, spangled the mud with golden chalices. He felt a passionate desire to embrace the budding earth and everything that stirred and swelled in it. He was irritated by the fact that he did not know the name of the bird, or of the yellow flowers. "I should like to give everything its right name, and to know why that name *was* the right one," he thought; the names of things had always seemed to him as closely and mysteriously a part of them as his skin or eyelashes of himself. What was the use of all he had been taught in college if the commonest objects on this familiar earth were so remote and inexplicable? There were botany manuals, and scientific books on the shapes and action of clouds; but what he wanted to get at was something deeper, something which must have belonged to flowers and clouds before ever man was born to dissect them. Besides, he wasn't in the mood for books, with this spring air caressing him. . . .

A little way down a lane to his right stood the tumble-down house in which Harrison Delaney, Floss's father, lived. Though Harrison Delaney, like Mr. Weston, was in the real estate business, his career had differed in every respect from his rival's, and Mr. Weston had been known to say, in moments of irritation, that the fact of Delaney's living at Crampton was enough to keep the boom back. Harrison Delaney was in fact one of the Awful Warnings which served to flavour the social insipidity of thousands of Euphorias. There wasn't a bright businessman in the place who couldn't put his finger on the exact causes of his failure. It had all come, they pointed out, of his never being on the spot, missing real estate transactions, missing business opportunities, deals of every sort and kind—just sort of over-sleeping himself whenever there was anything special to get up for.

Almost every family in Vance Weston's social circle could point to an Awful Warning of this type; but few were as complete, as singularly adapted for the purpose, as Harrison Delaney at fifty. You felt, the minute you set eyes on him, that nothing more would ever happen to him. He had wound his life up, as a man might wind up an unsuccessful business, and was just sitting round with the unexpectant look of a stockbroker on a country vacation, out of reach of the ticker. There—that was the very expression! Harrison Delaney always looked as if he was out of reach of the ticker. Only he wasn't worried or fretful, as most men are in such a case—he was just indifferent. No matter what happened he was indifferent. He said he guessed his making a fuss wouldn't alter things—it never had. So, when everybody was talking about Floss's going with that married drummer from Chicago, who turned up at Euphoria every so often in the year, and hired a car, and went off with her on long expeditions—well, her father just acted as if he didn't notice; and when the Baptist minister called, and dropped a hint to him, Harrison Delaney said he supposed it was Nature speaking, and he didn't believe he was the size to interfere with Nature, and anyhow he thought maybe one of these days the drummer would get a divorce and marry Floss—which of course he never did.

It was in going out to see his grandparents that Vance had first met Floss Delaney. That was before the trolley was running. Their bicycles used to flash past each other along the rutty road, and one day he found her down in the mud, with a burst tire and a sprained ankle, and helped her home. At first it was not the girl who interested him, but her father. Vance knew all about Delaney, the byword of Euphoria; but something in the man's easy indifferent manner, his way of saying: "Oh, come in, Weston, won't you?" instead of hailing his visitor as "Vance," his few words of thanks for the help rendered to his daughter, the sound of his voice, his very intonation—all differentiated him from the bright businessman he had so signally failed to be, and made Vance feel that failure also had its graces. Euphoria, he knew, felt this, however obscurely; it had to admit that he had the manners and address of a man born to make his mark. Even when he was finally down and out he was still put on committees to receive distinguished visitors. Somebody would lend him a black coat and somebody else a new

hat, because there was a general though unexpressed sentiment that on such occasions he was more at ease than their
most successful men, including even the president of the
college and the minister of the Alsop Avenue church. But all
this could not do away with the fact that he was a failure,
and could serve the rising community of Euphoria only as
the helots served the youth of Sparta. A fellow ought to be
up on Society and Etiquette, and how to behave at a banquet, and what kind of collar to wear, and what secret societies to belong to; but the real business of life was to keep
going, to get there—and "There" was where money was, always and exclusively.

These were the axioms that Vance had been brought up
on; but when, after Floss's accident, he dropped in from
time to time to ask how she was, he found a strange attrac-
tion in listening to Harrison Delaney's low, slightly drawling
speech, and noticing the words he used—always good English words, rich and expressive, with hardly a concession to
the local vernacular, or the passing epidemics of slang.

It was only when Floss began to get about again that
she exercised her full magic. One day when Vance called he
found her alone; and after that, instead of seeking out Harrison Delaney, he avoided him, and the pair met outside of
the house. . . . His body and soul still glowed with the
memory of it. But there was no use in thinking of that now.
She'd been going with another fellow all the time . . . he
knew it . . . and how she'd lied to him! He'd been a fool;
and luckily it was all over. But he still averted his eyes from
the house down the lane, where, only a few short months
ago, he used to hang about after dark till she came out. On
summer evenings they would go down to the maples by the
river; there was a clump of bushes where you could lie hidden, breast to breast, and watch the moon and the white
cloud reflections sail by, and the constellations march across
the sky on their invisible bridges. . . .

The Scrimsers' house had a Colonial porch, an open fireplace in the hall, and a view over the river. The door yard was always rather untidy; Mrs. Scrimser had planting plans, and meant some day to carry them out. But she would first have had to cut down a lot of half-dead bushes, and there never seemed to be anybody to do it, what with Grandpa's sciatica, and the hired man's coming so irregularly, and Grandma being engaged in tidying up everybody else's door yard, materially and morally.

When Vance reached the porch she was sitting there in her rocking chair, her blown hair tossed back from her broad yellowish forehead, and her spectacles benevolently surveying the landscape. A lawn mower straddled the path and she called out to her grandson: "It's the hired man's day, but he's gone to a big camp meeting at Swedenville, and your grandfather began to cut the grass so that we'd have everything looking nice when your father and mother come out on Sunday; but then he remembered he had an appointment at Mandel's grocery, so I don't see how it'll get done."

"Well, perhaps I'll do it when I cool off," said Vance, sitting down.

They all knew about Grandpa's appointments. As soon as he was asked to put his hand to a domestic job he either felt a twinge of sciatica, or remembered that he'd promised to meet a man at Mandel's grocery, or at the Elkington Hotel at Euphoria.

Mrs. Scrimser turned her eloquent gray eyes on her grandson. "Don't a day like this almost make you feel as if you could get to God right through that blue up there?" she said, pointing heavenward with a big knotted hand. She had forgotten already about the abandoned lawn mower, and the need of tidying up. Whenever she saw her grandson all the groping aspirations in her unsatisfied nature woke and trembled into speech. But Vance did not care to hear about

her God, who, once you stripped Him of her Biblical ver-
biage, was merely the Supreme Moralist of a great educa-
tional system in which Mrs. Scrimser held an important job.

"No, I don't feel as if anything would take me near
God. And I don't exactly want to get near Him anyhow;
what I want is to get way out beyond Him, out somewhere
where He won't look any bigger than a speck, and the god
in *me* can sort of walk all round Him."

Mrs. Scrimser glowed responsively: all the audacities
enchanted her. "Oh, I see what you mean, Vanny," she cried.
All her life she had always been persuaded that she saw
what people meant; and the conviction had borne her tri-
umphantly from one pinnacle of credulity to another. But
her grandson smiled away her enthusiasm. "No, you don't;
you don't see *my* god at all; I mean, the god in me."

His grandmother flushed up in her disappointment.
"Why don't I, Vanny? I know all about the Immanence of
God," she objected, almost resentfully.

Vance shook his head. It wasn't much fun arguing with
his grandmother about God, but it was better than hearing
eternally about new electric cleaners from his mother, or
about real estate from Mr. Weston, or the reorganization of
school grades from his sister Pearl. Vance respected effi-
ciency, and even admired it; but of late he had come to feel
that as a diet for the soul it was deficient in nourishment.
He wondered that Mrs. Weston, who was such an authority
on diet, had never thought of applying the moral equivalent
of the vitamin test to the life they all led at Mapledale. He
had an idea they were starving to death there without
knowing it. But old Mrs. Scrimser at least knew that she was
hungry, and his mind wandered back more indulgently to
what she was saying.

"The trouble is," he began, groping about in his limited
vocabulary, "I don't seem to want anybody else's God. I just
want to give mine full swing." And at this point he forgot

his grandmother's presence, and his previous experience of her incomprehension, and began to develop his own dream for his own ears. "And I don't even want to know what *he* is—not by reasoning him out, I mean. People didn't have to wait to learn about oxygen, and the way the lungs work, before they began to breathe, did they? And that's the way I feel about what I call *my* god—the sort of something in me that was there before I'd ever thought about it, and that stretches out and out, and takes in the stars and the ages, and very likely doesn't itself know why or how. What I want is to find out how to release that god, fly him up like a kite into the Infinite, way beyond creeds and formulas, and try to relate him to all the other . . . the other currents . . . that seem to be circling round you, a day like this . . . so that you get caught up in them yourself . . . and carried beyond Time and Space, and Good and Bad, to where the whole blamed thing is boiling over . . . Oh, hell take it, *I* don't know!" he groaned, and flung his head back despairingly.

Mrs. Scrimser listened, beaming, benedictory, her arms extended. "Oh Vanny, when you talk like that I do feel your call so clearly! You surely have inherited your grandfather's gift for speaking. You could fill the Alsop Avenue church clear away under the gallery, right now. 'The boy preacher' —they can often reach right down into the soul where the older men can't get a hearing. Don't you think, dear, such a gift ought to make you decide to go straight to Jesus?" She lifted her clasped hands with a *"Nunc dimittis"* gesture full of devotional sublimity. "If I could only hear you in the pulpit once I'd lay me down so peacefully," she murmured.

Vance's dream dropped with a crash to the floor of the porch, and lay there between them in rainbow splinters. The Alsop Avenue church! The pulpit! The ministry! This familiar way of talking about "Jesus" as if He were somebody waiting round the corner at Mandel's grocery for a

telephone call—and this woman, who had listened for forty
years to her husband's windy eloquence and sanctimonious
perfidies, and who was still full of faith in the power of
words and the magic attributes of Biblical phraseology! It
almost made Vance hate the Bible to hear her, though its
haunting words and cadences were the richest of his mental
possessions. . . . But why had he again let himself go, trying to carry her up with him to the dizzy heights of speculation, as if some tiny winged insect should struggle to lift the
lawn mower down there in the path? Vance looked sulkily
away at the straggling unkempt distances from which she
had managed to brush all the magic, so that where he had
seen flowers and heard birds he now beheld only a starved
horizon imprisoned behind crooked telegraph poles, and
partly blotted out by Mandel's grocery.

"Vance—I haven't said anything to offend you?" his
grandmother questioned, laying her big hand on his.

He shook his head. "No. Only you don't understand."

She took off her moist spectacles and wiped them.
"Well, I guess God created women so's to give the men
somebody to say that to," she remarked, with a philosophic
smile.

Her grandson smiled also. He never failed to appreciate
her humour; but today he was still quivering from his vain
effort at expression, and her misunderstanding of it; and he
had nothing more to say.

"Well, I guess I'll go along," he said, getting up.

Mrs. Scrimser never argued with her own family, and
she walked with him in silence down the path and halted at
the barricade of the mowing-machine. From there they
could look across a few vacant lots and, dodging Mandel's
grocery, bathe their eyes in the liquid gold of the sunset beyond the river.

"I used to think heaven was down *there*—on summer
nights!" the boy broke out, pointing toward the budding

maples by the river. In his own ears his words sounded sardonic, incredibly old and embittered; but the mention of heaven could evoke no such sensations in his grandmother's soul.

"I guess heaven is wherever we love Nature and our fellow beings enough," she said, laying her arm about his shoulder. It occurred to neither of them to remove the mower from the path, and they parted there, casually but fondly, as the habit was in Euphoria households, Vance bestriding the machine while his grandmother, arrested by it, stood gazing after him. "Only remember that, Vanny—that Love is everywhere!" she called after him. Large and full of benediction she stood between the lilac bushes and waved farewell.

Vance walked on in a fog of formless yearnings. His own words had loosened them, as the spring air and the yellow blossoms in the ditch had loosened his words. Twilight fell and the old spell of Crampton fell with it. He passed by the lane that led to Harrison Delaney's, but when he came to the field path descending to the river he paused, caught back into his early dream. Everything which had bound him to that scene was over and done with—he had served his sentimental apprenticeship and paid the price. But it was hard, at nineteen, and on a spring evening, to know this, and to feel himself forever excluded from the fellowship of the young and the happy. He supposed other fellows had been through it and survived—in books they told you so. But this evening his soul was like a desert.

He'd never looked at a girl since Floss—never meant to. Taken it out in writing poetry instead. Sometimes, for a few moments, doing that almost replaced her caresses, seemed to bring her as close as if words were warm and palpable like flesh. Then that illusion passed, and he was out again in the desert. . . . Once in a while, by way of experi-

ment, he would give himself a kind of mental pinch where
the ache had been, just to be sure he felt nothing—literally
nothing. But when the trees by the river budded, and the
buds were black against a yellow sky, the ache would spring
back and catch him in the heart as you see lumbago suddenly catch a man between the shoulders. For a long time
he stood gazing across the field and remembering how he
used to go and hide down by the river, and spy out through
the bushes for Floss. Or, oftener, she'd be there first, and
her strong young arms would pull him down to her. . . .
There was no danger now in remembering these things.
She had left Euphoria; he had heard she had a job in a department store at Dakin, on the other side of Chicago. He
suspected his father of having managed that. . . . The
scene of their brief passion was deserted, and for him it
would always remain so. That was life, he supposed. His
bitterness gradually passed; he remembered her kisses and
forgave her. Leaning on the fence, he pulled out a cigarette
and thought big manly thoughts about her, and about
Woman in general.

"Well," he interrupted himself suddenly, "I don't suppose you expected to be the only fellow to meet a girl down
under those bushes, did you, Vance Weston?" The remark
was provoked by the sight of a man sauntering across lots to
the edge of the maple grove. Even at that distance he had
the air of someone who would as soon not be seen, but is
doing all he can not to betray the fact. The sight instantly altered Vance's mood, and he continued to lean on the fence,
puffing ironically at his cigarette and whistling a vaudeville
tune. The light was growing faint, tht man was almost too
far away to be recognized; but as he approached, Vance
saw a tall spare figure moving with the jauntiness of an elderly man trying to look young who is jerked back at every
step by his stiff joints. The gait was familiar; so, as the figure
drew still nearer, was the frock coat flung open from a

crumpled waistcoat, and the sombrero brim of the felt hat. Presently he lifted the hat and wiped his forehead; and the last slant of sunset lit up his swarthy face, the dominant nose and weak handsome mouth, and the white-and-black mane tossed back from his forehead. Vance, amused and vaguely curious, stood staring at the apparition of his grandfather.

You never could tell about Grandpa—they all knew it in the family, and put up with the fact as you put up with the weather. Still, to come on him here, slinking along on the edge of the grove, and mopping his forehead as if he had been running to catch the trolley; well, it was funny. Something at once dashing and furtive about his air made Vance remember an occasion when, as a small boy, he had gone Christmas shopping with his mother, and they had run into Grandpa, mopping his forehead in the same way, and hurrying toward them round the corner of a certain street that Vance and his schoolmates were always forbidden to play in. The little boy had instantly guessed that something was wrong when his mother, instead of exclaiming: "Why, there's Grandpa!" had abruptly remembered that, good gracious, she'd never ordered the yeast from Sproul's Bakery, and had jerked Vance back there without seeming to notice Mr. Scrimser. Such subterfuges are signposts on the road to enlightenment.

Vance continued to smile sardonically at the remembrance of this episode, and the thought of how far behind him his guileless infancy lay. For a moment he felt inclined to hail his grandfather; then something about the old man's air and movements made him decide to turn away. "Guess it's about time to step round to Sproul's for the yeast," he chuckled to himself; but as he averted his glance it was arrested by the approach of another figure. The light was failing fast and Vance was a good hundred yards from the river; but in the thickest dusk, and at a greater distance,

he would have known the quick movements, the light outline, of the girl slipping through the trees toward Mr. Scrimser. . . . "But she isn't here . . . she isn't here . . . I
know she isn't!" stormed through the boy in a rush of useless
denial. He stood rooted to the earth while everything she
had ever been to him, every look and intonation, every scent
and breath and touch that had bound him to her, and made
them one, flooded over him in fiery remembrance. He had
never been able to imagine what excruciating physical pain
was like, the kind you felt when you were smashed under a
train, or torn by a whirling engine in a factory—but he
knew, he found out in the glare of that blinding instant, that
when the soul is smitten deeply enough it seems to become
one with the body, to share all the body's capacity for
suffering a distinct and different anguish in each nerve and
muscle. He saw—or thought he saw—the two figures come
together in the dimness, just where, so often, he had caught
Floss Delaney to his first embrace; then he stumbled away,
unseeing. A trolley swung along, making for the lights of
Euphoria. He hailed it and got on board.

❧ III ❧

THE FAMILY were at supper. The dining room was exquisitely neat. The Lithuanian girl shoved the dishes in hot
through the slide and set them down on the table without
noise: Grandpa always said his youngest daughter could
have taught an Eskimo to wait on table. The faces under
the hanging lamp reflected something of the comfort and
satisfaction of the scene. Pearl had got an advance of salary,
and Mr. Weston had put through the sale of an old business
building at a price even he had not hoped for.

"I guess we'll take that vacation at the Lakes you girls
are always talking about," he said, and glanced about the
table for approval. But Mrs. Weston wrinkled her mouth
(she frowned with her mouth as other people do with their
foreheads), and said, wouldn't they better let the Lakes
alone this year and put in that new electric cold-storage
affair the drummer had called about day before yesterday,
and taken the measures for? He said they'd get it at a big
reduction if they gave the order now, and paid down a third
of the amount when he called back.

Pearl, the eldest daughter, who was small and brisk,
with a mouth like her mother's, said, well, she didn't much
care, only she'd like to know sometime soon what they'd decided, because if they didn't go to the Lakes she thought
she'd go camping with a friend at the School of Hope, in
Sebaska County; but the younger, Mae, who was taller and
less compact, with an uncertain promise of prettiness, mur-

24

mured that the other girls' folks all got away to the Lakes for August, and she didn't see why they shouldn't without such a fuss.

"Well, we've got you and Vance to fuss about, for one thing," Mrs. Weston replied. "Here you are, seventeen and nineteen, and not knowing yet how you're going to earn your living, or when you're going to begin."

Mae, in an irritated tone, rejoined that she knew well enough what she wanted to do; she wanted to go to Chicago and study art, like Leila Duxberry—

"Oh, Chicago! There'll be an art school right here next year, in connection with the college, just as good, and nothing like as expensive," said Mrs. Weston, who was always jealous of any signs of independence in her flock.

Mae shrugged, and cast her eyes toward the ceiling, as if to say that conversation on any lower level had no further interest for her.

Mr. Weston drummed on the table, and took a second helping of pickles. "Well, and what about Advance G. Weston, Esq.? Got any idea what *you* planning to specialize in, sonny?"

Vance opened his lips to answer. He had always known that his father wanted him to be a real estate man, not only wanted but meant him to be, indeed could not conceive of any other career for him, whatever the women said, or the boy's own view of his vocation was, any more than a king on a well-established throne could picture any job but kingship for his heir. The *Free Speaker* had once headlined Mr. Weston as the King of Drake County Realtors and Mr. Weston had accepted the title with a modest dignity. Vance knew all this; but the time for temporizing was over. He meant to answer his father then and there, and to say: "I guess I'd better go on a newspaper." For he had made up his mind to be a writer, and if possible a poet, and he had never heard of any way to Parnassus save that which led through the columns of the daily press, and ranged from baseball reports to the exposure of business scandals. But as he was about to speak, something hot and choking welled up into his throat, and the brightly lit definite table with the dull definite faces about it suddenly melted into a mist.

He pushed back his chair uncertainly. "I've got a headache—I guess I'll go upstairs," he muttered to the whirling room. He saw the surprise in their faces, and became aware of Pearl vaguely detaching herself from the blur and moving toward him, anxious, inquisitive; but he pushed her back, gasping: "All right . . . don't fuss . . . Oh, just leave me alone, can't you, all of you?" and got himself out of the room, and upstairs to his own, where he fell on his bed in a storm of dry sobs without a tear. . . .

Two of the doctors said it was a malarial microbe; possibly he'd been bitten by an anopheles mosquito in those marshy fields out toward Crampton, or down by the river. The third doctor, a bacteriologist from the college laboratory, thought it was walking typhoid, and he might likely as not have picked it up drinking the river water, if he was in the habit of going out to Crampton—family living there? Oh, that it?—Well, the Crampton water was rank poison; they had a good many cases of the same sort every spring and summer. . . . That doctor was never sent for again; and the family noticed that Lorin Weston suddenly began to move once more in the matter of carrying the Euphoria water out to Crampton. The question was always a troublesome one; whenever it was raised it stirred up a hornet's nest of other matters connected with municipal and state politics, questions of the let-sleeping-dogs-lie sort; and it had been a relief to Mrs. Weston when her husband, the previous year, told her he had asked the Euphoria *Free Speaker* (the leading morning paper) to drop the Crampton Water Supply Investigation. The *Free Speaker* had done so, and the next week Mr. Weston had bought a new Buick, and remarked at table that he didn't know any greater waste of time than muckraking. Now the affair was all to be gone into again, and Mrs. Weston knew it was because of what that other doctor had said, the one who had not been asked to come back. But she kept her own counsel, as she always did where business or politics were concerned, and nursed her son, and told her husband not to be so nervous or he'd only make the boy worse. . . .

Vance caught a confused echo of this through the blur of those indistinct weeks—weeks of incessant tossings of the body, incessant gropings of the mind. The doctors said if it had been anybody but Mrs. Weston they'd have taken him right off to the fever ward of the hospital; but with Mrs. Weston they knew everything would be done just as well as if he'd been in the ward, that the disinfection would be attended to, and the fever chart accurately kept, and folks not allowed to barge in. . . . So he had been moved into the sepulchral spare room, which was the pride of Mrs. Weston's heart because nobody had ever inhabited it, or ever would, and because it had taken the place of that awful sanctuary of her youth, the unused "best parlour."

A month passed before Vance was strong enough to be moved back into his own room. He looked at it with alien eyes. He had been "down to normal" for some days, and that morning the doctors had told Mrs. Weston that she could unpin the chart from the foot of the bed, and give him a bit of broiled chicken. He ate it hungrily, and then lay back in the unutterable weariness of recovery.

He had begun to see the family again: his father first, awkward and inarticulate with the awe of a sorrow just escaped; Pearl concise and tactful, Mae as self-engrossed as ever, and having to be dragged away by her mother because she stayed too long and talked too much. Grandma was laid up with rheumatism, but sent messages and fresh eggs, and the announcement that she had been in constant communication with one of her household prophets, who was conducting a "Spirit of Service" meeting at the neighbouring town of Swedenborg, and that Vance had been remembered there daily in the prayers of the assistants.

Vance listened to it all as though he were dead and the family chatter came to him through his mound in the Cedarcrest cemetery. He had not known for how long, after recovery from illness, the mind continues in the airless limbo between life and death.

He was still drowsing there when his door opened, and he heard his grandfather's booming voice: "Say, old fellow, I guess you've had enough of the women praying over you by this time, haven't you, and it'll buck you up some to swap stories again with a man of your own age."

There he was, in the room, close to the bed, powerful, impending, the black-and-white mane tossed back boldly from his swarthy forehead, the white teeth flashing through the straggling drop of his dyed moustache, the smell of tobacco and eau de cologne emanating from the folds of his sagging clothes, from the tip of the handkerchief in his breast pocket and his long dark hands, which the boy saw spreading out over him as Mr. Scrimser bent paternally to the bed.

"Oh, Grandfather, don't—I say *don't!*" Vance raised himself on the pillows, the sweat breaking out over his weak body, his arms defensively outstretched. "Don't—don't! Go away—*go away!*" he repeated with the weak cry of a child, covering his eyes with his hands.

He heard Mr. Scrimser's movement of recoil, and bewildered stammer, and knew that in another moment Mrs. Weston or the girls would be summoned, and he would be hemmed in again by fever charts, thermometers, and iced compresses. He lowered his hands, and sitting upright looked straight into his grandfather's evasive eyes.

"You—you damned old lecher, you," he said in a low but perfectly firm voice. Mr. Scrimser stared, and he stared back. Gradually the grandfather lowered his piebald crest, and retreated across the narrow little room to the door.

"You're—you're sick yet, Vanny. Of course I won't stay if you don't want me to," he stammered. As he turned Vance said to himself: "He understands; he won't bother me anymore." His head fell back on the pillows.

For a few days he was less well. The doctor said he had seen too many people, and Mrs. Weston relieved her nerves by lecturing her husband and Mae on their thoughtlessness in tiring the boy out. It occurred to no one to incriminate Mr. Scrimser, who had just popped his head in and made one of his jokes. Mrs. Weston could have certified that her father had not been more than two minutes in the room. Mr. Scrimser was noted in Euphoria as a professional brightener-up. He was full of tact in the sickroom, and in great request to cheer the long hours of convalescence. As he left the house his daughter said: "You must pop in again tomorrow, Father, and get a laugh out of Vance"; and Mr. Scrimser rejoined in his rolling voice: "You can count on me, Marcia, if he's not too busy receiving visitors." But he did not return, and Mrs. Scrimser sent word that he had his sciatica back on him, and she was trying to see what prayers at the "Spirit of Service" meetings would do.

On the third day after his grandfather's visit, Vance, who was now sitting up in an armchair, asked his mother for paper and his fountain pen. Mrs. Weston, to whom all literary activities, even to the mere writing of a letter, represented untold fatigue, said protestingly: "What do you want to write for? It'll just make your head ache." But Vance said he was only going to jot down something, and she gave him what he wanted. When she was gone he took the pen, and wrote across the paper: "Damn him—I hate him—I hate—hate—hate—" He added a long line of obscene and blasphemous denunciation.

His hand was still unsteady, but he formed the letters

slowly and carefully, with a sort of morbid satisfaction in the doing. He had fancied that writing them out would in some mysterious way dispel the awful sense of loneliness which had repossessed him since he had come back to life. But after his first burst of anger he felt no relief, and dropped back again into the solitude which had isolated him from his kind ever since the afternoon when he had leaned against the fence and looked across the maple grove to the river. Yet relief he must have—and at once—or chuck up this too hideous business of living. He closed his eyes and tried to picture himself, when he was well again, taking up his usual pursuits and pleasures; and he turned from the vision, soul-sick. The fair face of the world had been besmirched, and he felt the first agony of youth at such profanation.

The oppression was intolerable. He was like a captive walled into a dark airless cell, and the walls of that cell were Reality, were the life he would in future be doomed to. The impulse to end it all here and now possessed him. He had tried out the whole business and found it wanting; been the round of it, and come back gorged with disgust. The negativeness of death would be better, a million times better. He got to his feet and walked unsteadily across the room to the door. He knew where his father's revolver was kept. Mrs. Weston had only one weakness: she was afraid of burglars, and her husband always had a revolver in the drawer of the night table between their beds. Vance made his way along the passage, resting his hand against the wall to steady his steps. The house was silent and empty. His mother and the girls were out, and the Lithuanian would be downstairs in her kitchen. He reached his parents' room, walked feebly to the table between the beds, and opened the drawer. The revolver was not there. . . .

Vance's brain reeled. He might have looked elsewhere, might have hunted . . . but a sudden weakness overcame him and he sat down in the nearest chair. Was it the weakness of his state, or a secret reluctance to pursue his quest, the unconfessed fear that he might find what he was looking for? He asked himself the question, and could not answer. But as he sat there he became conscious that, even in the halting progress from his room to the spot where he had supposed death waited—even during that transit, so short in space, so long in time, he had felt the arms of Life, the ancient mother, reaching out to him, winding about him, crushing him fast again to her great careless bosom. He was glad—he knew now he was glad—that he had not found the weapon.

He crawled back to his room and his armchair, pulled the blanket over his knee, and sat there, faint and frightened. His heart was still beating convulsively. It was incredible, what a coward illness had made of him. But he was resolved not to be beaten, not to accept any makeshift compromise between his fear of life and his worse fear of death. If life it was to be, well—he'd live!

The writing paper lay on the table at his side. He turned over the page on which he had scrawled his senseless curses, and sat with his pen over the blank paper; then he wrote out, slowly and carefully, at the top of the page: "One Day." Yes—that was the right title for the story he meant to tell. One day had sufficed to dash his life to pieces. . . .

He began hastily, feverishly, the words rushing from his pen like water from a long-obstructed spring, and as the paragraphs grew it seemed to him that at last he had found out a way of reconciling his soul to its experiences. He would set them down just as they had befallen him in all their cruel veracity, but as if he were relating the tragedy of somebody else.

≫ IV ≪

MRS. WESTON, turning over old Christmas cards in the course of the spring cleaning (which Vance's illness had deplorably delayed), came on one giving a view of Iceboating On The Hudson, and said: "Lucilla Tracy—why, now, I don't know's anybody's ever acknowledged that card. . . ."

The doctors said that Vance ought to get away for the hot weather—clear away, to a new place with new air and new associations. Nineteen was a nasty age to have a shake-up of that kind, they said; it took time to build up a growing body after such a tumble. The family'd better not talk to the boy about looking round for a job till the autumn—just let him lie fallow through the hot months, somewhere by the sea if it could be managed.

The sea seemed a long way off to the Weston family, and especially to Mrs. Weston, who could never understand why anybody whose parlour windows looked out on Mapledale Avenue, Euphoria, should ever want to go anywhere else, even to Chicago. But she had been frightened about the boy, and her husband, she knew, was frightened still. After consultation between the two it was decided to ask Vance himself where he would like to go. His father put the question, and Vance immediately said: "New York."

The announcement was staggering. New York was almost as far away as Europe; it was ten times more expensive; it was as hot in summer as Chicago; it was a place a man went to when he'd made his pile; a place you took your

family to for a week's blow-out when you'd been on the
right side of the market. It was Mr. Weston who piled up
these definitions; his wife, with nervous frowning lips, remarked that such a long journey would wear Vance out, and
do away beforehand with all the good of the rest he had
been ordered to take; and that, if the sea was too far off, she
didn't see why the air of the Lakes wasn't just as bracing.
And there he'd have the family to look after him; if he went,
that would make Father decide to take them all to the
Lakes, she guessed. She looked at her husband in a way that
made him so decide on the spot.

But Vance said, in that pale obstinate way he had acquired since his illness: "I want to go to New York. It's easy
enough to get down to the sea from there."

Mr. Weston laughed. "Yes, but it ain't so darned easy to
get there first." Vance was silent, and the family exchanged
perturbed glances. But just then Mrs. Scrimser came lum-
bering in, cured of her rheumatism (by the "Spirit of Service" prayers—which unhappily had not succeeded with her
husband), but moving heavily, as usual, with a stick to support her big rambling frame. She sat down among them in
the sleeping porch, where Vance now took his daily rest
cure, listened to their perplexity, and said with her dreamy
prophetic smile: "There's only once in a life when anybody
wants one particular thing so bad that nothing else on
earth'll do instead. I wouldn't wonder if wanting a thing
that way wasn't about the nearest we ever get to happiness."
She turned her softly humorous eyes on her grandson. "I
guess Vanny'll have to go East."

It was then that Mrs. Weston remembered her cousin
Lucilla Tracy's postcard. "That place of Lorburn Tracy's
isn't so far from New York," she remarked, "up there on the
Hudson. And Vance'd have good country air, anyhow, and
good milk. May be Lucilla'd be glad to take him in as a
boarder for a few weeks. I don't believe they're any too well

off, from what she said last time she wrote to me. Since Lorburn's death I guess she and the children have had pretty hard times making the two ends meet. Anyhow, I ought to answer that card. . . ."

Vance said nothing: the suggestion came to him as a surprise. He knew that Paul's Landing, where his mother's cousin lived, was not above an hour and a half by rail from New York, and his heart was beginning to beat excitedly, though he maintained an air of indifference.

But Lorin Weston was not indifferent. He seized on the suggestion as an unforseen way of indulging his son without too great an expenditure of money—an important consideration in view of the heavy cost of Vance's illness, and the complications and embarrassments likely to result from Weston's move in raising again the vexed question of the Crampton water supply.

"Say—why don't we ring Lucilla up right now," he suggested, getting to his feet with the haste of a man accustomed to prompt solution. Mrs. Weston raised no objection, and Mrs. Scrimser nodded approvingly. "That's great, Lorin. I guess Lucilla'll be only too glad. Her boy must be about Vanny's age, mustn't he, Marcia?" Marcia thought he must, and mother and daughter lost themselves in reminiscences of the early history of Lucilla Tracy, whom they had not seen since she had come out on a visit to them at Advance, years before, when Vance was a baby. The Tracys had been well-off then, and the young couple had been on their wedding trip to the Grand Canyon, and had stopped off on the way to see the bride's western relatives. Mrs. Scrimser and Mrs. Weston recalled Lucilla as having been very pretty, with stylish New York clothes; they thought Mr. Tracy's father owned a big "works" of some sort, on the Hudson; and he himself was editor of the principal newspaper at Paul's Landing, where there had always been Tracys and Lorburns, since long before the Revolution, so he told them.

"Dear me, don't it take you right back to Historic Times, hearing about things like that?" Grandma glowed reminiscently; but Mrs. Weston shivered a little at the opening of such interminable vistas. She liked to think of everybody living compactly and thrivingly, as she did herself, hemmed in by a prosperous present, and securely shut off from the icy draughts of an unknown past. "I guess the family's going way back like that don't always help the children to go forward," she said sententiously; and at that very moment her husband reappeared with an announcement which seemed to confirm her worst suspicions. It was simply that the Tracys had no telephone.

No telephone! The Westons had never heard of such a case before. Mrs. Weston began by saying it couldn't be possible, it must be a mistake, they were always making mistakes at the Information office; had Lorin said it was Mrs. *Lorburn* Tracy, at Paul's Landing, New York? Was he sure he'd heard right? It simply couldn't be, she reiterated, beginning to think that if it were, the Tracys must be "peculiar," and she wouldn't want to trust any child of hers to them, least of all Vance, after such an illness. She thought they'd better give up the idea altogether.

But Mrs. Scrimser was older, and her mind could reach back to days when, even in the enlightened West, she had known cases of people living in out-of-the-way places, or who were just simply too poor. . . .

"But I don't want Vance to go to an out-of-the-way place. Suppose he was sick, how'd they ever get hold of a doctor?"

"Well, if it's because they're not well enough off," her husband interrupted, 'it'll be a godsend to them to have Vance as a boarder, and I guess, from what I remember of Lucilla, she'll be real good to him, and get a doctor somehow, as quick as his own mother would."

Mrs. Weston looked at him witheringly. "What you

know of Lucilla Tracy is exactly nothing, Lorin; and you say that only because you remember she was pretty, and had on a showy pink dress with ruffles." But Mr. Weston, unperturbed, said, well, he didn't know as those were such bad points in a woman; and anyhow he'd go along to the telegraph office and wire, and then they'd see. He guessed they'd be pretty well able to judge by the answer.

At the Grand Central Station, a week later, Vance was met by his young cousin, Upton Tracy. Upton was a spindly boy of about sixteen, with wistful gray eyes and a pleasant smile. He told Vance he had a job with a nurseryman at Paul's Landing, but the manager had let him off for the afternoon so that he could come to New York to meet his cousin.

Vance hoped that Upton would not see how glad he was to be met. He was still weak after his illness, and the long railway journey—the first of that length that he had ever taken—had exhausted him more than he had expected. When he got into the train at Chicago his heart was beating so excitedly at the idea of seeing New York that he had nearly forgotten all his disgusts and disillusionments, and had secretly made up his mind to stop over for a night in the metropolis before going on to join his relatives at Paul's Landing. But now, in his tired state, and oppressed as he was by the sense of inferiority produced by untired conditions and surroundings, he felt unequal to coping with this huge towering wilderness of masonry where Vance Weston of Euphoria was of no more account to any one among the thousands inhabiting it than a single raindrop to the ocean.

He had been furious with his mother for suggesting that one of the Tracys should meet him at the station in New York, and had sworn that he would never again let his family treat him like a "softy"; but when Upton's wistful face appeared in the heedless indifferent throng on the platform, Vance felt the relief of a frightened child that has lost its way. "Comes of being sick," he grumbled to himself as his cousin pointed to the red carnation which was to identify him. Vance, who, at Euphoria, would have condescended to the shy boy at his side, now felt still shyer himself, and was grateful to Upton for having so little to say, and for assuming as a matter of course that they were just to wait in the station till the next train left for Paul's Landing. Luckily it left in half an hour.

His mother had said: "You just let me know if you see anything over there that's so much better than Euphoria," and he had smiled and made no answer. But the request came back to him with a shock of something like humiliation when he and Upton stepped out of the station at Paul's Landing. There was the usual bunch of Fords waiting there, and next to them, under the pale green shade of some crooked-boughed locust trees, a queer-looking group of old carts and carryalls, with drooping horses swishing off the flies and mournfully shaking their heads. The scene was like something in a film of the Civil War, one of those films that were full of horses with swishing tails and draggly manes. One of the horses, the oldest and mournfullest looking, with a discoloured white mane like a smoker's beard, was tied to a chewed-off post; Upton went up and unhitched him, and the horse shook his head in melancholy recognition.

"We're a good way from the trolley, so one of the neighbours lent me his team to come and get you," Upton explained, lifting Vance's luggage into the back of a buggy which seemed at least coeval with the horse. Vance could not have walked a step at that moment, much less carried the smallest of his two bags, so he was grateful to the unknown neighbour; but when he remembered how, if you went to stay with a chum at Swedenborg or Dakin, or anywhere in his home state, you buzzed away from the station in a neat Ford (if it wasn't in a stylish Chevrolet or the fam-

ily Buick), a sense of dejection was added to his profound
fatigue. His mother had said: "You wait and see—" and he
was seeing.

The old horse jogged them through Paul's Landing, a
long crooked sort of town on a high ridge, with gardens full
of big trees, and turfy banks sloping down from rambling
shabby-looking houses. Now and then a narrower street
dipped downhill to their left, and Vance caught a glimpse
of lustrous gray waters spreading lakelike to distant hills.
"The Hudson," Upton said, flicking his stump of a whip;
and at the moment the name stirred Vance more than the
sight of the outspread waters. They drove on down a long
street between shops, garages, business buildings, all more
or less paintless and dilapidated, with sagging awnings lowered against the premature spring heat; then uphill along a
rutty lane between trees and small frame houses even shab-
bier than the others, though some had pretty flowers before
them, and lilacs and syringas blooming more richly than
Grandma Scrimser's.

"This is it," said Upton, in a voice still shyer and more
apologetic. "It" was a small wooden house, painted dark
brown, with the paint peeling off, and a broken-down trellis
arbour in a corner of the front yard. There were shade trees
over the house, and a straggling rose on the verandah; but
the impression made by the whole place was of something
neglected and dingy, something left in a backwater, like the
sad Delaney house from which Vance still averted his
thoughts.

"You seem to have lots of trees around everywhere," he
remarked to Upton, wishing he could think of something
more striking to say.

"Aren't there as many out your way?" Upton rejoined.

"I dunno," Vance mumbled, suddenly on his guard
against admitting any inferiority in Euphoria, even to the
amount of shade afforded by its trees. "I suppose they're just
different—the way everything else is," he added.

Mrs. Tracy, who now appeared on the doorstep, was
certainly different—not only from the gay bride in showy
pink who had dazzled her western relatives on her wedding
tour, but also from any of the women of Vance's family. She
was small and slight, like Mrs. Weston, but without the latter's sharpness of outline and incisiveness of manner. There
was something fluctuant and shadowy about Mrs. Tracy, as
there was about her overshaded dooryard; but she had a
kind of phantom prettiness, something seen through a veil
not so much of years as of failure. She looked, not careless
of her beauty, like Grandma Scrimser, but disheartened
about it, as Vance suspected she was about everything else
in life. But the sweetness of her smile of welcome was something his own mother could not have compassed. "I guess
it'll be all right here," Vance thought, his contracted nerves
relaxing.

"You look very tired; the journey must have been awful. Come right in and have some supper," Mrs. Tracy said,
slipping her arm through his.

It was funny—but pleasant, too, as a novelty—sitting
around a table lit by a queer smelly oil lamp with an engraved globe on it, in a little dining room with a dark brown
wallpaper and an unwieldy protruding sideboard which had
evidently been picked up at a bargain because it wouldn't
fit in anywhere. Mrs. Tracy sat opposite, smiling at Vance
wistfully across the teacups, and asking gentle questions
about everybody out at Euphoria. She remembered what a
pretty little house the Westons had lived in at Advance,
when she'd gone there on her honeymoon, and Vance was a
baby; and when Vance smiled away her commendation, and
said they'd got a much bigger house now at Euphoria, she
replied that she supposed his mother'd made it all lovely,
and then rambled off to questions about the wonderful
Grandma Scrimser and Aunt Saidie Toler. Vance noticed
that she remembered a great deal more about all of them
than they did about her, and he said to himself that she had

what Grandma Scrimser called a Family Bible sort of mind.

Upton dropped into the seat between his mother and Vance, and while the meal was in progress a thin fair girl in a pale blue blouse and a very short skirt wandered into the room, shook hands awkwardly with the newcomer, and seated herself in the remaining chair.

"Laura Lou's always late—aren't you?" Mrs. Tracy said, in her tone of smiling acceptance. "I presume your sisters aren't always on time for meals, are they, Vance?"

Vance laughed, and said no, they drove his mother wild sometimes, and Laura Lou laughed too, but without looking at him, though his one glimpse of her heavy-lidded gray eyes with thick dark lashes made him desirous of another. Her face, however, was not pretty; too drawn and thin, like her brother's, and with rather high cheekbones which Vance thought ugly, and ash blonde hair flopping untidily over her forehead. She was not more than fifteen, he conjectured, an age essentially uninteresting to him; and as she refused to talk, and drooped her head sheepishly over her plate of cold meat and potatoes (which he saw she hardly touched), Vance's attention soon wandered from her. He had reached the stage of fatigue when everything about one is at once exciting and oppressive, and in spite of his friendly feeling toward his hosts he longed desperately for solitude and sleep.

But sleep was after all impossible. It was not the musty shut-up smell of his queer little room, nor the surprise of being unable to have a hot bath after his long cindery journey (the Tracy water supply being as primitive as their lighting and their means of locomotion); what kept him awake was something stronger even than youth's exhaustless faculty of self-repair, of sleeping through, and in spite of, any number of anxieties and discomforts—a burning inward excitement shadowed but not overcome by his sense of vague disappointment.

Vance did not know exactly what he had expected of the East, except a general superabundance of all the things he had been taught to admire—taller houses, wider streets, fresher paint, more motors, telephones, plumbing, than Euphoria possessed, or could ever imagine achieving. Yet here he was in a town close to New York, and in a house belonging to people of his own standing—and he had been brought thither in a broken-down buggy, and the house was the shabbiest he had ever seen except Harrison Delaney's, with none of the conveniences of civilized life, and kindly people who appeared too used to doing without them to make any excuse for their absence. Vance knew, by hearsay, of poverty; but almost all the people he had grown up among, if not as prosperous as his own family, were at least beyond any appearance of want; or rather, what they wanted, and felt the privation of, and hustled around to get were luxuries evidently not even aspired to by the Tracys. Vance supposed it came from the mysterious lack of vitality he felt in both Mrs. Tracy and her son; perhaps if Mr. Tracy hadn't died years ago it would have been different. Certainly they wouldn't have gone on ever since living in the same place and the same house—proof in itself of an absence of initiative which no Euphorian could understand. No, if Mr. Tracy had lived he would have got Upton onto a better job by this time (they left truck gardens to Poles and Dagoes at Euphoria), and he himself would have got a drive on, and moved to a live place, and done something to lift his family to the level where electric light, hot water, the telephone, a wireless, and a Ford in a cement garage are no longer privileges but necessities.

Not that Vance was a "softy"; he would have been indignant at the suggestion. Holiday camping in the backwoods had not only made him familiar with a rough life in the open but given him a passionate taste for it. When America had entered the war, Euphoria, true to her slogan

—"Me for the Front Row"—had also entered it with energy, and Vance, aged fifteen, had drilled, shouted, and scouted with all the other boys. Two or three times since then he had gone with his father prospecting in remote districts, in search of real estate ventures of a speculative kind, and they had lodged in the roughest of farmhouses, miles away from telephone or city water, and Vance had gloried in the discomfort and enjoyed his morning wash under the pump. But that was in the wilderness, the new country not yet captured and tamed by business enterprise; whereas Paul's Landing was like a place that enterprise of every sort had passed by, as if all its inhabitants had slept through the whole period of industrial development which Vance Weston had been taught to regard as humanity's supreme achievement. If Euphoria values were the right ones—and he had no others to replace them with—then the people who did not strive for them were predestined down-and-outers, as repugnant to the religion of business as the thief and the adulterer to the religion of Christianity. And here, in the very part of his immense country which represented all that western wealth strove for and western ambition dreamed of, Vance found himself in a community apparently unaware that such strivings and ambitions existed. "Seems as if they'd all slept right round the clock," Vance thought, remembering the torpid look of the main street, its draggled awnings and horse-drawn vehicles, and beginning to feel as if the Tracy house were not an isolated phenomenon but part of some huge geological accident. "As if they'd been caught centuries ago under a landslide, and just gone on living there, like those toads they find alive inside a stone—" and on this confused analogy the young traveller fell asleep.

❧ V ❧

VANCE SLEPT nearly as long as he had metaphorically accused the inhabitants of Paul's Landing of doing. When he woke he saw a pattern of rippling foliage on the ceiling of his room, and a bar of sunlight lying across the floor. The air that came in through the window was sultry with heat, and flies buzzed against the pane. Looking about him at the streaked and faded wallpaper, his clothes heaped up on a broken-down verandah chair, and the water jug with a chipped spout on the old-fashioned washstand, he felt a qualm of homesickness, and thought longingly of the spring sunsets across the fields at Crampton, and the perfume of his grandmother's neglected lilacs. So strong was the impression that the perfume was actually in his nostrils. He raised himself on his elbow, and there, on the pillow, lay a spray of white lilac, filling the room with June.

"Well, that's nice of them," Vance thought, burying his face in the ivory-coloured clusters. He remembered his grandmother's once saying, as they sat on the Crampton porch on a hot June evening: "I guess that box of ointment Mary Magdalen broke over our Lord's feet must have been made out of lilacs," and he had liked the fancy, and wished he knew how to make a poem out of it, rich and heavy with perfumed words. His grandmother's random fancies often stirred his imagination in this way.

Upton, he supposed, or perhaps Mrs. Tracy, must have come in while he was asleep, and dropped the flower on his

pillow because he had told them there were lilacs at
Grandma Scrimser's. "Upton most likely," he mused. "Good
little fellow—seems to have gardens on the brain." He took
another deep whiff of the flower, tumbled out of bed, filled
the cracked basin with water, and plunged his head into it.
After that the currents of activity reawoke, and he hurried
through his washing and dressing, impatient to be down, for
his watch told him it was after midday, and he was
ashamed to be so late on his first morning.

His window looked out on the back of the house. Close
to it were the trees which had drawn their fitful pencillings
on the ceiling above his bed; and beyond was a small patch
of vegetables, divided in oblongs by currant and goose-
berry bushes, and fenced off from other vegetable gardens
which sloped up the hillside to the irregular fringes of a
wood. More trees—trees everywhere, trees taller, fuller and
more heavy-branched, he thought, than those of his native
prairies. Up the hillside they domed themselves in great
bluish masses, one against the other, like the roofs of some
mysterious city built of leaves. Vance was pleased with that
fancy too, and would have liked to stop and put it into
verse, as well as his grandmother's idea about the lilacs. The
rhyming faculty, long abeyant, stirred in him again under
the spell of the unfamiliar scene, and the caress of the summer morning, and he forgot about his haste to leave his
room, and his scruples lest breakfast should have been kept
for him, and sat down at the table in the window, pulling
his pen and a scrap of paper from his pocket. Since his little-
boyhood his pockets had never been without scraps of paper.

"*Arcane, aloof, and secret as the soul*—" He liked that,
for the first line of the poem about the city built of leaves,
which was of course a forest. *Secret as the soul*. There were
times when his own soul was like a forest, full of shadows

and murmurs—*arcane, aloof*—a place to lose one's way in, a place fearsome, almost, to be alone in. And then: *secret.* That too was true. He often felt as if his own soul were a stranger inside of him, a stranger speaking a language he had never learned, or had forgotten. And there again was a good idea; the idea of the mysterious stranger within one's self, closer than one's bones and yet with a face and speech forever unknown to one. His heart was beating with a rush of inarticulate eloquence, words and waves of feeling struggling to fit into each other and become thought and music.

"Heavy with all the scent of summers gone—" how would that do for the lilac? No, *too* heavy. He wanted to say that the mere scent of the lilac was rich enough for bees to make honey out of it; to say that lightly, whirringly, like bees humming about before they settle. And then one organ note at the close, where the box of ointment is broken, and Christ likens the Magdalen's gesture to the perfume of holiness, the lovely fragrance it should give out, but so often does not. *Scentless holiness* . . . there too was something to write about. How one image beckoned another! And he couldn't stop them, often couldn't detain them long enough to trace their lineaments before they vanished. . . .

He scribbled on in the stuffy untidy room, beside his tumbled bed, the flies banging against the windowpane, the bar of hot sunlight wheeling slowly across the wall, scribbled on oblivious of time and place, of his wholesome morning hunger, of the fact that he was in a strange household where his nonappearance might be inconvenient or perplexing. Words for one poem, then for the other, continued to surge up, mingling, confused and exciting, in his half-awakened brain. Sometimes he lingered on one for the sake of its own beauty, and suddenly a new poem would bud from it, as if the word had been a seed plunged into the heated atmosphere of his imagination. Disconnected, unmeaning, alluring, they strung themselves out on one bit of paper after another, till he threw down his pen and buried his rumpled head in his hands.

Through his dream he heard a knock, and started up. It was Mrs. Tracy coming in with a cup of coffee. He mustn't mind about having slept so long, she told him at once—it was the best thing for him, after his illness and the long journey. "Sleep is the young people's best doctor," she said with one of her sad smiles. "But you didn't eat much last night, and you'd better drink this coffee right off, while it's hot. It won't keep you from wanting your dinner by and by, I hope." She put the tray down beside him while he stammered his excuses, and went on, in the same friendly tone, with a glance at the litter of paper at his elbow: "If you've got any work to get through, I guess you'll be cooler down on the back porch than here; there's a little breeze from the river. We always get one of these heat waves in June."

Vance thanked her, and said he would come down at once, and she added, designating the lilac blossom in his coat: "But I see you've been down already, haven't you? You're like me—you love lilacs."

"Then it wasn't she who brought it," he thought; and answered, colouring, that, yes, he thought they had the best smell of any flower he knew, but he hadn't been down yet, and he guessed Upton must have brought the flower in while he was sleeping.

Mrs. Tracy, he thought, coloured a little too; there was a hint of surprise in her eyes. "Why, maybe he did," she acquiesced; and slid away on her soft soles, leaving him to his belated coffee.

The day passed uneventfully. In spite of his long sleep Vance still felt the weariness of convalescence, and the excitement of his changed surroundings. Disappointment also, the feeling that he was somehow being cheated out of hoped-for experiences, oppressed his tired nerves and left him for the moment without initiative, so that after dinner he was glad to accept Mrs. Tracy's suggestion that he should return to the back porch and stretch out in the hammock.

Upton had hurried home for dinner, the nursery where he was employed not being far away; but Laura Lou's seat was empty. Mrs. Tracy explained that she usually returned from school for the midday meal, but that she had accepted an invitation from a friend that day, and would not be back till evening.

Upton, his shyness worn off, talked eagerly about his work; his employer was hybridizing gladioluses, he explained, and also experimenting in crosses between Japanese and European tree-peonies. All this evidently meant nothing to Mrs. Tracy, who had a stock set of questions ready (Vance perceived) for both of her children, and had learned how to interrogate Upton about his horticultural experiments, and Laura Lou about her studies, without understanding their answers, or even affecting to. She struck Vance as a woman who had lived all her life among people whose language she could not speak, and had learned to communicate with them by signs, like a deaf-mute, while ministering watchfully to their material needs.

Having settled Vance in the hammock she went off with a slatternly woman who came in from one of the next houses to help with the washing; and Vance lay in the warm shade, and dozed, or let his mind wander over his half-written poems. But whenever he tried to write poetry nowadays the same thing happened: after the first few lines, which almost wrote themselves, the inspiration died out, or rather he felt that he didn't know what to say next—that if his mind had contained more of the stuff of experience, words would have flocked of their own accord for its expression. He supposed it must take a good deal of experience to

furnish the material for even a few lines of poetry; and
though he was not prepared to admit that very little had
happened to him, he could not but remember that he was
only nineteen, and that there had not been time yet for any
great accumulation of events. He finished the Magdalen
poem about the lilacs, but haltingly, the expression flagging
with the vision—and when it was done he leaned back, lit a
cigarette, and thought with a smile what his restless inquisitive sister Mae would have said if she had known how he
was spending his first day within reach of New York. "Well,
I'll get there all the same, and get to a newspaper office
too," he thought, setting his teeth in a last effort at dogged-
ness before sleep once more overcame him.

That evening at supper Laura Lou again came in late.
She wore a faded yellow muslin which became her, and
looked flushed and animated; but she contributed no more
to the conversation than on the previous day. Mrs. Tracy
seemed tired, and more discouraged than ever—Vance supposed it was the washing. When supper was over, and they
were going back to the porch, she said she guessed she'd go
to bed early; and would Upton be sure to remember to put
out the lamp in the hall, and fasten the door chain when
they went upstairs? Upton said he would, and Mrs. Tracy
turned back to speak through the window of the dining
room, where she was clearing the table unaided by either of
her children. "Don't forget now, Upton; tomorrow's Saturday, and it's the Willows afternoon."

"All right, Mother; I won't."

"You say that; and then you get home hours late for
dinner," his mother insisted nervously. "I wouldn't wonder if
Miss Halo came down herself tomorrow," she added in an
anxious tone.

"Oh, no, she won't—not in this heat."

"You always say that too, Upton; and then when you
least expect it, she does come, or Mrs. Spear does, and

you're not there when they arrive. And of course they want to know where you are, and if we mean to keep on with the job or not; and I get all the blame. And I don't see how I can get to the Willows myself tomorrow, with all the ironing still to do. . . ."

"Well, you needn't, Mother. Laura Lou'll have to go with me; that's all."

"Oh, will I?" murmured Laura Lou. She spoke under her breath, but loud enough for Vance to hear, as she sat in the summer darkness close to the hammock to which he had returned.

"Yes, Laura Lou'll have to. You will, darling?" Mrs. Tracy, without waiting for the answer, which she perhaps feared would be negative, picked up a candlestick from the sideboard and slowly mounted the stairs.

Left alone, the young people relapsed into silence. Upton was evidently tired by his day's work, and Vance was embarrassed by the presence of an inarticulate schoolgirl whose replies to his remarks took the form of a nervous giggle. "I wish her mother'd made her go to bed too," he thought. He offered a cigarette to Upton, and then held out the packet to Laura Lou, who shook her head with another giggle.

"She's tried, but they made her sick," said Upton cruelly.

"Oh, Upton—"

"Well, they do." Her face wrinkled up as if she were about to cry. To change the subject, Vance questioned: "What did your mother mean by tomorrow being the afternoon for the Willows? What are the Willows?"

Upton answered indifferently: "It's old Miss Lorburn's place, out the other side of Paul's Landing. Nobody's lived there since she died, ages ago, and she left a funny will, and we have to go out once a fortnight and see to the house being aired and the knickknacks dusted. There's a sort of hired man lives on the place, but he isn't allowed into Miss Lorburn's rooms, and Mother and I have to see that they're kept clean, and just the way she left them."

"Was this Miss Lorburn a relative of your father's?"

"Oh, very distant, I guess. She left the place to one of her nephews, an old bachelor who never comes there; and it's he who arranged for Mother to keep an eye on things."

Vance meditated, his interest beginning to stir. "What sort of a place is it?"

"I don't know, nothing particular. Just an old house."

An old house! Upton spoke the words indifferently, almost contemptuously: they seemed to signify nothing to him. But they stirred Vance's blood. An old house! It occurred to him that he had never seen a really old house in his life. But Upton was young—a good deal younger than himself. What did he mean by the epithet? His perspectives were probably even shorter than Vance's.

"How old? As old as this house?" Vance questioned.

"Oh, ages older. My father used to go there when he was a little boy. It was an old house then. He could just remember seeing old Miss Lorburn, Mother says. She lived to be very old. She was a friend of my grandfather's, I believe. It's a dreary place anyhow. Laura Lou hates it. She says the rooms are full of ghosts, and she's scared of it. But I say it's because she hates missing her Saturday afternoon at the movies."

"Upton—" Laura Lou again protested.

"Well, you do. And Mother don't like you to go to the Willows because you break things. But you'll have to, to-morrow."

Laura Lou made no answer, and Vance pursued his interrogatory. "And who are those ladies your mother spoke about, who come in and raise a row?"

"Oh, Mrs. Spear and her daughter. Mrs. Spear was a

Lorburn. They won't come tomorrow—not in this heat. If they're here—and I'm not sure they are anyhow—"

"Here? At Paul's Landing?"

"Well, they live up at Eaglewood, another Lorburn place, a couple of miles from here, up the mountain. There's a grand view of the river from there. It's in the guidebooks. And they're supposed to come down to the Willows now and then, and keep an eye on us, the way we do on the hired man."

"How many Lorburn places are there round here?"

"They owned pretty near the whole place before the Revolution. Now there's only these two houses left."

"I suppose they had a big real estate boom, and got rid of everything?"

Upton chuckled incredulously in the dusk. "I don't believe there's ever been much boom of any kind about the Lorburns. They just got poorer and poorer and died off, I guess."

Vance was genuinely puzzled. "Well, I don't see why they couldn't have worked up a boom and unloaded the stuff on somebody," he murmured. Then he remembered Harrison Delaney's incapacity in the same line, and his grandmother's caustic comments on old families that have run to seed. He was glad that no aristocratic blood clogged his own lively circulation, and that, anyhow, there were no old families in a go-ahead place like Euphoria.

Upton got up and stretched his thin arms above his head. "Well, I'm going to get a move on toward bed. It was about 150 in that fernhouse this afternoon." He groped his way between them, and went into the hall, banging the screen door after him in the instinctive defence against mosquitoes. From where Vance lay in the hammock he could see Upton put the chain across the front door, and bolt it.

Suddenly, close to him in the darkness, he heard Laura

Lou say: "You've had that old lilac in your buttonhole all day. It smells all faded." She bent above him and snatched it out of his coat. Instinctively he put up his hand to prevent her; his poem had made the withered blossom sacred. "Oh, don't—" But his hand, instead of the lilac, caught her soft fingers. They quivered, frightened yet entreating, and the warmth of her touch rushed through him, tempting, persuading; but she was no more than a little girl, awkward and ignorant, and he was under her mother's roof. Besides, if it had not been for the heat and the darkness, and his mood of sensuous lassitude, he did not believe that even the touch of her soft skin would have roused him; the raw flapper had no charm for his unripe senses.

"Here—give it back! Listen to me, Laura Lou!" But she sprang out of reach with one of her maddening giggles, and he let her hand go, and the lilac with it, indifferently.

Upton came clumping back to the porch. "Going up to bed too?" he asked. Vance assented and tumbled out of the hammock. "All right. Then I'll put the lamp out. Come along, Laura Lou." To Vance he added: "Mother left a candle on the upper landing," and he reached up to the swinging lamp, pulled it down, and filled the passage with the stench of its extinction. Laura Lou had already slipped up ahead of them to her mother's room.

BOOK II

≫ VI ≪

"IT'S HERE," Upton said.

Vance had jokingly offered to accompany Upton to the Willows, and help him to dust Miss Lorburn's rooms, so that Laura Lou should not miss the movies. But Laura Lou, flushing crimson, replied in a frightened whisper that it wasn't true, that she wanted to go to the Willows, that she always did go when her mother couldn't—so Vance hired a bicycle at a nearby garage, and the three cousins set out.

Upton stopped before a padlocked gate overhung with trees. A deep green lane led up to it, so rutty and grassgrown that the cousins, jumping from their bicycles, climbed it on foot. Upton pulled out a key, unlocked the padlock of the gate, and led the way in, followed by Vance and Laura Lou. The house, which was painted a dark brown, stood at the end of a short grass-grown drive, its front so veiled in the showering gold-green foliage of two ancient weeping willows that Vance could only catch, here and there, a hint of a steep roof, a jutting balcony, an aspiring turret. The façade, thus seen in trembling glimpses, as if it were as fluid as the trees, suggested vastness, fantasy, and secrecy. Green slopes of unmown grass, and heavy shrubberies of unpruned syringa and lilac, surrounded it; and beyond the view was closed in on all sides by trees and more trees. "An old house—this is the way an old house looks!" Vance thought.

The three walked up the drive, their steps muffled by

the long grass and clover which had pushed up through the gravel. When the front of the house was before them, disengaged from the fluctuating veil of willows, Vance saw that it was smaller than he had expected; but the air of fantasy and mystery remained. Everything about the front was irregular, but with an irregularity unfamiliar to him. The shuttered windows were very tall and narrow, and narrow too the balconies, which projected at odd angles, supported by ornate wooden brackets. One corner of the house rose into a tower with a high shingled roof, and arched windows which seemed to simulate the openings in a belfry. A sort of sloping roof over the front door also rested on elaborately ornamented brackets, and on each side of the steps was a large urn of fluted iron painted to imitate stone, in which some half-dead geraniums languished.

While Upton unlocked the front door and went in with his sister, Vance wandered around to the other side of the building. Here a still stranger spectacle awaited him. An arcaded verandah ran across this front, and all about it, and reaching out above it from bracket to bracket, from balcony to balcony, a wistaria with huge distorted branches like rheumatic arms lifted itself to the eaves, festooning, as it mounted, every projecting point with long lilac fringes—as if, Vance thought, a flock of very old monkeys had been ordered to climb up and decorate the house front in celebration of some august arrival. He had never seen so prodigal a flowering, or a plant so crippled and ancient; and for a while it took his attention from the house. But not for long. To bear so old a climber on its front, the house must be still older; and its age, its mystery, its reserve, laid a weight on his heart. He remembered once, at Euphoria, waking in the night—a thing which seldom happened to him—and hearing the bell of the Roman Catholic church slowly and solemnly toll the hour. He saw the church every day on his way to school: a narrow-fronted red brick building with

sandstone trim, and a sandstone cross over the gable; and
though he had heard the bell time and time again its note
had never struck him. But sounding thus through the hush
of the night, alone awake in the sleeping town, it spoke to
his wakefulness with a shock of mystery.

The same feeling came over him as he stood in the long
grass before the abandoned house. He felt in the age and
the emptiness of it something of the church bell's haunting
sonority—as if it kept in its mute walls a voice as secret and
compelling. If only he had known how to pull the rope and
start the clapper swinging!

As he stood there the shutters were thrown back from
one of the windows on the ground floor, and Upton leaned
out to hail him. "Hul*lo!* Laura Lou thought the ghosts had
got you."

"They had—almost," Vance laughed. He went up to the
window and swung himself into the room. Upton had
opened all the shutters, and the afternoon light flowed softly
in. The room was not large, but its ceiling was high, with a
dim cobwebby cornice. On the floor was a carpet with a
design of large flower wreaths and bows and loops of faded
green. The mantelpiece, richly carved, was surmounted by a
mirror reaching to the ceiling; and here and there stood
pieces of furniture of a polished black wood inlaid with pat-
terns of ivory or metal. There were tall vases on mantel and
table, their flanks painted with landscapes in medallion, or
garlanded with heavy wreathes like those on the carpet. On
the mantelpiece Vance noticed a round-faced clock guarded
by an old man in bronze with a scythe and an hourglass;
and stiffly ranged about the room were armchairs and small
seats covered with a pale material slit and tattered with age.
As Vance stood looking at it all Laura Lou appeared from
another room. A long apron covered her from chin to knees,
and she had tied a towel about her head, and carried a large
feather duster.

"This is where she always sat," she whispered to Vance, signalling to him to follow. The room she led him into was more sombre than the other, partly because the wistaria had stretched a long drapery across one of the windows, partly because the walls were dark and had tall heavy bookcases against them. In a bow window stood a table with a velvet table cover trailing its faded folds and moth-eaten fringes on the floor. It bore a monumental inkstand, a bronze lamp with a globe of engraved glass, a work basket, and two or three books. But what startled Vance, and made him, in his surprise, forget everything else, was the fact that one of the books lay open, and that across the page was a small pair of oddly shaped spectacles in a thin gold mounting. It looked as if someone had been reading there a few minutes before, and, disturbed by the sound of steps, had dropped the book and spectacles and glided out of sight. Vance remembered Laura Lou's fear of ghosts, and glanced about him half apprehensively, as if the reader of that book, the wearer of those spectacles, might be peering at them from some shadowy corner of the room.

As he looked his eye fell on a picture hanging above the mantelpiece—a crayon drawing, he thought it must be, in a bossy and ponderous gilt frame. It was the portrait of a middle-aged woman, seen in three-quarter length. She leaned on a table with a heavy velvet cover, bearing an inkstand and some books—the very table and the very inkstand, Vance perceived, on which the picture itself looked down. And the lady, past a doubt, was Miss Lorburn: Miss Lorburn in her thoughtful middle age. She had dark hair, parted in heavy folds above a wide meditative forehead touched with highlights in chalk. Her face was long and melancholy. The lappets of her lace cap fell on her shoulders, and her thin arms emerged from the wide sleeves of a dark jacket, with undersleeves of white lawn also picked out in chalk.

The peculiar dress, the sad face, resembled nothing Vance had ever seen; but instantly he felt their intimate relation to all that was peculiar and unfamiliar in the house. The past—they all belonged to the past, this woman and her house, to the same past, a past of their own, a past so remote from anything in Vance Weston's experience that it took its place in the pages of history anywhere in the dark Unknown before Euphoria was. He continued to gaze up at the sad woman, who looked down on him with large full-orbed eyes, as if it were she who had just dropped her book and spectacles, and reascended to her frame as he came in.

Without surprise he heard Laura Lou say behind him: "This is the book she was reading when she died. Mr. Lorburn—that's her nephew—won't let us touch anything in this room, not even to dust it. We have to dust the things without moving them."

He had never heard Laura Lou make such a long speech; but he had no ears for it. He nodded, and she tiptoed away with her duster. Far off, down the inlaid wooden floors, he heard Upton clumping about in his heavy gardening shoes, opening other doors and shutters. Laura Lou called to him, and their voices receded together to some distant part of the house.

Vance stood alone in Miss Lorburn's library. He had never been in a private library before; he hardly knew that collections of books existed as personal possessions, outside of colleges and other public institutions. And all these books had been a woman's, had been this Miss Lorburn's, and she had sat among them, lived among them, died reading them —reading the very one on the table at his elbow! It all seemed part of the incomprehensible past to which she and the house belonged, a past so remote, so full of elusive mystery, that Vance's first thought was: "Why wasn't I ever told about the Past before?"

He turned from the portrait and looked about the room,

trying vainly to picture what this woman's life had been, in her solemn high-ceilinged house, alone among her books. He thought of her on winter evenings, sitting at this table, beside the oil lamp with the engraved globe, her queer little spectacles on that long grave nose, poring, poring over the pages, while the wind wailed down the chimney and the snow piled itself up on the lawns. And on summer evenings she sat here too, probably—he could not picture her out of doors; sat here in a slanting light, like that now falling through the wistaria fringes, and leaned her sad head on her hand, and read and read. . . .

His eyes wandered from the close rows of books on the shelves to the one lying open on the table. That was the book she had been reading when she died—died as a very old woman, and yet so incalculably long ago. Vance moved to the table, and bent over the open page. It was yellow, and blotched with dampness: the type was queer too, different from any that was familiar to him. He read:

"In Xanadu did Kubla Khan—"

Oh, what beautiful, what incredible words! What did they mean? But what did it matter what they meant? Or whether they meant anything but their own unutterable music? Vance dropped down into the high-backed armchair by the table, pushed the spectacles away from the page, and read on.

> *"In Xanadu did Kubla Khan*
> *A stately pleasure-dome decree:*
> *Where Alph, the sacred river, ran*
> *Through caverns measureless to man,*
> *Down to a sunless sea . . ."*

It was a new music, a music utterly unknown to him, but to which the hidden chords of his soul at once vibrated.

It was something for *him*—something that intimately belonged to him. What had he ever known of poetry before? His mind's eye ran over the verse he had been nurtured on: James Whitcomb Riley, Ella Wheeler Wilcox, Bliss Carman's "Songs from Vagabondia"; hackneyed old "pieces" from Whittier and Longfellow, in the Sixth Reader; Lowell's "Ode"—there were fine bits in that—Whitman's "Pioneers" (good, too, but rather jiggy); and then the new stuff he had got glimpses of here and there in the magazines, in one or two of the "highbrow" reviews (but these hardly ever came his way), and in his college paper. And he had taken it for granted that he had covered the field of poetry. . . .

And now—this! But this *was* poetry, this was what his soul had been alight for, this was what the word Poetry meant, the word which always made wings rustle in him when he read it. He sat with his head between his hands, reading on, passionately, absorbedly, his whole being swept away on that mighty current. He remembered that, as he looked up at the house from without, he had compared it to a long-silent bell, and had longed to set its sonorous waves in motion. And behold, the bell was swinging and clanging all about him now, enveloping him in great undulation of sound like the undulations of a summer sea.

But for that inner music the house was utterly silent. The steps and voices of his cousins had died away. The very afternoon light seemed to lie arrested on the page. He seemed to have been sitting there a long time, in this unmoving ecstasy, when something stirred near him, and raising his head he saw a girl standing in the door and looking at him.

"Oh, who wrote this?" he exclaimed breathlessly, pointing to the book.

It was only after he had asked the question, after his voice had sounded aloud in his own ears, that he became conscious of her presence as of something alien, substantial,

outside of his own mind, a part of the forgotten world of reality. Then he saw that she was young, tall, and pale, with
dark hair banded close under her drooping hat. There was
something about her, he saw also, that fitted into the scene,
seemed to mark her as a part of it, though he was instantly
aware of her being so young, not much older than himself,
he imagined. But what were time and space at that moment?

Without surprise, but merely smiling a little, she came
up and bent over the book, narrowing her lids slightly in the
way of the short-sighted. "That? Why—but Coleridge, of
course!" She chanted softly after him:

> " 'Through caverns measureless to man,
>   Down to a sunless sea.' "

Vance sat looking up at her. He had heard the "of
course," but without heeding it. All he cared for was that
she had given him the man's name—the man who had imagined that. His brain was reeling as if he were drunk. He had
not thought of moving from his chair, of naming himself to
the newcomer, or asking her name.

"Did he write a lot more?" he asked.

She stood by the table, her hands lightly resting on it,
and looked down on him with a faint smile. "Yes, he did,
worse luck."

"Worse luck—?"

"Because so very little was of that quality." Without
taking the book from him, or looking at the page, she went
on:

> " 'But O, that deep romantic chasm which slanted
>   Down the green hill athwart a cedarn cover...' "

Vance listened enthralled. Her rich voice, modelling the
words, gave them a new relief. He was half aware that her

way of speaking was unlike any he had ever heard, but too
much under the spell of what she was saying to separate it
from the quality of her utterance. He commanded imperi-
ously: "Go on—" and she continued, leaning slightly toward him and dropping the petal-like syllables with soft deliberation:

> "'A damsel with a dulcimer
> In a vision once I saw . . .'"

Vance leaned back and listened with deep-drawn breath
and lowered lids. "Honey-dew . . . honey-dew . . ." he
murmured as she ended, half consciously applying the
epithet to her voice.

She dropped down into a chair beside him and looked
at him thoughtfully. "It's queer—your caring as much as
that about poetry, and never having come across this."

He flushed up, and for the first time looked at her with
full awareness of her presence as a stranger, and an intruder
on his dream. The look confirmed him in the impression that
she was very young, though probably two or three years
older than himself. But it might be only her tallness and self-
assurance which made him think her older. She had dark
gray eyes, deeply lashed, and features somewhat too long
and thin in repose, but rounded and illumined by a smile
which flashed across her face in sudden sympathy or amusement. Vance detected amusement now, and answered
curtly: "I daresay if you knew me you'd think there was a
whole lot of things I'd never come across."

"I daresay," she agreed complaisantly. "But I might also
remember that you were probably too young even to have
heard of 'The Ancient Mariner.'"

"Coleridge? The 'Ancient Mariner' one? Was it the
same who wrote this?"

She nodded. "You know 'The Ancient Mariner,' then?

Sixth Reader, I suppose—or college course?" She laughed a little. "So culture comes."

He interrupted angrily: "What have I said to make you laugh?"

"Nothing. I wasn't laughing at you, but at the intelligence of our national educators—no, educationists, I think they call themselves nowadays—who manage to take the bloom off our greatest treasures by giving them to young savages to maul. I see, for instance, that they've spoilt 'The Ancient Mariner' for you." She continued to scrutinize him thoughtfully. "You're not one of the young savages—but the bloom has been rubbed off a good many things for you in that way, hasn't it?"

"Well, yes—some."

"Not that it matters—for *you*. You'll get it back. But I do so hate to think of mutilated beauty."

Mutilated beauty! How rich the words sounded on her lips—as if she swept the rubbish of the centuries from some broken statue, noble in its ruin! Vance continued to look at her, absently yet intently. He had drawn her into his dream.

But she stood up and pushed her chair aside. "And now," she said gaily, in a new voice, a light and humorous one, "perhaps you'll tell me who you are and how you got here."

The question seemed to come to him from so far off that he stared at her perplexedly before answering. "I—oh, I'm just the Tracys' cousin. I'm staying at their house. They're somewhere round dusting the other rooms."

Her look became more friendly. "Oh, you're the cousin from the West, who's been ill and has come to Paul's Landing for a change? Mrs. Tracy told me about you—only I can't remember your name."

"Vance Weston."

"Mine's Héloïse Spear. They call me Halo. The name

and the nickname are both ridiculous." She held out her hand. "And you've come to call on poor old Cousin Elinor? It's an attention she doesn't often receive from her own family." She glanced about the room. "I haven't been here in an age—I don't know what made me come today. At least I didn't—" she broke off with one of her fugitive smiles, letting her eyes rest on his and then turning away from him to inspect the books. "Some day," she said, as if to herself, "I must have the courage to take these down and give them a good cleaning."

Vance stood up also, beginning to speak eagerly. "Could I come and help you when you do—I mean with the books? I'd—I'd like it first-rate."

She turned back to him, her eyes brimming with banter and coquetry. "On account of the books?"

But he was too deep in his own emotion to heed the challenge. He answered simply: "I don't often get a chance at this kind." His eyes followed hers about the crowded shelves. "I've never before been in a house with a library—a real library like this."

She gave a little shrug. "Oh, it's a funny library, antiquated, like the house. But Cousin Elinor does seem to have cared for good poetry. When other ladies were reading 'Friendship's Garland' she chose Coleridge."

His gaze returned perplexed to her face. "Why do you call it a funny library?"

"Well, it's not exactly up-to-date. I suppose it's a fairly good specimen of what used to be called a 'gentleman's library' in my great-grandfather's time. With additions, naturally, from each generation. Cousin Elinor must have bought a good many books herself." She looked about her critically. "After all," she concluded with a smile, "the Willows is getting to have an atmosphere."

Vance listened, still perplexed. Her allusions escaped him—her smile was unintelligible—but he gathered that she attached no very great importance to the house, or to the books, and he dimly resented this air of taking for granted what to him was the revelation of an unknown world.

Involuntarily he lowered his voice. "It's the first time I've ever been in a very old house," he said, as if announcing something of importance.

"A very old house? The Willows?" The idea seemed a new one to her. "Well—after all, everything is relative, as what's-his-name said."

"Don't you call it a very old house?"

She wrinkled her dark eyebrows in an effort of memory. "Let me see. Father's great-uncle Ambrose Lorburn built it, I believe. When would that be?" She began to count on her fingers. "Say about 1830. Well, that *does* make it very nearly an old house for America, doesn't it? Almost a hundred years!"

"And the same folks always lived in it?"

"Oh, of course." She seemed surprised at the question. "The present owner is the first absentee—poor Cousin Tom! He thinks he ought to live here, but he says he can't come up to scratch. So he makes up for it by keeping everything unchanged." Again she surveyed the plaintive shadowy room. "I suppose," she mused, "the house will be getting to have an archaeological interest of its own before long. It must be one of the best specimens of Hudson River Bracketed that are left, even in our ultra-conservative neighbourhood."

To Vance she seemed still to be speaking another language, of which he caught only an occasional phrase, and even that but half comprehensible.

"Hudson River Bracketed?" he echoed. "What's that?"

"Why, didn't you know it was our indigenous style of architecture in this part of the world?" Her smile of mockery had returned, but he did not mind for he saw it was not directed against himself. "I perceive," she continued, "that you are not familiar with the epoch-making work of A. J.

Downing Esq. on Landscape Gardening in America." She
turned to the bookcases, ran her hand along a shelf, and
took down a volume bound in black cloth with the title in
gilt Gothic lettering. Her fingers flew from page to page, her
short-sighted eyes following as swiftly. "Here—here's the
place. It's too long to read aloud; but the point is that Mr.
Downing, who was the great authority of the period, sums
up the principal architectural styles as the Grecian, the Chinese, the Gothic, the Tuscan or Italian villa, and—Hudson
River Bracketed. Unless I'm mistaken, he cites the Willows
as one of the most perfect examples of Hudson River Bracketed (this was in 1842), and—yes, here's the place: 'The
seat of Ambrose Lorburn Esq., the Willows, near Paul's
Landing, Dutchess County, N.Y., is one of the most successful instances of etc., etc. . . . architectural elements in-
geniously combined from the Chinese and the Tuscan." And
so they were! What an eye the man had. And here's the picture, willows and all! How lovely these old steel engravings
were . . . and look at my great-uncle and aunt on the
lawn, pointing out to each other with pride and admiration
their fairly obvious copper beech . . . 'one of the first ever
planted in a gentleman's grounds in the United States.' "

They bent their heads together over the engraving,
which, as she said, reproduced the house exactly as Vance
had just beheld it, except that the willows were then slender
young trees, and the lawns mown, that striped awnings
shaded the lower windows, and that a gentleman in a tall
hat and a stock was calling the attention of a lady in bonnet
and cashmere shawl to the celebrated copper beech. From
Miss Spear's tone Vance could not tell whether pride or
mockery was uppermost in her comments on her ancestor's
achievement. But he dimly guessed that, though she might
laugh at the Willows, and at what Mr. Downing said of it,
she was not sorry that the house figured so honourably in his
book.

"There," she concluded with a laugh, "now you know

what the Hudson River Bracketed style was like, and why Uncle Ambrose Lorburn was so proud of his specimen of it." She handed him the volume, glanced at her wristwatch, and turned to nod to him from the threshold. "Gracious, how late it is! I must hunt up the Tracy children, and see how much crockery they've smashed."

She disappeared in the spectral shadows of the drawing room, and Vance heard her heels rapping lightly across the hall, and through unknown rooms and passages beyond. He sat motionless where she had left him, his elbows propped on the table, the book still open before him, his head pressed between his hands, letting the strangeness of the place and the hour envelop him like the falling light.

It was dusk in the book-lined room when he was roused by Upton's hobbledehoy tread and a tap on the shoulder. "What's become of you? I guess you've been sound asleep," his cousin challenged him.

Vance sat upright with a start. "No, I haven't been asleep." He got to his feet and looked about him. "Where's Miss Spear?"

"Miss Halo? Oh, did you see her? She's gone long ago. A gentleman friend called for her in his car. I don't know where they went. She never stays anywhere more than five minutes." Vance was silent, and Upton added: "Say, come along; Laura Lou's waiting. Time to lock up."

Vance reluctantly followed his cousin. As they left the house he realized that, instead of seizing the opportunity to explore every nook of it, he had sat all the afternoon in one room, and merely dreamed of what he might have seen in the others. But that was always his way: the least little fragment of fact was enough for him to transform into a palace of dreams, whereas if he tried to grasp more of it at a time it remained on his hands as so much unusable reality.

⊰ VII ⊱

THREE MEN and two ladies were sitting on the shabby paint-less verandah at Eaglewood at the end of a summer after-noon.

The place was full of the signs of comfortable but dis-orderly use. A low table was spread with tea things, a teapot of one make, cups of another, plates with fragments of stale-looking cake and cold toast. There were willow armchairs, some disabled and mended with string, but all provided with gaily striped cushions which had visibly suffered from sun and rain; there were also long deck chairs with tattered plaids or Indian blankets on them, and more cushions strewn on the floor, among a litter of magazines and news-papers. In one corner stood a tall earthen jar with branches of blossoming plum and shadbush, in another an easel with a study blocked out in charcoal, and everywhere were trails of ashes, and little accumulations of cigar and cigarette ends.

The low-studded old house of gray stone was throned on the mountainside so high above Paul's Landing that those who sat on the verandah missed the dispiriting sight of the town and of the cement works below, and saw only, beyond the precipitate plunge of many-tinted forest, the great sweep of the Hudson, and the cliffs on its other shore.

The view from Eaglewood was famous—yet visible, Héloïse Spear reflected, to none of those who habitually lived with it except herself. Her mother, she thought, had probably seen it for a while, years ago, in her first eager youth; then it had been lost in a mist of multiple preoccupations, literary, humanitarian, and domestic, from which it emerged only when visitors were led out on the verandah for the first time. "Ah, our view—*yes*," Mrs. Spear would then murmur, closing her handsome eyes as if to shut herself in with the unutterable, away from the importunities of spoken praise. And her guests would remain silent, too much impressed by her attitude to find the superlatives expected of them.

As for Mr. Spear, his daughter knew that he had simply never seen the view at all; his eyes had never been still long enough. But he had read of it in verse and prose; he talked of it with vivacity and emotion; he knew the attitude to strike, deprecating yet possessive, lighting a cigarette while the others gazed, and saying: "The poets have sung us, as you know. You remember Bryant's 'Eyrie'? Yes—that's the Eaglewood view. He used to stay here with my wife's great-grandfather. And Washington Irving, in his *Sketch Book*. And Whitman—it's generally supposed . . ." And at that point Mrs. Spear would open her eyes to interject: "Really? You didn't know that my husband knew Whitman? I always scold him for not having written down some of their wonderful talks together—"

"Ah, Whitman was a very old man when I knew him— immobilized at Camden. He never came here in my time. But from something he once said I gathered that Eaglewood undoubtedly . . . yes, I must really jot it all down one of these days. . . ."

Mr. Spear's past was full of the dateless blur of the remarkable things he had not jotted down. Slim, dark, well-preserved, with his wavy grayish hair and cleverly dyed moustache, he was the type of the busy dreamer who is forever glancing at his watch, calling impatiently for time-tables and calendars (two articles never to be found in the

Spear household), calculating and plotting out his engagements, doubting whether there will be time to squeeze in
this or that, wondering if after all it will be possible to
"make it," and then, at the end of each day, groaning as he
lights his after-dinner cigar: "Devil take it, when I got up
this morning I thought of a lot of rather important things I
had to do—and like a fool I forgot to jot them down." It
was not to be expected, Halo thought, that a man as busy as
her father should ever have time to look at a sunset.

As for Héloïse's brother Lorry (Lorburn, of course)
who sat extended in the hollow of a canvas chair, his handsome contemptuous head tilted back, and his feet on the
verandah rail, Lorry, the fool, *could* see the view when he
chose, and out of sheer perversity and posing, wouldn't—
and that was worst of all, to his sister's thinking. "Oh, for
God's sake, Halo, don't serve up the view again, there's a
good girl! Shan't I ever be able to teach you *not to have
taste?* The world's simply dying of a surfeit of scenery—an
orgy of beauty. If my father would cut down some of those
completely superfluous trees, and let us get a line on the
chimney of the cement factory . . . It's a poor little chimney, of course, but it's got the supreme quality of ugliness.
In certain lights, you know, it's almost as ugly as the Willows
. . . or the Parthenon, say. . . ."

But unless there were visitors present Lorry seldom got
as far as the Parthenon in his monologue, because he knew
his family had long since discounted his opinions about
beauty, and went on thinking of other things while he was
airing them—even old George Frenside did nowadays,
though once the boy's paradoxes had seemed to amuse
him.

George Frenside was the other man on the verandah.
There he sat, behind his sempiternal cigar, glowering into
the tender spaces of the sky as if what he saw there were an
offense to the human race; yet Halo wondered if one could

say of those small deep-sunk eyes, forever watchful behind their old-fashioned pince-nez, that anything they
rested on escaped them. Probably not; for in certain ways
he was sensitive to beauty, and not afraid of it, like Lorry.
Only, to move him, it had to be beauty of man's making,
something wrung by human genius out of the stubborn elements. The sunset and the woodlands were nothing to him
if they had not fed a poet or a painter—a poet preferably.
Frenside had often said to Halo: "No, my child; remember
I'm not a vegetarian—never could digest raw landscape."
But that did not mean that he did not *see* it, did not parcel
it out into its component parts with those cool classifying
eyes. George Frenside was aware of most things; little escaped him of the cosmic spectacle. Only for him the beauty
of the earth was something you could take apart, catalogue,
and pigeonhole, and not the enveloping harmony it was to
the girl who sat beside him looking out on the sunset opal-
escence at their feet.

George Frenside was an institution at Eaglewood, and
wherever else the Spears set up their tents. His short stocky
figure, his brooding Socratic head, his cigar and eyeglasses,
figured among Halo's earliest recollections, and she had always seen him as she saw him now: elderly, poor, unsuccessful, and yet more masterful, more stimulating, than anyone else she had known. "A fire that warms everything but
itself," she had once defined him; but he had snapped back:
"I don't warm, I singe."

Not a bad description of his relation to most people;
but she, who knew him so well, knew also the communicative glow he could give out, and often wondered why it had
never lit up his own path.

She was familiar with Frenside's explanation: the critical faculty outweighed all others in him, and, as he had
often told her, criticism won't keep its man. He saw (he also
said) the skeletons of things and people: he was a walking

radiograph. God knows he didn't want to be—would rather
not have had a decomposing mind. But it was the one allot-
ted to him, and with it he had lingered on the outskirts of
success, contributing fierce dissections of political and literary ideas to various newspapers and reviews, often refusing
to write an article when it was asked for—and especially
when a good sum was offered for it—and then suddenly
dashing off a brilliant diatribe which no one wanted, and
which came back to him from one editor after another. He
had written, a good many years earlier, a brief volume of
essays called *Dry Points,* which had had a considerable success in the limited circle of the cultivated, and been enthusiastically reviewed in England. This had produced a handsome offer from a publisher, who asked Frenside for a revolutionary book on education: a subject made to his hand.
The idea delighted him, he wanted the money badly, he had
never before had the offer of so large a sum; and he sat para-
lyzed by the completeness of the opportunity. One day he
found a title which amused him—The Art of Imparting Ignorance—and that was the only line of the book he ever
wrote.

"It's one of the surest signs of genius to do your best
when you're working for money," he told Halo. "I have only
talent—and the idea of doing a book to order simply benumbed me. What the devil can I do but keep on hack-writ-
ing?" But even that he did only intermittently. Nevertheless,
he held jealously to his pecuniary independence, and,
though he frequently accepted the hospitality of the Spears,
and of a few other old friends, he was never known to have
borrowed a penny of any of them, a fact which Halo Spear's
own brief experience led her to regard as unusual, and almost unaccountable. But then, she thought, there was nothing about George Frenside that wasn't queer, even to his
virtues. . . .

Her eyes wandered back to the landscape. It lay before

her in the perfect beauty of a June evening: one of those evenings when twilight floats aloft in an air too pure to be penetrated by the density of darkness. What did it all mean, she wondered—that there should be this beauty, so ever-varying, so soul-sufficing, so complete, and face to face with it these people who one and all would gladly have ex-changed it for any one of a hundred other things; her mother for money enough to carry them to the end of the year, her father for his New York club and a bridge table, Lorry of course for money too (money was always the burn-ing question in the Spear family), and George Frenside for good talk in a Bohemian restaurant?

The girl herself shared, or at least understood, the hereditary antagonism toward Eaglewood of those who lived there. To the last two generations of Lorburns Eagle-wood had embodied all the things they could not do because of it. The only member of the family who idealised it (and even he only theoretically) was Mr. Spear, who had "mar-ried into" it, and still faintly glowed with the refracted hon-our of speaking of "our little old place on the Hudson."

Old it was, for an American possession. Lorburns had lived there for considerably over two hundred years: the present house had been built in 1680. It was too long, per-haps, for Americans to live in any one place; and the worst of it was that, when they had, it became a sort of tribal ob-ligation to go on doing so. Sell Eaglewood? Which one of them would have dared to? When Pittsburgh and Chicago fell upon the feudal Hudson, and one old property after an-other was bartered for a mess of pottage, the Lorburns sat apart with lifted brows, and grimly thanked Providence that Paul's Landing was too far from New York to attract the millionaires. Even now, had fashion climbed to their solitary height it is doubtful if any of them—not excepting Lorry—would have dared to mention aloud the places they could have gone to, and the things they could have done, if only

they had been free of Eaglewood. As it happened, no such
danger threatened, for fashion had passed them by; but had
the peril been imminent, Mr. Spear would have opposed it
with all the force of his eloquence.

Mr. Spear regarded Eaglewood with the veneration of
the parvenu for a recently acquired ancestor. When he married the beautiful Miss Lorburn, New York said: "He's very
clever, of course; but still, who would have expected to see a
Spear at Eaglewood?" And he knew it, and was determined
to show New York that a Spear could be perfectly at home
even at that altitude.

He was himself the son of the Reverend Harold Spear,
the eloquent and popular divine who for years had packed
Saint Ambrose's with New York's most distinguished con-
gregation. Dr. Spear, as popular out of the pulpit as in it,
had married a distant cousin of the Van der Luydens, thus
paving the way for his son's more brilliant alliance; but still
it required a certain courage on the part of the heiress of
Eaglewood to accept a suitor whom her friends alluded to
as "merely clever." Sometimes Héloïse, thinking over the
phrase (which her mother had once quoted to her in derision), smiled to note how exact it was. After all, those dull
old Lorburns and their clan must have had a nice sense of
nuances: her father, whom she loved and laughed at, was
exactly that—he was merely clever. It was perhaps because
his wife belonged to the same category (though, being a
Lorburn, she had never been placed in it, since a Lorburn
woman might be beautiful, or masterful, or distinguished,
but never anything so ambiguous as "clever") that she had
had been attracted by young Spear, and had married
him in spite of the family opposition. Emily Lorburn,
brought up in an atmosphere of rigid social conformity, had
become passionately nonconforming; her husband, educated after the strict rule of Episcopalian orthodoxy, had
read Strauss and Renan in secret before going over openly

to Darwin and Haeckel. The young people, dazzled by each
other's audacities, had perhaps expected, by pooling them,
to form a nucleus of intellectual revolt; but the world had
revolted without waiting for them. Their heresies were too
mild to cause any excitement outside of their own circle,
and their house, instead of being the centre of incendiarism
they had imagined, was merely regarded as one where one
was likely to meet agreeable people.

All this, though long since patent to their children, was
still but dimly apprehended by Mr. and Mrs. Spear, and
Halo knew that her mother secretly regarded Eaglewood,
the obligations it entailed and the privations it necessitated,
as the chief obstacle to the realizing of her ambitions. Mrs.
Spear felt that what both she and her husband needed to
produce the revolutionary effect they aimed at was a house
in New York; and for years all her energies had been bent
on getting it. These had been the years of Halo's little girl-
hood and first youth: economical years marked by a series
of snowbound winters at Eaglewood, and (whenever the
place could be let) European summers in places dingily aesthetic. But in spite of these sacrifices the unequal struggle
had had to be given up; the visionary house in New York
had shrunk to a small flat, the flat to six weeks in a family
hotel, with Eaglewood for the rest of the year; and at present, as Halo knew, her mother was anxiously calculating
whether, with the growing cost of everything, and Lorry's
perpetual debts, and perpetual inability to find a job, it
would not be necessary to renounce even a month in the
family hotel.

There were times when to the girl herself Eaglewood
was as much of a prison as to her elders. But the fact that it
was easier for her than for her parents to get away made the
being there less irksome; and besides, she loved the place for
itself, instead of being proud of it for family reasons, and

hating it for every other. The house depressed her, in spite of its portraits and relics, and the faded perfume of old days, because it was associated with the perpetual struggle to keep the roof dry, the ceilings patched, the furnace going, the curtains and carpets turned and darned, the taxes paid. But poverty and lack of care could not spoil what lay outside the house: the acres of neglected parkland with ancient trees widening their untrimmed domes over lawns that had lapsed into pasture, the woods beyond, murmuring and glinting with little streams, and that ever-renewed view on which the girl's eyes never rested without the sense of inner communion which all the others had missed.

Ah, that view . . . suddenly she thought: "I believe the boy I saw down at the Willows last week has the only eyes I know that would really see it as I do—"; and the thought, rousing her out of her dream, brought her to her feet with a jerk.

"Oh," she exclaimed, with a cry in which amusement mingled with consternation; for she saw nearly everything in life first on the amusing side, even to her own shortcomings.

George Frenside lifted his head from the newspaper and turned his ironic eyeglasses on her. "What's up?"

"Only that I've forgotten an engagement."

"What? Again?"

She nodded contritely. "I'm a perfect beast—it was simply vile of me!" She was talking to herself, not to Frenside. As for her own family, they were all too used to her frequent outbursts of compunction over forgotten engagements to let her remorse disturb their meditations.

For a moment she stood brooding over her latest lapse; then she turned to re-enter the house. As she disappeared Mrs. Spear, roused from some inner calculation which had wrinkled her brows and sharpened the lines about her mouth, sat up to call after her in a deep wailing voice: "But Lewis Tarrant—have you *all* forgotten Lewis Tarrant? Who's going to fetch him from the station?"

Whenever Mrs. Spear emerged thus suddenly from the sea of her perplexities, her still lovely face wore a half-drowned look which made Halo feel as if one ought to give her breathing exercises and other first-aid remedies.

"Don't look so upset, darling. Why should you think I'd forgotten Lewis? I'm going down presently to meet him; his train's not due for another hour."

But Lorry Spear, with an effort, had pulled himself to his feet and cast away his cigarette end. "You needn't, Halo. I'll go," he said in a voice of brotherly self-sacrifice.

"Thanks ever so, Lorry. But don't bother—"

"No bother, child. I'll call at the post at the same time, and pick up Mother's arrowroot at the grocer's."

This evoked a languid laugh from Mr. Spear and Frenside, for the grocery at Paul's Landing was the repository for all Mrs. Spear's daily purchases, and whenever she suggested that, yes, well, perhaps they *had* better call there on the way home, because she believed she had ordered a packet of arrowroot, the motor would invariably climb the hill from the town groaning with innumerable parcels.

Halo paused in the glass door leading into the hall. "I want the car for myself, Lorry," she said decisively, and turned to go in. Behind her, as she crossed the hall, she heard her brother's precipitate steps. "See here, Halo—stop! I'm going down to meet Lewis; I want to."

She faced him with her faint smile. "Oh, certainly. Come with me, then."

"What's the use of your going?" His handsome irresolute mouth grew sulky and resentful. "Fact is I rather want to see Lewis alone. We've got a little matter—"

His sister's eyebrows rose ironically. "So I supposed. How much this time, Lorry?"

"How much—?"

"Yes. Only don't exaggerate. I've told you I want the car for myself. How much were you going to ask Lewis to lend you?"

Her brother, flushing up, began to protest and ejaculate. "Damned impertinence—" But Halo lifted her arm to examine her wristwatch. "Don't splutter like Father when he says he's going to denounce an outrage in the papers. And don't be exorbitant either." She fumbled in the shabby antelope bag which hung from her other wrist. "Here—will this do?" She took out two ten-dollar notes and held them toward her brother.

"Hell, child—" he stammered, manifestly tempted and yet furious.

"You know you wouldn't get as much out of Lewis. Better take it."

He stood with his hands in his pockets, his chin down, staring at the notes without moving.

"Come, Lorry; I tell you I'm in a hurry." She made a slight motion as though to reopen the bag and put back the money.

"I'll go down myself to fetch Lewis," he mumbled, all the fluid lines of his face hardening into an angry obstinacy.

"You won't!"

"Won't I? You'll see, then—" He caught her by the wrist, and they stood glaring at each other and breathing hard, like two angry young animals. Then Halo, with a laugh, wrenched her hand free, and reopening the bag drew out another ten dollars. She tossed the three notes on the table, and walked across the hall and out of the front door. No footsteps followed her, and she deemed it superfluous to glance back and see if the money had been removed from the table.

⚛ VIII ⚛

IN THE cobwebby coach-house of the old stable she found the man-of-all-work, Jacob, who was chauffeur when he was not gardener and dairyman, lying on the floor with his head under the car. He emerged at her call, and said he guessed there was something wrong again, because Mr. Lorry had had trouble getting her up the hill, and maybe he'd better take her to pieces while he was about it.

"Not on your life. I'm going down to Paul's Landing in her this minute."

Jacob stared, but without protesting. "You won't get back, very likely," he merely observed, and Halo scrambled into the motor with a laugh and a shrug. The motor, she said to herself, was like life in general at Eaglewood: it was always breaking down, but it always managed to keep on going. "Tied together with string and patched up with court plaster: that's been the way with everything in the family ever since I can remember." She gave a little sigh as she slipped down the overgrown drive, heading for the stone pillars of the gateway. The motor, she knew, would be all right going down the hill to Paul's Landing—and after that, at the moment, she didn't particularly care. If she and Lewis Tarrant had to walk back to Eaglewood in the dark— well, Lewis wouldn't mind, she imagined. But meanwhile she had to catch up somehow with her forgotten engagement.

In a few minutes the winding road down the mountain

brought her to the sad outskirts of Paul's Landing, and
thence to the Tracys' house. She jumped out, ran up the
steps and knocked, looking about her curiously as she did
so. She seldom went to the Tracys', and had forgotten how
shabby and humble the place was. The discovery increased
her sense of compunction and self-disapproval. How could
she have forgotten that clever boy there for so long! If he
had been one of her own group it would never have happened. "If there's anything I hate," she reflected, "it's seeming casual to people who live like this." And instantly she
decided that one ought to devote one's whole life to the
Tracys and their kind, and that to enjoy the world's goods,
even in the limited and precarious way in which they were
enjoyed at Eaglewood, while other lives like these were
being lived at one's door, denoted a vulgarity of soul which
was the last fault she would have cared to confess to. What
made it worse, too, in the particular case, was the Tracys'
far-off cousinship with the Lorburn family; the fact that two
or three generations ago a foolish (and elderly) Lorburn
virgin had run away with farmer Tracy's son, who worked
in the cement factory down on the river, and being cast off
by her family had dropped to the level of her husband's,
with whom affairs had not gone well, and who had left his
widow and children in poverty. Nowadays all this would
have signified much less, as far as the family's social situation went; but in the compact life of sixty years ago it was a
hopeless fall to lapse from the height of Eaglewood to the
depth in which the small shopkeepers and farmers of Paul's
Landing had their being. It was all wrong, Halo mused,
wrinkling her young brows like her mother's in the effort to
think out, then and there, while she waited for her ring to
be answered, the quickest way of putting an end to such injustice.

The development of her plan was interrupted by the
appearance of young Upton, who looked at her with such

surprise that she felt more acutely than ever her suddenly discovered obligation toward his family.

"Oh, Upton, how are you? I know I've interrupted you at supper! I hope your mother won't be very angry with me."

"Angry—?" young Tracy echoed, bewildered. He passed the back of his hand over his mouth in the effort to conceal the fact that she had rightly suspected him of coming from supper. "I thought mebbe there was something wrong at the Willows," he said.

"The Willows! No. Or rather, yes, it is about the Willows—" She burst out laughing. "Don't look so frightened, poor Upton! The wrongdoing's mine, all mine. I believe I promised to meet your cousin there this afternoon, to let him take a look at the books. . . ." She looked interrogatively at Upton, and caught his motion of assent. "Didn't I? Yes. Well—and I didn't go. It was all my fault. The fact is I was . . . prevented . . . at the last minute. I should so like to see him and explain. . . ."

"Oh," said Upton, with evident relief. He glanced about him timidly, away from her sweeping searching eyes: "If you'll step into the parlour, Miss Halo—"

She shook her head. "No, I won't do that, or your mother'll feel she ought to leave her supper to receive me. And I've only got a minute—I'm meeting a friend at the station," she reminded herself with a start, for that also she had been near forgetting. "So if you'll just ask your cousin—Vance, that's his name, isn't it?—ask him to come out here and say two words to me . . ."

"Oh, certainly," Upton agreed. He turned back into the house, but the visitor caught him by the sleeve. "Upton! Listen. Don't mention my name; don't tell Vance I'm here. Just say it's somebody with a message—*somebody with a message*," she repeated, trying with her sharp italics to bore the fact into the youth's brain.

"Oh, certainly," Upton repeated. He walked away to

the back of the house, and Héloïse, already partly rid of her burden of self-reproach, as she always tended to be the moment she had given it expression, stood looking absently over the garden, the broken-down fence, and the darkness already gathering in the folds of the hills.

She heard another step, and saw Vance Weston. He stood gazing at her with wide open eyes, his face small and drawn from his recent illness. In the twilight of the library at the Willows he had not looked so boyish; now she was struck by his frailness and immaturity, and felt sorrier than ever that she had failed to keep her promise.

"It's me, Vance. I've come to apologize about this afternoon."

"Oh—" he began, as awkwardly as Upton.

"You went to the Willows after lunch, and waited for me?" He nodded without speaking.

"Waited *hours?*"

"I didn't mind. I sat in the porch. I liked it."

"Well, it was hideous of me—hideous! I don't know how . . ."

He looked at her in surprise. "How could you help it? Upton said something prevented you—"

"Ah—then he told you I was here?" She laughed with amusement, and relapsed into self-accusal. "It was worse, much worse! What I told Upton wasn't true. Nothing prevented me—and nobody. I simply forgot. The day was so heavenly—wasn't it? I went off alone, up the mountain, to bathe in a pool in the woods; and I took some books and the dogs; and I forgot everything. . . . Can you ever forgive me?" She stretched her hands out, but he stood and looked at them, bewildered, as if not believing such a gift could be meant for him, even for the space of a touch.

"A pool in the woods . . . is it anywhere near here? Could I get to it?" he questioned eagerly.

"Of course you could. I'll take you. It's the divinest

place! In weather like this it's better even than books. . . .
But you shall see the books too," she added, suffusing him in
her sudden smile.

He reddened slightly, with the flush of convalescence,
which leaves the face paler when it goes. "I—that's awfully
kind . . ."

"No. I'm never kind. But I like to share my treasures—
sometimes." She continued to look at him, noting with a sort
of detached appreciation, as characteristic of her as the outward glow, the good shape of his head with its shock of
rumpled brown hair, the breadth and modelling of his forehead, and the strong planting of the nose between his
widely set eyes, the gray eyes which sometimes seemed to
bring his whole self to their surface, and sometimes to draw
it back into an inaccessible retreat, as when she had surprised him over "Kubla Khan" at the Willows. Decidedly,
she thought, in saying that she had not gone too far. She
was jealous of what she called her treasures; but here was
someone with whom they might be shared. Yes, she would
let him see the pool. . . . But when? Her life was always
crowded with projects, engagements, fragments of unfinished
work; there were always people arriving at Eaglewood, or
opportunities to dash off from it (with visitors who had
motors), or passionately absorbing things to be dealt with
on the spot—as she was dealing with the Weston boy now.
Yes, better do it at once, before other things crowded in. It
would be the friendliest way of wiping out her forgetful-
ness. . . .

"Do you get up early?" she asked. "Do you care about
sunrises?"

He coloured again, with pleasure, as it seemed. Her
elliptic interrogatory seemed to have no fears for him. "Yes.
I guess the pool would be great then," he said.

"Oh, well, we'll see the Hudson first. You can't see it
from here, can you?" She felt a sudden contempt for the un-

imaginativeness of living like the Tracys. "You've no idea
what it is from Eaglewood—and better still from up above
—from the ridge of Thundertop. The river's like a sea at
that hour. You don't speak German?" He made a negative
gesture, and she added: "I was only going to quote something from *Faust*—you'll read it some day—but now just listen to the sound:

> *" 'Die Sonne tönt nach alter Weise*
> *In Brudersphären Wettgesang.*
> *Und ihre vorgeschriebene Reise*
> *Vollendet sie mit Donnergang.*
> *Ihr Anblick giebt den Engeln Stärke*
> *Wenn keiner sie ergründen mag,*
> *Die unbegreiflich hohen Werke*
> *Sind herrlich wie am ersten Tag.'*

"Isn't that beautiful to you, just as mere music, without
any meaning? Besides, that whole question of *meaning* in
poetry . . . I have an old friend I wrangle with about it by
the hour . . ." She broke off, and gathering up her whole
attention, poured it for a moment into the gaze she shed on
him. "I have an idea! If you're not afraid of getting too tired
(you've been ill, I know), what do you say to my bringing
the car down to the corner of the lane tomorrow, about half
an hour before sunrise? I'll run you up to Thundertop first,
and we'll have a picnic breakfast by the pool. Does that
tempt you? Only you'll have to get up—when? Half-past
two, I suppose! And we'll see the stars fade like flowers, and
a new world born—don't you feel it's a new world every
morning? And it will be all ours, with no one to interfere, or
spoil it—Oh, Vance," she broke off, lifting her wrist to her
short-sighted eyes. "I do believe my watch has stopped! The
brute! Can you tell me the time? I've got to meet a friend at
the station, and it's nearly dark, and the car's only going on

one leg. . . ." He pulled out a new-looking watch, and gave her the hour. "Oh, misery! can I make it? Well, I'll have to try, or Lewis won't have his suitcase till tomorrow; and he loathes borrowing pyjamas." She stood poised in the dusk of the porch as if her outcry had given her wings; then she turned and held out her hand. This time Vance took it in his. "Well—so long. Don't oversleep yourself! I'll be on the stroke tomorrow," she laughed.

She ran down the steps and scrambled into the car, and the Providence which cares for the improvident carried her to the station just in time for the arrival of the train from New York.

A perspiring throng was pouring out of the station, but she had to wait for some time before she was joined by a fair-haired young man in a light gray suit, whose movements had the deliberation of a nervous traveller determined to keep cool.

The two greeted each other with friendly familiarity. "I was afraid you'd get tired of waiting, and run away before I turned up," the young man said, as he put himself and his suitcase into the motor, "but I didn't want to get mixed up with that dripping crowd."

She replied with a laugh that running away was the last thing the motor was thinking of, and that it was doubtful if they wouldn't have to push her up the hill or drop her at a garage for repairs. But this did not seem to dismay him.

"I suppose Lorry's been out in her again," he merely remarked; and Miss Spear rejoined that it was no use trying to hide the family secrets from him. He settled himself comfortably at her side, and she put her hand on the wheel. The car, after making a spasmodic dash, hovered a moment between arrest and movement, and then spurted up the mountain as if nothing in the world had been the matter with it. As they bumped up the road under the dark arch of overhanging trees Halo lapsed into silence, her attention seem-

ingly absorbed in the delicate task of persuading the motor
to forget its grievances till they were safely landed at Eaglewood. In reality her mind was still lingering over her talk
with young Weston, and his curious way of leaping straight
at the gist of things, as when, at the Willows, he had asked
her as soon as she appeared in the doorway who had written
"Kubla Khan," and just now had seized upon her mention of
a mountain pool, instantly crying: "Could I get to it?" That
way of disposing of preliminaries, brushing them aside with
an impatient shake, as he tossed the tumbled hair from his
forehead—what a sense it gave of a latent power under his
unformed boyish manner. And what a wonderful thing life
would be without idle preliminaries—as clear of smoke and
rubbish as the crystal world of sunrise she was going to
show him from the mountain! Getting at once to the heart
of things: that was the secret. But how many people know
it, or had any idea where the heart of things really was?
. . .

She felt a touch on her arm. "Penny, Halo."

"My thoughts? I don't know. . . . Well, yes." She gave
a little laugh. "I was thinking I'd spent thirty dollars this
afternoon, and what I'd bought with it."

"New hat?"

She laughed. "Exactly. A new hat—a wishing-cap!"

He laughed too, with an easy vague air of assent and
approval. "Though why you women keep on buying new
hats as you do, when you all of you go bareheaded—"

"Ah," she murmured, "that's what makes it such fun.
Art for art's sake. Besides, as it happens, my new hat's invisible, and I've got it on at this very minute. . . ."

"Well, if you have it's awfully becoming," he rejoined.

"How silly! When you know you can't see it—"

"I don't so much care about that, if I can see what's
going on underneath it." She fell suddenly silent, and he
added in the same quiet voice: "Halo, can I?"

"Just what is it you want to see?"

"Well—just if you think we're engaged."

She drew away slightly from his gesture. "When you think we are it always makes me think we're not."

"Oh well—I'll try not to think about it at all then," he rejoined good-humouredly.

To this at the moment she made no answer, and they drove on again in silence under the overhanging boughs; but as she turned the motor in at the gate she said, with another of her fugitive laughs and eyes bent on his: "You see, Lewis, I'm as like this old car as her twin sister. When she says she won't she almost always does."

⚜ IX ⚜

THE SUMMER darkness rustled with the approach of dawn. At the foot of the lane below the Tracys' Vance Weston felt the stir as if it were one with the noise in his own temples: a web of sounds too tenuous to be defined or isolated, but something so different from the uniform silence which had enveloped the world an hour earlier that every blade of grass and feather of bird now seemed sighing and ruffling in the darkness.

Vance had crept unheard out of the sleeping house, and now, in the obscurity of the lane, sat on a stone under a twisted thorn tree and listened for the splutter of the Eaglewood motor. Miss Spear might forget him again, as she had forgotten him (how he liked her for owning it!) the day before; or the car, which she had said was going on one leg, might fall dead lame, and leave her stranded before she could get down the mountain. But he did not really believe that either of these things would happen. There are days which give you, in the very moment of waking, the assurance that they were born for you, are yours to do as you please with; this was one of them for Vance.

He had been, not offended, but hurt and a little bewildered, at Miss Spear's failure to come to the Willows the previous afternoon, after sending him word that if he met her there she would let him spend a long afternoon with the books. She had taken the trouble to ask for Upton at the nursery, where she had called to pick up a basket of plants

89

for her mother, and had instructed him to tell his cousin
Vance to be at the Willows punctually at three, and to let
her know in case he could not come. It was the tenth day
after Vance's arrival, and that very morning he had made
up his mind to go to New York. He was going alone, for
Upton could only get away on Sundays; moreover, Vance
knew by this time that as a guide his cousin would be of
little use. All that Upton seemed to know of the metropolis
was where the wholesale seedmen and nurserymen had
their offices; as a means of introducing Vance to the world
of journalism Laura Lou would have been about as helpful.
Vance therefore meant to go alone, not with any hope of arriving within speaking distance of an editor, but to slake his
curiosity with a sight of the outside of some of the big newspaper offices, and get an impression of the general aspect of
the city. He had waited for over a week, partly because of
the oppressive heat (his mother was right, it was worse than
Chicago) and his own lingering physical weakness, but
chiefly because his afternoon in the library at the Willows,
and the brief apparition there of the girl who might have
been old Miss Lorburn's reincarnation, had thrown him into
a sort of prolonged daydream, which was broken only by intervals of frenzied composition.

When the summons came from Miss Spear to meet
Miss Spear again at the Willows he threw New York to the
winds, and lived through the next twenty-four hours in a
tremor of expectation. Long before three he was unlocking
the gate of the deserted place and pushing his bicycle
through the grass and clover of the drive. The day was
cooler—it would have been a good day for New York—and
the green air under the willows trembled with a delicious
freshness. Vance sat down on the doorstep. From where he
sat he could get a glimpse of the gate through the shimmering branches, and watch the shadows of the trees wheel
slowly across the lawn. The air was rich with the smell of

syringas, that smell which is so like the sound of bees on a
thundery day. Vance leaned his head back against a pillar
of the porch and waited. . . .

He had been sincere in saying to Miss Spear that while
he waited he had not been impatient or angry. He had always had a habit of rumination unusual at his age, and everything in this new life was so strange, so unreal, that even
in its disappointments and denials he found food for his
imagination. The spell of Miss Lorburn's house was stronger
now than on his first visit, because in the interval he had
lived among people, plain unimaginative people, who nevertheless took old houses for granted, took age and permanence for granted, seemed in fact to live with one foot in
the grave of the past, like the people pushing back their
tombstones in a queer stiff sculpture of the Last Judgment
that he had seen reproduced in some illustrated travel
paper. The fact that the Tracys, who never thought of anything but the present, were yet so tacitly imbued with the
past, so acquiescent in its power and its fatality, that they
attached such a ritual significance to phrases like "a very
long time ago," and "it's always been so," and "nothing will
be changed as long as any of the family are alive," had completely altered Vance's perspective, transforming his world
from the staring flatness of a movie "close-up" to a many-
vistaed universe reaching away on all sides from this empty
and silent house. Even the thought of the books inside the
house, so close yet inaccessible, did not long tantalize him.
It was enough to sit there waiting, listening for the noise of
the motor, and in the intervals straining his ear to catch the
secret coming and going of the Past behind the barred
threshold.

It was only when dusk fell that he roused himself to the
fact that Miss Spear had failed him. Then his boyish pride
reasserted itself, and for a moment he felt sore and humiliated. He remembered things Upton had said: "She never

stays anywhere more than five minutes. . . . A gentleman
friend called for her in his car. . . ." and subsequent allusions picked up from Mrs. Tracy, who had been speechless
with surprise when she learned that Miss Spear intended to
devote an afternoon to showing Vance the books at the Willows. "Well, I never! Anyhow, she's got the right to—I guess
some day the place will be hers," was one of the things Mrs.
Tracy had said; and Laura Lou, breaking her habitual silence, had added in her quick fluttering way: "I don't believe she'll ever live at Paul's Landing. She says she means
to travel all the time when she's married. . . ."

All this wove itself into Vance's own picture of the pale
dark-haired young woman who had appeared to him so
suddenly, and taken up the verse of "Kubla Khan" in her
rich chanting voice. He had assumed her to be some years
older than himself, and at nineteen, and to a mind as ignorant of class distinctions as his, such a difference of age
put a much greater distance between them than the fact
that Miss Spear lived at "the big house" (as the Tracys
called Eaglewood), or even that she was to inherit the Willows, or meant to travel all the time when she was married.
. . . Vance thought of her as goddesslike and remote, mistress of the keys of knowledge and experience; her notice
had flushed him with pride, but it seemed a part of the mysterious unreality of everything in this new world. As he got
to his feet and walked back to the gate of the Willows he
felt his first pang of wounded pride. She had forgotten him;
forgotten him because he was too young and insignificant to
be remembered; because fellows called for her and carried
her off in their cars; because she never stayed anywhere
more than five minutes. . . .

Ah, how differently he thought of her now! Since her
breathless arrival at the Tracy house on the previous evening, her summoning him out to the porch to accuse and excuse herself, the goddess had become woman again, and he

was sure that the woman was to be trusted. She still seemed
to him a good deal older than himself, but that now gave
him a happy sense of ease and freedom, instead of the feverish excitement which the advances of a girl of his own
age would have occasioned. . . .

As he waited in the darkness the early noises of awak-
ening life began to stir. He heard the long eerie scream of a
train far away; then the rumble of a motor truck down the
turnpike at the foot of the hill, followed by the jolt of a lame
farm horse coming in with garden produce; and lastly, close
by, the cluck-cluck of the Eaglewood motor—and she was
there.

"Vance!" she called gaily, half under her breath, as
though instinctively adapting her voice to the whispered
sounds of the hour. He had his hand on the door of the car,
and in a moment was sitting at her side. "Now if she'll only
start!" the girl sighed. The car kicked and jibbed and stood
stock still, as it had the evening before; then it was off with
a rush, as if aware of the challenge to its powers, and
amused at so unusual an adventure.

Vance was too full of happy emotion to speak. When
Miss Spear said: "Did you think I was going to forget you
again?" he merely answered: "No," and she laughed, as if
the simplicity of the answer pleased her, and then fell silent
too.

When they started up the wooded road to the mountain there still lingered so much of night under the branches
that she had to turn on the headlights, and the white stretch
of illumination on each side of the motor was filled with
layer upon layer of delicately drawn motionless leaves, between which the ruts of the road seemed to Vance to rise up
and meet them as they climbed. All these details burnt
themselves into his brain with a curious precision, as if he
had been crawling at a snail's pace through an eternity of
overarching foliage, while at the same time the wheezy car

seemed to be whirling him breathlessly to unknown distances; so that when the headlights painted the sudden picture of two gateposts of gray stone flanking a drive he was startled to hear Miss Spear say: "There's Eaglewood," for he thought they must long since have reached the ridge of the mountain above it.

They still mounted; the air was growing cooler; at last it was almost cold. The headlights paled gradually in the imperceptible growth of dawn, and when Miss Spear remembered to turn them out the road was scarcely less distinct, though everything appeared farther away and softer to the eye. At last the motor came out of the woodland, high up on a stretch of rough country road between fields. The sky arched overhead dim and pallid, with here and there a half-drowned star like a petal in gray water. They passed once more under trees, the world grew all dark again, and Miss Spear, stopping the motor, said: "Here."

They were in a tree-shadowed trail leading from the road to the foot of a steep overhanging rock. "There's Thundertop," Miss Spear said. She jumped out, and Vance after her. They scrambled up from ledge to ledge and finally reached a projecting rocky spur from which they saw, far below and around, the outspread earth, its lonely mountain masses and habitable slopes, and hollows still indistinct, all waiting inanimate for the light.

"If it shouldn't happen!" Miss Spear exclaimed. Vance turned to her in wonder. She had spoken his very thought; and to youth such coincidences are divine.

"Or if it had never happened before—if we were actually looking at the very first. . . . Ah!" she broke off on a deep breath; for a faint vibration, less of light than of air, a ripple of coming life, had begun to flow over the sky and the opposite mountains, hushing every incipient sound. There was a lull after that first tremor; a lull lasting so long that it seemed as if, after all, nothing in the landscape had moved or altered. Then Miss Spear, laying her hand on Vance's shoulder, turned him about toward a break in the swarthy fell of the eastern mountains; and through it came the red edge of the sun. They watched in silence as it hung there apparently unmoving; then they glanced away for a moment, and when they looked back they saw that it had moved; saw the forerunning glow burn away the ashen blur in the forest hollows, the upper sky whiten, and daylight take possession of the air. Again they turned westward, looking toward the Hudson, and now the tawny suffusion was drawing down the slopes of the farther shore, till gradually, very gradually, the river hollows also were washed of their mists, and the great expanse of the river shone bright as steel in the clear shadow.

Vance drew a deep breath. His lips were parted, but no word came. He met Miss Spear's smiling eyes with a vague stare. "Kubla Khan?" she said. He nodded.

"You'd never seen one of our sunrises?"

"No, only over the prairies."

"Well, that must be rather splendid too. But very different—like seeing it over the sea."

He made no response, for he had never seen the sea, and there was no room in his soul for more new visions.

"It's less of an effort to see the sun rise in Illinois, I suppose?" Miss Spear continued. "You only have to look out of your window. Here it involves mountaineering, and it's given me a mountaineer's appetite; hasn't it you?"

He didn't know; he supposed so; but he hardly heard what she said. His whole sentient self was still away from him, in the blue and gold of the uprolling. He would have liked to lie down there on the edge of Thundertop between the misty splendours below and the pure light above, and let the hours drift by while the chariot of the day described its great circuit before him. At such moments he was almost disembodied.

"Come along, Vance! I'm ravening. Ham and eggs over a gipsy fire!" She slipped a comrade-arm through his, and they started to scramble down from their eminence, leaving at each step a fragment of the mighty spectacle behind them. Vance, reluctantly following, thought to himself: "She never stays anywhere more than five minutes—"

But by the time they had reached the motor hunger had seized him too, and he was laughing with her while she made sure that the lunch basket and thermos were somewhere among the odds and ends under the seat, and thinking he had never met anybody who made things so easy, yet was somehow so gaily aloof. With a fresh expenditure of persuasion and violence she got the motor going, and they backed out of the trail, and started down the mountain. About halfway of the descent Miss Spear turned into another trail, deeply shadowed, and they took out their provisions, and began to climb through the forest. Presently the little woodland noises, twitter of birds and stir of leaf, were all merged in the tinkle of an unseen brook, and a little farther on they met the brook itself, leaping down wet ledges in a drip of ferns and grasses, till it led them to the rocky pool encircled with turf of which Miss Spear had told him. There she unpacked the basket, and Vance brought two stones, and some twigs to lay across them; but they could find no dry fuel in that mossy dripping place, and had to eat their eggs raw, and munch the ham between slices of stale bread. Luckily the coffee was piping hot, and when Vance had drained his cup his tongue was loosened, and there poured from him all that he had been revolving in his mind, and thirsting to utter, since his first encounter with Miss Spear at the Willows. He could hardly keep the thread of the talk in his hands, so quickly did one idea tumble out after another, and so many new trains of thought did Miss Spear's answers start in the coverts of his mind.

Afterward, in looking back at the adventure, he wondered at the fact that he had hardly been conscious of his companion's age or sex, hardly aware of the grave beauty of her face, had felt her only as the mysterious vehicle of all the new sensations pouring into his soul—as if she had been the element harmonizing the scene, or a being born of the sunrise and the forest.

Yet afterward he saw nothing ethereal or remote about her; to his memory she became again a dark-haired girl with thoughtful eyes and animated lips, who leaned back, her hat tossed off, her bare arms folded behind her head, and plied him with friendly questions. The trouble was that every one of the questions, though to her so evidently simple and matter-of-course for him, called a new vision out of the unknown, as the car's headlights, while they climbed the mountain, had kept on painting pictures on the darkness. The simplest things she said presupposed a familiarity with something or other that he was ignorant of: allusions to people and books, associations of ideas, images and metaphors, each giving an electric shock to his imagination, and making him want to linger and question before she hurried him on to the next point.

What she wanted, for her part, was evidently just to be helpful and friendly. She had guessed, perhaps, that there was not much nourishment for him in life at the Tracys', and wondered what direction he would take when that interval was over, as she assumed it would be soon. He acknowledged that he had accepted his parents' proposal to send him to his cousins for his convalescence because it was a way of being brought nearer New York, which at the moment was the place he most wanted to get to; and when she asked why—whether just as a big sight, or with some special object? he answered, feeling himself hot from feet to forehead at the confession, yet unable to hold it back, that yes, what he wanted was to live in New York and be a writer.

"A writer? I see. But that's interesting." Miss Spear raised herself on her elbow and reached for a cigarette, while her eyes continued to rest on his crimson countenance. "Tell me more about it. What do you want to write?"

He threw back his head and gave back her look with a thumping heart. "Poetry."

Her face lit up. "Oh, but that's splendid! You've written a lot already, I suppose?"

"Not a lot. Some." How flat the monosyllables sounded! And all the while his brain rustled with rich many-branching words that were too tangled up with each other to be extricated. Miss Spear smiled, and said: "This is just the place for poetry, isn't it? Do repeat something of yours."

Vance's heart dropped back to silence. No one had ever before asked him to recite his verses. The inside of his mouth grew parched and there was a buzzing in his head. This girl had commanded him, here in this magical place, to recite to her something he had written! His courage began to ebb away now that he was confronted with this formidable opportunity.

He moistened his dry lips, closed his mind's eyes as if preparing to leap into space, and said: " 'Trees.' "

"Is that the title?"

"Yes. They were the first things that struck me when I got here—the trees. They're different from ours, thicker, there are more of them . . . I don't know . . ."

"Yes, and so—"

He began: *"Arcane, aloof, and secret as the soul . . ."*

She sat motionless, resting her chin on her lifted hand. Her cigarette went out, and dropped to the damp mosses of the poolside. *"Secret as the soul,"* she murmured. "Yes." She nodded softly, but did not speak again, and at times, as he went on, he forgot her presence and seemed alone with his own imagination; then again he felt her so close that her long meditative face, drooping slightly, seemed to interpose itself between his eyes and what he was saying, and he was chilled by the thought that when, in a moment, he ceased reciting, the face would be there, unescapable, rhadamanthine, like death at the end of life. He poured out the last words of the poem in a rush, and there was a long silence, an endless silence, it seemed to the poet, before his hearer spoke.

"You recite too fast; you swallow half the words. Oh, why aren't people in our country taught—? But there are beautiful things . . ." She paused, and seemed to muse discriminatingly upon them. "That about the city of leaves . . . I wish you'd write it out for me, will you? Then I can read it over to myself. If you have a bit of paper, do write it now."

Vance had the inevitable bit of paper, and the fountain pen from which he was never parted. He pulled out the paper, spread it on a stone, and began to write. He was mortified that she thought his reading so bad, and his hand shook so that he feared she would hardly find the poem more intelligible than when he had recited it. At last he handed her the paper, and she held it to her short-sighted eyes during another awful interval of silence.

"Yes—there are beautiful things in it. That image of the city of leaves . . . and the soul's city being built of all the murmurs and rustlings of our impressions, emotions, instincts . . ." She laid the page down, and lifted her head, drawing her eyelids together meditatively. "By the way, do you know what the first temple at Delphi was built of?" She paused, smiling in expectation of his enjoyment. "Of birds' feathers and honey. Singing and humming! Sweetness and lightness! Isn't that magical?"

Vance gazed at her, captivated but bewildered. Did he understand—or did he not? Birds' feathers and honey? His heart beat with the strange disturbing beauty of the metaphor—for metaphor it must be, of course. Yet bodying forth what? In his excitement over the phrase, his perplexity at the question, he felt himself loutish and unresponsive for not answering. But he could not think of anything to say.

"The First Church of Christ at Delphi? Christian Science, you mean? I'm afraid I don't understand," he stammered at length.

She stared as if she didn't either; then she gave a little laugh. "Well, no, nothing quite so recent. The legend is about the first temple of Delphi—(I mean the *Greek* Delphi, the famous shrine, where Apollo's oracle was)—well, the legend is that the first temple was only a hut of feathers and honey, built in that uninhabited place by the bees and birds, who knew there was a god there long before man came and discovered him. . . ." She broke off, and folded up the paper. "That's a subject for another poem, isn't it? . . . But this one," she added, rousing herself, and turning again to Vance with her look of eager encouragement, "this I do like immensely. You'll let me keep it? I have a great friend who really cares for poetry, and I want to show it to him. And won't you repeat another? Please do. I love lying here and listening to beautiful words all mixed up with the sound of water and leaves . . . Only you know, Vance," she added, fixing him suddenly with a piercing humorous glance, "I should leave 'urge' as a noun to the people who write blurbs for book jackets; and 'dawn' and 'lorn' do *not* rhyme in English poetry, not yet. . . ."

A silence followed. The girl's praise and understanding —above all, her understanding—had swung Vance so high above his everyday self that it was as if, at her touch, wings had grown from him. And now, abruptly, her verbal criticism, suggesting other possibilities of the same kind, hinting at abysses of error into which he might drop unawares at any moment, brought him down like a shot bird. He hardly understood what she meant, did not know what there was to find fault with in the English of the people who wrote for book jackets—it was indeed the sort of thing he aspired to excel in some day himself—and still less understood what she meant when she attacked the validity of rhymes as self-evident to the ear as "lorn" and "dawn." Perverse and arbitrary as she evidently was—and sound-deaf, probably—she might as well have said (very likely would, if challenged) that "morn" and "gone" did not rhyme in English poetry! He was so passionately interested in everything concerning the material and the implements of his art that at another time he would have welcomed a discussion of the sort; but in this hour of creative exaltation, when his imagination was still drenched with the wonder of the adventure, and the girl's praise, as she listened, had already started a twitter of new rhythms and images in his brain, it was like falling from a mortal height to have such praise qualified by petty patronizing comments, which were all the more disturbing because he found no answer to them.

"Don't rhyme—in English poetry?" he stammered, paling under the blow. But Miss Spear had sprung to her feet and stood looking down on him with the sportive but remote radiance of some woodland spirit.

"Oh, but what does all that matter? I don't know what made me even speak of it." She continued to look at him, and as she did so, the anxious groping expression of her short-sighted eyes, as she tried to read his, suddenly humanized her face and brought her close again. "It was just my incurable mania for taking everything to pieces. Gilding the lily—who was the fool who said *that* wasn't worth doing? . . . But I shouldn't have spoken, you know, Vance, if I didn't believe you have the gift . . . the real gift . . . 'the sublime awkwardness that belittles talent,' as George Frenside calls it . . ."

His heart swelled as he listened. How she knew how to bind up the hurts she made! "The sublime awkwardness . . ." He trembled with the shock of the phrase. Who talked or wrote like that, he wondered? Was it anyone he could see, or whose books he could get hold of—in the Willows library, perhaps? "Who's that you spoke of?" he asked breathlessly.

"The man who can talk to you better than anybody else about English poetry."

"Oh, do you know him? Can I see him? Is he alive?"

To each question Miss Spear, still looking down on him, nodded her assent. "He's the friend I spoke of just now. He's staying at Eaglewood. He's the literary critic of *The Hour.*" She watched the effect of this announcement with her sleepy narrowed glance. "I'll bring him down to see you some day—the day I show you the Willows library," she said.

Vance had never heard of Frenside, or the paper called *The Hour;* but the assurance with which she pronounced the names stamped them with immediate importance. His heart was beating furiously; but such shining promises were no longer enough for him. Upton's allusions to Miss Spear's unreliability and elusiveness came back to him; and he remembered with a new resentfulness his hours of waiting at Miss Lorburn's door. Perhaps something of this incredulity showed in his eyes, for Miss Spear added, with one of her sudden touches of gentleness: "I can't tell you now just what day; but I'll leave word with Upton at the nursery, I promise I will. And now come, Vance, we must pack up and start. Our sunrise isn't ours any longer. It belongs to the whole stupid world. . . ."

❧ X ❦

WAKING NEAR noon that day from the sleep into which she had fallen after the vigil on Thundertop, Héloïse Spear sat up in bed and thought: "What's wrong?"

She stretched her arms above her head, pushed back her hair from her sleepy eyes, and looked about her room, which was cooled by the soft green light filtered through the leaves of the ancient trumpet creeper above her window. For a moment or two the present was drowned in the re-membered blaze of the sunrise, and the enjoyment of the hunger satisfied beside the pool; but already she knew that —as was almost invariable in her experience—something disagreeable lurked in the heart of her memories: as if every enjoyment in life had to be bought by a bother.

"That boy has eyes—I was right," she thought; and then, immediately: "Oh, I know, the motor!" For she had remembered, in the act of re-evoking young Weston, that on the way home the car had stopped suddenly, a mile or more above Eaglewood, and that, after a long struggle (during which he had stood helplessly watching her, seemingly without an idea as to how he might come to her aid,) they had had to abandon it by the roadside, and she had parted with her companion at the Eaglewood gates after telling him how to find his way home on foot. She herself had meant to take a couple of hours of sleep, and then slip out early to catch the man-of-all-work before the household was up, and persuade him to get the delinquent motor home somehow. But as soon as she had undressed, and thrown herself on her bed, she sank into the bottomless sleep of youth; and here it was nearly lunchtime, and everybody downstairs, and the absence of the motor doubtless already discovered! And, with matters still undecided between herself and Lewis Tarrant, she had not especially wanted him to know that she had been out without him to see the sunrise—the more so as he would never believe she had gone up to Thundertop unaccompanied.

Ah, how she envied the girls of her age who had their own cars, who led their own lives, sometimes even had their own bachelor flats in New York! Except as a means to independence riches were nothing to her; and to acquire them by marriage, and then coldly make use of them for her own purposes, was as distasteful to her as anything in her present life. And yet she longed for freedom, and saw no other way to it. If only her eager interest in life had been matched by some creative talent! She could half paint, she could half write—but her real gift (and she knew it) was for appreciating the gifts of others. Even had discipline and industry fostered her slender talents they would hardly have brought her a living. She had measured herself and knew it—and what else was there for her but marriage? "Oh, well," she thought, for the thousandth time, "something may turn up . . ." which meant, as she knew, that her mother's cousin, old Tom Lorburn, might drop off at any moment and leave her the Willows, with enough money to get away from it, and from Paul's Landing, forever.

She heard her mother's fluttering knock, and Mrs. Spear came in, drooping, distressed, and dimly beautiful.

"Oh, Halo—asleep still? I'm sorry to disturb you, darling, but it's after eleven" ("I know, I know," grumbled Héloïse, always impatient of the obvious), "and something so tiresome has happened. The motor has disappeared. Jacob says somebody must have got into the garage in the night. The cook says she saw a dreadful-looking man hang-

ing about yesterday evening; but the trouble is that the garage lock wasn't broken open—only it so seldom is locked,
as I told your father. Your father says it's Lorry again; he's
made such a dreadful scene before Lewis. . . . It's not so
much the fact of Lorry's being out all night; but your father
thinks he's sold the car. And if he *has* we shall never see a
penny of the money," Mrs. Spear added, confusedly struggling to differentiate the causes of her distress, of which fear
about the money was clearly by far the most potent.

Héloïse sat up in bed and gazed at her mother's troubled countenance. "Even now," she thought, "her eyes are
beautiful; and she doesn't screw them up in the ugly way
that I do." Then she roused herself to reality. "What nonsense—nobody stole the motor," she said.

"It *was* Lorry, then? He's told you—?"

"He's told me nothing." She paused, letting her imagination toy for a moment with the temptation to be silent;
then she said: "The motor's a mile up the road, toward
Thundertop. It broke down, and I left it there myself early
this morning." The idea of allowing Lorry to bear the brunt
of the storm had lasted no more than the taking of breath
between two words; but it had stirred in her an old re-
siduum of self-disgust. Yet she did wish she had got the car
safely under cover before all this fuss!

Her mother stood staring at her with astonished eyes.
"You, Halo? You had the car out in the middle of the
night?"

"Yes. I had the car out. I went up to Thundertop to see
the sunrise."

"With Lewis, darling?" Mrs. Spear's face brightened
perceptibly; then it fell again. "But no, he was there just
now when your father scolded poor Lorry, and of course if
he'd been with you—"

"He wasn't with me. He doesn't know anything about
it."

"Halo!" her mother moaned, "And you chose this time

—when he'd just arrived!" She paused with a gesture of despair. "Who *was* with you?"

Halo, sliding out of bed, got her feet into her flopping Moroccan slippers, and began to gather up her sponge and towels preparatory to an advance to the bathroom. "Oh, nobody in particular. Just that young boy from the Tracys'—"

Mrs. Spear gasped out her perplexity. "Boy from Tracys'? You don't mean Upton?"

"Of course not. How ridiculous! I mean the cousin from the West that they've got staying there—the boy who's had typhoid fever. Didn't I tell you about him? He's rather extraordinary; full of talent, I believe; and starving to death for want of books, and of people he can talk to. I promised to spend an afternoon with him at the Willows, and let him browse in the library, and then I forgot all about it, and to make up for having chucked him I slipped out early this morning and ran him up to Thundertop to see the sunrise. It was glorious. And he read me some of his poems—he means to be a poet. I do believe there's something in him, Mother."

While Mrs. Spear listened the expression of her beautiful eyes passed from anxiety to a sympathetic exaltation. As her daughter was aware, one could never speak to Mrs. Spear of genius without kindling in her an irrepressible ardour to encourage and direct it.

"But, my dear, how interesting! Why didn't you tell me about him before? Couldn't George Frenside do something to help him? Couldn't he publish his things in *The Hour*? I do hope you asked him to come back to lunch?"

Héloïse laughed. Her mother's enthusiasms always amused her. To hear of the presence, within inviting distance, of a young man of talent (talent was always genius to Mrs. Spear) was instantly to make her forget her family and financial cares, however pressing, and begin to wonder anxiously what the cook could scrape together for lunch—a sincere respect for good food being one of the anomalies of her oddly assorted character, and a succulent meal her instinctive homage to celebrity. "What time did you tell him to come—one or half-past? I believe Susan could still manage a cheese *soufflé*—but it's nearly twelve now."

"Yes; I know it is—and you must give me a chance to take my bath. And how could I ask him to lunch? It wouldn't be decent, when he's staying with the Tracys, who, after all, are distant connections of ours, and whom we certainly don't want to invite—do we?"

Mrs. Spear, at this reminder, clasped her long expressive hands self-reproachfully. "Oh, those poor Tracys! Yes, they *are* distant relations. But if Lorburn Tracy, who was a poor sort of man anyhow, and less than nobody on his father's side, chose to marry the gardener's daughter at the Willows, we could hardly be expected, could we . . . ? Not that that sort of thing really matters in the least. Why should it? Only—well, perhaps we've been snobbish about the Tracys, darling. Do you think we have? There's nothing I hate so much as being snobbish. Do you think we ought to send Jacob down now with a note, and ask them *all* up to lunch with this young novelist you speak of? Not a novelist —a poet? What a head I've got! My dear, I really believe we ought to. Is there any notepaper here? There so seldom is, in your room . . . but if you can find a scrap, do write a line to Mrs. Tracy, and say . . . say . . . well, put it as nicely as you can . . . and say that Jacob is at their door, with the car, waiting to bring them up; oh, with the young man, of course! Remind me again of the young man's name, my dear."

"Well, if I said all that, Mother, part of it would hardly be true, as the car's a mile or more up the Thundertop road at this minute, and refuses to budge." Héloïse let her mother's outcries evaporate, and continued quietly: "Besides, you know perfectly well that we can't ask the Tracys to lunch.

We never have, and why should we now? They'd hate it as much as we should. They're plain working people, and they have nothing on earth to say to us, or we to them. Why should we suddenly pretend the contrary?"

"Oh, Halo, how *vulgar* of you! I wonder how you can even think such things. All human beings ought to have things to say to each other, if only they meet on the broad basis of humanity and . . . and . . ."

"Well, the Tracys wouldn't; how could they? They've never heard of the broad basis of humanity. If we had them here with Lewis and George Frenside, or any of our other friends, what on earth should we find to say to each other? They talk another language, and it can't be helped. But this boy is different, and I've promised to take him to the Willows to go through the books, and to bring George down to see him there some day. So let's let it go at that. . . ." And Héloïse, followed by her mother's reproaches and ejaculations, made a dive for the door and dashed down the passage to the bathroom.

When she descended the worn shallow steps of the old staircase the lunch gong was sounding, and Mr. Spear was pacing the hall in a state of repressed excitement. Halo and Lorry, as children, had found in a popular natural history book a striking picture of a bristling caterpillar sitting upright on its tail, with the caption: "The male Puss-Moth when irritated after a full meal." They instantly christened their progenitor the Puss-Moth, but modified the legend by explaining to strangers that he was more often irritated *before* a full meal than after—especially when kept waiting for it. Today Mr. Spear was unusually perpendicular and bristling, and his small, rather too carefully modeled features were positively grimacing with anger. To his daughter long habit made the sight more comic than impressive; but she was vexed that the question of the motor had to be dealt with.

"Halo, I suppose you know the car was taken out of the garage last night, *without the door lock's being broken,* and that it has not since been seen? Your mother tells me—"

Halo nodded. "Mother knows. I've explained."

"Explained! I don't know what you call—"

"Hullo, Lewis—good morning." Halo interrupted her father's diatribe to greet Lewis Tarrant, who came lounging in from the verandah, followed by George Frenside munching his eternal cigar. "Good morning, Frenny—if it's still morning? Are you all coming to assist at my execution?" she laughed.

"We want to hear the argument for the defence," Frenside retorted, in his deep voice with the queer crack in it.

"Isn't any. I plead guilty. I had the car out in the small hours, and busted her coming down the Thundertop road. I had to get home on my own feet, and that's all."

"All—all? You say it was you who was out in the car in the middle of the night?" Mr. Spear swung round on young Tarrant. "Lewis—was she?"

Lewis Tarrant's fair complexion, which so curiously matched his very fair and very clear light gray eyes, grew sallow with surprise and embarrassment.

"I—why, of course, sir, if she says so," he stammered.

" 'Says so'? Were you with her—or weren't you? If you weren't she's only shielding her brother for the hundredth time; and God knows where the car's gone to, by this time."

"Send Jacob up the road to see," Héloïse interrupted impatiently. She had meant to carry the thing off with a light hand, laughing at them all, turning the affair into a good story to be served up to future guests; they were great, at Eaglewood, on collecting good stories for social purposes. But she had been put off her balance by the expression of Lewis Tarrant's face, the intonation of his voice. Evidently he too supposed she was lying to shield her brother, and like the gentleman he was he was going to shield her; and the business was not in the least to his liking. ("Well, he knows what we're like; why does he keep on coming here?" she thought, almost putting the question aloud to him.) She swung away from both men with one of her quick rebellious movements.

"And now, for goodness' sake, Father, don't go on keeping everybody waiting for lunch. Their interest in this affair is purely one of politeness. They don't care a hang who had the car out last night, and they know it's not the first time she's broken down, especially when I've been driving her."

"No—as to that, sir, Halo's right, you know," Tarrant corroborated laughingly, and at the same moment Mrs. Spear appeared, her face brightening as she caught the echo of the laugh. But her exhilaration did not last. "I do think, Halo, we ought to have invited the Tracys here long ago," she began, the lines forming again about her eyes and mouth.

"The Tracys—the Tracys—who on earth do you mean by the Tracys?" Mr. Spear broke in, glad of a new vent for his irritation. "Not Tom Lorburn's caretakers at the Willows, I take it?"

"Why, you know, Harold, the Tracys really are related to Tom Lorburn and me, and I'm afraid we've been dreadfully distant to them, never going near them except to see whether they'd looked after the Willows properly—and now Halo says they have a young cousin from the West staying there—a painter, no, I mean a poet, who's really a genius. And so I thought . . ."

Mrs. Spear's confused explanation was interrupted by the convulsive splutter and angry pause of a motor outside of the house. So familiar were the sounds to all present that Héloïse merely said with a shrug: "What did I tell you?" and turned toward the dining room door, in the hope that the sight of food would cut short the investigation of her nocturnal trip.

"Well, Jacob?" Mr. Spear exclaimed, pausing halfway

across the hall; and his daughter, turning, met the reproach-ful gaze of the family factotum, who stood in the doorway mopping the moisture from his perpetually puzzled wrin-kles.

"Well, I've got her," Jacob said. He glanced about him somewhat apprehensively, and then, fixing his eyes again on Héloïse: "I found a fellow sitting in her. He said he'd lost his way and gone to sleep. He was going to cut and run, but I told him he'd have to come here with me and tell you folks what he was doing in the car anyhow."

Jacob fell back, and over his shoulder Héloïse caught sight of a slim boyish figure with white face and rumpled hair, and deep eyes still bewildered with sleep.

"Is this Eaglewood?" Vance Weston asked of the as-sembled company; then he saw Miss Spear behind the oth-ers, and his pallor turned to crimson.

Halo came forward. "Vance—how wonderful. Mother was just asking why I hadn't brought you back to lunch; and here you are!"

He looked at her as if only half understanding. "I couldn't find my way home, so I came back up the road, and when I saw the car was still there I got into it to wait until somebody came along—and I guess I must have fallen asleep."

"Well, that's all right; it's even providential. You've saved Jacob the trouble of going all the way down the hill to get you. Mother, Father, this is Vance Weston, who's staying at Paul's Landing with the Tracys. Mother, can't we have something to eat? You've no idea how inhumanly hun-gry sunrises make people—don't they, Vance? Oh, and this is Mr. Frenside, whom I've told you about: who writes for *The Hour.* And this is Mr. Lewis Tarrant—and here's my brother Lorburn. I suppose you're our cousin, too, aren't you, Vance? Lorry, this is our new cousin, Vance Weston."

As she performed this rapid ceremony Halo's eyes

dwelt a moment longer on Lewis Tarrant's face than on the others. Ah, he was taking his dose now—a nasty brew! "Shielding" her again; much she cared about being shielded! He would know now that she really had been out in the car in the night, that this unknown boy had been with her, that she didn't care a fig who knew it, and that the escapade had taken place at the very moment when he, Lewis Tarrant, had come to Eaglewood for the weekend, on her express promise that she would tell him definitely, before the end of his visit, if she were going to marry him or not. . . .

Lorry Spear was the first to break the silence which had followed on young Weston's entrance. "I see that our new cousin has done us the doubtful service of preventing that rotten old car from being stolen. At least we might have collected the insurance on her. . . . Glad to see you all the same, Weston; don't bear you the least grudge." He held out his hand to the increasingly bewildered Vance.

"How absurd, Lorry . . . as if anybody had really thought . . ." Mrs. Spear broke in, the cloud lifting from her brow as she saw that her son was helping to carry the thing off (he didn't always; but when he did he was masterly).

"And all this time, my dear Vance," Mrs. Spear continued turning her beautiful eyes on her guest, "you must be wondering what we're all talking about, and why lunch is so late. But it's providential, as Halo says; for we shouldn't have had the pleasure of having you with us if that stupid old motor hadn't broken down. Now come into the dining room, my dear boy, this way. I'm going to put you next to Mr. Frenside, our great critic, whom you know by reputation—of course you read *The Hour?* George, this is Halo's friend, the young novelist . . . no, poet . . . poet, isn't it, Vance? You happy being!" Mrs. Spear laid her urgent hand on his shoulder and drew him toward the luncheon table.

❧ XI ❦

It was so still in the dim book-lined room that had the late Miss Lorburn reappeared upon the scene she might have mistaken for a kindred ghost the young man in possession of her library.

Vance, for the last few days, had been going over the books at the Willows, wiping them with a soft towel and carefully putting one after another back in its proper place. Halo Spear, in one of her spasmodic bursts of energy, had swooped down from Eaglewood the first morning to show him how to do it; for in the reverent and orderly treatment of books (handling them, Mrs. Weston might have put it, as gingerly as if they were "the best china"!) Vance was totally untaught. Miss Spear, with those swift and confident hands of hers, had given him one of her hurried demonstrations, accompanied by a running commentary of explanation. "Don't *shake* the books as if they were carpets, Vance; they're not. At least they're only magic carpets, some of them, to carry one to the other side of the moon. But they won't stand banging and beating. You see, books have souls, like people: that is, like a few people. . . . No, I wouldn't ask the Tracys to help; they don't know much about books. You and I will manage it by ourselves. Look: wipe the edges gently, like this, and then flutter the pages ever so lightly—as if you were a bee trying to shake open a flower —just to get the dust out. . . . Ah, but how lovely this is! Listen:

" 'Ah, what avails the sceptred race,
And what the form divine?
What every virtue, every grace?
Rose Aylmer, all were thine . . .' "

And then, in the midst of her dusting and reading (the former frequently interrupted by the latter), she had glanced abruptly at her wristwatch, exclaiming: "Oh, Lord, there's Lewis waiting—I'd forgotten!" and had dashed out of the house, crying back advice, instructions and adieux.

Vance scarcely noticed her departure. It was exciting— almost too exciting—to have her there; but he did not want more excitement just then. What he wanted was in some way to be kept outside of time and space till his fury of intellectual hunger was, not indeed sated, but at least calmed. The mere sense of all those books about him, silent witnesses of an unknown and unsuspected past, was almost more agitating than he could bear. From every side their influences streamed toward him, drawing him this way and that as if he had been in the centre of a magnetic circle. To continue the work he was there to do soon became manifestly impossible. Why, even Miss Spear had broken off every few minutes to read and admire, often dropping the book in her hand while she darted on to another, oblivious, in her hummingbird greed, of the principles of order she was inculcating. And yet to her these volumes, or the greater number of them, were old friends. She must long since have surmounted the shock of surprises with which Vance was tingling; while to him nearly all the books were new and unknown, and the rest bore names just familiar enough to sharpen his hunger. How could he attempt to remember from which shelf he had taken one book or the other, once it had opened its golden vistas to him?

He did not try for long. He already had a fairly definite sense of values, and could not delude himself with the idea that dusting a dead woman's books was, for him or anybody else, a more vital and necessary act than reading them. This was his chance, and he was going to take it.

If only he had known better how to! The pressure of this weight of wisdom on his ignorance was suffocating: he felt like a girl Miss Spear had told him about, the girl who was so greedy for gold that she betrayed Rome, and the fellows she betrayed it to despised her so that they crushed her under their golden shields. These books were crushing Vance like that. If only there were some way of climbing the slippery trunk of the Tree which dangled its fruit so far above him!

He turned to the corner from which Miss Spear had taken the books, and his hand lit on a shabby volume: *Specimens of English Dramatic Poets contemporary with Shakespeare*. He settled himself in Miss Lorburn's Gothic armchair and read:

> *"Is this the face that launched a thousand ships*
> *And burnt the topless towers of Ilium?"*

My God! Who wrote it? Who could have? Not any of the big fellows he knew about . . . this was another note: he knew it instinctively. And the man's name? Marlowe . . . and he'd lived, why, ever so long ago, two or three hundred years before this old house of Miss Lorburn's was built, or the funny old mouldy *Half Hours* book published —and the English language, in this Marlowe's hands, was already a flower and a flame. . . . Vance rambled on from glory to glory, slowly, amazedly, and then, out of sheer gluttony, pushed the book under his chair, like a dog hiding a bone, and wandered back to the magic shelves for more.

> *"When she moves, you see*
> *Like water from a crystal overflowed,*

*Fresh beauty tremble out of her, and lave
Her fair sides to the ground . . ."*

Vance dropped the little volume, and pressing his
hands against his eyes let the frail music filter through him.
This poetry had another quality of newness quite its own—
something elusive as the shy beauty of a cold spring evening. Beddoes . . . that was the name. Another unknown!
Was he a contemporary of those others, Marlowe and Ford,
who lived so long before the Willows was built, almost before the Hudson River had a name? Or was he not, rather
with an exquisite new note, trying to lure back the earlier
music? How could a boy from Euphoria hope to find his
way through this boundless forest of English poetry, called
hither and thither by all these wild-winged birds pouring
down their music on him?

As he stood groping and gazing, in the litter and confusion of the ravaged shelves, his eyes fell on a title which
seemed to hold out help. *Half Hours with the Best Authors*
—stoutish volumes in worn black cloth, with queer pin-
nacled gilt lettering. Well, at least they would tell him who
were supposed to be the best authors when the book was
written—put him wise on that, anyhow. He reached for a
volume, and settled himself down again.

The book was not, as Vance had expected, a series of
"half hour" essays on the best authors. Charles Knight (that
was the man's name) had simply ranged through a library
like Miss Lorburn's, about eighty years ago, gathered this
bloom and that, and bound them together with the fewest
words. Vance, accustomed to short-cuts to culture, had expected an early version of the "five-foot shelf"; he found, instead, the leisurely selections of an anthologist to whom it
had obviously not occurred that he might have readers too
hurried to dwell on the more recondite beauties of English
literature. The choice of the poetry did not greatly interest

Vance, after Lamb's *Specimens* and the Beddoes volume;
but as his eye travelled on he found himself receiving for
the first time—except when he had first read his Bible as
literature—the mighty shock of English prose.

For the moment it affected him almost more powerfully
than the poetry, such a sense it gave of endlessly subtle in-
tricacies of rhythm and movement, such a great tidal pressure as he could feel only, and not define. "Methinks I see in
my mind a noble and puissant nation rousing herself like a
strong man after sleep, and shaking her invincible locks;
methinks I see her as an eagle nursing her mighty youth,
and kindling her undazzled eyes at the full mid-day beam;
purging and unscaling her long abused sight at the fountain
itself of heavenly radiance. . . ." "The light of the world in
the turning of the creation was spread abroad like a curtain,
and dwelt nowhere, but filled the *expansum* with a dissemi-
nation great as the unfoldings of the air's looser garment, or
the wilder fringes of the fire, without knots, or order, or
combination; but God gathered the beams in his hand, and
united them into a globe of fire, and all the light of the
world became the body of the sun."

What a fellow could say, if he had the chance, and the
habit of words and sentences like that!

Vance shut the volume and sat gazing ahead of him.
The blood was beating in his temples. The walls of dark
musty books seemed to sway and dissolve, letting him into
that new world of theirs—a world of which he must somehow acquire the freedom. "I must find out—I must find
out." He repeated the words chantingly, unmeaningly, as if
they had been an incantation. Then slowly his mind began
to clear, to become again able to follow its own movements.
What he needed, no doubt, to enter that world, was
education—the very thing he thought he already had!

It was not only the books into which he had been dip-
ping that told him of his need. Every word, every allusion

caught at the Eaglewood lunch table had opened new vistas of conjecture. Of course each human agglomeration, down to the smallest village, had its local idioms, its own range of allusions, its stock of jokes and forms of irony. At the Tracys', for instance, you heard the Paul's Landing vernacular, as you heard that of Euphoria at Vance's family table; but all that was different. Vance had known instantly that the language, the intonations, the allusions of Eaglewood did not belong peculiarly to Paul's Landing, were indeed hardly concerned with it, but embraced, though so lightly flitting, great areas extending not only to New York and beyond, but backward through this mysterious past which was so much newer to Vance than any present. These easy affable people could talk—did talk—about everything! Everything, that is, but the exclusively local matters which had formed the staple of the only conversation Vance had ever heard. What they talked of was simply *all the rest;* and he could see that they did it without the least intention of showing-off, the least consciousness that their scope was wider than other people's—did it naturally, carelessly, just as his mother talked about electric cookers, his father about local real estate, Mrs. Tracy about Laura Lou's school picnics and Upton's job at the nursery. The inference was, not that the Spears and their friends were an isolated group, parading their superior attainments before each other, but that they belonged to a class, a society, a type of people, who naturally breathed this larger air, possessed this privilege of moving freely backward and forward in time and space, and were so used to it all that they took the same faculty for granted in others—even in a boy like Vance Weston.

Well, there was no reason why a boy like Vance Weston shouldn't, some day or other, acquire a like faculty. He had been brought up in the creed that there was nothing a fellow from Euphoria, the cradle of all the Advantages, couldn't attain to. Only—how? It seemed to him that the gulf was untraversable. If only he could have been left alone in that library, left there for half a year, perhaps. . . . But even so, he felt that he needed some kind of tuition to prepare him for the library. The Past was too big, too complicated, too aloof, to surrender its secrets so lightly.

College again? College meant to him sports and more sports, secret societies, class scraps and fraternity rushing, with restricted intervals of mechanical cramming, and the glib unmeaning recital of formulas—his courses provided a formula for everything! But all that had nothing to do with all *this*. . . .

Besides, thinking about college was a waste of time. Even had he been willing to submit again to the same routine, he hadn't the means to re-educate himself, and he could not ask his father to pay his expenses twice over. Mr. Weston, Vance knew, regarded him as an investment which ought already to be bringing in something. After the boy's illness his father had recognized the necessity of his taking a holiday; and being a man who always did things handsomely when his doing so was visible to others, he had agreed, besides paying the trip to New York and back, and Vance's board at the Tracys', to allow him a hundred dollars a month for four months. Vance had received half the sum before starting, with a warning to be careful and not make a fool of himself; and his father's gesture, which became generally known on Mapledale Avenue, was thought very liberal, and worthy of Lorin Weston.

But Vance, at the same time, was given to understand that as soon as his summer's rest was over he was to "make good." His father, having reluctantly come round to the idea of his going into journalism instead of real estate, had obtained the promise of a job for him on the *Free Speaker*, and was already swaggering at club meetings about the nuisance of having a literary fellow in the family. "Problem

most of you fellows aren't up against, I guess? Fact is, Mrs.
Weston has a way-back culture complex in her family, and
it's a microbe you can't seem to eradicate." This was all
very well—and nobody liked swaggering better than the
silent Lorin Weston; but Vance knew that he liked to have
his swagger justified with the least possible delay.

The only hope lay in returning as often as he could to
this silent room, and trying to hack a way through the dense
jungle of the past. But he was not sure it would be possible.
He was aware that Mrs. Tracy, though she made no comment, wondered at his meetings with Miss Spear at the
Willows, and at the permission given him to range among
the books. He had spent two whole days there since his
lunch at Eaglewood, and on this second day no one had
come down from the "big house," as Mrs. Tracy called it, to
let him in, and he had been obliged to go back to Paul's
Landing and ask her for the keys. "I don't know as I ought
to," Mrs. Tracy had said as she handed them over; and
then: "Oh, well, I suppose it's all right if *they* say so." She
referred to the Spears as "they," with a certain tartness,
since she had learned of Vance's having lunched at Eaglewood. "Well, I never! Mebbe some time they'll remember
that Upton and Laura Lou are related to them too." Vance
felt that in asking for the keys he had vaguely offended her,
and he was sorry; but he could not give up the books.

New York had completely vanished from his thoughts.
He had the sense to understand that, to a boy like himself,
New York could offer no opportunity comparable to this.
He must learn something first—then try his luck there.
When he had found himself, at the Eaglewood lunch table,
seated next to the literary critic whose name, in his confusion, he had not caught, he had acted at once on the deep
instinct which always made him seize on what was meant
for his own nourishment, in however new and unfamiliar
surroundings. Here, at least, he said to himself, was an

editor—a journalist! He had no idea if *The Hour* were a
daily (as its name seemed to imply), or some kind of highbrow review (as he feared); but whatever it was, it might
give him his chance—and here he was sitting next to the
very man who had the power to open its columns to him.

But he found it less easy than he had imagined. The
great man (whom they all addressed simply as "George" or
"Frenny") was evidently trying to be friendly, in his dry sardonic way; but he paid no heed to Mrs. Spear's allusions to
"our young poet," and his remarks to Vance were merely
perfunctory questions as to his life in the West, and his
present sojourn at the Tracys'. Once indeed he asked, blinking absently at the boy through his glasses: "And what's the
next move to be?" but on Vance's answering: "I want to get
onto a newspaper," his interest seemed to flag. "Oh, of
course," he merely said, as who should imply; "What's the
use of expecting anything different in a world of sameness?"
and the blood which had rushed to Vance's face ebbed back
to his heart. A few hours earlier, as he talked of his poetry
with Halo Spear by the mountain pool, everything had
seemed possible; now he thought bitterly: "When it comes
down to hardpan girls don't know anything anyhow." And it
gave him a grim satisfaction to class his mountain nymph in
the common category.

But when she reminded him of his promise to help her
with the books his feeling veered to adoration, and her appearance at the Willows, vivid and inspiring, instantly lifted
him to the brow of Thundertop. "She carries that pool
everywhere with her," he thought, and was seized by the
desire to embody the fancy in a new poem; and when she
broke off in her dusting and sorting to say: "I gave your poetry to George Frenside to read last night," he was too much
agitated to thank her, or to put a question. A moment later,
she seemed to forget what she had said, carried away by a
dip into Andrew Marvell (What—he didn't know "The Coy

Mistress"? Oh, but he must just listen to this!); and finally, after whirling him on from one book to another for an hour or so, she vanished as suddenly as she had come to join the mysterious "Lewis," the fellow she was going to marry, Vance supposed.

She came back the next day, and the next. On the fourth she promised to leave her keys with him and to meet him again at the Willows the next morning; but she carried the keys off with her, and he had to get the hired man, who scrutinized him sulkily, to lock up. And the fifth day there had been no sign of her . . . and now twilight would soon be falling, and it was time to go.

Show his poetry to George Frenside (if that was the man's name)? Much chance he'd ever hear of that again . . . likely as not she'd never even done it; just meant to, and forgotten. For if she had, wouldn't she have had something to report—even if unfavourable? It wasn't likely she'd stick at telling him a few more home truths, after the stiff dose she'd already administered! Perhaps on second thoughts she'd decided the stuff wasn't worth showing. And yet, hadn't she told him in so many words that she *had* shown it? No, what she had said, literally, was: "I gave Frenside your poetry to read." Well, the great critic probably hadn't taken advantage of his opportunity—perhaps she'd put him off in advance with her comments. "Urge" not a noun! And that nonsense about "dawn" and "lorn" not being good rhymes! God, to see a tone-deaf woman laying down the law—and all Eaglewood kowtowing! Well, he had to laugh at the thought of those stuffed oracles sitting up there and telling each other what was what. . . . What the hell'd he care for their opinion, anyhow—of his poetry, or of himself? Lot of self-opiniated amateurs . . . he had to laugh. . . . Well, he'd go to New York the next day, and look round on his own, and see what the professionals thought about him. . . . After all, he could describe himself as being on the staff of the *Free Speaker*.

Suddenly a shadow cut off the western sunlight slanting on his book, and he saw one of the young men from Eaglewood leaning on the window and looking in at him—not the fair dissatisfied-looking one they called "Lewis," but the other: Halo's brother Lorburn. Lorburn Spear put his hand on the sill, said "Hullo—still at it?" and vaulted into the room. In the middle of the floor he paused, his hands in his pockets, and gazed about with an amused smile and ironically lifted brows. He was slim and dark, like Halo, with the same carefully drawn features as his father, but more height and less majesty than Mr. Spear. An easy accessible sort of fellow; a fellow Vance felt he could have taken a liking to if only—if what? Perhaps it was that his eyes were too close together. Grandma Scrimser always used to say: "Don't you ever trust a man whose eyes are near enough to be always whispering to each other." And then she went and trusted everybody—even Grandpa! Fact was, Grandma liked axioms the way you like olives; it never occurred to her they were meant for anything but to roll under your tongue. . . .

"Well," said Lorry Spear pleasantly, "this is luck, finding you still in the mausoleum. I suppose Halo set you the job and then chucked you? Thought so. She promised to pick me up by and by, but will she? Have you made any amusing finds? Cigarette? No?" He drew out his own, lit one, and dropped into the chair nearest Vance's. "There ought to be things here, you know," he went on sending his eyes sharply about him while his attention still seemed to be centred on Vance.

"Things?" Vance echoed excitedly: "I should say so! See here—do you know this?" He pushed across the table the volume of *Half Hours,* open at Beddoes. Lorry Spear stared, took the book up, glanced at the title page and threw it

down. "Well—I don't believe there'd be any bids for that
unless it took the ragpicker's fancy."

"The ragpicker—?"

The young men stared at each other, and Lorry
laughed.

"Oh, I see: you're a reader. Halo told me. It's a conceivable branch of the business, of course."

"Business—?"

"Business of book-collecting. That's what books are for,
isn't it? Even people who read 'em have to collect them. But
personally I've never thought they were meant to be read.
You can get all the talk you want—and too much—from live
people; I never could see the point of dragging in the dead.
The beauty of books is their makeup: like a woman's.
What's a woman without clothes and paint? Next to nothing, believe me, after you've worn off the first surprise. . . .
And a book without the right paper, the right type, the right
binding, the right date on the title page; well, it's a blank to
me, that's all." He got up again, cigarette in hand, and
lounged across the room. "Don't suppose there's much here,
anyhow. I've always meant to take a look, and never had
time. . . . There might be some Americana—never can tell.
The best thing about these ancestors was that they never
threw anything away. Didn't value things; didn't know
about them; but just hung on to them. I shouldn't wonder—
Oh, see here! *Hullo!*" He stretched his long arm toward an
upper shelf, reached down a volume, and stood absorbed.

Vance watched him curiously. He had never seen anyone so easy, self-assured, and yet careless as this brother of
Miss Spear's. "Thought you didn't care about reading," he
remarked at length, amused at his visitor's absorption.
Young Spear gave a start, and laid the book down. "Oh, I
was turning out paradoxes—they madden my family, but
amuse me. Trouble about reading at Eaglewood is that
whatever you get hold of everybody's been there before

you. No discoveries to be made. But *you* don't read, do you
—you write? You'll find nobody can do both. What's your
line? Poetry?"

Vance was trembling with excitement, as he always did
when anyone touched on his vocation. But his recent experiences had caused a sort of protective skin to grow over his
secret sensibilities—or was it that really the eyes of this good-
looking young man were too close together? Vance could
imagine having all kinds of a good time with him, but not
talking to him of anything that lay under that skin. "Oh, I
guess there'll be time for me to choose a line later," he said.
"I'm in the reading stage still. And this old house interests
me. Where I come from everything's bran' new—houses and
books and everything. We throw 'em out when they get
shabby. And I like looking at all these things that folks have
kept right along—hung onto, as you say."

Lorburn Spear looked at him with interest, with sympathy even, Vance thought. For a second his smile had the
fugitive radiance of his sister's. "Why, yes, I see your point:
what you might call the novelty of permanence. And this
place certainly has character, though old Tom Lorburn is
too stupid to see it. And our Cousin Elinor had character
too! Good head, eh?" He glanced up at the portrait, still
with that odd air of keeping hold of Vance while he looked
away from him. "You know she did a good deal to the house
when she inherited it. This room expresses one side of her;
her maturity, her acceptance. But when she did the drawing
rooms she was frivolous, she still dreamed of dancing—she'd
read Byron on the waltz, poor girl! What an appetizer it
must have been to those women to have so many things forbidden! Seen the rest of the rooms? No? Oh, but they're
worth it. Come along before it gets too dark."

Gaily, with his long free step, he led the way across the
patterned parquet, and Vance followed, captivated by the
image of a young Miss Lorburn who still dreamed of danc-

ing, and to whom so many things were sweet because forbidden. "Yet she ended in her library. . . ." he thought.

Lorry Spear was a stimulating guide. His quick touches woke the dumb rooms to life, lit the dusky wax candles in chandeliers and wall brackets, drew a Weber waltz from the slumbering piano, peopled the floor with gaily circling couples, even made Vance see the dotted muslins and billowy tarlatans looped with camellias of the young women with their ringlets and sandalled feet. He found the cleverest words, made it all visible and almost tangible, knew even what flowers there would have been in the ornate porcelain vases: mignonette and pinks, with heavy pink roses, he decided: "Yes—I ought to have been a theatrical decorator; would be, if only the boss would put up the cash. But to do that they'd have to sell Eaglewood—or marry Halo to a millionaire," he added with an impatient laugh.

Upstairs he took Vance over the funny bedrooms, so big and high-ceilinged, with beds of mahogany or rosewood, and the lace-looped toilet tables (like the ladies' balldresses) with gilt mirror frames peeping through the festoons, and big marble-topped washstands that carried carafes and goblets of cut glass, porcelain basins and ewers with flower garlands. In one of the dressing rooms (Miss Lorburn's) there was a specially ornate toilet set, with a ewer in the shape of a swan with curving throat and flattened wings, and a basin like a nest of rushes. "Poor Elinor—I supposed she dreamed of a Lohengrin before the letter, and hoped to find a baby in the bulrushes," Lorry commented; and Vance, understanding the allusions, felt a pang of sympathy for the lonely woman. At the end of the passage, in one of the freakish towers, was a circular room with blue brocade curtains and tufted furniture, the walls hung with large coloured lithographs of peasant girls dancing to tambourines, and young fellows in breeches and velvet jackets who drove oxcarts laden with ripe grapes. "The Italy of her day," Lorry smiled. "She must have done this boudoir in the Lohengrin stage. And she ended in spectacles, cold and immaculate, reading Coleridge all alone. Brr!" He broke off, and turned to the window. "Hullo! Isn't that Halo?"

The hoarse bark of the Eaglewood motor sounded at the gate. "Come along down," Lorry continued. "You'd better take advantage of the lift home. Besides, it's too dark to do much more here."

They started down the stairs, but in the hall Vance hesitated. "I've left the books piled up anyhow. Guess I'd better go back and put them on the shelves." He realized suddenly that for the last two days he had done neither dusting nor sorting, and wondered what Miss Spear would say if she saw the havoc he had created.

"Not on your life!" Lorry enjoined him. "You could hardly see a yard before your nose in the library by this time, and lighting up is strictly forbidden. Might set the old place on fire. If it was mine I'd do it, and collect the insurance; but old Tom don't need to, curse him." He stopped short, and clapped his hand on his waistcoat pocket. "I must have left my cigarette case in there. Yes, I remember. You wait here—"

He spun down the polished floor of the drawing-rooms and disappeared. Vance waited impatiently. Although the June sky outside was still full of daylight it was dark already in the hall with its sombre panelling and heavy oak stairs. Now and then he heard the croak of the Eaglewood motor and he wondered how much longer Miss Spear would deign to wait. Between the motor calls the silence was oppressive. What could young Spear have done with his cigarette case? Once Vance thought he heard the banging of a window in the distance. Could it be that he had forgotten to close the windows in the library? But he was sure he had not; and the sound took on the ghostly resonance of unexplained noises. Perhaps that silly Laura Lou was right to be scared—as dusk fell it became easier to believe that the Willows might be haunted. Vance started back across the echoing parquet to the library; but halfway he met Lorry returning.

"Couldn't find the damn thing," he grumbled. "Got the keys, eh?" Vance said he had, and they moved toward the door. On the threshold Lorry paused, and turned to him again with Halo's smile. "You haven't got ten dollars you don't know what to do with? Like a fool I let Lewis and Frenside keep me up half the night playing poker. . . . Well, that's white of you. Thanks. Settle next week. And don't mention it to Halo, will you? The old people are down on poker . . . and on everything else I want to do." Vance turned the key in the front door, and the two walked through the long grass to the gate.

Vance felt grown-up and important. It put him at his ease with Lorry's sister to have a secret between men to keep from her.

BOOK III

⫷ XII ⫸

VANCE TURNED over slowly, opened his eyes, pushed back
his rumpled hair, and did not at first make out where he
was.

He thought the bed was a double one, black walnut
with carved ornaments and a pink mosquito net, on the wall
facing him a large photograph of a fat man with a Knights
of Pythias badge and a stiff collar, and a gramophone
shrieking out the Volga Boat Song somewhere below.

Then the vision merged into the more familiar one of
his neat little room at Euphoria, of college photographs and
trophies on the walls, and the sound of early splashing in
the white-tiled bathroom at the end of the passage. But this
picture also failed to adapt itself to his clearing vision, and
gradually he thought: "Why, I'm back at Paul's Landing,"
and the sloping ceiling, the flies banging against the pane,
the glimpse, outside, of a patch of currant bushes backed by
sultry blue woods, came to him with mingled reassurance
and alarm. "What the hell—" he thought.

Oh—he knew now. That baseball game over in New
Jersey had been Upton's idea. It was a Saturday, the day after Lorry Spear's visit to the Willows. When Vance got back
to the Tracys' Upton had been waiting at the gate, his
eyes bursting out of his head. A fellow had given him
tickets: Bunty Hayes, a reporter on the Paul's Landing paper. They could leave next morning by the first train, take a
look round in New York, and reach the field in good time.

131

As it was a Saturday there would be no difficulty in Upton's getting off. Vance was struck by the change in him: his pale face flushed, his shy evasive eyes burning with excitement, his very way of moving and walking full of a swagger and self-importance which made him seem years older.

Indoors, under Mrs. Tracy's eyes, he relapsed at once into the shy shambling boy with callous hands and boots covered with mud from the nursery. Mrs. Tracy did not oppose the plan, or did so only on the ground of Vance's health. They had a long hot day before them, and could not get home till ten or eleven o'clock at night. He must remember that he was just getting over a bad illness. . . . But Vance refused to be regarded as an invalid, or even as a convalescent. He was well again, he declared, and equal to anything. Mrs. Tracy could not but acknowledge how much he had gained during his fortnight at Paul's Landing; and she finally gave a colourless assent to the expedition, on condition that the two youths should take the earliest possible train home, and keep out of bad company—like that Bunty Hayes, she added. Vance and Upton knew it was not her way to acquiesce joyfully in any suggestion which broke the routine of life, and after giving her the requisite assurances they began their preparations lightheartedly.

In the morning, when they came down to gulp the cold coffee and sandwiches she had laid out overnight, Vance was astonished to find Laura Lou in the kitchen, in her refurbished yellow muslin, with a becoming shade-hat on her silvery-golden head. "You're going to take me, aren't you? I've warmed the coffee and boiled some eggs for you," she said to Vance in her childish way; and it caused him a pang when Upton, with a brother's brutality, reminded her that she knew Bunty'd only given him two tickets. Her lower lip began to tremble, her big helpless gray eyes to fill: Vance asked himself with inward vexation whether he ought to surrender his ticket to this tiresome child. But before he had made up his mind Upton cut short his sister's entreaties. "We're going with a lot of fellows: you know Mother wouldn't hear of it. What's all the fuss about anyway? You've got that school picnic this afternoon. That's what you were doing up your dress for yesterday. Don't you take any notice of her, Vance." She ran from the room, crimson and half crying; and Vance ate his eggs with compunction and relief. He didn't want any girl on his hands the first day he saw New York. . . .

They were there only a couple of hours, and there was no use trying to hunt up an editor. The most he could achieve was a distant view of the most notable skyscrapers, a gasp at Fifth Avenue and a dip into Broadway, before dashing to the Pennsylvania Station for the Jersey train. From that moment they were caught up in the baseball crowd, a crowd of which he had never seen the like. Life became a perspiring struggle, a struggle for air, for a foothold, for a sight of anything but the hot dripping napes and shoulder blades that hemmed them in. Finally, somehow, they had reached the field, got through the gates, found their places, discovered Bunty Hayes nearby with a crowd of congenial spirits, and settled down to the joys of spectatorship—or such glimpses of it as their seats permitted. It was a comfort to Vance to reflect that he had been right not to give his ticket to Laura Lou; such a frail creature could hardly have come alive out of the battle.

The oddest thing about the adventure was the transformation of Upton. Vance would have imagined Upton to be almost as unfitted as his sister for such a test of nerve and muscle; but the timorous youth of Paul's Landing developed, with the donning of his Sunday clothes, an unforeseen audacity and composure. The fact that Vance didn't know the ropes seemed to give Upton a sense of superiority; he said at intervals: "Come right along; stick to me; don't let 'em put it over on you," in a tone of almost patronizing reas-

surance. And when they joined Bunty Hayes, who was one
of the free spirits of Paul's Landing, Vance was struck by
the intimacy of his greeting of Upton, and by the "Hullo,
Uppy boy"—"Say, that the Tracy kid?" of his companions.
It was evident that Upton had already acquired the art of
the double life, and that the sheepish boy who went about
his job at the Paul's Landing nursery, and clumped home
for supper with mud and manure on his boots, was the pale
shade of the real Upton, a dashing blade with his straw hat
too far back on his pale blond hair, and a fraternity ribbon
suddenly budding in his buttonhole. "Wonder if Laura Lou
knows?" Vance speculated, and concluded that she did, and
that brother and sister carried on their own lives under Mrs.
Tracy's unsuspecting eye. He was rather sorry now that they
hadn't brought Laura Lou after all; it would have been
curious to see her blossom out like her brother. But Vance
soon forgot her in the exhilaration of watching the game. It
was his first holiday for months; for the dull business of convalescence had nothing to do with holiday-making. The
noise and excitement about him were contagious, and he
cheered and yelled with the rest, exchanged jokes with
Bunty Hayes and his friends, and felt himself saturated with
the vigour of all the young and vigorous life about him. But
when the game was over, and the crowd began to scatter,
the vitality seemed to ebb out of him as the spectators
ebbed out of the stadium. It was still very hot; he had
shouted himself hoarse; they had ahead of them the struggle
at the station, the struggle to get into a train, the stifling
journey home—and Vance began to feel that he was still a
convalescent, with no reserves of strength. At Euphoria, after a ball game, a dozen people would have been ready to
give him a lift home; but here he knew no one, Upton
seemed to have no acquaintances but Bunty Hayes and his
crowd, and Paul's Landing, where they all came from, was a
long way off.

"See here—you look sick," said Bunty Hayes, touching him on the shoulder.

Vance flushed up. "Sick? I'm hot and thirsty, that's all." He wasn't going to have any of that lot of Upton's treating him like a sissy.

"Well, that's easy. Come round with us and have a cool-off. We're all going to look in at the Crans', close by here. This is their car: jump in, sonny"

Suddenly a motor stood there: Vance remembered piling into it with Upton, Bunty Hayes, and some other fellows; they sat on each other's laps and on the hood. A girl who laughed very much and had blown-back hair, dyed red, was at the wheel. Where were they going? Who was she? Vance didn't care. As the motor began to move the wind stirred in his own hair, driving it back like the girl's, and life flowed through him again. He began to laugh, and tried to light a cigarette, but couldn't, because there wasn't enough elbow-room for a sardine. The others laughed at his ineffectual attempt, and another girl, perched somewhere behind him, lit a cigarette and leaned forward to push it between his lips. They were going to the Crans', and he found out, he didn't know how, that these two were the Cran girls —Cuty with the dyed hair at the wheel, and the younger, 'Smeralda they called her, sitting behind him on the hood between two fellows, so that his head rested against her knees, and he felt, through his hair, the warm flesh where her scant skirt had slipped up. Once or twice, after they had left the state highway, the overloaded motor nearly stuck in the deep ruts of the country road, and everybody laughed and cheered and gave college yells till Cuty somehow got them going again.

Ah, how good the cool drinks were when they got to the Crans'! It was at the back of the house, he remembered, under an arbour of scarlet runners that looked out on a long narrow yard where clothes were drying. Some of the clothes

were funny little garments with lace edgings and holes for
ribbon, and there was a good deal of joking about that, and
he remembered Cuty Cran crying out: "No, it ain't! No, I
don't! Mine are crepp-de-sheen. . . . Well, you come upstairs and see, then. . . ." But Cuty was not the one he fancied; and anyhow, since Floss he'd never . . . and he had
young Upton to look after. . . .

As the shadows lengthened it grew quiet and almost
cool under the arbour. The girls had the house to themselves, it appeared, Mr. and Mrs. Cran having been called
away that morning to the bedside of a grandmother who
had been suddenly taken sick somewhere upstate. "Real ac-
commodating of the old lady to develop stomach trouble
the day before the game," Bunty commented to the sisters,
who responded with shrieks of appreciation. "Not the first
time either," he continued, winking at his admiring audience, and the sisters shrieked afresh. The redhaired one was
the current type of brazen minx—but the younger, 'Smeralda, with her smouldering eyes and her heavy beauty of
chin and throat—ah, the younger, for his undoing, reminded Vance of Floss Delaney. She had the same sultry
pallor, the same dark penthouse of hair. . . .

Presently some other girls turned up, and there were
more drinks and more jokes about Mr. and Mrs. Cran being
away. "Guess some of us fellows ought to stay and act
watchdog for you two kiddies," Bunty humorously suggested. "Ain't you scared nights, all alone in this great big
house?" A general laugh hailed this, for the Cran homestead
was of the most modest proportions. But it stood apart in
the fields, with a little wood behind it and the girls had to
admit that it *was* lonesome at night, particularly since somebody'd poisoned the dog. . . . More laughs, and a bur-
lesque confession from Bunty that he'd poisoned the dog for
his own dark ends, which evoked still shriller cries of

amusement. . . . Bunty always found something witty and unexpected to say. . . .

There was a young moon, and it glinted through the dusk of the bean leaves and silvered their edges as darkness fell. Bunty and Cuty, and the other girls and fellows, wandered off down into the wood. Vance meant to follow, but he was very tired and sleepy, and a little befuddled with alcohol, and his broken-down rocking chair held him like a cradle.

"You're dead beat aren't you?" he heard one of the girls say, and felt a soft hand push back his hair. He opened his eyes and 'Smeralda's were burning into his.

"Come right upstairs, and you can lay down on Mother's bed," she continued persuasively.

He remembered saying: "Where's Upton?" with a last clutch at his vanishing sense of responsibility, and she answered: "Oh, he's down in the woods with Cuty and the others," and pulled Vance to his feet. He followed her upstairs through the darkening house, and at the top of the landing she slid a burning palm in his. . . .

As his vision readjusted itself and he found that he was in a narrow iron bedstead, instead of a wide one of black walnut, with a portrait of Mr. Cran facing him, he began to wonder how he had got from the one couch to the other, and how much time had elapsed in the transit. . . . But the effort of wondering was too much for him; his aching head dropped back. . . .

The recollection of Upton shot through him rebukingly; but he said to himself that Upton hadn't needed any advice, and would probably have rejected it if offered. "He ran the show—it was all fixed up beforehand between him and the Hayes fellow. . . . I wonder if his mother knows?" The thought of Mrs. Tracy was less easy to appease. He remembered her warning against Hayes, her adjuration that they should avoid bad company and come home before night; and he would have given the world to be in his own bed at Euphoria, with no difficulties to deal with but such as could be settled between himself and his family. "If I only knew the day of the week it is!" he thought, feeling more and more ashamed of the part he had played, and more and more scared of its probable consequences. "She'll cry—and I shall hate that," he reflected squeamishly.

At last he tumbled out of bed, soused his head in cold water, got into his clothes, and shuffled downstairs. The house was quiet, the hour evidently going toward sunset. In the back porch Mrs. Tracy sat shelling peas. There was no sign of emotion on her face, which was sallow and stony. She simply remarked, without meeting his eyes: "You'll find some fried liver left out on the table," and bent again to her task.

"Oh, I don't want anything—I'm not hungry," he stammered, longing to question her, to find out from her all that remained obscure in his own history, to apologize and to explain—if any explanation should occur to him! But she would not look up, and he found it impossible to pour out his excuses to her bent head, with the tired-looking hair drawn thinly over the skin, like the last strands of cotton round one of his mother's spools. "Funny women should get to look like that," he thought with a shiver of repulsion. To cut the situation short, he wandered into the dining room, looked at the fried liver and sodden potatoes, tried in vain to guess of what meal they were the survival, and turned away with the same sense of disgust with which the top of Mrs. Tracy's head had inspired him.

In the passage he wavered, wondering if he should go up again to his room or wander out in the heat. If Mrs. Tracy had not been in the porch his preference would have been to return there and go to sleep again in the hammock.

Then he determined to go back and have it out with her.

"Can't I help with those peas?" he asked, sitting down beside her. She lifted her head and looked at him with eyes of condemnation. "No, I don't want any help with the peas. Or any help from you, anyhow. You'd better go upstairs and sleep off your drunk before Miss Spear and Mr. Lorburn come round again—"

"My drunk?" Vance flushed crimson. "I don't know what you mean—"

"The words are English, I guess. And you'll want all your wits about you when you see Mr. Lorburn."

"Who's Mr. Lorburn? Why should he want to see me?"

"He's the owner of the Willows. He'll tell you soon enough why he wants to see you."

Vance felt a sinking of the heart. "I don't know what Mr. Lorburn's got to say to me," he muttered, but he did.

"Well, I presume *he* does." Mrs. Tracy pushed aside the basket of peas and stood up. Her face was a leaden white and her lower lip twitched. "Not as I care," she continued, in a level voice as blank as her eyes, "what he says to you, or what you feel about it. What's a few old books, one way or another? I don't care if you did take his books—"

"Take his books?" Vance gasped; but she paid no heed.

"—When what you took from me was my son. I trusted him with you, Vance; I thought you'd had enough kindness in this house to feel some obligation. I said to you: 'Well, go to that game if you're a mind to. But swear to me you'll be back the same night, both of you; and keep away from that Hayes and his rough crowd.' And you swore to me you would. And here I sat and waited and waited—the first time Upton was ever away from me for a night, and not so much as knowing where he was. And then a second night, and no sign of you. I thought I'd go mad then. I began life grand enough, as your folks'll tell you; and now everything's gone from me except my children. And when you crawled in yes-

terday evening, the two of you, I knew right away where
you'd been, and what you'd been doing—and leading Upton into. It's not the first time you've been out all night since
you came here, Vance Weston; but I wasn't going to say
anything about the other time, if only you'd have let Upton
alone. Now I guess you'd better tell your folks the air here
don't agree with you. And here's the money your father sent
me for your first fortnight. Take it."

She held out the money in a twitching hand, and Vance
took it because at that moment he would not have dared to
disobey any injunction she laid on him. And, besides, he
could understand her hating that money. There was something much more alarming to him in the wrath of this mild
creature than in the explosions of the choleric. When Mr.
Weston was angry Vance knew it bucked him up like a
cocktail; but Mrs. Tracy's anger clearly caused her suffering
instead of relief, was only one more misery in a life made up
of them. "If it hurts her to keep that money I'd better take
it," he thought vaguely.

"You mean I'd better go?" he asked.

"You'd better go," she flung back with white lips.

"I'm sorry," was all he could think of saying. It was
awfully unjust about Upton, but the boy *was* his junior by
two or three years, and of course, if his mother didn't
know . . .

"All right, I'll go if you say so. Is this Monday or Tuesday?"

"It's Tuesday, and near suppertime," said Mrs. Tracy
contemptuously. "I trust you've enjoyed your sleep." She
gathered up the basket of pods and the bowl of shelled
peas, and walked into the kitchen. Vance stood gazing after
her with a mind emptied of all willpower. It seemed incredible that three nights should have passed since he and Upton had set out so lightheartedly for the ball game. He had
always hated the idea of drunken bouts—had never been in

one like this since his freshman year. His self-disgust seemed to cling to every part of him, like a bad taste in the mouth or a smell of stale tobacco in the clothes. He didn't know what had become of the Vance of the mountain pool and of the library at the Willows. . . .

The Willows! The name suddenly recalled Mrs. Tracy's menacing allusion. What had she meant by saying that he had taken old Mr. Lorburn's books? She must have lost her head, worrying over Upton. He *had* left the books in a mess, the evening before the ball game; he remembered that. He had wanted to go back and straighten them out, and Lorry Spear had dissuaded him; said it was too dark, and it wouldn't do, in that old house, to light a candle. And now it would seem that the absentee owner of the place, who, according to Miss Spear, never came there, had turned up unexpectedly, and found things in disorder. Well, Vance had to own that the fault was his; he would have liked to see Miss Spear, and tell her so, before leaving. But the pale hostility of Mrs. Tracy's face seemed to thrust him out of her door, out of Paul's Landing. He thought to himself that the easiest thing would be to pack up and go at once—he did not want to sit at the table again with that face opposite to him. And Upton, the dirty sneak, would be afraid, he felt sure, to say a word in his defence . . . to tell his mother that the Hayes gang, and the Cran girls, were old acquaintances. . . . "No, I'll go now," Vance thought.

He went up to his room, packed up his clothes, and jammed his heap of scribbled papers in on top of them; then he leaned for a moment in the window and looked out to the hills. Up there, behind that motionless mask of trees, lived the girl with whom he had wandered in another world. He would have liked to see her again, to be with her just once on those rocks facing the sunrise. . . . Well . . . and how was he going to get his things down to the station? He guessed he was strong enough by this time to lug them down the lane to the trolley . . . He started downstairs with the suitcase and the unwieldy old bag into which his mother, at the last moment, had crammed a lot of useless stuff. The sound of the bags bumping against the stairs brought Mrs. Tracy to the kitchen door. She stared at Vance, surprised: "Where are you going?"

Vance said he was going to New York. She looked a little frightened. "Oh, but you must wait till tomorrow. I didn't mean—"

"I'd rather go today," he answered coldly.

She wiped her hands on her apron. "There's no one to help you to carry your things to the trolley. I didn't mean—"

"I guess I'll go," Vance repeated. He walked a little way down the garden path and then turned back to Mrs. Tracy. "I'd like to thank you for your kindness while I've been here," he said; and she stammered again: "But you don't understand . . . I didn't mean . . ."

"But I do," said Vance. He shouldered his bags and walked to the gate. Mrs. Tracy stood crying in the porch, and then hurried in and shut the door behind her. Vance trudged along the rutty lane, measuring his weakness by the way the weight of his bags increased with every step. The perspiration was streaming down his face when he reached the corner of the turnpike, and he sat down under the same thorn tree where, so short a time ago, he had waited in the summer darkness for Halo Spear. Even the memory of that day was obscured for him by what had happened since. He did not even like to think of Miss Spear's touch on his arm as she turned him toward the sunrise, or of the way she had looked as she sat by the pool leaning her head on her hand and listening while he recited his poems to her. All that seemed to belong to the far-off world of the hills, the world he had voluntarily forsaken, he didn't know why. . . .

The trolley came, and he scrambled in and was carried to the station. When he got there he found that the next

train for New York was not leaving for an hour and a half.
He deposited his property in the baggage room and, wandering out again, stood aimlessly in the square, where the
same tired horses with discoloured manes were swinging
their heads to and fro under the thin shade of the locust
boughs. It seemed months since he had first got out of the
train, and seen that same square and those old-fashioned
vehicles and languid horses. He remembered his shock of
disappointment, and was surprised to find that he now felt a
choking homesickness at the idea of looking at it all for the
last time. Suddenly it occurred to him that he might still be
able to walk as far as the Willows and have a last glimpse at
its queer bracketed towers and balconies. He could not have
told why he wanted to do this: the impulse was involuntary. Perhaps it was because his hours in that shadowy library had lifted him to other pinnacles, higher even than
Thundertop.

He walked from the station to the main street, and at
the corner was startled by the familiar yelp of the Eaglewood motor. His heart turned over at the thought that it
might be Miss Spear. He said to himself: "Perhaps if she
sees me she'll stop and tell me she's sorry for what's happened"; and he softened at the memory of her lavish atone-
ments. But when the motor disengaged itself from the traffic
he found there was no one in it but Jacob. Vance was about
to walk on, but he saw Jacob signalling. The thought started
up: "He may have a message—a letter," and his heart beat
in that confused way it had since his illness. Jacob drew up.
"See here, I was looking for you. I've been round to the
Tracys'. You get right in here with me."

"Get in with you—why?"

" 'Cos the folks've sent me to bring you over to the Willows. They're waiting for you there now. They said I was to
go to your place and tell you you was to come right off."

The blood rushed to Vance's forehead, and his softened

mood gave way to resistance. Who were these people, to order him about in this way? Did they really suppose that he was at their beck and call? "Waiting for me? What for? I'm leaving for New York. Mrs. Tracy has the keys of the Willows. I've got nothing to do with it."

Jacob took off his straw hat and scratched his head perplexedly. "Miss Halo she said you was to come. She said: 'You've got to bring him, dead or alive.'"

Jacob's face expressed nothing; neither curiosity nor comprehension disfigured its supreme passiveness. His indifference gave Vance time to collect himself. He burst into a laugh. "Dead or alive—" the phrase was so like her! "Oh, I'm alive enough. And I'll come along with you if she says so." In his heart he knew Miss Spear was right: it was his business to see her again, to explain, to excuse himself. He had failed her shamefully . . . he hadn't done the job she had entrusted him with . . . he had left the books in disorder. "All right—I'll go," he repeated. He knew there was a train for New York later in the evening. "Anyhow," he thought, "I'm done with the Tracys. . . ."

❧ XIII ❧

THE DOOR of the house stood wide. The afternoon radiance gilded the emerald veil of willows, shot back in fire from the unshuttered windows, rifled the last syringas of their inmost fragrance. Vance, even through his perturbation, felt again the spell of the old house. That door had first admitted him into the illimitable windings of the Past; and as he approached the magic threshold compunction and anger vanished.

"Oh, Vance!" he heard Miss Spear exclaim. He caught in her rich voice a mingling of reproach and apology—yes, apology. She was atoning already—for what?—but she was also challenging. "I knew you'd come." She put her hand on his arm with her light coercive touch. "Our cousin Mr. Tom Lorburn is here—he arrived unexpectedly on Sunday to see the Willows. It's years and years since he's been here. . . ."

"A surprise visit," came a voice, an old cracked fluty voice, querulous and distinguished, from the drawing room. "And I *was* surprised. . . . But perhaps you'll bring the young man in here, Halo. . . . Whatever you have to say to him may as well be said in my presence, since I am here . . ."

The little tirade ended almost in a wail, as the speaker, drooping in the doorway, looked down on Vance from the vantage of his narrow shoulders and lean brown throat. Vance looked up, returning the gaze. He had hardly ever

145

seen anyone as tall as Mr. Lorburn, and no one, ever, as plaintively and unhappily handsome. A chronic distress was written on the narrow beautiful face condescending to his, with its perfectly arched nose, and the sensitive lips under a carefully trimmed white moustache; and the distress was repeated in the droop of Mr. Lorburn's shoulders under their easily fitting homespun, in the hollowing of his chest, and the clutch of his long expressive brown hand (so like Mrs. Spear's) on the bamboo stick which supported him.

"Since unhappily I *am* here," Mr. Lorburn repeated.

Miss Spear met this with a little laugh. "Oh, Cousin Tom—why unhappily? After all, since you've come, it was just as well you should arrive when we were all napping."

Mr. Lorburn bent his grieved eyes upon her. "Just as well?"

"That you should know the worst."

"Ah, *that* we never know, my child; there's always something worse behind the worst. . . ." Mr. Lorburn, shaking his head, turned back slowly through the drawing room. "There's my health, to begin with, which no one but myself ever appears to think of. A shock of this kind, in this heat . . ."

"Well, here's Vance Weston, who has come, as I knew he would, to clear things up."

Mr. Lorburn considered Vance again in the light of this fresh introduction. "I should be glad if he could do that," he said.

"Then," said Miss Spear briskly, "let's begin by transporting ourselves to the scene of the crime, as they say in the French law reports."

She slipped her arm in Mr. Lorburn's, and led him through the two drawing rooms, his long wavering stride steadied by her firm tread. Vance followed, wondering.

In the library the shutters were open, and the western sun streamed in on the scene of disorder which Vance had left so lightheartedly three days before. He wondered at his own callousness. In the glare of the summer light the room looked devastated, dishonoured; and the long grave face of Miss Elinor Lorburn, with its chalky highlights on brow and lappets, seemed to appeal to her cousin and heir for redress. "See how they have profaned my solitude—that, at least, my family always respected!"

Mr. Lorburn let himself down by cautious degrees into the Gothic armchair. "At least," he echoed, as if answering the look, "if I never came here, I gave strict orders that nothing should be touched . . . that everything should remain absolutely as she left it."

The words were dreadful to Vance. His eyes followed Mr. Lorburn's about the room, resting on the books pitched down on chairs and tables, on the gaping spaces of the shelves, and the lines of volumes which had collapsed for lack of support. Then he looked at the cigarette ashes which Lorry Spear had scattered irreverently on the velvet table cover, and his gaze turned back to Mr. Lorburn's scandalized countenance. He felt too crushed to speak. But Miss Spear spoke for him:

"Now, Cousin Tom, that all sounds very pretty; but just consider what would have happened if we'd obeyed you literally. The place would have been a foot deep in dust. Everything in it would have been ruined; and if the house hadn't been regularly aired your precious books would have been covered with green mould. So what's the use—"

Vance lifted his head eagerly, reassured by her voice. "The books did need cleaning," he said. "But I was wrong not to put them back after I'd wiped them, the way you told me to. Fact is, I'd never had a chance at real books before, and I got reading, and forgot everything. . . ." He looked at Miss Spear. "I'm sorry," he said.

Mr. Lorburn, leaning on his stick, emitted a faint groan. "The young man, as he says himself, appears to have forgotten everything—even to return the books he has taken from here."

Again Mrs. Tracy's accusation! Vance turned his eyes on Miss Spear; but to his bewilderment her eloquence seemed to fail her. She met his glance, but only for a moment; then hers was averted. At last she said in a low voice: "I'm sure he'll tell you the books are at Mrs. Tracy's . . . that he took them away to finish reading something that interested him . . . without realising their value. . . ."

"I'm waiting to hear what he has to tell me," Mr. Lorburn rejoined. "But I must remind you, Halo, that, according to your own statement, Mrs. Tracy has looked everywhere for the books, and been forced to the conclusion—as you were—that when the young man disappeared from her house he took them with him. Perhaps he will now say if he has been obliging enough to bring them back."

Mr. Lorburn revolved his small head on his long thin neck and fixed his eyes on Vance.

Vance felt the muscles of his face contracting. His lips were so stiff that he could hardly move them. These people were suggesting that he had taken away books from the Willows—valuable books! This Mr. Lorburn, apparently, was almost accusing him of having stolen them! What else could he mean by the phrase "When he disappeared from Mrs. Tracy's he took them with him"? Vance felt as defenceless as a little boy against whom a schoolmate had trumped up a lying charge; in his first bewilderment he did not know what to say, or what tone to take. Then his anger rushed to his lips.

"What's this about taking books away and disappearing? I never disappeared. I went with Upton to a ball game." He felt himself redden at the memory. "I never took a single book away from here, not one."

Miss Spear interrupted eagerly: "I told you so, Cousin Tom . . . I was sure. . . ."

Mr. Lorburn leaned more heavily on his stick. "Where are they then?" Her head drooped, and she turned from him with an appealing gesture. "Vance?—"

"What books?" Vance asked again.

Mr. Lorburn drew himself to his feet and began to move across the room with shaking sideway steps, his stick pointed first at one shelf, then at another. As he did so he reeled off a succession of long titles, all too unfamiliar to Vance for his ear to hold them. He heard "rare Americana," and did not know if it were the name of a book or a reference to some literary category he had never met with. At last he said: "I never even heard of the names of any of those books. Why on earth should I have taken them?"

"Never heard of them?" Mr. Lorburn spluttered. "Then some accomplished bibliophile must have given you a list." He looked pale and gasping, like a fish agonizing for water. "Oh, my heart—I should never have let myself to be drawn into this." Sitting down again, he closed his lids and leaned his head against the knobby carving of the armchair.

Vance was alarmed by his appearance; but he noticed that it did not affect Miss Spear. She continued to fix her anxious gaze upon himself. "Just try to remember exactly what happened." She spoke as if reassuring a child. Her voice was too kind, too compassionate; his own caught in his throat, and he felt the tears swelling.

"Of course I didn't take any books," he repeated. "And I didn't disappear—I went with Upton. . . ."

"Of course," she said. "But the books are gone. There's the point. Very valuable ones, unluckily."

("The most valuable," Mr. Lorburn interjected, his eyes still closed.)

"Think, Vance; when you left last Saturday night, didn't you forget to shut this window?" She pointed to the window near which she stood.

The definiteness of the question cleared Vance's mind.

"No, I didn't. I fastened all the shutters and windows before I left."

She paused, and he saw a look of uncertainty in her face. "Think again, please. On Sunday morning this one was found open, and the shutter had been unhooked from the inside. Someone must have got in after you left, and taken the books, for they're really gone. We've hunted everywhere."

Vance repeated: "I fastened all the shutters; I'm sure I did. And I locked the front door." He stopped, and then remembered that when he left the house Lorburn Spear had been with him. "Ask your brother; I guess he'll remember."

As he spoke, there came back to him the sensation he had experienced as he waited in the dusk of the hall for Lorry Spear, who had gone back to the library to find his cigarette case. He had been a long time finding it, and while Vance waited he had heard that mysterious sound somewhere in the distance: a sound like a window opening or a shutter swinging loose. He had thought of Laura Lou's childish fears, smiled them away, and nevertheless turned back to see. . . .

"My brother? Yes, I know he was with you," Miss Spear said, almost irritably. Her face looked expressionless, cold. "He says it was you who attended to closing the house."

"Well, doesn't he say I closed everything?"

"He says he doesn't remember." She paused, and then began, in a hasty authoritative tone: "Someone must have broken in. Someone has taken the books. Try to remember what happened when you were leaving—try again, Vance," she urged, more gently.

Mr. Lorburn still sat with closed eyes, and the gasping fishlike expression. He murmured again: "I ought not to have let myself be drawn into this—" and then was silent.

Vance looked resolutely at Miss Spear. Her eyes wavered, as if trying to escape from him; then they bathed him in a fluid caress. The caress poured over him, enveloping, persuading. The words were on his lips: "But after we left the library your brother went back to it alone—while he was there I heard a window opened . . . or thought I did. . . ." *Thought you did?* But only *thought,* her smile whispered back, silencing him. How can you suggest (it said) . . . and anyhow, what use would it be? Don't you see that I can't let you touch my brother? Vance felt himself subdued and mastered. . . . He couldn't hurt her . . . he couldn't. He had the sense of being shut in with her in a hidden circle of understanding and connivance.

"Of course a burglar broke in somehow and stole the books," he heard her begin again with renewed energy. "Come, Cousin Tom; why should we stay any longer? It's just upsetting you. . . . This is a job for the police."

She held out her hand to Vance. "I'm sorry—but I had to ask you to come."

He said of course she had to . . . he understood; but the only thing he really understood was that she had bound him fast in a net of unspoken pledges. As they reached the door she turned back. "We'll see you again soon—at Eaglewood? Promise. . . ."

But he had given her his last promise. "I don't know. I'm going to New York. . . . Maybe I'll have to go back home. . . ."

Mr. Lorburn had descended the steps and was walking unsteadily along the drive. Miss Spear looked at Vance. "Yes, go," she said quickly, "but come back someday." Her face was sunned over with relief; for a moment she reminded him of the girl of the mountaintop. "Don't forget me," she said, and pressed his hand. She unlocked the gate and sprang into the car after Mr. Lorburn. Vance watched them drive away. Then he walked slowly down the lane without once looking back at the old house. He felt sick at heart, diminished and ashamed, as he had at Crampton the day he had seen his grandfather prowling by the river.

≈ XIV ≈

VANCE WESTON had started from Euphoria with two hundred dollars; and to what was left of that sum there was added the money Mrs. Tracy had thrust back at him as they started. After he had sat for a while in the train, dazed from the shock of his last hour at the Willows, he remembered that henceforth he must subsist on the balance of his funds, and he drew the money out and counted it. He had bought a ten-dollar wristwatch for Upton in New York, the day they went to the ball game, and a rainbow-coloured scarf for Laura Lou, to console her for not coming; the scarf, he thought, had cost about three-seventy-five. On the eve of their ill-fated expedition he had lent ten dollars to Lorburn Spear; and at the ball game, and afterward at the Crans', had stood drinks, soft and hard, a good many times. He remembered also that the fellows, with a lot of laughing and joking, had clubbed together to buy the Cran girls a new watchdog; and good watchdogs, it appeared, came pretty high. Still, it gave him an unpleasant shock of surprise to find that he had only ninety-two dollars left, including the money returned by Mrs. Tracy. He could not recall where the rest had gone; his memory of what had happened at the Crans' was too vague.

Ninety dollars would have carried him a long way at Euphoria. In New York he didn't know how far it would go —much less, assuredly. And he didn't even know where to turn when he got out of the train, where to find a lodging for the night. In the car there were people who could no doubt have told him, friendly experienced-looking people; but no familiar face was among them, and a rustic caution kept him from questioning strangers on the approach to a big city. As the train entered the Grand Central he hurriedly consulted the black porter, and the latter, after looking him over with a benevolent eye, gave him an address near the station. He found a narrow brick hotel squeezed in between tall buildings, with a dingy black-and-gold sign over the door. It looked dismal and unappetizing enough; but his bed there, and his coffee next morning, cost him so much that he decided he must not remain for another night, and wandered out early in search of a rooming house.

The noise and rush of traffic, the clamour of the sign-boards, the glitter of the innumerable shops distracted him from his purpose, and hours passed as he strayed on curiously from street to street. Some faculty separate from mind or heart, something detached and keen, was roused in him by this tumult of life and wealth and energy, this ceaseless outpour of more people, more noises, more motors, more shopfuls of tempting and expensive things. He thought what fun it would be to write a novel of New York and call it *Loot*—and he began to picture how different life would have seemed that morning had he had the typescript of the finished novel under his arm, and been on his way to the editorial offices of one of the big magazines. The idea for a moment swept away all his soreness and loneliness, and made his heart dilate with excitement. "Well, why not? . . . I'll stay here till I've done it," he swore to himself in a fever of defiance.

He halted before a shop window displaying flowers in gilt baskets, or mounted in clusters tied with big pink bows. The money Mrs. Tracy had returned was burning in his pocket, and he said to himself that he could not keep it another minute. In one corner of the window was an arrangement which particularly took his fancy: a stuffed dove perched on the gilt handle of a basket of sweet peas and maidenhair fern. It recalled to him Miss Spear's description of that temple to Apollo, somewhere in Greece, which had been built by the birds and bees; and looking at the burnished neck of the dove he thought: "That might have been one of the birds." There was a good-natured-looking woman in the shop, and he ventured to ask her the price of the object he coveted. She smiled a little, as if surprised. "Why, that's twenty-five dollars."

Vance crimsoned. "I was looking for something for thirty."

"Oh, were you?" said the woman, still smiling. "Well, there's those carnations over there."

Vance didn't care for the carnations; the bird on the basket handle was what attracted him. "Laura Lou'll like it anyhow," he thought. And suddenly an idea occurred to him, and he asked the woman whether, for thirty dollars, she would have the basket carried for him that very morning to the house of a lady at Paul's Landing. She looked still more surprised, and then amused, and after they had hunted up Paul's Landing in the telephone book, she said, yes, she guessed she could, and Vance, delighted, pulled out thirty dollars, and his pen to write the address. She pushed a card toward him, and after a moment's perplexity he wrote: "I thank you, Cousin Lucilla," addressed the envelope, and walked out with a lighter step. The woman was already wrapping up the dove.

He was beginning to feel hungry, and the instinct of clinging to the relatively familiar drew him back to the Grand Central, where he knew he could lunch. As he entered he almost ran into a motherly-looking woman with a large yellowish face and blowsy gray hair, who wore a military felt hat with a band inscribed: "The Travellers' Friend." Vance went up to her, and her smile of welcome reassured him before he had spoken. He wanted to know of a nice quiet rooming house? Why, surely—that was just what she was there for. Country boy, she guessed? Well, why wouldn't he bring his things right round to Friendship House, just a little way off, down in East Fiftieth—she fumbled in her bag and handed him the address on a card with: "Bring your friend along—always room for one more," in red letters across the top. That, she explained, was the men's house; she herself was in the station to look after women and girls, and there was another house for them not far off; but Vance had only to mention her name to Mr. Jakes and they'd find a room for him, and give him the addresses of some respectable rooming houses. She shook his hand, beamed on him maternally, and turned away to deal with a haggard bewildered-looking woman who was saying: "My husband said he'd sure be at the station to meet me, but I can't find him, and the baby's been sick in the cars all night. . . ."

At Friendship House Vance was received by an amiable man with gold teeth, given supper of coffee and bread and butter, and assigned to a spotless cubicle. Not till he was falling asleep did it occur to him that Mrs. Tracy had a row of sweet peas in her own garden, and that a stuffed dove could hardly compensate her for the cost of his fortnight's board. He felt ashamed of his stupidity, and was haunted all night by the vision of the dreary smile with which she would receive his inappropriate tribute. Probably even Laura Lou would not know what to do with a stuffed dove. Yet that basket, with the lustrous bird so lightly poised on it, had seemed all poetry when he chose it. . . .

The weeks passed. After Vance's regulation twenty-four hours at Friendship House he was recommended to a rooming house which was certainly as respectable as they had promised, but offered few other attractions, at least in hot weather. During those first lonely suffocating days and nights Vance's weak body and sore spirit yearned for his neat room at home, the glitter of the bath, the shade of the Mapledale Avenue trees. But since he was determined to hold on till he got a job he dared not risk taking a better room; and the thought of going home was more hateful than his present misery. Yet loneliness was the core of that misery; incessant gnawing loneliness of mind and heart. He was benumbed by the feeling that in the huge wilderness of people about him not one had ever heard of him, or would take the least interest in his case if he should appeal for understanding; not one would care a straw that within him all the forces of the universe were boiling. He felt the same desolation, the sense of life being over for him, as when he had staggered down the passage to his parents' room and groped for the absent revolver. . . .

But the returning tide of vitality did not mount as rapidly as it had then. The situation was different. Then he had made up his mind to wait till life gave him another chance; and life had given him that chance—magnificently—and what had he made of it? His rage against Mrs. Tracy, against Upton and the Spears, was a mere passing flare-up; it soon gave place to a lasting sense of failure. He had been at fault, and he only. Upton was a sly little fool, but he, Vance, was the older of the two, and being the more experienced should have been the stronger. He should have resisted the temptation to loaf and drink with those wasters and flashy girls, should have remembered his promise to Mrs. Tracy to come home with Upton after the game. If he had, everything might have been different, for early the next morning he would have hurried back to the Willows, have noticed that the books were gone, and perhaps prevented his own disgrace and Miss Spear's unhappiness. . . . He could not forget how unhappy she had looked when it first flashed on her that her brother had probably taken the books. Vance ached with that more than his own wretchedness. His only comfort was that he had seen at once what was passing through her mind, had caught her signal and obeyed it. He knew she had perceived this, and been grateful; and the fact that she had sacrificed him to her brother did not offend him—it seemed to create a new tie between them. . . .

All this worked out gradually in his mind, and meanwhile he waited, and reflected on his situation. His first impulse had been not to let his whereabouts be known to anyone. He lived in dread of being dragged back to Euphoria when his parents learned that he had left the Tracys. What he longed for was to vanish into space, to get off into a universe of his own where nothing associated with his former life could reach him. It was what he had tried to do after he had seen his grandfather and Floss Delaney by the river; only this time his suicide would have taken the form of losing himself in a big city, to re-emerge from it when he had made himself a new existence. But he soon came to his senses and realized that Mrs. Tracy, frightened by his departure, would be sure to write to his family, and that, if he gave them no sign, they would be frightened also, and would set all the machinery of police research in motion. It was not easy for a fellow with an anxious family to lose himself in these times; and Vance had not had the presence of mind to give a fictitious name at his lodgings.

He wrote briefly to his mother, telling her he was doing well; and wouldn't his folks please let him alone and give him a show in New York, now he'd got there? He said he'd left Paul's Landing because he felt quite strong enough to take a job on a paper, and didn't care to loaf around any longer at the Tracys', where it was a good deal hotter than in the city, anyhow. He added that he had money enough left, and had already made the acquaintance of a famous editor (and so he had, though he would rather have starved than appeal to George Frenside); and he arranged with the good-natured secretary at Friendship House to receive his letters, so that his family should be reassured by the address.

Accident favoured him. His sister Mae wrote that his father had just left for a Realtors' Congress at Seattle and would not return for a month or more; and that though Mrs. Weston was upset and anxious at the idea of his being alone in New York she had been persuaded by Grandma Scrimser not to interfere, but to let him try his luck, at any rate till his father got back. This being settled, Vance turned his mind to the means of holding out—for he was sure that, until he got a job, his father would not think of sending him more money. His promised allowance had been meant to see him through his convalescence at Paul's Landing; if he didn't choose to stay there, and was strong enough to work—well, let him.

Meanwhile he had New York to himself, and his first business was to collect his wits and try not to miss this chance as he had the other. The main thing was to see how long he could make his remaining dollars last; and he bent his mind on this, foregoing all amusements which had to be paid for, eating at the cheapest places he could find, often going without a midday meal, and wandering about the streets for hours staring at the strange confused spectacle which remained so mockingly unaware of him.

But all his moments were not lonely. A few days after his arrival he happened to emerge upon Fifth Avenue just opposite the public library. Awed by its rhetorical façade, so unlike a haunt of studious peace, he stood wondering if it were one of the swell hotels he'd heard about—the Ritz or the St. Regis—till looking more closely he read its designation. Instantly he dashed up the vast steps, entered the doors unabashed, and asked the first official he met if he could go in and read. . . . He could, it appeared, and without paying a cent, and for many hours of the day. At first he was perplexed as to his next step; but where books were concerned some instinct seemed to guide him, and presently he had been made free of a series of card catalogues, and was lost in them as in the murmurs of a forest. . . . True, the place lacked the magic of the Willows, since the reader had to know beforehand what he wanted, and could not roam at will from shelf to shelf, subject to the mysterious, the almost physical appeal of books actually visible and accessible. That joy was one he could not hope to find again till—well, till he had made money enough to have his own library. But meanwhile it was wonderful enough to sit in a recess of a quiet room, with a pile of volumes in front of him, his elbows on the table, his hands plunged in his hair, his soul immersed in a new world. . . .

The weeks passed, and though his hours at the public library cost him nothing, those spent in his rooming house were using up his funds. In spite of what he had written to his mother he had not as yet looked up a newspaper job. He wanted first to acquaint himself a little more with New York, its aspect, its ways, its language; to appear less of a hayseed and an ignoramus. That, at least, was what he told himself; but in reality his hours at the library were so engrossing, and his ignorance had revealed itself on a scale so unsuspected and overwhelming, that each day drew him back to the lion-guarded gates of knowledge. To cheat himself into thinking that he could live thus indefinitely he began to plan his novel of New York; nor did it strike him till afterward that a raw boy whose experience was bounded by a rooming house and a library would find it even harder to weave a tale out of the millions of strands of a great city's activities than to evolve copy for a newspaper. Everything that appealed to his creative instinct always seemed to become a part of his experience, and he sat down with a pas-

sionate eagerness to block out his dream. But he knew that
this novel, even if he could do it, would take an immense
time in the doing; and meanwhile he must find the means to
live.

Drifting from dream to dream, eating daily less, studying daily for longer hours, he entered into the state of
strange illumination which comes to ardent youth when the
body hungers while the intelligence is fed. His shaking fingers filled page after page with verse and prose; it seemed
as though every difficulty of thought and language were
overcome, and he could conceive and formulate whatever
his restless intellect willed. The veil of matter had grown so
transparent that the light of eternity shone through it, and
in that pure radiance he could see with supernatural clear-
ness the images of gods walking among men, and angels
going up and down the heavenly ladder. But Jacob's pillow
is a hard one for a young head still weak from fever; and
one morning when after a night of tossing misery he
crawled to his table and pulled out his papers, his mind was
a blank, and he could hardly decipher what he had written
the day before. He looked up and saw in the blotched looking glass a face so bloodless and shrunken that he thought
he must be on the verge of another illness; and when he
counted his money he found he could not hold out, even on
a starvation diet, for more than a week.

The world grew light and dizzy about him, as if the air
had turned into millions of shimmering splinters. He managed to dress and get out to the nearest eating house, and
for the first time in days he ordered hot coffee and a couple
of eggs. After eating he felt better, but so tired and heavy
that he crawled home and threw himself on his unmade
bed; and there he slept dreamlessly for hours. When he
woke he understood that he must have more food, and that
the only way to get it was to try for a job. He felt too weak
to think much more than that; but he gave himself another

good meal, and the next day started out on his round. He went from one newspaper to another, was received either civilly or the reverse, was asked to state his qualifications, and saw his name and address taken down; but no one showed any interest in him, and he turned away hopeless from the last threshold. With no one to recommend him, and no past experience of newspaper work, what chance was there of his getting a job? The only alternative was Euphoria; but he was too disheartened to let his mind dwell on that.

There was just one other chance; that Mr. Frenside, in spite of his gruff sneering way, had not been unfriendly. He knew of Vance's aspirations, and perhaps would be willing to advise him—unless unfavourable rumours had reached him from Eaglewood. But Vance remembered Halo Spear's kindly glance when she took leave of him, heard her say: "Go now—but come back some day," and guessed that, however bent she was on screening her brother, she would not let Vance suffer unjustly. He had found out by this time that *The Hour,* as he had suspected, was a mere highbrow review, and therefore not to his purpose; but Frenside must have relations with the newspaper world, and would be able to tell him where there was hope of an opening for an untrained outsider. At any rate, it was the only thing left to try.

⪧ XV ⪦

THE HOUR was modestly housed on an upper floor of a shabby ex-private house; no noiseless lift, plate-glass doors or silver-buttoned guardians led to its threshold. But the typewriter girl in the outer office, who said, no, Mr. Frenside wasn't the editor, but only literary adviser, added that she guessed he was there that morning, and presently returned to show Vance into a stuffy cell full of cigar smoke where Frenside leaned on an ink-spattered table and fixed Vance with his unencouraging stare.

"Oh, yes—Weston your name is? Well, sit down."

He smoked and stared for a while; then he exclaimed: "By George, I saw you up at Eaglewood, didn't I? Why, yes —that business of the books. . . . Miss Spear'll be glad I've run across you. The books were found, she wanted you to know. . . ."

"The books?" Vance looked at him vaguely. In this shimmering dubious world in which he had lately lived the story of the books at the Willows had become as forgotten and far-off a thing as the song in one of those poems Miss Spear had read to him; Miss Spear herself was only a mist among mists; all Vance could think of now was that he must get this taciturn man behind the cigar to find him a job.

"Why, yes, the books turned up," Frenside repeated.

"How?" Vance asked with an effort.

"I don't know the particulars. It seems Lewis Tarrant— you remember that fair young man who's always up at

162

Eaglewood?—well, he managed to buy them back . . . ad-
vertised, I believe . . . offered a reward. . . . They never
caught the thief; but that didn't so much matter. The main
thing was to get the books. So that question's closed."

"Well, I'm glad," Vance forced himself to say. And he
knew he would be, in the other world of solid matter, if ever
he got back to it. . . .

He felt that Frenside was looking at him more attentively. "That's not what you came for, though? Well, let's
hear." He settled back in his chair, listening in silence to
what Vance had to say, and drumming on the table as if he
were rapping out his secret thoughts on a typewriter.

Vance stammered through the tale of his vain quest,
and wondered if perhaps Mr. Frenside could recommend
him to a newspaper—but the other cut him short. He hadn't
any pull of that sort; sorry; but Vance had better go straight
home if he had an opening on a newspaper there. Vance
turned pale and made no answer; he cursed himself inwardly for having appealed, against his better judgment, to
this man who cared nothing for him and was perhaps prej-
udiced by what had happened at the Willows.

"All right, sir, thank you," he said, getting to his feet,
and turning to the door. As he did so, Frenside spoke. "See
here—going home's a nasty dose to swallow sometimes, isn't
it? I remember . . . at your age. . . . Why do you want to
go on a newspaper, anyhow?"

Vance, leaning against the doorway, answered: "I want
to learn to be a writer."

"And that's the reason—" Frenside gave a gruff laugh.

Vance looked at him curiously. "Is there any other
way?"

"There's only one way. Buckle down and write. Newspapers won't help you."

Vance felt the blood rush to his forehead. "I have . . .
I have . . . tried to write. . . ."

Frenside reached for a match, relit his cigar, and once more said: "Sit down." Vance obeyed. "What have you written? Got it in your pocket, I suppose? Let's see."

Vance, with a feverish hand, pulled out a bundle of papers—the poems he had written at Paul's Landing, and some of the stuff which had poured from his pen in the long hungry hours at the rooming house. He laid them on the desk, and Frenside adjusted his eyeglasses. It seemed to Vance as if he were fitting his eyes to an exceptionally powerful microscope.

"H'm—poetry. All poetry?"

"Most of what I've written is."

"Well, poetry won't earn your keep: it's pure luxury. Like keeping a car."

Silence followed. At intervals it was broken by what sounded to Vance like the roar of the sea, but was in reality the scarce audible rustle as Frenside unfolded one sheet after another. He was doubtless not accustomed to reading manuscript, and to Vance's agony of apprehension was added the mortification of not having been able to type his poems before submitting them. In most editorial offices, he knew, they wouldn't look at handwritten things; presenting the poems to Frenside in this shape would probably do away with their one chance. Vance thought of offering to read them aloud, remembered Miss Spear's comment on his enunciation, and dared not.

The roar of unfolding pages continued.

"H'm," said Frenside again. He spread the papers out before him, and puffed in silence.

"Well, you're at the sedulous age," he continued after a pause. (What did that mean?) "Can't be helped, of course. Here's the inevitable Shakespeare sonnet: 'What am I but the shape your love has made me?'—and the Whitman: 'Vast enigmatic reaches of ocean beyond me'—just so. It *is* beyond you, my dear fellow, at least at present. Ever seen the ocean?"

Vance could hardly find his voice. He shook his head.

"Not even at Coney Island?" Frenside shrugged. "Not that that matters. Look here; this is all Poets' Corner stuff. Try it on your hometown paper. That's my advice. There are pretty things here and there, of course; you like the *feel* of words, don't you? But poetry, my son, is not a halfway thing. I remember once asking a book-learned friend if he cared for poetry, and he answered cautiously: 'Yes, up to a certain point.' Well, the devil of it is that real poetry doesn't begin till beyond that certain point. . . . See?"

Vance signed that he saw: somehow he liked that definition of poetry, even at the cost of having to sacrifice his own to it.

"How about prose; never written any?"

The unexpectedness of the question jerked Vance out of the clouds. "I—I'm writing a novel."

"Hullo—are you? What about."

"About life in New York."

"I thought so," said Frenside grimly. There was another silence. "Never tried an article or a short story?"

"Never anything—good enough." Vance got wearily to his feet. "I guess I'll take these things and burn 'em," he said, putting out his hands for the poems.

"No, don't do that. Keep 'em, and reread 'em in a couple of years. That requires more courage, and courage is about the most useful thing in an artist's outfit." Vance was beginning to think it must be.

"Well," Frenside continued, "if ever you try a short essay, or a story, bring them along. Don't forget." He smiled a little, as if to bind up the wounds he had inflicted. "You never can tell," he concluded cryptically.

He held out his hand. The interview was over.

The interview was over; but when Vance reached the foot of the stairs he perceived its repercussions were only just beginning. He wandered on through a street or two, found himself in Union Square, and sat down under the meagre shade of its starved trees. The other people on the bench with him, listless sodden-looking men, collarless and perspiring, seemed like companions in misery who had preceded him a flight or two down the steep stairs of failure. Perhaps they too—or at least one among them—had tried for the impossible, as he was doing. He shivered a little at the sense of such kinship.

But gradually a luminous point emerged out of the enveloping fog. "Newspapers won't help you," Frenside had said; and Vance was suddenly aware that the dictum chimed with his own deep inward conviction. It had always seemed to him that newspapers, as he knew them, were totally unrelated to literature as he had always dreamed of it, and as he now knew that it existed. Yet was Frenside right —was he himself right? Everyone always said: "Nothing like newspaper work as a training if a fellow wants to write. Teaches you not to waste time, to go straight to the point, to put things in a bright snappy way that won't bore people. . . ." Ugh, how he hated all the qualities thus commended! What a newspaper man like Bunty Hayes, for instance, would have called wasting time seemed to Vance one of the fundamental needs of the creative process. He could not imagine putting down on paper anything that had not risen slowly to the verge of his consciousness, that had not to be fished for and hauled up with infinite precautions from some secret pool of being as to which he knew nothing as yet but the occasional leap, deep down in it, of something alive but invisible. . . . And this Frenside, whom he did not like, whose manner offended him, whose views awoke his instinctive antagonism, had yet, in that one phrase, summed up his own obscure feeling. "Buckle down and

write"; yes—he had always felt that to be the only way. But
to do it a fellow must be quiet, must have enough to eat,
must be fairly free from material anxieties; and how was he
to accomplish that? He didn't know—but he was so grateful
for the key word furnished by Frenside that nothing else
seemed much to matter; not the disparagement of his
poems, the shrug at his novel, or the assumption that his
aspirations were bound to be exactly like those of any other
young fool who presented himself to an editor with a first
bundle of manuscript. He walked slowly back to his rooming
house, uncertain what to do next, but feeling that at least
the darkness was not total.

His first impulse was to go through all his accumulated
papers, to resee them in this new faint ray. He skimmed over
the pages of his novel, found it shapeless, helpless—more so
even than he had feared—and remembered another tonic
phrase of Frenside's: the curt "I thought so," in reply to
Vance's confession that he was attempting a novel, and then
the injunction: "If ever you try a short story send it along."
What a pity he hadn't tried one, instead of this impossible
unwieldy novel! And then, as he sat there, fumbling with
fragments of dead prose, his hand lit on a dozen typed
pages, clipped together, and a little frayed at the edges.
He'd forgotten he had that with him. . . . "One Day"—the
thing he'd written in a kind of frenzy, after his fever, when he
couldn't find his father's revolver. How long ago all that
seemed! There had been weeks when he couldn't have
looked at those pages, could barely have touched them; and
now he was turning on them an eye almost as objective as
George Frenside's. . . .

You couldn't call it a short story, he supposed. It was
just the headlong outpouring of what he had felt and
suffered during those few hours—like a fellow who'd been
knocked down and run over trying to tell you what it felt
like. That was all. But somehow the sentences moved, the

words seemed alive—if he'd had to do it again he didn't know that he'd have done it very differently. It didn't amount to much, but still he felt as if it was his own, not the work of two or three other fellows, like the novel. A sudden impulse seized him: he wrapped up the manuscript, addressed it to Frenside, put his own name and address below, and carried the packet back to the office of *The Hour*. He hadn't the courage to go in with it, but slipped it into the letter box and walked away.

Three days afterward—the last but two of his week—he came in one afternoon and found that a letter had been pushed under his door. On the corner of the envelope was stamped *The Hour*. Vance's hands turned cold. He stood for a few seconds looking at that portentous name; then he tore open the envelope and read: "Dear Sir, The editor of *The Hour* asks me to say that he will be glad to take your story, 'One Day,' though *The Hour* does not usually publish short stories. I enclose a cheque for $50." There followed a vague secretarial signature, and underneath, untidily scrawled with a blunt pencil: "Better go back home and write more like it. Frenside." Vance stood a long time motionless, the letter in his hand. At first he was not aware of any sensation at all; and when it did come it seemed too strong for joy. It was more as if he had been buffeted in a crowd and had the wind knocked out of him, as he had on the day when he and Upton fought their way to the Crans' car after the ball game. . . .

"I want to go and see the ocean," he suddenly said aloud. He didn't know where the words had come from, but the force of the impulse was overwhelming. Perhaps he had unconsciously recalled Frenside's sneer: "Ever seen the ocean? Not even from Coney Island?" Well, he thought, he was going to see it now. . . . He put the cheque in his pocket and went out again. With that talisman on his breast he felt strong enough to conquer the world. What might it not have bought for him? Well, first of all it was going to buy him one of the greatest things in the universe. . . . He went round to Friendship House, found the friendly manager, and got his cheque cashed. Then he decided to leave the money in the manager's safe; it was no use risking it in crowded trains. And he meant to take a train that very minute, and get down to the Atlantic shore before it grew dark. He didn't know where—but he asked, and the manager said, smiling: "Why, we've got a camp of our own down on Long Island, not far from Rockaway. It's pretty near empty in the middle of the week; you might as well go down there, I guess. I'll give you a line to the man in charge—you look as if a good swim would pick you up. . . ." He scribbled a card. "Don't forget to come for your money, though," he said.

It was nearly sunset when the train reached the little station where Vance was to get out. He saw only a cluster of frame houses among scrubby sandhills, and a skyline criss-crossed by telephone and telegraph wires, like the view across the fields from Crampton. The man at the station said the camp was some way down the road. Vance followed the indication. The road, little better than a sandy trail, ran level for a bit, drifted past a colony of shacks and bathhouses, and then lifted him to a ridge of sand and left him face to face with the unknown. Before him more sandhills, sparsely tufted, sloped down imperceptibly to bare sand. The sand spread to a beach which seemed to stretch away right and left without end, and beyond the beach was another surface, an unknown element, steel gray in the cloudy twilight, and breathing and heaving, and swaying backward and forth with a shredding and rending of white yeasty masses ceaselessly torn off from that smooth immensity. Vance stood and gazed, and felt for the first time the weight of the universe upon him. Even the open sky of the plains, bending to the horizon on all sides, and traceried and buttressed, up aloft, with the great structure of the stars, seemed less huge, less immemorial, less incomprehensible to the finite mind than this expanse which rested not yet moved not, except in a rhythmic sway as regular as the march of the heavens. Vance sat down on a hillock and gazed and gazed as twilight fell; then in the last light he scrambled across the dunes to the sands, reached the stones of the beach, knelt close to that long incoming curve, and plunged his hands into it, as if in dedication.

BOOK IV

≫ XVI ≪

HALO SPEAR in a world of shifting standards, had always held fast to her own values. Such and such things were worth so much! a great deal, perhaps; yet no more than so much. It was good, for instance—necessary, indeed—to have a comfortable amount of money; enough to grease the machinery of life, to prevent recurring family wrangles, or worse; but even for that there was a price not worth paying. That price was herself; her personality, as the people about her would have called it; the something which made Halo Spear and no other. Of that something, she often told herself, she would never surrender the least jot.

Looking back now, after three years, she remembered old Tom Lorburn's perturbed face as she left the Willows with him, the day the loss of the books was discovered. She had said to herself then: "This business about the books is going to make him change his will," and, immediately afterward: "Well, it won't make me change my mind about Lewis." For even if her hopes of an inheritance were gone she was not going to offset the disappointment by marrying Lewis Tarrant. She was sure she would make life unbearable to any man she married for such a reason, and Lewis was too good a fellow to be her victim. It was a pity, of course—for Cousin Tom did die within a few months, and did change his will, leaving the Willows to a distant relative who knew no more what to do with it than he had; and the blow was a bad one for Mr. and Mrs. Spear. Lorry being predestined to ruin them, they had always regarded it as Halo's rôle to restore their fortunes; they would never have asked her to sacrifice her happiness to do so, but they told her (always in reference to other couples) that when it came to marriage a community of tastes and interests—well, such as there was between herself and Lewis, say—was the only guarantee of happiness, once the first rapture was over. "I know, but I want the first rapture," Halo would answer them inwardly; and to Lewis she said with a smiling firmness: "If I married you you'd want to murder me in a month."

Yet she had been his wife for nearly three years now, and they had not only spared each other's lives, but arrived at some kind of mutual understanding, so that, had she been suddenly called on to leave her husband's roof and return to the precarious existence at Eaglewood she would have hesitated, and not only on his account. Habit had wound its benumbing web about her, and she was no more the girl she had been than he was the man she had imagined. . . .

"Happy?" she said one day to Frenside, with her quick smile. "No, I've never been happy; but I'm content. And being content is so jolly that I sometimes think I couldn't have stood being happy. . . ."

"Ah, it's a destructive experience," Frenside agreed.

Not for a moment would she have admitted to anyone else that her marriage had not brought her happiness, for no one but Frenside would understand, as she did, that life may be "strengthened and fed without the aid of joy." But the relief of saying it to him was deep; it took her out of a world of suffocating dissimulations into a freer air. She looked at him curiously, at his bumpy tormented forehead above the thick blunt nose and ironic mouth, the eyes barricaded by his eternal glasses, the heavy shabby figure. "Yet he speaks about happiness as if he'd known it—poor old George." Her impulse was to say: "Oh, Frenny, tell me what it's like!" But though she had once gone up so boldly to every new riddle she shrank from this one. "I suppose we each of us have our different Sphinx," she thought. She had grown a coward, no doubt.

"Life's so full of things anyhow, isn't it?" she continued evasively. "I've often thought I shouldn't have time to crowd in anything more . . . even happiness. . . ." She laughed a little, and getting up out of her deep armchair by the fire walked across the library and stood looking out at the sweep of the East River glittering far below through the autumn haze in its forest of roofs and spires and chimneys. The Tarrant flat was high up in one of the new buildings overhanging the mighty prospect on which New York had till so lately turned its back. A wide low window filled almost the whole eastern wall of the room; the other three were of a sober grayish-green wherever they were revealed by a break in the bookshelves. Halo Tarrant's association with the sturdy old house at Eaglewood had saved her from the passing extravagances of fashion. Her room depended for its character on the view from its window, the books on its walls, and the friendly grouping of its lamps and chairs. It seemed neither to exclude experiment nor invite it, but to remain outside the flux of novelty like some calm natural object, tree or field.

Frenside said nothing more, and Halo wandered across the room, pausing absently to straighten a paper cutter on the big table laden with books; then her glance travelled to an oil sketch of her husband which Vuillard had done in Paris, the first year of their marriage: just the head, half averted, with the thin sensitive nose, the dissatisfied mouth —dissatisfied still—and that excessive fairness of hair and complexion which singled Tarrant out in any group, even before the delicacy of his features was perceptible. Halo stood in front of the picture, her hands clasped behind her, retravelling the way that he and she had come.

"Well?—" Frenside queried.

She turned back to him. "I was thinking how lucky it is that *The Hour* happened to be for sale, and that I had the nerve to urge Lewis to buy it. It's going to be exactly the kind of job he likes. I only wish you'd stayed on it, Frenny."

Frenside shook his head. "Better not. I'm always available as an adviser, if he needs one. But new blood all round was what was wanted. And now we'll see—"

Halo looked up at him a little sharply. "See—?"

"What he's going to make of it."

Her lips parted, as if on a quick retort; then they closed again, and with a slight shrug she dropped back into her chair. "Of course he'll make mistakes—"

"Of course. But that's sometimes stimulating."

She interrupted: "The great thing for a man like Lewis, with rather too much money, and decidedly too many talents, is to canalize both—isn't it? He's never before been able to make up his mind, to find anything that entirely suited him. I believe this does; I believe it's going to group his scattered interests, and hold him to his job as no . . . no vague sense of duty would. . . ."

"Bless you, the sense of duty is prehistoric; even that idea of our first duty being to ourselves, which seemed so mad and bad in the 'nineties, wouldn't interest a baby nowadays. But I daresay Tarrant'll take hold—for a while—"

"Ah, you underrate him!" Halo flashed out, rising again nervously. People were right, after all, when they said Frenside's way of encouraging you was like a doctor's saying: "Nothing will make any difference now."

But she was vexed with herself as soon as the words were spoken. She held no brief for her husband; she didn't have to. Everyone knew Lewis was brilliantly clever—even those who were put off by his indifference, his lack of enthusiasm, recognized his superiority. "A fellow who'll make his mark, my son-in-law," Mr. Spear described him, leaning back comfortably in an armchair of the cosy little flat provided by Lewis for his parents-in-law, and puffing at a Corona of the thousand Lewis had sent him for Christmas. Being able to escape from Eaglewood for the winter months had singularly softened Mr. Spear's view of human nature, and lent an added lustre to his admiration for Halo's husband. "Anyone who doesn't recognize Tarrant's ability is simply envious of it, that's all. . . ." Ah, how Halo loved her father for saying that! Poor Frenside's congenital lack of generosity always prevented his predicting for others the success he himself had missed; but Mr. Spear, now that he and his wife had their own little nook in New York, and could gather about them the dowdy middle-aged conformists whom Mrs. Spear still called revolutionaries—Mr. Spear had become tolerant and even benignant. He still wrote to the papers to denounce what he called crying evils, such as the fact that the consumption of whole wheat bread was not made compulsory ("If I may cite my own humble experience," that kind of letter always said), or that no method had been devised for automatically disinfecting the tin cups attached to public fountains. ("An instance of this criminal negligence may actually be found within a hundred feet of my own door," was the formula in such cases—thus revealing to his readers that Mr. Spear *had* a New York door.) But all this was rather by way of a literary exercise than to relieve a burning indignation; now that his life had been reshaped to his satisfaction Mr. Spear was disposed to let others do their own protesting. "After all, there's something to be said for the constituted authorities," he had been known to declare, smiling indulgently across his daughter's dinner table; and if Mrs. Spear's short-haired satellites (women, Mr. Spear now called them, who had been sexually underfed) had not been forever challenging him to take up his pen in denunciation of one outrage or another—"you really ought to, Mr. Spear, with your marvellous way of putting things"—the ink would have coagulated in his Waterman.

Prosperity had affected Mrs. Spear differently. It had

made her more indignant, more agitated, more emaciatedly beautiful; while a rising plumpness rounded Mr. Spear's waistcoat his wife's garments hung more slackly from her drooping shoulders and restless arms. While there was so much misery in the world, how was it possible, she asked her daughter, for those in happier circumstances not to strain every nerve . . . ?

"But you strained yours to a frazzle long ago, mother; and the world still goes on in its old juggernaut way."

"Halo! I hate to hear you echo that cheap cynicism of George Frenside's. As long as I have a voice left to protest with I shall cry out against human savagery in all its forms." Mrs. Spear had just discovered from a humanitarian leaflet that the truffle-hunting pigs of southwestern France perform their task in muzzles, and are never permitted the least morsel of the delicacies they unearth. ("Well, I should hope not," murmured Mr. Spear, unfolding his napkin at the approach of a crab-mayonnaise, "and anyhow, in the raw state in which the poor animals would eat them, they'd probably taste like old india-rubber.") And George Frenside added, with a malicious glint behind his glasses: "What seems to me a good deal worse is the fate of the cormorants in the China seas. . . . You know the Chinese train them to catch fish . . . carry 'em on their wrists like hawks. . . ." "Well?" Mrs. Spear gasped, in anguished anticipation. "No cormorant is ever allowed to taste a fish—much less a mayonnaise of crab," Frenside grinned, with a side-glance at Halo.

The recollection of the little scene flashed through Halo's mind as she looked up at Vuillard's sketch of her husband. It was for the sake of her parents that she had married him; she was too honest to disguise it from herself; and whenever she saw Mr. Spear sipping his champagne critically but complacently, and Mrs. Spear, in black velvet and old lace, bending her beautiful shortsighted eyes above an appetizing dish, or lifting them to heaven in protest at some

newly discovered cruelty to pigs or cormorants, Halo said to
herself that it had been worthwhile. For Mrs. Spear's woes
had become as purely a luxury as Mr. Spear's cigars and
champagne. They could treat their indignations like pet animals, feeding them on the fat of the land till they became
too bloated to be disturbing; and Halo, looking back on the
hard rasping years when her parents' furious concern for the
public welfare had been perpetually fed by personal worries
and privations, reflected that there could hardly be a pleasanter life than that of retired reformers. "And at least now,"
she added, "they've stopped borrowing from Lewis; I'm almost sure they have."

The extent of their borrowings (discovered suddenly,
at the precise moment when she had decided to break her
engagement) had in fact been the direct cause of Halo's
marriage. Tarrant had stepped into the breach more often
than she had guessed; had not only bought back the books
so mysteriously lost from the Willows, but had helped Lorry
Spear to start as a theatrical decorator, besides filling in the
ever-widening gap in the Spear budget. And he had done it
all so quietly that when the facts became known to Halo her
first movement of exasperation was followed by an unexpected feeling of admiration. If he were like that, she
thought, she ought to be able to love him; at any rate, she
knew she could never willingly cause him any pain. And on
this basis they were married. . . .

The years that followed had represented the interest on
her husband's advances. He was far too much of a gentleman to let her feel that she, or any of hers, was in his debt;
but there the fact loomed, the more oppressively because of
his studied ignoring of it. She had gradually found out that
it had not altered his real nature; but it had imposed on her
the obligation to view him always in the light of an accidental magnanimity. It was dreadful, she thought in her rebellious moods, to know exactly what one would have to think

of one's husband till one's dying day. But these rebellions were rare with her. Every morning she told herself anew that he had been incredibly generous to her people, and that the only return she could make was to throw herself with ardour into every new scheme which attracted, and reject with promptitude any enterprise which ceased to please him. Some day, perhaps, he would find his line—and *then* people would see, then even Frenside would have to confess . . .

Poor Frenside! It was natural, she thought, that his own inability to stick to a job should add venom to his comments on the instability of others. "Everything I touch turns cold on my hands," he had once confessed; and that had been the fate of *The Hour*. After a dazzling start it had grown querulous, faddish, and then dull; one could feel the creeping chill of inanition as one turned its pages. Subscribers fell off, and the owners, discouraged, offered the paper for sale. Frenside, understanding his own share in the failure, resigned, and went back to free-lance articles for various newspapers and reviews. It was nonsense, he said, his acting as literary adviser to anybody, when his honest advice would almost always be: "To the wastepaper basket." *The Hour* languished along, unread and unbought, for another year; then it occurred to Tarrant to pick it up as a bargain, and once purchased it acquired in his eyes the importance inherent in anything that belonged to him. "Funny— perhaps what I was really meant for was to be an editor," he said to his wife, with depreciatory smile which disguised such a fervour of self-esteem. "Not a very dazzling career— I suppose I might have looked rather higher; but it may give me the chance to make myself known. . . ."

"Of course, Lewis; it's what I've always wanted for you."

"It is? You've thought—?" he began with his look of carefully suppressed avidity.

"Why, for a man who wants a hearing, and has something new to say, I can't imagine a better chance than an open arena like *The Hour*." She could reel off things like that as long as he wanted them; and besides, she did think, had forced herself to think, after his various unsuccessful experiments, first in architecture, then in painting, that letters might really be his field. Not creative work, probably (though she knew he aspired to be a novelist), but literary criticism, literary history, perhaps—provided he had the patient to pursue any line of investigation far enough. "If only he hadn't any money!" she sometimes found herself reflecting, confronted with the bewildering discovery that abundance may hamper talent as much as privation does. "But what is talent made of, then?" she wondered. "Is it really like some shoddy material that can't stand either rain or sun?"

Frenside still mused by the fire. "Yes; I shouldn't wonder if Tarrant made something out of *The Hour*, if only he gets the right people for the routine work." It was unusually generous of Frenside to say that; yet Halo tingled with resentment.

"You mean he'll never have the perseverance himself?"

"My dear child, don't make me out worse than I am. I mean exactly what I say. Every business enterprise is built on drudgery—"

"Yes, and he's too brilliant. He *is* brilliant, Frenny." She stood looking at her old friend with confident insistent eyes; it always fortified her faith in her husband to impress it on others. And really she did believe in *The Hour*, and in what he and she were going to make of it. . . .

The door opened, and there he was, slender, distinguished, handsomer than ever, she thought, as her eyes challenged the calm face under which she knew such a hunger for approbation burned.

"Hallo, Frenside—" Lewis Tarrant nodded to his wife

and strolled up to the fireplace with his unhurried step. "Cold as the devil outdoors." He bent over the flame, stretching his nervous transparent hands to it. ("With hands like that," Halo mused, "why isn't he a poet?")

Tarrant dropped into an armchair near the tea-table. "No—a cocktail, please. I'm frozen to the marrow. Cursed climate!"

She handed him the cocktail, and in passing laid her hand on his shoulder. "You're tired, Lewis—you've been overworking." It did her good to be able, in all sincerity, to rebuke him for that!

"Well, it *is* hard work—straightening things out. But I think I begin to see my way." He spoke with the cold sparkle of voice and face which was his nearest approach to enthusiasm. "By the way, though—it wasn't all just hacking and hewing. I've made a find." He picked up a bundle of papers he had thrown down, and extracted from them a copy of *The Hour*.

"What about this, Frenside? I never heard of it before —it must have come out while we were honeymooning, Halo."

The word startled her, on his lips. Was it all so long ago that he seemed to be speaking a dead language? She shook off the chill and put out her hand for the review—an old number, as Lewis said, battered from long kicking about in the office. "What? Oh—this: 'One Day'? A story, is it?" She wrinkled her brows over her shortsighted eyes. "Lewis! Why, it's by that boy: the Tracys' cousin. The one . . ." She broke off, and felt the colour rising to her temples. Vance Weston—she had not thought of Vance Weston since her marriage. Yet what a score he had against her! She had never been able to acquit herself of that; if ever the chance to do so arose, how gladly she would seize it! She bent above the page, curious, excited, with the little half articulate murmurs of the born reader. "How queer that I never heard of this. . . . Yes, it came out the winter we were in Egypt." (Her chronology of her married life was more topographic than sentimental.) She looked up at Frenside. "I suppose he sent it to you, Frenny, after that time you met him at Eaglewood?"

Frenside seemed to be groping in a heap of dusty recollections. "Yes—sure enough. It comes back to me. He turned up at the office one day, and unloaded a lot of fool poetry." (Halo remembered too, and winced.) "Then, when I told him the stuff wouldn't do, he pulled this out. Let me see: yes, that's it. I thought it better than most things of the kind; and anyhow the boy looked so starved and scared that I took it. Never saw him but that once, as well as I can remember."

Halo was no longer listening: she had plunged again into her reading. Yes; Frenside was right—the poetry, though it had possibilities (or seemed to, by that mountain pool at sunrise) was a poor parrotlike effort compared to this blunt prose, almost telegraphic in its harsh directness. She read on, absorbed.

"Well—?" Lewis queried, triumphant.

She came back to him from a long way. "What a strange thing it is—how terrible!"

"Fine, though? That fellow ought to be watched. Don't you think so, Frenny?"

Frenside rose, throwing his cigar end into the embers. "Well, it's a toss-up. This is the early morning 'slice-of-life'; out of the boy's own experience, most likely. Wait and see what happens when he tackles something outside of himself. That's where the test comes in."

Halo asked: "Didn't he send anything else?" and Frenside, rummaging among more faded memories, thought that, yes, he had—articles and stories, all raw stuff, unusable. That was the general rule; any chap with a knack could usually pull off one good thing at the start. . . .

"This shows more than knack."

Frenside shrugged, said he hoped so, wished them goodbye, and shuffled out into the hall, getting grumblingly into his overcoat with the help of Tarrant, who came back rubbing his hands and smiling. "Well, my dear, there's your great critic: couldn't even remember when and how he'd got hold of a thing like this, or whether the boy had sent him anything else as good! No knowing what we've lost —or how to get hold of him now. Not a trace of his address on the books. The way that paper was run—!" He sank down by the fire with a dry wrinkling of lips and nostrils. "I rather flatter myself things will go differently now . . ."

"Oh, Lewis! But of course—with your *flair.*"

He stroked his slight moustache lingeringly, using his hand, as she knew, to mask a satisfaction that might have appeared too crude. "Well, I suppose one *has* the instinct or one hasn't. . . ." he murmured.

"I'm so glad, dear, that you have it. You saw at once what this was worth, didn't you? But we must get at the boy —a young man now, I suppose," she mused. "How long ago it all seems! I wonder how we can run him down? Why, through the Tracys, of course! I'll write to Mrs. Tracy now."

She started up and went to the writing table, pulling out paper and pen with an impatience doubled by her husband's. "Oh, we'll wire," he said in a tone of authority; "I'll get it off at once. We want something from him for our New York number." And she thought, deep in herself: "Nothing will be too good for Vance Weston now that he's Lewis's own discovery," and then tingled with shame at her lucidity. She dashed off the telegram at her husband's dictation, and while Tarrant went out to send it, dropped down again into her armchair.

"If my boy had lived—" she said to herself, covering under that elliptical sweep of regret all the things she might

have judged differently, all the things she might have for-
borne to judge, if between her and her husband there had
been a presence, warm and troublesome and absorbing, to
draw them closer yet screen them a little from each other.

⤳ XVII ⤲

ONE RAW autumn evening when Vance came in, tired and dispirited, from the office of the *Free Speaker,* his elder sister, Pearl, who was always prying and investigating, bounced out into the hall with: "Here's a letter for you from a New York magazine."

Vance followed her into the overheated room where the family were waiting for Mr. Weston to go in to supper. Mr. Weston was generally late nowadays: real estate was in a slack phase at Euphoria, and he was always off somewhere, trying to get hold of a good thing, to extend his activities, especially to get a finger into the pie at Swedenville, which had recently started an unforeseen boom of its own.

There seemed to be a great many people in the brightly lit room, with its large pink-mouthed gramophone on a table with a crochet lace cover, its gold-and-gray wallpaper hung with the "Mona Lisa" (Mae's contribution), "The Light of the World" (Grandma's), and the palm in a congested pink china pot on a stained oak milking stool.

On chilly evenings the radiator was the centre of the family life, and the seat nearest it was now always occupied by a very old man with a yellowish waxen face and a heavy shock of black hair streaked with gray, who sat with a helpless left arm stretched on the shawl that covered his knees, and said at intervals, in a slow thick voice: "Feels . . . good . . . here . . . after . . . Crampton. . . ."

Grandpa and Grandma Scrimser had moved into Ma-

pledale Avenue after Grandpa's first stroke. The house out
at Crampton was too cold, and the Nordic help, always
yearning for Euphoria or Swedenville, could not be persuaded to wait on a paralytic old man and his unwieldy
wife. Lorin Weston had accepted the charge without a
murmur: he was a great respecter of family ties. But the
presence of the old couple had not made things easier at
Mapledale Avenue. It was an ever-recurring misery to Mrs.
Weston to have the precise routine of her household upset
by Mrs. Scrimser's disorderly ways; she did not mind
nursing her father nearly as much as "picking up" after her
mother. But the crowning grievance was the invasion of her
house by Grandma's followers—all the "inspirational" fad-
dists, the prophets, seers, and healers who, having long enjoyed the happy-go-lucky hospitality of the Scrimser table,
now thronged to Mrs. Weston's, ostensibly to pray with
Grandma and over Grandpa, but always managing, as Mrs.
Weston remarked, to drop in round about mealtimes.

Grandpa's stroke had come within the year after
Vance's return to Euphoria. Vance had not seen much of
Mr. Scrimser during the months preceding the latter's illness. Going out to Crampton was something the young man
still shrank from. Everything in Euphoria, when he returned
there from New York, seemed so small and colourless that
he strayed about in it like a ghost in limbo; but the first time
he walked out to see his grandmother, the old nausea
caught him as he passed the field path leading to the river;
and when his grandfather mounted the steps of the porch
where Vance and Mrs. Scrimser were sitting, stiff-jointed
but jaunty as ever, his hat tilted back from his black curls,
his collar rolled away from his sinewy throat, the boy felt
himself harden to a stone. . . . And then, one evening at
the *Free Speaker*, a voice at the telephone had summoned
Vance to the Elkington—and there in the glaring bar lolled
the old man, like a marionette with its wires cut, propped

on the sofa to which they had hurriedly raised him. . . .

The accident did not reawaken Vance's love for his grandfather, but it effaced the hate. If this was what a few years brought us to, the sternness of the moral law seemed cruelly out of proportion to the brevity of life; he acknowledged the grinning truth of the old man's philosophy. Hitherto Vance had never regretted having written, or sold for publication, the tale into which he had poured all his youthful indignation; but now, though he felt sure that no one at Euphoria had ever heard of *The Hour,* or would have connected his tale with any actual incident, yet he would have been glad to wipe those pages out of existence, and still more glad to blot from his memory the money they had brought him. . . .

"Well, I guess your father's going to be later than ever tonight, and that Slovak girl says she won't stay another week if she don't ever know what time to dish up for meals," Mrs. Weston murmured, looking up from her towel-hemming as her son entered.

"Well, Vance's got a letter from a New York magazine," Pearl exulted, disregarding her mother.

Mrs. Scrimser looked yearningly from the corner where she sat by her husband, the last number of *Spirit Light* on her knee. ("What your grandmother wastes, subscribing to all those come-to-Jesus papers, is something that passes me. She could hire a nurse with the money," Mrs. Weston frequently lamented to her children.)

"Oh, Vanny, open it quick!" his grandmother besought. "I wonder if it's from *Spirit Light?* I was just reading to Grandpa about a twenty-five dollar prize they're offering for a five-hundred-word appreciation of Jesus Christ, to be sent in before the last of the month. What are we now?"

No one answered, and Vance went up to the lamp and opened his letter. Below the letterhead of *The Hour* a rush

of words poured out at him. "Another story on the lines of
'One Day' . . . Review in new hands . . . editor would
like to have first call on anything you may turn out during
the coming year . . . Liberal terms . . . first story if possible in time for January number . . . wants to know if any
chance of your being in New York within few weeks to consider possibility of permanent connection with review . . ."

Another story on the lines of "One Day"—that was
what first struck him. He read the phrase over several times;
then, involuntarily, he turned and glanced at the marionette
with its wires cut that cowered in the armchair by the radiator. How strange it was, Vance mused—that poor creature
had first taught him the meaning of pain, and out of the terrible lesson the means of deliverance had come!

His future . . . here was his future secure. And the
people at *The Hour* regretted having lost sight of him for so
long—and the review was in new hands! He glanced back
at the letterhead, and saw: "Editor: Lewis Tarrant." But
surely that was the blond fellow who was always hanging
about Miss Spear and going off in the motor with her? Cor-
respondence between Paul's Landing and Mapledale Avenue had ceased after a somewhat acrimonious exchange of
letters at the time of Vance's departure from the Tracys';
since then he had heard nothing of the household at Eaglewood. Two or three curt notes from the editorial office of
The Hour, rejecting the tales and essays he had sent at
Frenside's suggestion, had been the last of his communications with New York; and for nearly two years now his horizon had been so shut in by Euphoria that he was beginning
to feel as if he had never left there.

"*Is* it about the *Spirit Light* competition, Vanny?" Mrs.
Scrimser asked; and Pearl ejaculated: "Father may be late,
but I guess he'll be here before Vance condescends to tell
us!"

"Tell us what?" Vance's father questioned, banging the front door shut, and dropping his outer garments in the ingle-nook before joining his family.

"His news from New York," Pearl snapped.

Lorin Weston came in, casting his cautious tired eyes about the room. His son suddenly noticed how much older and thinner he looked; his dapper business suit hung on him. "Well, what's your news, son?"

"I've got a job in New York," Vance announced, hardly believing that the voice he heard was his own.

"Feels . . . good . . . here . . . after . . . Crampton. . . ." the marionette crooned from its corner.

On the train to New York Vance had the same sense of detachment as when he had gone thither three years before. Again it was as though, in leaving his home, he took his whole self with him, like a telephone receiver unhooked and carried on a long cord into another room. The years at Euphoria had taught him something, he supposed; he felt infinitely older, felt mature, "hardboiled" as the new phrase was: he smiled with pity at the defenceless infant he had been when he made his first assault on the metropolis.

But how had the process of maturing been effected? He had felt himself an alien from the moment of his return to Euphoria; there had been no retightening of loosened links, no happy boyish sense of homecoming. He could imagine that a fellow might feel that, getting back to one of those old Lorburn houses, so impregnated with memories, so thick with tangible tokens of the past; but his own recollections could only travel back through a succession of new houses, each one a little larger and with a better bathroom and a neater garage than the last, but all without any traces of accumulated living and dying: shells shed annually, almost, like a crab's. He even felt, as he sat in the spick-and-span comfort of Mapledale Avenue, the incongruity of an old

man's presuming to die there. "Seems like there's no past
here but in the cemeteries," he mused one day, looking pity-
ingly at his grandfather. . . .

And now he was getting away from it again, getting
back into an atmosphere which to him seemed charged with
the dust of ages. When he had been in New York before he
had hardly noticed the skyscrapers, which were merely
higher than those he already knew; but on one of his last
days before leaving he had gone down to Trinity Church,
and slowly, wonderingly, had roamed about the graveyard,
brooding over names and dates. . . . The idea that there
had been people so near his own day who had lived and
died under the same roof, and worshipped every Sunday in
the same church as their forebears, appealed in an undefin-
able way to his craving for continuity. And when he entered
the church, and read the epitaphs on the walls above the
very seats where the men and women commemorated had
sat, it was like feeling a heart beating through the grave
wrappings of one of the mummies he had seen in the mu-
seum. The ocean and Old Trinity—those were the two gifts
New York had given him. . . .

And now he was going back full of hope to the place
which seemed to have become his spiritual home. The long
cold weight of discouragement had fallen from him at the first
word of the summons from *The Hour*. This time he knew he
could make good. Never in journalism: his experience on
the *Free Speaker* had taught him that. If his father hadn't
owned stock in the newspaper Vance knew he could never
have held down even his insignificant job there. But there
was nothing to regret in all that. He was going to be a
writer now: a novelist. A New York review had opened its
doors to him; he had only to reread the editorial letter for
his brain to hum with new projects and ambitions. "A big
novel—I'll do a big novel yet," he thought; but meanwhile
he would give them all the short stories they wanted. Sub-

jects were swarming about him, opening paragraphs writing themselves on the curtains of his sleeper. All night he lay awake in an ecstasy of invention, rocked by the rhythm of the train as if the great Atlantic rollers were sweeping him forward to his fate.

This mild November day was all jewelled with sunlight as Vance pushed his way out of the Grand Central. Grip in hand, he was starting for the rooming house where he had lodged before. He did not know where else to go; but no doubt at *The Hour* he would find someone to advise him. Meanwhile he would just drop his bags (they were bulging with manuscripts), and get a quick wash-up before presenting himself at the office. It was nearly ten o'clock, and he had wired announcing his visit for that day at eleven.

It was the day after Thanksgiving, and the huge station was humming with the arrivals and departures of weekend crowds. Outside, close to the curb, a row of long "rubber-neck" cars was drawn up, and with an absent eye Vance watched a band of sightseers, mostly girls, scrambling into one of them. He thought he had never seen so many happy unconcerned faces: certainly the mere air of New York seemed to wake people up, make them sparkle like the light on this balmy day. Vance, always amused by thronged streets and pleasurable activities, lingered to watch; and as he stood there he saw a girl in a close-fitting blue hat spring into the car in front of him. Her movement was so light and dancing that no term less romantic could describe it. She was absorbed into a giggling group, and under the blue brim Vance caught only a glimpse of cropped straw-coloured hair and a face so translucent that the thin brown eyebrows looked dark as the velvet crescents on a butterfly. His sense of bouyant renewal seemed to find embodiment in this morning vision, and he forgot his bag, forgot *The Hour*, forgot even his healthy morning hunger. All he wanted was to know if there was a seat left in that car. A man in a long light ulster, a lettered band on his cap, stood near the driver's seat, giving orders or instructions. Vance touched his arm. "See here—" The man turned, and Vance was face to face with Bunty Hayes, the former reporter of the Paul's Landing paper.

Bunty Hayes had not changed; he was the same trim tight-featured fellow with impudent eyes and a small mouth with a childlike smile; but he had thickened a little, and the black-and-gold lettering on his cap gave him an air of authority.

"Say—why, if it ain't Vance Weston!" he exclaimed.

If anything could have troubled Vance in his present mood, it would have been an encounter with Bunty Hayes. The name had only disastrous associations, and he had always thought the man contemptible. But the tide which was sweeping him forward could not be checked by anything as paltry as Bunty Hayes; and Vance, with no more than a moment's hesitation, put his hand into the other's, and made one of his abrupt plunges to the point. "Say—you going for a ride in this car?"

"Going for a ride in her?" Bunty echoed with his easy laugh. "Looks like as if I was. Say, why I'm the barker for her, sonny. Thought I was still up at Paul's Landing, did you, doing write-ups for that cemetery of a paper? No, sir, that was in the far away and long ago. I been showing New York for nearly two years now. Hop right in—got a capacity load, but I guess the girls'll make room for you. (I'm taking round Saint Elfrida's select boarding school, from Peapack —yes, sir; six front rows; bunch of lookers, ain't they? Primarily an art trip; we take in the Lib'ry, the Metropolitan, the Cathedral and the Palisades.) See here, pile in, Vance; never mind about your grip. 'Gainst the rules, I know; but shove it under the seat while the chauffeur's looking at her appendix. There—in you go; this row. Say, there's a girl at the other end that'll give you a squeeze-in next to her; there, the one with the blue hat."

The barker caught Vance under the elbow to launch him on his way; and then, as he moved forward, called after him stentorianly: "Say, Vance, I want you to meet my feean*cee;* yes, that's her in the blue hat. Laura Lou, meet Mr. Weston. . . . Gee, Vance, but ain't you Laura Lou's cousin? Say, well, if I didn't clean forget you and me'd got acquainted at the Tracys'. . . . Laura Lou, here's your cousin Vance Weston, come all the way from Illinois to see you. Now then, ladies and gentlemen, all aboard, *please!*"

Vance found himself climbing past a row of exposed pink knees. A flutter of girlish exclamations greeted him, and he slipped into a crack between a stout Jewish-looking young woman in rimless glasses and the girl under the blue hat, whose flexible young body seemed to melt against his own as she made room for him.

"Laura Lou!" he exclaimed as the car swayed out into the street. He could hardly believe that this little face with the pale rosy mouth and the delicately traced eyebrows could be that of the sulky flapper of Paul's Landing. Yet he remembered that one evening when she came in for supper, late and a little flushed, in a faded yellow muslin the colour of her hair, he had thought her almost pretty. *Almost pretty* —crude fool that he'd been, craving only such coarse fare as Floss Delaney and 'Smeralda Cran! Time had refined his taste as it had his cousin's features; and he looked at her with new eyes. . . .

"Vance!" she said, in her shy drawling voice, but without a trace of shyness in her own eyes, which rested on him with a sort of affectionate curiosity.

The eyes too were different; instead of being like blurred gray glasses they were luminous as spring water; and they met his with full awareness of the change. It seemed as if, without self-consciousness or fatuity, she knew herself lovely and was glad, as simply as a flower might be. The sight absorbed Vance's senses; he hardly heard what she was saying, was conscious only of her nearness, burning and radiant, yet so frail, immaterial almost, that she might vanish at a rash word or motion.

"Why, Vance, isn't it funny? I didn't know you were in New York," she said; and he thought: "I used to think her cheekbones too high; and now the little shadow under them is what makes her look like those marble heads of Greek priestesses with the smile under their lids. . . ." (He had seen photographs of them in some book on ancient art, in the Euphoria college library.)

"It's three years since I was here; you're grown-up now, aren't you?" he said; and she conceded: "Why, I s'pose I am," with a laugh that made her mouth break open on her teeth like a pink pod on pearly seeds.

"Three years—" he echoed; and suddenly he remembered her bending over him as he lay in the hammock, on his first evening at the Tracy's, and snatching from his buttonhole the spray of lilac he had found on his pillow that morning. "Why, it was you that put the lilac on my pillow before I was awake!" he exclaimed, the words breaking from him before he knew it. He was looking at her intently and she did not avert her gaze; but a light like a rosy reflection stole from her throat to her temples. "Of course it was," he triumphed. "Why, you're like a tropical shell with the sun shining through it," he cried; and she answered: "Oh, Vance, you always did say such killing things. I'll die laughing if you don't quit. . . ." It was only when she drew away her soft bare hand that he realized he had held it clutched ever since he had pushed his way to her. . . .

"This vacant lot on your right," Bunty Hayes was bellowing as the car rolled up Fifth Avenue, "was formerly the site of Selfridge B. Merry's five-million-dollar marble mansion, lately sold to the Amalgamated Searchlight Company, who are about to erect on it a twenty-five-million-dollar sky-scraper of fifty stories, with roof gymnasium, cabaret terrace, New Thought church and airplane landing. . . . The artistic Gothic church on your left is the Reformed Methodist. . . ."

Vance caught back Laura Lou's hand and pressed it in both of his. "For God's sake . . . that's all a joke about your being engaged to him, isn't it?"

She cast down her lashes, which were of the same velvet texture as her eyebrows, but a darker brown, the colour of brown pansy petals. Her hand still lay confidingly in Vance's. "Why, I guess he kinder thinks I am. . . ." she said.

"Oh, *let* him!" cried Vance derisively. He took a quick glance at the Jewish girl in rimless glasses, saw that she had turned away to pass a box of Fuller's marshmallows down the line, and flinging his arm about Laura Lou, kissed her fervently.

She paled a little and shrank back, but so submissively, with such an air of leaving herself on his lips even though she withdrew her own, that he thought exultantly: "She knows she belongs to me," and had there been room in his breast for any feeling but rapture it would have been pity for the tight-faced young man bellowing through his megaphone: "We are now approaching the only remaining private residence on Fifth Avenue, belonging to one of the old original society leaders known throughout the world as the Four Hundred."

❧ XVIII ❧

THE NEXT day, when Vance got out of the train at Paul's Landing, the old horses in the broken-down carry-alls were still standing in the station square, shaking their heads despondently.

He jumped on board a passing trolley and was carried out of the town. At the foot of a familiar lane overhung by bare maple boughs he got out and began to climb to the Willows. Laura Lou had said she would bring the key of the gate with her. She couldn't let him into the house, she explained: since the theft of the books (which had been brought back, as she supposed Vance knew) Mrs. Tracy had kept the house key hidden away where no one could get it. But Vance was determined at least to see the garden and the outside of the house again, and the day was so windless and mild that they would be able to sit in the sun on the verandah. He wanted to relive his first visit to the Willows, when he had accompanied Laura Lou and Upton, and had lingered spellbound in the library while Laura Lou, her hair covered with a towel, went off with Upton to dust and air the rooms. That day Vance had hardly noticed her, had felt her presence only as that of a tiresome schoolgirl, butting in where she wasn't wanted, like his own sisters, Pearl and Mae—especially Pearl. And now—!

She was at the gate already; he caught sight of her through the branches, in the powdery gold of the autumn light. She waved to him, and opened the gate; and he followed her in. "No, you mustn't!" she whispered, as his arms went out, and added, laughing: "With all the leaves off the bushes—and that hired man around."

"Curse the hired man! Can't we go and talk quietly somewhere?"

He was looking at her as though to store up the sight against a coming separation, and yet he knew already that he never meant to leave her again. "Can't I hold your hand, at least?" he asked, awed by something so tender and immature in her that it curbed his impetuousness.

"Oh, well—" she conceded; and hand in hand, like two children, they began to walk toward the house. Barely screened by its tracery of leafless willows it stood out more prominent and turreted than he had remembered; but if less romantic, it still seemed to him as mysterious. Treading noiselessly on the rain-flattened yellowish grass they passed around to the other front, where the projecting verandah and obliquely set balconies, clutched in the bare gnarled arms of the wistaria, stood out like the torso of an old Laocoön.

A few oaks still held their foliage, and the evergreen clumps stood out blue-black and solid. But the fall of the leaves revealed, at the end of a path, a rickety trellised arbour which Vance had never before noticed. "Let's go and sit there." They crossed the wet cobwebby lawn and entered the arbour. The old hired man was nowhere to be seen, and Vance drew Laura Lou to him and laid his lips on her eyelids. "Ever since yesterday I've wanted to kiss your eyes." She laughed under her breath, and they sat close to each other on the mouldy bench.

"You never used to take any notice of me in old times," she said; and he answered: "I was nothing but a blind puppy then. Puppies are all born blind. . . ." He wanted to let his kiss glide down to her lips, but she put him from her. The gentleness of her touch controlled him; but he whispered rebelliously: "Why—why?"

She answered that all she had promised was to come and talk things over with him, and he mustn't tease, or she'd have to go away; and why couldn't they just sit there quietly, when there was so much to say and so little time? He hardly heard what she said, but there was a power in her softness—or in her beauty, perhaps—which held him subdued. "Your hand, then—?" "Yes." She gave it back, with one of those smiles which made her mouth like the inside of a flower. Oh, idle metaphors! . . .

"Now tell me." And she told him how upset her mother had been when he went away so suddenly ("She never meant you to, Vance—but she got frightened. . . ."), and how surprised they were when the basket of flowers with the dove was brought the next day, and how Mrs. Tracy had first been angry, and said: "Is he crazy?" and then cried, and said: "But he must have spent all the money I gave him back," and then been angry again because she was so sure he'd be the cause of their losing their job at the Willows—and they did lose it, and only got it back after Miss Halo had intervened, and the books were returned, and old Mr. Lorburn had been quieted down again. ("But the dove was lovely, Vance. I've got it over my looking glass. . . .") And at the thought of this miraculous reward he had to clench her hand hard to keep himself from warmer endearments. How little he had dreamed, when he bought it, that the dove would be Venus's messenger!

She went on to say that things had been very hard for a time, because they had been out of their job for six months. It wasn't so much the money, though they needed that too; he gathered that Mrs. Tracy's pride had been wounded, and that she had declared, when Miss Halo tried to fix it up, that it was no use, as she would never let her children go back to the Willows if they had forfeited their cousin's confidence. But Miss Halo always somehow managed to put things right, and had finally persuaded Mrs. Tracy to relent; and

she had continued to help them after that, and had found a
fine situation for Upton as undergardener with some friends
of hers who had a big place at Tarrytown. So everything
was going better now; and she, Laura Lou, was at Saint Elfrida's School, at Peapack, for a six months' course, to learn
French and literature and a little music—because her
mother wanted her to be educated, like her father's folks
were. . . .

Laura Lou was not endowed with the narrative gift;
only bit by bit, in answer to Vance's questions (when he
was not too absorbed in her to put any) did she manage, in
fragmentary communications, to bridge over the interval
which had turned the gawky girl into the miracle of young
womanhood before him.

When she wanted to hear what had happened to him
since they had parted he found it even harder to tell his
story than to piece hers together. While she talked he could
spin about her a silken cocoon of revery, made out of her
soft drawl, the throb of her hand, the fruitlike curve of her
cheeks and eyelids; but when he tried to withdraw his attention from her long enough to put his words in order he
lost himself in a blur. . . . Really, he said, nothing much
had happened to him, nothing that he specially remembered. He'd been a reporter in the principal Euphoria newspaper, and hated it; and he had taken a post-graduate
course in philosophy and literature at the state college; but
the lecturers somehow didn't get hold of him. Reading in a
library was what suited him, he guessed. (Her lashes were
planted like the double row of microscopic hummingbird
feathers in a South American embroidery he'd seen somewhere. . . .) But Euphoria was over and done with; he'd
got a job in New York . . . a job on a swell magazine, a
literary review they called it, but they published short stories too, they'd already published one of his, and wanted as

many more as he could write . . . and the editor, Lewis Tarrant, had written to him to come to New York. . . .

"Lewis Tarrant! But he's the one Miss Halo married!" Laura Lou exclaimed.

"Did she?" Vance absently rejoined. All his attention was on her hands now; he was separating the fingers one by one, lifting them up and watching them drop back, as though he were playing on some fairy instrument. He hardly noticed the mention of Halo Spear.

"Why, didn't you know? They were married the year you went away, I guess. I know it was ever so long ago."

"Does it seem to you ever so long since I went away?"

"Oh, Vance, I've told you you mustn't . . . or I'll have to go. . . ."

He drew back, dropping her hands, and restricting himself to the more delicate delight of looking at her. "What's the use of trying to write poetry, when she *is?*" he mused. Yet in another moment he was again seeking rhymes and metaphors for her. He tried to explain to himself what it was that kept him thus awestruck and submissive, as if there were a latent majesty in her sweetness. With that girl on Thundertop it had been different; the shock of ideas, the stimulus of the words she used, the allusions she made, the sense of an unknown world of beauty and imagination widening about him as she talked—all this had subdued his blood while it set his brain on fire. But when Laura Lou spoke she became a child to him again. His allusions to his literary plans and ambitions filled her eyes with a radiant sympathy, but evoked nothing more definite than: "Isn't that too lovely, Vance?" Yet his feeling for her was not the sensual hunger excited by girls like Floss Delaney. It was restrained by something new in this tender creature; as if the contending elements of body and soul were so harmonized in her that to look at her was almost to clasp her.

But the air grew chilly; Vance noticed that she had turned paler; she coughed once or twice. The instinct of protection woke in him. "See here, we mustn't go on sitting here till you catch cold. Where'll we go? Why don't we walk back to the town to warm ourselves up, and have a cup of hot coffee before I catch my train?" She assented, and they turned toward the gate. As Laura Lou stooped to the padlock Vance looked back yearningly at the old house. "We'll come here often now, won't we?"

The gate had closed on them, and Laura Lou walked on a few steps before answering. "Oh, I don't know about coming again, Vance. I had hard work getting the key out of Mother's drawer without her seeing me. . . . Besides, I'm not here weekdays; I'm at school."

"Your mother can't object to our coming here after we're married," Vance tranquilly rejoined.

"Married?" she stood still in the lane and looked at him with wide incredulous eyes. Her pale pink lips began to tremble. "Why, how can we be, Vance?"

"Why can't we be, I'd like to know? I'll be earning enough soon." (He was sincerely convinced of it.) "See here, Laura Lou, I want to begin life in New York married to you. I'm coming out to tell your mother and Upton about it tomorrow. You won't go back to school till Monday, will you? Can I come out early tomorrow, and have dinner with you?"

A shade of apprehension crossed her face. "Oh, Vance darling—not tomorrow."

"Why not?"

"Because it's Sunday, and Sunday's Bunty's day." She made the statement with a sort of tragic simplicity, as a fact to be neither disguised nor eluded.

"Bunty's day?" Wrath descended on him like a thunderclap. "How dare you, after this afternoon—how dare you speak to me as if you belonged to that fellow and not to me?

Don't you know we're each other's forever, Laura Lou? Say you do—say you've always known it!" he commanded her.

"Well, I *was* engaged to him," she murmured, with her gentle obstinacy.

"If you were, you're not now. How could your mother ever have let you go with a fellow like that anyhow? She thought poorly enough of him when I was with you."

"Well, she didn't fancy him at first; she thought he was a bad companion for Upton. But you don't know how changed he is, Vance. He helped Mother when she lost her job here; and it's him who's paying for my year at Saint Elfrida's. You see, he's real cultured himself, and he wants I should be cultured too, so that by and by we can take those personally conducted parties to Europe for one of the big travel bureaus, and earn a lot of money. That's what first reconciled Mother to him, I guess, his being so cultured. She's always wanted I should marry somebody in the same class as Father's."

Vance stood listening in a tumult of anger and amazement. He had never heard her say as much at one time, and every word she spoke was pure anguish to him. He had the same sense of the world's essential vileness as had swept over him that day by the Crampton riverside. Life tasted like cinders on his lips. At length his indignation broke out in a burst of scattered ejaculations. "He's been paying for you at school—that lowdown waster? Laura Lou, you don't know what you're saying! Culture—him? In your father's class? Oh, God! You'd make me laugh if it wasn't so sickening. . . . I'm coming back to see your mother tomorrow whether you want me or not—understand? And if that Hayes fellow wants to come too, let him. I'll be there to talk to him. And I'll work day and night till I pay him back what he's paid your mother for you. And you've got to leave that school tomorrow, Laura Lou . . . do you hear me?"

"No, no, Vance." Her little pale face had grown curiously resolute, and her voice too. "You mustn't come tomorrow—it would kill me if you did. You must give me time . . . you must do as I tell you. . . ."

"What *are* you telling me? That I'm not to see you till it suits this gentleman's convenience? Is that it?"

Her head drooped, and there was a glitter of tears on her lashes; but in a moment she looked up, and her gaze rested full on his. "Vance, if you'll give me your promise not to come tomorrow I'll promise to go and see you next week in New York. I'll slip off somehow. . . . Because now, Vance," she cried, "whatever happens, I'll never marry anybody but you—never, never, not even if we have to wait for each other years and years."

Dizzy with joy, he stood looking at her as if he were looking into the sun; then he caught her to him, and their youth and passion flowed together like spring streams. "Laura Lou . . . Laura Lou . . . Only we won't wait any years and years," he cried; for at that moment it really seemed to him that achievement lay in his hand.

THREE YEARS of marriage had not been needed to teach Halo Tarrant that when her husband came home to lunch it was generally because something had gone wrong. She had long known that if he sought her out at that hour it was not to be charmed but to be tranquillized, as a man with a raging headache seeks a pillow and a darkened room. This need had been less frequent with him since he had bought *The Hour* and started in on the exciting task of reorganizing it. Usually he preferred to lunch near the office, at one of the Bohemian places affected by Frenside and his group; probably it was not indifferent to him, as he made his way among the tables, to hear: "That's the fellow who's bought *The Hour*. Lewis Tarrant; tall fair chap; yes—writes himself. . . ." Every form of external recognition, even the most casual and unimportant, was needed to fortify his self-confidence. Halo remembered how she had laughed when Frenside, long before her marriage, had once said: "Young Tarrant? Clever boy—but can't rest unless the milkman knows it." Nowadays she would not have tolerated such a comment, even from Frenside; and if she made it inwardly she tempered it by reminding herself that an exaggerated craving for recognition often proceeds from a morbid modesty. Morbid—that was what poor Lewis was at bottom. She must never forget, when she was inclined to criticize him, that her faculty of rebounding, of drawing fresh energy from discouragement, had been left out of his finer organization—for her own support she had to call it finer.

And now, on the very Friday when he was expecting his new discovery—the Tracys' young cousin from the West —Tarrant had suddenly turned up for lunch. When his wife heard his latchkey she supposed he had brought young Weston back with him, and she had been pleased, and rather surprised, since it would have been more like him to want to parade his new friend among his colleagues. Possibly Weston had not turned out to be the kind to parade— though his young poet's face and profound eyes had lingered rather picturesquely in her memory. Still, it was three years since they'd met, three years during which he'd been reporter on a smalltown newspaper. Perhaps the poetry had not survived. . . .

Her husband came in alone, late, and what she called "rumpled-looking," though no outward disorder was ever visible in his carefully brushed person, and the signs she referred to lurked only about his mouth and eyes.

"Any lunch left? I hope there's something hot—never mind what." And, as he dropped into his seat, and the parlourmaid disappeared with hurried orders, he added, unfolding his napkin with a sardonic deliberation: "Well, your infant prodigy never turned up."

Ah, how well she knew that law of his nature! Plans that didn't come off were almost always ascribed (in all good faith) to others; and the prodigy who had failed him became hers. She smiled a little to see him so ridiculously ruffled by so small a contretemps. "Genius is proverbially unpunctual," she suggested.

"Oh, *genius*—" He shrugged the epithet away. She might have that too, while she was about it. "After all, he may never do anything again. One good story doesn't make a summer."

"No, and mediocrity is apt to be unpunctual as genius."

"*Unpunctual?* The fellow never came at all. Fixed his own hour—eleven. I put off two other important appointments and hung about the office waiting till after half-past one. I'd rather planned to take him round to the Café Jacques for lunch. A young fellow like that, from nowhere, often thaws out more easily if you feed him first, and encourage him to talk about himself. Vanity," said Tarrant, as the maid approached with a smoking dish, "vanity's always the first button to press. . . . *Eggs?* Good Lord, Halo, hasn't that cook learnt yet that eggs are slow death to me? Oh, well, I'll eat the bacon— What else? A chop she can grill? The inevitable chop! Oh, of course it'll *do*." He turned to his wife with the faint smile which etched little dry lines at the corners of his mouth. "I can't say you've your mother's culinary imagination, Halo."

"No, I haven't," she answered good-humouredly; but a touch of acerbity made her add: "It would be rather wasted on a digestion like yours."

Her husband paled a little. She so seldom said anything disagreeable that he was doubly offended when she did. "I might answer that if I had better food I should digest better," he said.

"Yes, and *I* might answer that if your programme weren't so limited I could provide more amusing food for you. But I'd sooner admit at once that I never did have Mother's knack about things to eat, and I don't wonder my *menus* bore you." It was the way their small domestic squabbles usually ended—by her half contemptuously throwing him the sop he wanted.

He said, with the note of sulkiness that often marred his expiations: "No doubt I'm less easy to provide for than a glutton like Frenside—" then, furtively abstracting an egg from the dish before him: "It's a damned nuisance, having all my plans upset this way. . . . And a fellow I was hoping I might fit into the office permanently. . . ."

Halo suggested that perhaps the young man's train had been delayed or run into—that perhaps at that very moment he was lying dead under a heap of wreckage; but Tarrant grumbled: "When people break appointments it's never because they're dead"—a statement her own experience bore out.

"He's sure to turn up this afternoon," she said, as one comforts a child for a deferred treat; but the suggestion brought no solace to Tarrant. He reminded her with a certain tartness (for he liked her to remember his engagements, if he happened to have mentioned them to her) that he was taking the three o'clock train for Philadelphia, where he had an important appointment with a firm of printers who were preparing estimates for him. There was no possibility of his returning to the office that day; he might even decide to take a night train from Philadelphia to Boston, where he would probably have to spend Saturday morning, also on business connected with the review. He didn't know when he was going to be able to see Weston—and it was all a damned nuisance, especially as the young fool had given no New York address, and they had hoped to rush a Weston story into their coming number.

Time was when Halo, as a matter of course, would have offered to interview the delinquent. Now she knew better. She had learned that in such matters she could be of use to her husband only indirectly. The very tie she had most counted on in the early days of their marriage—a community of ideas and interests—had been the first to fail her. She knew now that the myth of his intellectual isolation was necessary to Tarrant's pride. Nothing would have annoyed him more than to have her suggest that she might take a look at young Weston's manuscripts. "Of course you could, my dear; it would be the greatest luck for the boy if you would—only, you know, I must reserve my independence of judgment. And if you were to raise false hopes in the poor devil—let yourself be carried away, as I remember you were once by his poetry—it would be a beastly job for me to have

to turn him down afterward." She could hear him saying
that, and she knew that the satisfaction of asserting his superiority by depreciating what she had praised would out-
weigh any advantage he might miss by doing so. "Oh,
young Weston will keep," she acquiesced indifferently, as
Tarrant got up to go.

The door closed on him, and she sat there with the
golden afternoon on her hands. She said to herself: "There
has never been such a beautiful November—" and her imagination danced with visions of happy people, young, vigorous, self-confident, draining with eager lips the last drops of
autumn sunshine. Always in twos they were, the people she
pictured. It used not to be so; she had often had her solitary
dreams. But now that she was hardly ever alone she was so
often lonely. Lonely! It was a word she did not admit in her
vocabulary—but the sensation was there, cold and a little
sickening, gnawing at the roots of her life. . . . What nonsense! Why, she was actually robbing poor Lewis of the
proud prerogative of isolation! As if a girl with her resources
and her spirits hadn't always more than enough to pack the
hours with! She leaned in the wide window of the library
and looked over the outspread city, and thought how when
she had first stood there all its myriad pulses seemed to be
beating in her blood. . . . "Am I tired? What's wrong
lately?" she wondered. . . . Should she call up the garage
where her Chrysler was kept and dash out for the night to
Paul's Landing, where her family had lingered on over
Thanksgiving? It would be rather jolly, arriving at Eaglewood long after dark, in the sharp November air, seeing the
glitter of lights come out far ahead along the Hudson, and
entering, muffled in furs, the shabby drawing room where
Mr. and Mrs. Spear would be sitting over the fire, placidly
denouncing outrages in distant lands. . . . No, not that
. . . It was sweet to sit in New York dreaming of Eaglewood; but to return there now was always a pang. . . .

She began to muse on the woods in late summer, *her* woods, when their foliage was heaviest, already yellowing a little here and there, with premature splashes of scarlet and wine colour on a still-green maple, like the first white lock in a young woman's hair . . . Of days on Thundertop, sunrise dips in the forest pool, long hours of dreaming on the rocky summit above the Hudson—how beautiful it had been that morning when she had stood there with young Weston, and they had watched light return to the world with a rending of vapours, a streaming of radiances, like the first breaking of life out of chaos! "He felt it too—I could see it happening all over again in his eyes," she thought; those eyes had seen it with hers. Perhaps that was why, when he recited his poetry to her, in spite of his shyness and his dreadful drawl, she had fancied she heard the authentic note. . . . Had she been mistaken? She didn't know. But surely not about the story Lewis had brought home the other day. She was sure that was the real thing; and she was glad Lewis had felt it too, felt it at once—she was always glad when they saw things together. Perhaps the boy *was* going to be a great discovery; a triumph for Lewis, a triumph for *The Hour!* She remembered that as she leaned back against the mossy edge of the pool the pointed leaf shadows flickered across his forehead and seemed to crown it like a poet's. . . . Poor little raw product of a standardized world, perhaps never to be thus laurelled again! . . .

She turned and wandered back to the fire, gazing, as she went, at the books her own hands had arranged and catalogued with such eager care. "What I want today is the book that's never been written," she thought; and then: "No, my child, what you really want is an object in life. . . ." She was grimly amused to find that she was talking to herself as so often, mentally, she talked to her husband. . . .

Oh, well—it was nearly dusk already; one more day to

tick off the calendar; and at five there was a concert at the Vanguard Club—something new and exotic, of course; she'd mislaid the programme. . . . She went to her room and pulled out her smart black coat with the gray fur, and the close black turban that made her face look long and narrow and interesting. There were sure to be amusing people at the concert. . . .

The concert was dull; the amusing people were as boring as only the amusing can be; Halo came home late and out of sorts to find a long-distance from her husband saying he was going to Boston that night, and she was to notify the office that he would not reappear till Monday. . . .

Next morning she rang up the office and gave her message; then, after a pause, she added: "By the way, did Mr. Weston turn up yesterday—Vance Weston, the storywriter, you know?" Yes; they knew; they were expecting him. But he had not appeared, and there had been no message from him. No; they hadn't his address. . . . She thought: "After all I was a fool not to go out to Eaglewood last night." Another radiant day—the last before winter, perhaps! Why shouldn't she dash out now, just for a few hours? A tramp in the woods would do her more good than anything. . . . But she lacked the energy to get into country clothes and call for the Chrysler. . . . "Besides, very likely that boy will turn up. . . ." Not that she meant to see him; but she could at least report to Lewis if he called at the office, and give whatever message he left. . . . It was rather petty of Lewis, she thought, not to have told her to see young Weston. . . .

Before twelve she rang up the office again. No; no sign of Weston; no message. How very queer. . . . Yes, it *was* queer. . . . Well, look here—that's you, Mr. Rauch? Yes. Well, if he should turn up today after the office was closed —supposing he'd forgotten it was a Saturday—would Mr.

Rauch leave word with the janitor to tell him to come to see her? Yes, at the flat; she'd be in all the afternoon. He was just to be told to ask for Mrs. Tarrant. (In the end, Lewis would probably be grateful—though he'd never go as far as acknowledging it.)

"I think I'll try and do some painting," she said to herself as she hung up. Lewis had fitted up a rather jolly room on the roof—a sort of workshop-study, in which he had reserved a corner for her modelling and painting. He always encouraged her in the practice of the arts he had himself abandoned, and while gently disparaging her writing was increasingly disposed to think there was "something in" her experiments with paint and clay. But it was months now since she had attempted either. . . . She mounted to the roof studio, pulled a painting apron over her shoulders, rummaged among canvases, fussed with her easel, and got out a bunch of paper flowers which she had manufactured after reading somewhere that Cézanne's flowers were always done from paper models. "Now for a Cézanne!" she mocked.

Whenever she could persuade herself to work she still had the faculty of becoming engrossed in what she was doing, and the hours hurried by as she struggled with the mystery of mass and values. At that moment, really, she believed she was on the eve of learning how to paint. "Perhaps Lewis is right," she thought.

Just as the light was failing the maid appeared. There was a gentleman downstairs—young gentleman, yes; his name was Weston. Halo dropped her brushes and wiped her hands hurriedly. She had forgotten all about young Weston! But she was glad that, now it was too dark to paint, he was there to fill in the end of the day.

Would she find him the same? Or had he changed? Would she still catch the shadow of the laurel on his forehead? As she entered the library her first impression was that he was shorter—smaller, altogether—than she had remembered; but then she had lived in the interval with a man of dominating height. This youth—how young he still looked!—met her eyes on a level. He had broadened a little; his brown hair with the slight wave in it had grown darker, she thought. This was all she had time to note, for before she could even greet him he had exclaimed: "There must be more books here than at the Willows!" Ah, how that brought him back—that way of going straight to his object, dashing through all the customary preliminaries, yet so quietly, so simply, that it seemed the natural thing to do.

She looked at him with a faint smile. "You care for books as much as ever?"

Instead of answering he said: "Can I borrow some of these, do you think? I've got to buckle down to work at once. I see they're classed by subjects; ah, here's philosophy. . . ." Half annoyed, half amused at being treated like a librarian (an assistant librarian, she ironically corrected herself) she asked him if philosophy were what he was studying, and he said, yes, chiefly; that and Italian—so as to be able to read Dante.

"Dante?" she exclaimed. "We lived in Italy a good deal when I was a child. Perhaps I could help you with Dante."

His face lit up. "Oh, could you? Say, could I come round evenings, three or four times a week, and read him with you after supper?"

A little taken aback she said she was not sure she could be free as often as that in the evening. They went out a good deal, she and her husband, she explained—to the theatre, to concerts . . . in a big place like New York there were always so many things to do in the evening. She forbore to mention that frequent dining-out was among them. Couldn't he, she suggested, come in the early afternoon instead—she was often free till four. But he shook his head, obviously disappointed. "No, I couldn't do that. I've got to stick to my own writing in the daytime."

Ah, to be sure—his own writing! That was what he'd come about, she supposed, to see her husband? Her husband unluckily was away on business. He had expected Mr. Weston at the office the morning of the day before; she believed Mr. Weston had fixed his own hour for coming. And her husband had waited all the morning, and he hadn't turned up. Her tongue stumbled over the "Mr. Weston"; it sounded stiff and affected; she remembered having called him "Vance" as a matter of course the first time she had seen him, at the Willows. But something made her feel that she was no longer in his confidence, or perhaps it was that he had simply forgotten what friends they had been. . . . The idea disconcerted her, and made her a little shy. It was as if their parts in the conversation had been reversed. "My husband expected you, but you never came," she repeated, gently reproachful.

No, he said, he hadn't come. He'd meant to, the day before, as soon as his train got to New York; but he hadn't been able to. He stated the fact simply, without embarrassment or regret, and left it at that. Halo felt a slight flatness, an uncertainty as to how to proceed.

"And this morning—?"

"This morning I couldn't either. I called round at the office half an hour ago, but it was closed, and the janitor told me to come here instead."

"Yes, I left word—as my husband's away."

She suddenly perceived that they were still in the middle of the room, exchanging their explanations on the particular figure of the rug where he had been standing when she entered. She signed to him to take one of the armchairs by the fireplace, and herself sank into the other. Twilight had gathered in the corners of the bookwalled room, and the fire flowed more deeply for the shadows. Her visitor leaned to it. "I never saw such a beautiful fire—why, that's real wood!" he exclaimed, and fell on his knees on the hearth, as if to verify the strange discovery.

"Of course. We never burn anything else."

This seemed to surprise him, and he lifted his firelit face to hers. "Because it's so much more beautiful?"

"Because it's alive."

His gaze returned to the hearth. "That's so; it's alive. . . ." He stretched his hands to the flame, and as she watched him she remembered, a few days before, looking at Lewis's hands as he held them out in the same way, and thinking: "Why isn't he a poet?"

This boy's hands were different: sturdier, less diaphanous, with blunter fingertips, though the fingers were long and flexible. A worker's hand, she thought; a maker's hand. She wondered what he would make.

The thought reminded her once more of the object of his visit—or at least of hers in sending for him, and she said: "But you've brought a lot of things with you, haven't you? I hope so. I want so much to see them."

"Manuscripts?" He shook his head. "No, not much. But I'm going to write a lot of new stuff here." He got to his feet and stood leaning against the mantelshelf, looking down at her with eyes which, mortifyingly enough, seemed to include her as merely part of the furniture. "What is he *really* seeing at this moment?" she wondered. Aloud she said: "But my husband wrote you were to be sure to bring everything you'd written. He's so much interested . . . we both think 'One Day' so wonderful. I understood he'd asked you to bring all the stories and articles *The Hour* had rejected. You see it's in new hands—my husband's—and he means to pursue a much broader policy. . . ." (Why was she talking like a magazine prospectus? she asked herself.)

Vance Weston shook his head. "I didn't bring any of

those old things; they're no good. *The Hour* was dead right to refuse them."

"Oh—" she exclaimed, surprised and interested. It was a new sound in that room—the voice of honest self-disparagement! She looked at him with a rising eagerness, noting again the breadth of his forehead, and the bold upward cut of the nostrils, and the strong planting of his thick-ish nose between the gray eyes, set so deeply and widely apart.

"Authors are not always the best judges. Perhaps what you think no good might be just what a critic would admire."

"No, that man Frenside's a critic, isn't he? Anyhow, the objections he made were right every time; I know they were." He spoke firmly, but without undue humility. "My head's always full of subjects, of course. But he said I hadn't accumulated enough life-stuff to build 'em with; and I know that's right. And I know I can do a lot better now. That's why I want to get to work at once."

She felt disappointed, foreseeing her husband's disappointment. It would have given him such acute satisfaction to reverse one of Frenside's judgments! "You think by this time you've accumulated the life-stuff?" Her tone was faintly ironical.

"Well," he said with simplicity, "I guess time keeps on doing that—the months and years. They ought to. I'm three years older, and things have happened to me. I can see further into my subjects now."

She noticed the lighting up of his eyes when he began to speak of his writing, and felt herself more remote from him than ever. She longed to know if he remembered nothing of their talks and she rejoined more gently: "I suppose it seems a long time to you since you read your poems to me on Thundertop."

"Yes, it does," he said. "But you taught me a lot that

day that I haven't forgotten—and at the Willows too." He paused, as if groping for the right phrase. "I guess you were the first to show me what there was in books."

The joyous colour rushed to her face. At last he had recovered the voice of the other Vance! "Ah, I was young then too," she said with a wistful laugh.

"Young? I guess you're young still." Relapsing into friendly bluntness, he added: "I'm only twenty-two."

"And I'm old enough to be your mother!"

"Say—I guess you're about twenty-five, aren't you?"

She shook her head with a mournful grimace. "You must add one whole year to that. And such heaps and heaps of useless experience! I don't even know how to turn it into stories. But tell me—haven't you at least brought one with you today?"

"A story? No, I haven't brought anything."

She sat silent, inconceivably disappointed. "Shall I make a confession? I hoped you'd want me to see something of yours . . . after all our talks. . . ."

"Well, I do; but I want to be sure it's good enough." He moved away from the fire and held out his hand. "I want to go right home now and write something. This is generally my best hour."

She put her hand reluctantly in his. "I suppose I mustn't keep you then. But you'll come back? Come whenever you feel that I might help."

"Surely," he said with his rare smile; she was not sure she had ever seen him smile before. It made him look more boyish than ever. "I suppose I can see your husband on Monday?" he added.

Yes, she thought he could; but she repeated severely that he must be sure to telephone and make an appointment. "Editors are busy people, you know, Vance," she added rather maternally, slipping back into her old way of addressing him. "If you make another appointment you must be sure to keep it—be on the stroke, I mean. My husband was rather surprised at your not coming yesterday, at your not even sending word. His time is—precious."

He met this with a youthful seriousness. "Yes, I presume he would be annoyed; but he won't be when I've explained. I couldn't help it, you see; I had to see the girl I'm going to marry before I did anything else."

Halo drew back a step and looked at him with startled eyes. She felt as if something she had been resting on had given way under her. "You're going to marry?"

"Yes," he said, with illuminated eyes. "That's the reason I've got to get to work as quick as I can. I guess your husband'll understand that. And I'll be sure to be at the office whatever time he wants me on Monday."

When he had gone Héloïse Tarrant sat down alone and looked into the fire.

❧ XX ❧

TARRANT DID not reappear till Monday evening. He had telephoned to his wife from Boston that on returning to New York he would go straight to the office of *The Hour,* and that she was not to expect him till dinner. They were dining alone at home, and she had already got into her tea gown and was waiting to hear his latchkey before ringing for dinner. She knew that Lewis, who liked to arrive late when he chose, also liked his food to be as perfectly cooked as when he was on time; and she sometimes felt despairingly that only her mother could have dealt with such a problem.

He came in, hurried and animated, with the slight glow which took the chill from his face when things were prospering. "All he wants to make him really handsome," his wife mused, "is to have real things to do."

"Hullo, my dear; not late, am I? Well, put off dinner a bit, will you? I've been on the jump ever since I left. Here's something to amuse you while I'm changing." He threw a manuscript into her lap, and she saw Vance Weston's name across the page.

"Oh, Lewis! He turned up, then?"

"He condescended to, yes—about an hour ago."

"Well—is it good? You've had time to read it?"

Little non-committal wrinkles formed themselves about his smile as he stood looking down at her. "Yes, I've read it; but I'd rather wait till you have before I tell you what I

219

think. I want your unbiassed opinion—and I also want to jump into my bath." The door closed on him, and she sat absently fingering the pages on her knee. How well she knew that formula: "Your unbiassed opinion." What it meant was, invariably, that he wasn't sure of himself, that he wanted someone else to support his view, or even to provide him with one. After that his judgments would ring out with such authority that people said: "One good thing about Tarrant is that he always knows his own mind."

Héloïse sent the cook a disarming message—she knew how long it took Lewis to dress. Then she drew her armchair to the lamp. She was aware, as she began to read, of a certain listlessness. Was it possible that her opinion would not be as unbiassed as her husband supposed? Had she felt an interest in Vance's literary career only because she hoped to renew her old relation with the eager boy who had touched her imagination, to resume the part of monitress and muse which she had played during their long sessions at the Willows? When he had said: "You were the first to show me what there was in books," her contracted heart had glowed and unfolded; when, a moment later, he told her he was engaged, and she had seen an unknown figure intrude between them, something in her shrank back, a door was closed. Well, why not? She was lonely; she had looked forward to the possibility of such comradeship as he might give her. But though she had been fated to disappointment that was surely not a reason for feeling less interest in his work. . . . As she took up the manuscript she tried to arouse in herself the emotion she had felt a few days earlier, when her eyes lit on the opening paragraph of "One Day."

The new tale was different; less vehement, less emotional, above all less personal. Was he already arriving at an attitude of detachment from his subject? If so, Halo knew, Frenside would see a future novelist in him. "If he goes on retailing the successive chapters of his own history, as they happen to him, they'll be raw autobiography, or essays disguised as novels; but not real novels. And he probably won't be able to keep it up long." That would be what Frenside would say in such a case. It was his unalterable conviction that the "me-book," as he called it, however brilliant, was at best sporadic, with little reproductive power. Well, the charge of subjectivity could hardly be brought against the tale she had just read. Boy as he was, the writer had moved far enough away from his subject to see several sides of it. And it was an odd story to have interested a beginner. It was called "Unclaimed," and related an episode brought about by the sending home of the bodies of American soldiers fallen in France. Myra Larcom, the beauty of her prairie village, had become engaged in 1917 to Ben Purchase, a schoolmate and neighbour. Ben Purchase was killed at the front, and Myra became the heroine as well as the beauty of Green Lick, which happened to have no other fallen son to mourn. When the government offered to restore its dead soldiers to their families for burial, Myra of course accepted. Her Ben was an orphan, with no relations near enough to assume the expense of his translation; and besides, she said, she would never have allowed anyone else to have the privilege. . . . But the dead heroes were slow in returning. Months passed, and before there was any news of the warrior's approach, another hero—and alive—had come back and won her. It appeared that her engagement to Ben Purchase had been a last-minute affair, the result of a moonlight embrace the night he started; indeed, she was no longer very sure that there had been an actual engagement; and when at length his body reached New York there was no one to claim it; and no one to pay for its transport, much less for the funeral and gravestone. But Tullia Larcom, Myra's elder sister, had always been secretly in love with Ben, though he had never given her a glance. She was a plain girl, a predestined old maid, the drudge and butt of the family. She had put by a little money as the village seamstress, but not much—there were so many demands on her. And it turned out to be an expensive business—a terribly expensive business—to bring home and bury a dead hero. And the longer you left him in the care of his grateful government the more expensive it became. . . . "Unclaimed" was the simple and unsentimental relation of how Tullia Larcom managed to bring Ben Purchase's body back to Green Lick and give him a grave and a headstone. . . . When Halo finished reading she had forgotten about her husband, forgotten about the cook, forgotten even about her own little emotional flutter over Vance Weston. . . . All her thoughts were with Tullia at Ben Purchase's grave. . . .

"How did he know . . . how did he know?" she murmured to herself. And the fact that he did know seemed warrant of future achievement.

"Halo, are you never coming?" her husband's voice called from the dining room. "You seem to forget that a hard day's work makes a fellow hungry. . . ."

At dinner he went into all sorts of details about his new printing contract, and his interviews in Boston, where he had gone to secure various literary collaborations. All that he said was interesting to Halo. She began to see that *The Hour* would bring a new breath of life into her world as well as her husband's. It would be exciting to get hold of the budding geniuses; and once she had let Lewis discover them, she knew they would be handed over to her to be tamed and amused. She had inherited her mother's liking for the company of clever people, people who were doing things and making things, and she saw the big room in which she now spent so many solitary hours peopled by a galaxy of new authors and artists, gathered together under the banner of *The Hour.*

"If only nobody calls it a *salon* Lewis won't mind," she thought.

There was so much to hear and to say that Vance Weston was not mentioned again till dinner was over and they returned to the library. Tarrant lit his cigar and settled down in his own particular easy chair, which had a broad shelf for his coffee cup and ashtray. "Well, how does it strike you?" he said, nodding in the direction of the manuscript.

"Oh, Lewis, you've discovered a great novelist!" She prided herself on the tactfulness of the formula; but enthusiasm for others was apt to excite her husband's suspicions, even when it implied praise for himself.

"Novelist? Well—we'll let the future take care of itself. But this particular thing—"

"I think it's remarkable. The simplicity, the unselfconsciousness. . . ."

"H'm." He puffed at his cigar and threw back his head in meditation. "To begin with, war stories are a drug in the market."

She flashed back: "Whose market?" and he replied, with a hint of irritation: "You know perfectly well that we can't afford to disregard entirely what the public wants."

"I thought you were going to teach it what it ought to want."

As this phrase was taken from his own prospectus it was too unanswerable to be welcome, and his frown deepened. "Little by little—certainly. But anyhow, doesn't it strike you that this story—which has its points, of course—is . . . well, rather lacking in relief? A trifle old-fashioned . . . humdrum? The very title tells you what it's about."

"And you want to have it called 'What Time Chronos?' or 'Ants and Archangels' ?" She broke off, remembering the risk of accusing him of wanting anything but the rarest and highest. "Of course I know what you mean . . . but isn't there another point of view? I mean for a review like *The Hour?* Why not try giving your readers the exact opposite of what all the other on-the-spot editors are straining to pro-

vide? Something quiet, logical, Jane Austen-y . . . obvious,
almost? A reaction from the universal paradox? At the very
moment when even *Home and Mother* is feeding its million
readers with a novel called *Jerks and Jazzes,* it strikes me
that the newest note to sound might be the very quiet—
something beginning: 'In the year 1920 there resided in the
industrial city of P——a wealthy manufacturer of the name
of Brown. . . .' That's one of the reasons why I've taken
such a fancy to Vance's story."

Adroitly as she had canalized her enthusiasm, she did
not expect an immediate response. She knew that what she
had said must first be transposed and become his own. He
laughed at her tirade, and said he'd make a note of her titles
anyhow—they were too good to be lost; but the fact remained that, for the opening number of *The Hour* under its
new management, he thought they ought to have something
rather more showy. But he'd think it over . . . he'd told
Weston to come back in a day or two. "Queer devil—says he
wrote the thing white hot, in forty-eight hours after getting
here; must be about ten thousand words. . . . And it jogs
along so soberly."

The bell rang, and Halo said: "That must be Frenny."
Frenside was incapable of spending an evening alone. His
life of unsettled aspirations and inconsecutive work made
conversation a necessity to him as soon as he had shaken off
the daily task, and he often drifted in to sit with Halo for an
hour after his club or restaurant dinner.

He entered with his usual dragging step, stooping and
somewhat heavier, but with the same light smouldering under the thick lids behind his eyeglasses.

"Hallo, Lewis—didn't know you were back," he grumbled as Tarrant got up to welcome him.

"There's a note of disappointment in your voice," his
host bantered. "If you were led to think you'd find Halo
alone I advise you to try another private enquiry man."

"Would, if they weren't so expensive," Frenside bantered back, settling down into the armchair that Tarrant pushed forward. "But never mind—let's hear about the new *Hour.* (Why not rechristen it that, by the way?) Have you come back with an argosy?"

"Well, I've done fairly well." Tarrant liked to dole out his news in guarded generalities. "But I'm inclined to think the best of my spoils may be here at your elbow. Remember how struck I was by that story, 'One Day,' by the boy from the West whose other things you turned down so unmercifully?"

"Not unmercifully—lethally. What about him?"

"Only that I rather believe he's going to make people sit up. I've got something of his here that strikes an entirely new note—"

"*Another?*" Frenside groaned.

Tarrant's lips narrowed; but after a moment he went on: "Yes, the phrase is overworked. But I don't use it in the blurb sense. This boy has had the nerve to go back to a quiet, almost old-fashioned style: no jerks, no paradoxes— not even afraid of lingering over his transitions; why, even the title . . ."

Halo, mindful of Frenside's expectation of a whiskey and soda, rose and went into the dining room to remind the maid. She reflected, not ill-humouredly, that it would be easier for Lewis to get through with the business of appropriating her opinions if she stayed out of hearing while he was doing it; and she lingered a few minutes, musing pleasurably over the interest of their editorial venture, and of the part Vance Weston might be going to play in it. She had believed in him from the first; and her heart exulted at the thought that he was already fulfilling his promise.

"If he keeps up to this standard he may be the making of *The Hour;* and when he finds himself an important literary figure he'll take a different view of his future. We're not likely ever to hear of his engagement again," she thought, irresistibly reassured; and she decided that she must manage, as often as possible, to keep an evening free for their Dante readings. When Lewis went to his men's dinners it would be easy. . . .

As she re-entered the library she heard Frenside's gruff laugh, and her husband saying: "Damned cheek, eh? Just told me in so many words he couldn't come to the office that day because he had to go and see his girl. . . . Seems the poor devil's going to be married; and who do you suppose she is? Why, one of those down-at-the-heel Tracys at Paul's Landing. . . . Halo, my dear, did you know you were going to have your new genius for a cousin?"

❧ XXI ❦

"WHERE ARE we going? You'll see," Vance said with a confident laugh.

He stood with Laura Lou on the doorstep of a small gingerbread-coloured house in a rustic-looking street bordered with similar habitations. Her bare hand lay on his sleeve, and the gold band on her fourth finger seemed to catch and shoot back all the fires of the morning.

It was one of those windless December days when May is in the air, and it seems strange not to see grass springing and buds bursting. The rutty street lay golden before Vance and Laura Lou, and as they came out of the Methodist minister's house they seemed to be walking straight into the sun.

Vance had made all his plans, but had imparted them to no one, not even to his bride. The religious ceremony, it was true, had been agreed on beforehand, as a concession to her prejudices, and to her fear of her mother. When Mrs. Tracy learned of the marriage it must appear to have been performed with proper solemnity. Not that Vance had become irreligious; but, since his elementary course in philosophy had shown him that the religion he thought he had invented was simply a sort of vague pantheism, and went back in its main lines to the dawn of metaphysics, he had lost interest in the subject, or rather in his crude vision of it. What he wanted now was to learn what others had imagined, far back in the beginnings of thought; and he could see no relation between the colossal dreams and visions amid which his mind was moving and the act of standing up before a bilious-looking man with gold teeth, in a room with a Rogers statuette on the sideboard, and repeating after him a patter of words about God and Laura Lou—and having to pay five dollars for it.

Well, it was over now, and didn't much matter anyhow; and everything to come after was still his secret. Laura Lou had not been inconveniently curious: she had behaved like a good little girl before the door opens on the Christmas tree. It was enough for her, Vance knew, to stand there looking up at him, her hand on his arm, his ring on her finger; from that moment everything she was, or wanted, was immersed and lost in himself. But his own plans had been elaborately worked out; he was in the state of lucid ecstasy when no material detail seems too insignificant to be woven into the pattern of one's bliss.

"Come," he said, "there's just time to catch the train." They hurried along the straggling streets of the little Long Island town, and reached the station as the last passengers were scrambling to their places. They found two seats at one end of the car, where they could sit, hand locked in hand, while the train slid through interminable outskirts and finally reached an open region of trees and fields. For a while neither spoke. Laura Lou, her head slightly turned toward the window, was watching the landscape slip by with a wide-eyed attention, so that Vance caught only the curve of her cheek and the light shining through the curls about her ear. There was something almost rigidly attentive in her look and attitude, as though she were a translucent vessel so brimming with happiness that she feared to move or speak lest it should overflow. The fear communicated itself to him, and as they sat there, hand in hand, he felt as if they were breathlessly watching a magic bird poised just before them, which the least sound might put to flight. "My dove," he thought, "we're watching my dove. . . ."

At length she turned and said in a whisper (as if not to frighten the dove): "Mother'll come home soon and find the letter."

He pressed her hand more tightly. The letter was the one she had written to tell Mrs. Tracy that she was not going to marry Bunty Hayes—that she would already be married to Vance when her mother opened the letter. She had been utterly unable to find words to break the news, and Vance had had to tell her what to say. In the note he had put a hundred-dollar bill, on which was pinned a slip of paper with the words: "On account of B. Hayes's loan." For the idea of the thousand-dollar loan, which Bunty Hayes had made to poor Mrs. Tracy to enable her to send Laura Lou to school, was a torture to Vance. *The Hour* had paid two hundred dollars for "Unclaimed," and he had instantly enclosed half the amount in Laura Lou's letter. It was perhaps not exactly the moment to introduce the question of money; but Vance could suffer no delay. He hoped to wipe out the debt within two or three months; then the last shadow would be lifted from his happiness. Meanwhile it had tranquillized him to do what he could.

"Oh, look—the sea!" cried Laura Lou; and there it was, beyond scrub oak and sandhills, a distant flash of light under a still sky without clouds. Vance's heart swelled; but he turned his eyes back to Laura Lou, and said, with seeming indifference: "That's nothing. . . ."

The gleam vanished; the train jogged on again between trees and fields. Houses cropped up, singly, then in groups, then in streets; the train slowed down by rural platforms, people got in and out. An hour later, as the usual clanking and jarring announced another halt, Vance said: "Here!" He reached for their joint suitcase, took Laura Lou by the arm, and pushed her excitedly toward the door. A minute later they were standing on a shabby platform, while the train swung off again and left them alone in a world of shanties and sandhills. "We'll have to walk," Vance explained, pick-

ing up the suitcase, which seemed to him to weigh no more
than a feather. As soon as they had left the station every rut
of the road, every tussock of grass and hunched-up scrub
oak cowering down against the wind, started up familiarly
before him. If he lived to be a thousand, he thought, he
would never forget an inch of that road.

Laura Lou seemed to have cast aside her apprehensions. She swung along beside him, saying now and then:
"Where are we going?" and laughing contentedly at his joyous: "You'll see." There was no sense of winter in the air;
but as they advanced a breath of salt and seaweed made
their faces tingle, and Vance, drawn by it, started into a run.
"There's not a minute to lose!" he called back; and Laura
Lou raced after him, stumbling on her high heels among the
sandy ruts. They scrambled on, speechless with haste, drunk
with sun and air and their own hearts; and presently he
dragged her up the last hillock, and there lay the ocean. He
had sworn to himself that one day he would come back and
see it with the girl he loved; but he had not known that the
girl would be Laura Lou. He felt a little awed to think that
the hand of Destiny had been on his shoulder even then;
and as he gazed at the heaving silver reaches he wondered
if they had known all the while where he was going, and if
now they saw the path that lay ahead.

When, three years earlier, he had come down in summer to that same beach, lonely, half starved, dazed with discouragement, fevered from overwork, the sea had been a
gray tumult under a sunless sky; now, on this December
day, it flashed with summer fires. "Like my life," he thought,
putting out his arm to draw Laura Lou to the ridge on
which he sat. "There," he said, his cheek on hers, "there's
where our bird's mother was born."

Her bewildered eyes turned to him under their hummingbird lashes. "Our bird's mother?"

"Venus, darling. Didn't you know the dove belonged to

Venus? Didn't you know Venus was our goddess, and that
she was born out of the waves, and came up all over foam?
And that you look so like her that I feel as if you'd just been
blown in on one of those silver streamers, and they might
pull you back any minute if I didn't hold tight onto you?"
He suited the act to the words with a vehemence that made
her laugh out in rosy confusion: "Vance, I never did hear
such things as you make up about people."

He laughed back and held her fast; but already his
thoughts had wandered again to the ever-heaving welter of
silver. "God, I wish a big gale would blow up this very
minute—I'd give anything to see all those millions and millions of waves rear up and wrestle with each other."

Laura Lou shivered. "I guess we'd be frozen if they
did."

"Why—are you cold?" he wondered, remembering
how, as afternoon fell, she had grown pale and shivered in
the garden of the Willows.

She shook her head, nestling down against him. "No—
but I'm hungry, I believe."

"Hungry? Ye gods! So am I. You bright child, how did
you find out?" He caught her close again, covering with
kisses her eyes and lips and her softly beating throat.

He had pitched the suitcase down at their feet, and he
stooped to open it, and pulled out a greasy-looking parcel.
"What about picnicking here? I've always wanted to have
the wild waves at my wedding party." He was unwrapping,
and spreading out on the sand, beef sandwiches, slices of
sausage and sticky cake, cheese, a bunch of grapes and a
custard pie, all more or less mixed up with each other; and
he and Laura Lou fell on them with hungry fingers. At last
she declared: "Oh, Vance, we mustn't eat any more—oh, no,
no, I *couldn't* . . ." but he continued to press the food on
her, and as her lips opened to morsel after morsel the returning glow whipped her cheeks to carmine. Then he dug

again into the suitcase, extracted a half bottle of champagne and a corkscrew—and looked about him desperately for glasses. "Oh, hell, what'll I do? Oh, child, there's nothing for us to drink it out of!"

Rocking with laughter, she followed the pantomime of his despair. But suddenly he sprang up, slid down the hillock, and running along the beach came back with a big empty shell. "Here—our goddess sends you this! She sailed ashore in a shell, you know." He flourished it before her, and then bade her hold it in both hands, while she laughed and laughed at his vain struggles with the corkscrew and the champagne bottle. Finally he gave up and knocked off the neck of the bottle, and the golden foam came spiring and splashing into the shell and over their hands. "Oh, Vance . . . oh, Vance . . ." She tilted her head back and put her lips to the fluted rim, and he thought he had never seen anything lovelier than the pulse beat in her throat when the wine ran down. "Ever taste anything like that?" he asked, licking his fingers; and she giggled: "No, nothing, only ginger ale," and sat and watched while he refilled their chalice and drank from it, carefully putting his lips where hers had been. "It's like a gale of wind and with the sun in it—that's what it's like," he declared. He did not confess to her that it was also his first taste of champagne; unconsciously he had already decided that part of his duty as a husband was to be older and stronger than she was, and to know more than she did about everything.

"Here's our house," Vance said, swinging her hand to cheer her up. He knew by her dragging step that the walk had seemed long to her. To him it had appeared, all the way from the beach to the cluster of deserted buildings they were approaching, as if the racing waves had carried him. But he forced himself to walk slowly, taking his first lesson in the duty of keeping step.

The house, a mere shanty, had a projecting porch roof

which gave it a bungalow look. When Vance, bitten with the idea of spending his honeymoon by the sea, had hunted up the kindly manager at Friendship House, the latter, amazed and then diverted at the idea—"Land alive—in December?"—had said, why yes, he didn't know why Vance shouldn't have the keys of the bungalow where the camp manager and his wife stayed when the camp was open. The camp had been run up near a farm, for the convenience of being in reach of milk and country produce, and he guessed the farmer's wife would put some fuel in the bungalow, and see if the old stove would draw. They could get milk from her too, he thought, and maybe they could take their meals at the farm. She was pretty good-natured, and at that time of year she might like a little company for a change.

Once in most lives things turn out as the dreamer dreamed them. This was Vance's day, and when he pushed open the door there was the stove, with a pile of wood and some scraps of coal ready for lighting, and a jug of milk and loaf of bread on the table. The bare boarded room, which looked like the inside of a bathhouse, was as clean as if it had been recently scoured, and the drift of sand and crinkled seaweed on the floor merely suggested that a mermaid might have done the cleaning. Vance laughed aloud for joy. "Oh, Laura Lou, isn't it great?"

She stood on the threshold, looking shyly about her, and he turned and drew her in. The table bearing the provisions carried also a candle in a tin candlestick; and against the wall stood a sort of trestle bed with two pillows and a coarse brown blanket. Two kitchen chairs, a handful of broken crockery on a shelf, a cracked looking glass, and a pile of old baskets and cracker boxes in a corner completed the furniture. Over the bed hung a tattered calendar, of which the last page to be uncovered was dated September 15, and bore the admonition: *Little Children, Love One Another.*

Vance burst out laughing; then, seeing a faint tremor

about Laura Lou's lips, he said: "See here, you sit down
while I get at the fire." He began to fear their frail shanty
might be too cold for her as night fell; and he dropped on
his knees and set to work cramming fuel into the stove. Decidedly it was his day; the fire lit, the stovepipe drew. But as
he knelt before it he felt a faint anxiety. Laura Lou sat behind him. She had not spoken since they had entered the
shanty, and he wondered if she had felt a shock of disappointment. Perhaps she had expected a cosy overheated
room in a New York or Philadelphia hotel, with white sheets
on the bed and running water—oh, God, he thought suddenly, how the hell were they going to get washed? There
wasn't a basin or pitcher, much less soap or towel. In summer, no doubt, the manager and his wife just ran down to
the sea for a dip. . . . Vance began to be afraid to look
around. At length he heard a sound behind him and felt
Laura Lou's hands on his shoulders. He turned without rising, and her face, flushed and wet with tears, hung close
over him.

"Why, what is it, darling? The place too rough for you
—too lonely? You're sorry we came?" he cried remorsefully.

She gave him a rainbow smile. "I'll never be sorry
where you are."

"Well, then—"

"Only I'm so tired," she said, her voice grown as small
as a child's.

"Of course you are, sweet. Here—wait till I make the
bed comfortable and you can lie down." He shook up the
meagre pillows, and after she had taken off her shoes he
covered her with her coat and knelt down to chafe her cold
feet. She looked so small and helpless, so uncomprehending
and utterly thrown on his mercy, that his passion was held
in check, and he composed her on the bed with soft fraternal hands. "There—the fire'll warm the place up in no time;
and while you're resting I'll step across to the farm and see
what I can bring back for supper."

"Oh, Vance, I don't want any supper."

"But I do—and piping hot," he called back with a facti-
tious gaiety, wondering that he had not guessed the place to
take her to would have been a hotel with an imitation marble restaurant, and a good movie next door where she could
read her own romance into the screen heroine's.

He grimaced at the thought, and then, lighting the
candle, so that the place might look as cheerful as possible,
went out and walked across a stubbly field to the farm. The
farmer's wife, a big good-natured Swedish woman, received
him with friendly curiosity. She'd known one or two young
fellows to come down as late as December, she said, but
she'd never had a honeymoon before. The idea amused her,
and she started at once warming up a can of tomato soup,
and offered Vance a saucepan to heat the milk for breakfast.
While she warmed the soup he sat in the window of the
kitchen and looked out to the sea. What a place to live in
always—solitude and beauty, and that great unresting Presence calling out night and day with many voices! ("Many
voices"—where'd he read that?) There, the woman said; she
guessed the soup was good and hot; maybe he'd like some
crackers with it? Oh, he could settle when he went away—
that was all right. She even rummaged out a tin of prepared
coffee, left there with some of the camp stores; he could
have that too, and a couple of towels. Soap was more difficult to come by, but she decided that they could have her
youngest boy's, as he was off clamdigging for a week, and
no great hand at washing anyhow. Carrying the pot of hot
soup carefully, his other supplies in his pockets, Vance
walked back through the twilight. . . .

Outside of the door he said softly: "Lou!" There was
no answer, and he lifted the latch and went in. The room
was dark, except for the cloudy glow through the stove-door
and the unsteady candle flicker; at first he had a sense of
entering on emptiness. Then he saw that Laura Lou was
lying as he had left her, except that she had flung one bare

arm above her head. Shading the candle he went up to the bed. Her little face, flushed with the sea wind, and tumbled over with rumpled straw-coloured hair, lay sideways in the bend of her arm. She was sound asleep, the hummingbird lashes resting darkly on her clear cheek with the hollow under it, and her breath coming as softly as if she were in her own bed at home. For the first time Vance felt a faint apprehension at what he had done, at his own inexperience as well as hers, and the uncertainty of the future. He had bound himself fast to this child, he, hardly more than a child himself in knowledge of men and in the mysterious art of getting on . . . and for one stricken instant he asked himself why he had done it. The misgiving just flashed through him; but it left an inward chill. With those other girls he had been tangled up with there had been no time for such conjectures; they sucked him down to them like quick-sands. But now he seemed to be bending over a cool moonlit pool. . . .

"What shall I say," he thought, "when she wakes?" And, at that moment her lids lifted, and her eyes looked into his. The candle slanted in his shaking hand; but Laura Lou's face was still. "Oh, Vance . . . I was dreaming about you," she said, with a little sleep-fringed smile.

About dawn he woke and got up from her side. He moved with infinite caution lest he should disturb her, drawing on his clothes and socks, and picking up his shoes to put them on outside in the porch. From the threshold he looked back. In the pale winter light she lay like a little marble image; the serenity of her attitude seemed to put the whole weight of the adventure on his shoulders, and again he thought: "Why did I do it? What can come of it?" and stood dazed before the locked mystery of his own mind. In those short hours of passion the little girl who had seemed so familiar to him had suddenly become mysterious too; closest part of himself henceforth, yet utterly remote and inexpli-

cable; a woman with a sealed soul, but with a body that
clung to his. . . . The misgiving which had passed in a
flash the night before now fastened on him with a cold
tenacity. "What do I know about her? What does she know
about me?" he questioned in a terror of self-scrutiny. He
looked at her again, and the startled thought: "What if she
were lying there dead?" flashed through his mind. How
could such a horrible idea have come to him? In an instant
his wild imagination had seized on it, and he saw himself
maimed, desolate, crushed—but free. Free to open that
door and go out, straight back to his life of two days before,
without the awful burden of responsibility he had madly
shouldered. . . . The vision lasted but the flicker of a lid,
but like lightning at night in an unknown landscape it lit up
whole tracts of himself that he had never seen. The horror
was so strong that he half turned back to wake her up and
dispel it. The faint stir of her breast under her thin night-
dress reassured him, and he unlatched the door and went
out. . . . Instantly the horror vanished, and as he saw before him the great motionless curves of sea and sky, and
thought that all the while they had been there, hushed and
secret, encircling his microscopic adventure, a sense of uni-
fying power took possession of him, as it used to in his boyhood. "And all the time there was *that!*" he thought.

He pulled on his shoes and raced down to the sea. The
air was still mild, and he stood by the fringe of little waves
and looked eastward at the bar of light reddening across the
waters. As he stood there, all the shapes of beauty which
had haunted his imagination seemed to rise from the sea
and draw about him. They swept him upward into the faint
dapplings of the morning sky, and he caught, as in a mystic
vision, the meaning of beauty, the secret of poetry, the sense
of the forces struggling in him for expression. How could he
ever have been afraid—afraid of Laura Lou, of fate, of himself? She was the vessel from which he had drunk this di-

vine reassurance, this moment of union with the universe. Whatever happened, however hard and rough the road ahead, he would carry her on his heart like the little cup of his great communion. . . .

❧ XXII ❦

FOR TWO more balmy days they lingered, ecstatic children, by the sea; but on the third the air freshened. Laura Lou began to cough, and Vance, frightened, packed up their possessions and carried her back to civilization. He had made up his mind to give her twenty-four hours at a New York hotel, with a good evening at the movies or a cabaret show (should her imagination soar so high), after which—though he had not confessed it—he knew no more than she where they were going.

He had no pressing anxiety about money. His mind was teeming with visions, and in his state of overwrought bliss every dream seemed easy to capture and interpret. His preference would have been to sit down by the sea and write an immensely long poem; but he knew that Laura Lou, the inspirer of this desire, was also the insuperable obstacle to its fulfilment. He would write stories instead; after the acceptance of "Unclaimed" he felt no doubt that he could sell as many as he chose. And he had promised, as soon as possible after his marriage, to call on Tarrant, and talk over the plan of becoming a regular contributor to *The Hour*. Still, to live in New York with Laura Lou would be a costly if not impossible undertaking. She was as much of a luxury as an exotic bird or flower: that she might help him in wage earning or housekeeping had never entered his mind. He had simply wanted her past endurance, and now he had her; and exquisite as the possession was, he was abruptly faced with the cost of it.

He found a hotel showy enough to dazzle her without
being too exorbitantly dear; and they had dinner in a sham
marble restaurant where every masculine eye was turned to
them, and she glowed in innocent enjoyment of the warmth
and light, and the glory of sitting with him, as his wife, at a
pink-candle-shaded table. Afterward, with a charming assumption of superiority, she decided on a theatre rather
than the pictures. It was a good deal more expensive—but,
hang it, he'd write another story: it was wonderful, how the
unwritten stories were accumulating on the shelves of his
mental library. It was he who selected the play: *Romeo and
Juliet,* with a young actress, tragically lovely, as Juliet; and
presently they were seated in the fashionable audience,
Vance with mind and eye riveted on the stage, Laura Lou
obviously puzzled by the queer words the actors used and
the length of their speeches, and stealing covert glances
(when what was going on became too incomprehensible) at
the fashionable clothes and exquisitely waved heads all
about them. Between the acts she sat silent, brimming with
a happy excitement, her hand close in her husband's, as if
that contact were the only clue to life. As at the restaurant,
many glances were drawn to her small head with its silvery-
blonde ripples and the tender moulding of brow and cheek;
but Vance saw that she was wholly unaware of attracting
attention, and enclosed in his nearness as in a crystal world
of her own.

Gradually this barrier was penetrated by what was
happening on the stage: the beauty of the young actress,
the compelling music of the words, seemed to stir in Laura
Lou some confused sense of doom, and Vance felt her anguished clutch on his arm. "Oh, Vanny, I'm sure it's going to
end bad," she whispered, and a tear formed on her lashes
and trembled down.

"You darling—" he breathed back, wondering why on

earth he had chosen *Romeo and Juliet* for a honeymoon out-
ing; but when the tragedy rose and broke on them he saw
that even her tears, now flowing in a silver stream, were
part of the happiness in which she was steeped to the weeping lashes. "It's too dreadful . . . it's too lovely . . ." she
moaned alternately as the play moved deathward, and with
a furtive movement she dried her wet cheek against his
sleeve. And brooding on those beautiful dead lovers they
went home to another night of love.

The next morning Vance presented himself at the office
of *The Hour*. As he sprang up the stairs he almost ran into
Frenside, who was coming slowly down. The older man
stopped and looked at him curiously.

"Going up to settle about your job?"

"Well, I hope so, sir."

"All right. Good luck." Frenside nodded and passed on.
From a lower step he turned to call back: "I wouldn't tie
yourself up too far ahead—especially your fiction."

Vance, new at such transactions, stared a moment, not
quite understanding.

"Keep free—keep free as long as you can," Frenside repeated, hobbling down with a heavy rap of his stick on
each step. And Vance turned in to the office.

He found a cordial welcome from Tarrant. Everybody
on the staff had read "Unclaimed," and great hopes were
founded on its appearance in the coming number. Tarrant
produced cigarettes and cocktails, and introduced Eric
Rauch, the assistant editor. Eric Rauch was a glib young
Jew with beautiful eyes and a responsive smile, who had
published an obscure volume of poetry: *Voodoo,* and a
much talked-of collection of social studies: *Say When.* For
the first time Vance found himself talking with an author,
and treated by him as one of the tribe. When Rauch said:

"You've struck out on a new line," the praise rushed through Vance like fire, and he longed to hurry back to the hotel and tell Laura Lou. But what would it have meant to her?

After these agreeable preliminaries Tarrant looked at his watch, said: "Half-past one, by Jove—and I'm due at the Century, to lunch with old Willsdon." Willsdon, the historian, had promised *The Hour* an article on "A New Aspect of Benjamin Franklin," and Tarrant hurried off, saying: "You and Eric'll be able to fix up details. Come round again soon, won't you?"

Eric Rauch proposed that Vance should lunch with him at the Cocoanut Tree, a nearby lunchroom, and they walked there, Vance's steps dancing down the street as if the dull pavement were the seashore. Talking to a fellow like Rauch was something as new to him as his first sight of the ocean, and almost as exciting. . . .

At the Cocoanut Tree they met other fellows who were writing or painting, or doing something with the arts. To Vance, whose horizon had greatly widened in the interval since his first visit to New York, the names of two or three of the older men were familiar; but the ones Rauch took most seriously—vanguard fellows, he explained—who looked as youthful as Vance himself, the latter had never heard of. They all greeted him good-humouredly, and one, a critic named Redman, said: "See here, when are you going to give us a novel?"

"*The Hour*'s going to see to that," Rauch rejoined briskly; and another young man, with bruised eyelids in a sallow illumined face, and a many-syllabled name ending in "ovsky," adjured Vance with ardent Slav gestures: "For God's sake tackle something big—colossal—cosmic—get away from the village pump . . ." while a shabbily dressed girl with a greasy mop of black hair and bold gay eyes pushed up to the table, exclaiming: "Eric, why don't you introduce me? I'm the sculptress Rebecca Stram, and I want to do your head one of these days," she explained to Vance.

"Well, I guess you will, if you want to," said Rauch humorously; "only let the poor devil have something to eat before you begin to feel his bumps."

It all sent a novel glow through Vance, and he thought how wonderful life would be, spent among these fellows who talked of art as freely and familiarly as his father did of real estate deals. Eric Rauch explained who they were, what they had written or painted or carved ("That Stram girl—she's a regular headhunter; bright idea, doing all the new-comers . . ."), and which ones were likely to "get there." For the first time Vance was inducted into the world of lit-erary competitions and rewards. Eric Rauch said there was a big campaign on already for this year's Pulsifer Prize; hadn't Vance heard of it? Best short story of the year . . . Two thousand dollars; and of course *The Hour* was going to try for it for "Unclaimed." "And, by the way, what have you got on the stocks now?" And then the business talk began.

Rauch said he had been charged by Tarrant to come to an understanding with Weston. They believed in him at *The Hour*—their policy was forward-looking; they wanted to make their own discoveries, not to butt in where some-body else had already staked out a claim. Weston, now—he wouldn't mind Rauch's saying frankly that as a writer he was utterly unknown? Because, unluckily, owing to muddle-headed mismanagement, his first story, "One Day," had been allowed to fall flat, drop out of sight as completely as if it had never been written. And they would have to build up his reputation all over again with "Unclaimed," which, they thought, was quite as remarkable as the other; though of course they couldn't guarantee the public's taking to it, with the silly prejudice there was against war stories. Any-how, it was a good gamble, and they were glad to risk it. And to prove their faith in Weston, they were willing to go farther; willing to take an option on his whole output, arti-

cles, short stories and novels, for the next three years. Rauch
didn't know if Weston realized what a chance that was for a
beginner, who—well, wasn't in a position, let's say, to order
himself an eight-cylinder Cadillac . . . for the present, anyhow. . . .

But Tarrant wanted to do more. He understood that
Weston was just married, and he knew that when a man
takes on domestic responsibilities there's nothing like a
steady job, even a small one, for making his mind easy. *The
Hour* therefore proposed to let Vance try his hand at a
monthly article on current literary events. They'd find a racy
title, and let him have full swing—no editorial interference
if the first articles took. A fresh eye and personal views were
what they were after—none of the old mummified tradi-
tions. And for those twelve articles they would guarantee
him a salary of fifteen hundred a year for three years, without prejudice to what he earned by his fiction: say a hundred and fifty for the next two stories after "Unclaimed,"
and double that for the following year, if he would guarantee three stories a year, or possibly four. Only, of course, he
was to pledge himself not to write for any other paper or
publisher—no other publisher, because *The Hour*'s solicitude included an arrangement for book publication with
their own publishers, Dreck and Saltzer. Tarrant had gone
into all that so that Weston should be able to get to work at
once, free from business worries. He'd had some difficulty in
getting a publisher to look at it that way and sign for three
years, but he'd fought it out with them, and as Dreck and
Saltzer were great believers in *The Hour* they'd finally
agreed, and had the contract ready. "So now all you'll have
to do is to lie back and turn out masterpieces," Rauch cheer-
fully concluded, lighting a final cigarette. "Say though, it's
pretty near time to get back to the office," he added, with a
glance at his watch. "Shall we go now and settle things on
the spot?"

Vance sat flushed and brooding, his brows drawn together in the effort to calculate his yearly income on the basis suggested. Figures always puzzled him, and a fortnight earlier he would have acquiesced at once, to get rid of troublesome preliminaries. But with Laura Lou in the background it was different. . . . He tried writing out the figures mentally on the tablecloth, but when it came to adding them up they became blurred and vanished. . . .

"Well, I guess that wouldn't total up to much over two thousand dollars a year, would it?" he ventured, trying to give his voice a businesslike sound.

Erich Rauch arched his eyebrows in a way that signified: "Well—for a beginner? For a gamble?" Then, as Vance was silent, he threw off: "There's nothing to prevent your writing a novel, you know."

"What would you give me for a novel?" Vance asked.

Eric Rauch's eyebrows flattened themselves out meditatively. "What sort of a novel would you give us?" Then, with a laugh: "See here, I don't see that we need look as far ahead just yet. . . . A novel takes time; but meanwhile there's the Pulsifer Prize, don't forget. We're going to put up a big fight to get that for you."

Vance looked at him, perplexed. The Pulsifer Prize— two thousand dollars for the best short story of the year! He could pay off Bunty Hayes at a stroke, and live on Easy Street with the balance . . . buy Laura Lou some pretty clothes, and have time to think over subjects, and look round. . . . His heart beat excitedly. . . . But what could *The Hour* do about it? he asked.

"Why, boom you for all we're worth. You can get even a short story into the limelight nowadays with money. And we mean to spend money on 'Unclaimed.'"

"But I don't understand. Who gives this Pulsifer Prize anyhow?"

"Oh, a rich society woman: widow of old Pulsifer, the railroad man. It's the event of her life—"

"Why, does she award the prize herself?"

"Bless you, no: it's done the usual way. Bunch of high-brows as judges." Rauch paused, and added with his exquisite smile: "Even judges are human. . . ." He let the rest of the smile drift away through his cigarette spirals.

Vance understood and winced. The use of the business vocabulary was what he recoiled from. That there should be "deals," transactions, compromises in business was a matter of course to him. That *was* business, as he understood it; his father's life was a labyrinth of such underground arrangements. But Vance had never taken any interest in business, or heard applied to it the standards of loyalty which are supposed to regulate men's private lives, and which he had always thought of as prevailing in the republic of letters. To him an artist's work was essentially a part of the private life, something closer than the marrow to the bone. Any thing that touched the sanctity, the incorruptibility, of the creative art was too contemptible to be seriously considered. As well go back to doing write-ups for the *Free Speaker*. . . . Vance looked at the clever youth behind the smoke wreaths, and thought: "Queer that a fellow who writes poetry can care for that sort of success . . ." for the poets seemed to him hardly lower than the angels.

He said curtly that he didn't care a darn for prizes, and Eric rejoined: "Not for two-thousand-dollar ones?"

Vance, a little dizzy, nevertheless echoed: "Not a darn—"

"Well, *The Hour* does, then. It's something you owe us if we take you on—see? A beginner . . . Everything's a question of give and take . . . fair play. Not that I mean . . . of course little O'Fallery may pull off the prize anyhow, with "Limp Collars." Shouldn't wonder if he did. His publisher's hustling round for him—I know that. And we don't guarantee anything . . . See?"

The last phrase brought a vague reassurance to Vance. Of course they couldn't guarantee anything . . . of course little O'Fallery might get the prize. Vance had read "Limp Collars," and thought it well-named . . . pretty poor stuff. . . . Seemed a pity. . . . Anyhow, he saw with relief that he must have misunderstood Rauch. Of course *The Hour* wasn't going to try to corrupt the judges—what an absurdity! They were simply going to direct public opinion: that was what "limelight" meant. Any fellow's publisher had a right to commend his goods. . . .

Laura Lou had been captivated by a girl who sat near them at the theatre in a peach-coloured silk . . . or lace, or something . . . not a patch on Laura Lou, the girl wasn't, but even Vance could see there was a look about the dress. . . . His Laura Lou! There wouldn't be one of 'em could touch her if only he could give her togs like that. . . .

> "When she moves, you see
> Like water from a crystal overflowed,
> Fresh beauty tremble out of her, and lave
> Her fair sides to the ground . . ."

He shut his eyes on the vision and thought: "And yet even the ones that look like that want finery!"

"Of course I'd like that prize first-rate," he mumbled.

"Well, I guess it's yours—on the merit of the story alone. Only, our job is to get that merit known," Eric Rauch explained patiently, as they rose to get their hats and coats. They walked back together to the office, and before Vance left he had signed the two contracts which lay ready for him on Tarrant's desk: one surrendering to *The Hour* all his serial rights for three years, the other pledging him for the same period of time to Dreck and Saltzer for book publication.

On the way downstairs, late in the afternoon, he remembered meeting Frenside coming down the same stairs in the morning, and recalled his warning: "Keep free."

"Oh, well," Vance said to himself, "what's he made of his life, anyway?" For Frenside already seemed to him as remote as old age and failure. His head was brimming with ideas for his article, and for others to follow, and it was agreed (at his suggestion) that the series should appear under the caption of "The Cocoanut Tree," in memory of the spot where the bargain had been struck. "I want a tree to climb, to get a bird's-eye view from," Vance had said, laughing; and Rauch replied that he was sure the title would take Tarrant's fancy. He pressed a copy of his poems on Vance, and the latter set off, his heart beating high at the thought of announcing to Laura Lou that he was a member of the editorial staff of *The Hour,* had signed a three years' contract with a big publisher. "She won't understand what it's all about, but it'll sound good to her," he thought. And so it did to him.

Laura Lou showed the radiant incomprehension he had foreseen. "Oh, Vance, isn't it great?" She clung to him and worshipped; then, loosening her arms, drew back and lifted ineffable eyes to his. "Oh, Vanny—"

He laughed and recaptured her. "Guess you're thinking already what show we'll pick for tonight, aren't you?" He grew reckless. "And, say, darling, if there's anything particular you want to buy . . ." He knew there would be no pay till the end of the coming month, but time seemed as negligible as age while she lifted her trembling smile to him.

"Oh, Vanny . . . I wonder, could we go out and buy something to take back to Mother?"

"Sure." He laughed with relief. Mrs. Tracy's wants could be more inexpensively supplied than her daughter's; and besides, he liked Laura Lou's not instantly asking for something for herself. Then he looked again and noticed a shadow of anxiety on her radiance. He saw that she *was* asking for something for herself, but inwardly, because she dared not speak it. "What is it, sweet? Anything bothering you?"

Yes, something was: her mother. They'd been gone four days now, she reminded Vance, and Mrs. Tracy didn't even know where they were, and must have been fretting dreadfully over that letter her daughter had left; and what Laura Lou wanted, oh, beyond anything, was to start right off for Paul's Landing—oh, Vance, truly, couldn't they?—and surprise her mother with the splendid news, and make everything all right that very day. Oh, wouldn't Vance help her to pack up at once, and maybe they could catch the five o'clock express, and pop in on Mrs. Tracy just as she was clearing away supper?

Their hotel was close to the train, their packing was soon done. Secretly, Vance was relieved by his wife's suggestion. The rush of his happiness had swept away all resentment against Mrs. Tracy, and he felt obscurely in the wrong in having persuaded Laura Lou to marry without her mother's knowledge. Only the certainty of Mrs. Tracy's opposition had made him do so; but he could not shake off his compunction, for he knew her life had been full of disappointments, and that Laura Lou's flight would be the bitterest. Now it was all different; with his two contracts in his pocket he could face his mother-in-law with head erect. She would surely rather see Laura Lou married to the assistant editor of *The Hour* than to the barker of a sightseeing car; and if Vance should capture the Pulsifer Prize the Hayes debt would be cancelled at once. They paid in haste and hurried to the station, finding time on the way to select for Mrs. Tracy a black silk bag mounted in imitation amber. "She never has anything pretty," Laura Lou explained, as if excusing so frivolous a choice; and Vance, remembering the basket of sweet peas with the stuffed dove, mused once more on the mysterious utility of the useless.

❧ XXIII ❧

MRS. TRACY's forgiveness turned out harder to win than they had imagined. When they came on her that evening clearing away her lonely supper, as Laura Lou had predicted, their arrival provoked a burst of tears and an embrace in which Vance managed to get included. But the rousing of Mrs. Tracy's emotions did not affect her judgment. The exchange of acrimonious letters between Paul's Landing and Euphoria, at the time when she had ordered Vance out of her house, had sown ineradicable seeds. Even had her son-in-law's prospects impressed her as much as he had hoped, her view would not have changed; but, as Vance soon perceived, she remained unimpressed by the documents so proudly spread before her. "I guess newspaper work's more reliable than magazines," she merely remarked, no doubt mindful of the dizzy heights to which journalism had lifted Bunty Hayes.

But these were secondary considerations; for she now regarded Vance as the corrupter of both her children. Vance had taken Upton to a "bad house" (so Upton, the sneak, had never shouldered his part of the blame!); Vance had made Laura Lou deceive her mother and break her promise to Bunty Hayes, the promise on the strength of which Mrs. Tracy had accepted a loan that it might take years to repay. Vance had wounded her in her pride and her affection; and the double humiliation was not effaced by this vague talk about a review that was going to give him a hundred dollars a piece for articles he hadn't even written.

"Mr. Hayes wanted she should be brought up like a lady, as her father's daughter ought to be," Mrs. Tracy said over and over again, during her first private talk with Vance, on the day after their return to Paul's Landing.

"She doesn't have to be in Hayes's pay to learn to be a lady—I guess God made her that," Vance retorted. Mrs. Tracy, with a cold patience, said he knew well enough what she meant—she meant, educated like a lady, the way all the Lorburns had been; the way she couldn't afford to educate her children because of her husband's misfortunes, and his dying just when things were going against them. . . . Mr. Hayes had understood, and had wanted to help them, and had acted as a gentleman would. . . .

"Well, I guess you can trust me to act as well as he did," Vance said, too happy not to be generous, and feeling how poor a case he could make out for his own behaviour. But Mrs. Tracy only answered that, whatever she might feel about the matter, Laura Lou was not free to break her engagement till that thousand dollars was paid back.

"Why, see here, there's been a law in the United States for some years now against trading in flesh and blood," Vance broke out, his irritation rising again; but the resentment in Mrs. Tracy's eyes showed him the uselessness of irony.

"I guess I understand well enough how you feel," he began humbly. "But Laura Lou loved me, and didn't love Hayes; that's about the only answer. Anyhow, I've told you I mean to pay back that loan as soon as ever I can. I've got the promise of a salary of fifteen hundred dollars, and I'm going to get right to work earning it, and as much over it as I can; and every cent I can put by each month will go to paying off Hayes. You couldn't seriously expect Laura Lou and me to let a thousand dollars separate us, could you?"

Mrs. Tracy replied, obliquely, that she supposed he knew by this time what his own folks intended to do for him; and this brought Vance up with a jerk, for he had not yet told his parents of his marriage. He stood before Mrs. Tracy flushed and irresolute while she added: "I guess a thousand dollars isn't the mountain to them it is to me. But maybe they don't fancy your getting married so young."

"I—I haven't heard yet," Vance stammered, and she said, evidently perceiving her advantage, and enjoying the chance to exercise a grim magnanimity: "Well, I guess you and Laura Lou'd better stay here till you hear what your family mean to do."

Vance and Laura Lou knew she was secretly thankful to have them there. Upton's new job made it impossible for him to live at Paul's Landing, and his mother was nervous alone in the house, yet reluctant to leave because of her monthly allowance for the care of the Willows; so that, her resentment once expressed, she found it easier to keep the offenders than to send them away.

Vance, when he carried off Laura Lou, had never thought of the possibility of having to live at Paul's Landing. Vague visions of life in a New York boarding house had flitted through his mind, or rather lurked scarce-visible on its edge; but till he had persuaded Laura Lou to come to him nothing had seemed real or near at hand save the bliss he craved, and before four days of that bliss were over he understood that he lacked the experience and the money to make any sort of home for her. They were lucky to have Mrs. Tracy to turn to; her conditional forgiveness, and the shelter of her tumbledown roof, were the best they could expect—unless Mapledale Avenue should intervene. But Vance had small expectation of help from home. He had been startled back to a sense of reality by Mrs. Tracy's question; for he had not meant to conceal his marriage from his parents, but had simply forgotten all about them. From the very moment—less than a fortnight ago—when he had stepped out of the Grand Central and seen Laura Lou in the rubberneck car, he had thought of nothing else—hardly even of his art. The sight of her, the sound of her voice, the touch of her hand had rapt him away from common values and dimensions into that mystic domain to which he sometimes escaped from the pressure of material things. To that domain Laura Lou at the moment held the key, as hitherto great poetry had held it, the sunrise from Thundertop, his first sight of the sea, his plunge into the past in the library at the Willows, or any of the other imaginative shocks that flung open the gates of wonder. But the world to which Laura Lou admitted him seemed to comprise all the others, and it was not till he woke from his first ecstasy that he saw she herself was not an extra-terrestrial joy but a solid earthly fact, capable of apprehending only the earthly bounds out of which her beauty had lifted him. Laura Lou, dispenser of raptures, was merely a human being to be fed, clothed, cherished—what was it the minister had said?—in sickness and in health, till death should them part. And as long as they were together it could be only (to her at least) in the world of food, clothes, salary, sickness or health, prosperity or failure, mothers-in-law or boarding houses. As Vance went up to bed, after a drawn battle in the cold dimly lit dining room with his first "Cocoanut Tree" article, he reflected: "Well, anyway, I know it makes her happy to be back here," and bent his impetuous neck to the yoke.

At first the yoke proved less heavy than he had expected. While he was at work Laura Lou had her mother's companionship. During their brief days alone his wife's tenderness had begun to frighten him, not its ardour but its submissiveness. He had not imagined that one human life could be so swiftly and completely absorbed into another. It was like a blood transfusion: body and soul, he seemed to have taken her into himself; whenever he returned, after an absence of a few hours, only her lovely ghost awaited him, and his presence had to warm her back to life. Now it was different. Her love was quieted by the return to the daily routine in familiar surroundings. She, who had formerly done so little to help her mother, was now eager to share in the household labours; Vance guessed that she was trying to learn how to make a home for him. Already she sternly defended his working hours, and had once or twice reproved Mrs. Tracy for asking him to bring up the coal or clear out the roof gutter. Luckily, if clumsy he was willing, and had no objection to undertaking the tasks which had been Upton's, if only the women would let him alone while he wrote. This was not very difficult, since he worked in the afternoon and after they had gone to bed; and the first weeks at Paul's Landing passed peacefully.

One day Upton came over. He had grown broader and stronger, and his new job had given him an air of importance which at first amused and then irritated Vance, to whom he was still the shifty boy of three years ago. Upton did not appear much more pleased with Laura Lou's marriage than his mother, nor more impressed by Vance's literary credentials. While the women were in the kitchen he followed Vance back to the dining room, where the latter had been given a corner for his desk and papers, shut the door solemnly, and asked: What about Bunty Hayes? Vance laughed, and said he guessed Bunty Hayes wasn't going to bother them much, and anyhow he'd had three weeks now to stir things up, and they hadn't heard from him.

"Oh, but you will," Upton said, a little apprehensively. "He was in California when Laura Lou and you went off, and I don't believe he knows anything yet. His job in New York ended after Thanksgiving, and the firm that employs him sent him West to look over some winter and spring routes. I guess he'll be back any day," he added.

Vance laughed again. "Well, what do you think he'll do?" Upton coloured uncomfortably, and said: "I'd feel bet-

ter if Mother hadn't taken the money." Vance rejoined that
he would too, but as it had been taken the only thing was to
pay it back. He understood Saint Elfrida's School wouldn't
refund an advance if the pupil had taken part of the course,
and he was going to do his best to get the loan paid off as
quickly as his earnings permitted. He was getting bored
with the subject, and tried to change it, but Upton, scratch-
ing his head, insisted dubiously: "I wish't you could have
raised the whole thousand right away. He's the kind to turn
ugly."

"Oh, I thought he was a friend of yours," Vance rapped
back, exasperated; but Upton answered: "Well, I guess
you'd better try and stay friends with him too, if you don't
want him coming round and raising hell."

Vance would have been angry if he had not seen that
Upton, under his commanding manner, was still the scared
boy of old. The discovery made him smile, and rejoin:
"Well, I guess I'd better get to work right now, and try to
earn some money for him,"—at which Upton sulkily withdrew.

Vance became aware, after this, that the only thing to
restore his credit with Mrs. Tracy would be the approval of
his family. If they were pleased with his marriage they
would do something handsome; and the something handsome would help to wipe out the Hayes loan. Vance shared
her view, but not her hope; he knew what his family would
think. The exchange of acrimonious letters had left traces no
less deep in Mapledale Avenue than at Paul's Landing. His
people would regard it as folly for him to marry at his age,
and be indignant with him for marrying the Tracy girl after
the way the Tracys had treated him. These considerations
weighted his pen when he wrote home to announce his marriage; and he was less surprised than Mrs. Tracy at the time
which elapsed before he had an answer.

The first sign came from Grandma Scrimser, who sent

him a beautiful letter, a Bible, and a year's subscription to *Spirit Light,* to which she and her daughter Saidie Toler were now regular contributors. Grandma thought it lovely and brave of him to get married right off. She hoped that Laura Lou was as pretty and high-minded as her mother, when Mrs. Tracy had come out to see them years ago, on her wedding tour, and that Vanny would bring his bride to Euphoria right away, and that their married life would be full of spiritual benedictions.

A few days later Mrs. Weston wrote. She said they had been so taken aback by Vance's news that they didn't know what to say. They'd all supposed Vance would have too much pride ever to set foot in Mrs. Tracy's house again, and now first thing they knew he'd married her daughter, without even telling them, or asking their advice or approval. His father had been so hurt and upset that at first she didn't know how she'd ever bring him round, and even now he couldn't make up his mind to write; but she, Mrs. Weston, had finally persuaded him to let her do so, and he had told her to say that if Vance chose to bring his wife out to Euphoria and get a job there, the couple would be welcome to the spare room to live in, and Mr. Weston would see what he could do to get Vance taken back on the *Free Speaker,* though of course he couldn't guarantee anything—only Vance might be able to do something if he was on the spot, so Mrs. Weston thought they'd better come out as soon as they could. She added in a postscript that Mr. Weston had showed the terms of Vance's contract with *The Hour* to the celebrated authoress, Yula Marphy, who was over from Dakin visiting with friends at Euphoria, and Miss Marphy had said, why it looked to her like a downright swindle, for she could get five hundred dollars any day for a story in the big magazines, and she'd never heard of *The Hour* anyhow, and she guessed it was one of those highbrow papers that run at a loss for a year or so, and then fizzle out. And what she advised was for Vance to come straight back West, where he belonged, and take up newspaper work again, and write pure manly stories about young fellows prospecting in the Yukon, or that sort of thing, because the big reading public was fed up with descriptions of corrupt society people, like there was a demand for in the East. Mrs. Weston added that his sisters sent him their love, and hoped his marriage would make him very happy; and would he be sure and telegraph when to expect him, as they presumed Mrs. Tracy was still without a telephone?

The sting of this did not escape Vance. The social classifications of Euphoria were based on telephones and bathtubs; but he had already guessed that elsewhere other categories prevailed. His irritation made it easier to answer than if the letter had been more cordial. He wrote that he didn't suppose his father would seriously advise him, even if he were willing to break his contract, to give up a good opening in New York for a problematic job at Euphoria. He thanked his parents for offering his wife and himself a room, but added that his mother-in-law had already given them a home at Paul's Landing. And he posted this letter without telling either Mrs. Tracy or Laura Lou that he had heard from his mother. To his grandmother he wrote affectionately; he knew that a Bible and a year's subscription to *Spirit Light* were the best she could afford, and the tone of her letter touched him. She was the one human being at Euphoria who had dimly guessed what he was groping for: their souls had brushed wings in the twilight. . . .

The weeks passed. He took his first article—"Coleridge Today"—to *The Hour,* and Eric Rauch was enthusiastic, but said Vance must tackle a contemporary next time. Rauch suggested his own volume of poems, *Voodoo,* and Vance reddened and mumbled at the suggestion. The little book had interested and puzzled him; he was surprised to watch, under its modern bluster, so many half-familiar notes. He

said he didn't believe he was ready yet to tackle the new
poetry; hadn't read enough or understood enough of it; Eric
Rauch rejoined, with his compelling smile: "Why, that's just
what we're after for *The Hour:* a fellow's first reactions, *before* he's ready. We want to wipe out the past and get a
fresh eye on things. We can get standardized reviewing by
the bushel." Vance travelled home heavyhearted, trying on
the way to distract his thoughts by thinking up subjects for
his next story.

Not subjects: they abounded—swarmed like bees,
hummed in his ears like mosquitoes. There were times when
he could hardly see the real world for his crowding visions
of it. What he sought was rather the development of these
visions; to discover where they led to. His imagination
worked slowly, except in the moments of burning union
with the power that fed it. In the intervals he needed time
to brood on his themes, to let them round themselves within
him. And he felt also increasingly, as his life widened, how
small his provision of experience was. He needed time for
himself—time to let his mind ripen, to have things happen
to himself, and watch them happen about him, without
being in haste to interpret or develop what he saw. He did
not want to cut down all his trees for firewood. All this was
still confused and unexpressed in him; he felt it most clearly
when, after his imagination had seized on a subject and was
preparing to plunge to its heart, he was brought up short by
inexperience, by his inability to relate the thing he had fastened on to the rest of the world. Experiences, for him, were
not separable entities; everything he saw, and took into
himself, came with a breaking away of tendrils, a rending of
filaments to which the soil of life still clung—and he was
familiar, as yet, with so few inches of that soil. The rest was
alien territory. He never seemed able to get to the heart of
his subjects. . . . And then, when he got out of the train at
Paul's Landing, there was Laura Lou in the winter dusk, a

little pinched by the cold, but with eyes of blue fire, lips that burned on his—and he wondered if he hadn't been meant to be a poet. . . .

Two or three times a week he went up to the office of *The Hour*. Tarrant would have liked him to come every day; but that would have put an end to his writing. He had never been able to work except in solitude; and besides, the journey back and forth was a clear waste of time and money.

He soon found that even these absences preyed on Laura Lou. She did not reproach him; she simply pined when he was not there. When he got back he had to tell her everything that had happened to him, describe the people he had met, repeat everything that everyone had said or done; and in doing so he measured again her mental limits, and saw that the things which counted for him would never count for her. She smiled them away as oddities, like a wise little wife humouring a cranky husband; and her smile almost made him feel that endearments were enough for a soul to live on. Almost, not quite. From his childhood there had been in him an irreducible core of selfness (he found no other word for it), a hidden cave in which he hoarded his secretest treasures as a child hoards stony dead starfish and dull shells of which he has once seen the sea glitter, though he can make no one else believe in it. Even Laura Lou's ignorance, even Laura Lou's embraces, could not cheapen that treasure.

He had been coming and going in this way for about three weeks when one evening, on his return from town, not finding his wife below stairs, he ran up to her. She lay on the bed, asleep, in the attitude of trustful composure which had moved him on their first wedded morning. Near the bed he saw a crumpled paper on the floor. Laura Lou's sleep was so sound that he picked up the paper and smoothed it out under the lamp without waking her. It was a letter, bearing the address of a drummer's hotel at Seattle, and it began: "Well, in a few more days now, little sweet, I'll be back home again, and I guess we'll have some good times round about Christmas, if Bunty Hayes is the man I take him for. Say, honey, how long do they let you off that school for the holidays . . . ?"

Vance read no further. He stood motionless, looking at his wife. She had not told Bunty Hayes; Mrs. Tracy had not told him. Vance saw that both women had been afraid, and pity and wrath struggled in him, the wrath mostly for Mrs. Tracy, the pity—well, yes, the pity for Bunty Hayes. The women hadn't treated him squarely. . . . Vance let the letter fall where he had found it. . . .

The next day—his last at the office before Christmas—he handed in his article on Eric Rauch's *Voodoo*. He wasn't satisfied with it; he knew it wasn't good. And he hated it because it was part of what he was expected to do for *The Hour* in return for the salary he had to have.

Tarrant, evidently, didn't care for the article either; though he was prepared to do so later, Vance suspected, if good reasons were forthcoming. Vance had already learned that his chief's opinions were always twenty-four hours late. At first he had thought it was because they matured as slowly as his own; but he had begun to suspect a different reason. Somebody, not always immediately available, did Tarrant's thinking for him—Vance wondered if it were his wife. He had not had much time to think of Mrs. Tarrant since his encounter with her on the afternoon when she had offered to read Dante with him. He had heard no more of her since; she never came to the office, and he had no time to go and see her, even had the idea occurred to him—which it never did. At most, he thought enviously now and then of the rows and rows of books in the room where she had received him. . . .

"Of course," Tarrant said, "there are things about it
. . . certainly. . . . Only, perhaps . . . well, I see you're a
traditionalist at heart. . . ." He wavered. "Not a bad thing,
perhaps . . . the *tabula rasa's* getting to be an old story,
eh? Well, I don't deny . . ."

"Somebody asking for Mr. Weston," a voice came
through the door of the editorial retreat. Tarrant looked relieved at not being obliged to commit himself farther, and
Vance, surprised at the summons, went back to the outer
office.

Bunty Hayes stood there. He was crimson and shiny in
the face, as if from cold or drink, and looked larger than life
in the cramped space. He glared at Vance furiously. "That
you, is it? Doing the highbrow act, eh? Call yourself a magazine editor, do you? Well, I'll tell you what I call you." He
did so, in a rush of oaths and imprecations.

Vance received them in silence, and his silence had the
effect of increasing the other's exasperation. "Well, haven't
you got anything to say, take it all lying down, will you?
Well, I'll give you something that'll keep you from getting
up again. . . ." His fist, red and shiny as his face, flew out
and caught Vance under the ear. . . . The blow was violent but unsteady—Vance noticed that at once. The fellow
was half drunk—drunk enough to be pitiable, though not
(Vance also perceived) to be undangerous. But to Vance he
would have been pitiable even if he had been sober.

"You damn dirty thief, you . . . Steal women, do
you?" Vance saw him squaring himself for another blow,
and his own fighting instinct flamed up. By this time Bunty's
denunciations had summoned the slender staff of *The Hour*
to the outer office. The typewriter girl wailed, "It's a hold-
up," but the men laughed and reassured her. . . . "Let 'em
alone—it's their funeral," Vance heard, as Bunty's fist leapt
out at him again. His own was raised to parry it. He was the
lighter and swifter, and he was sober—he had all the ad-

vantages. His arm dropped, and he drew back against the wall. "Better go home now—I'll see you wherever you want," he said, his hands in his pockets, the welt of his first blow spreading up his cheek like fire.

"Ho, a coward too, are you? Standing there to take your licking as if you were sitting for your portrait? I'll make a portrait of you, by God. . . . See me do it, boys. . . ."

Tarrant's door opened and he came out. He was very pale, and his thin lips were drawn together in a narrow line of disdain.

"Weston—what's all this? I'll thank you to do your fighting elsewhere. . . ."

Bunty Hayes broke into a rusty laugh. "Fighting? He won't fight. This is a licking he's going to get. . . ." Somebody echoed the laugh, and Tarrant's cold eyes turned again to Vance. "Do you know this man?"

"Yes," said Vance.

"Know me? God, that's the trouble with him. And I've given him a chance at a stand-up fight, and he won't take it. That so?" he challenged Vance. Vance, his hands in his pockets, repeated: "That's so." He saw the disdain on Tarrant's lips turn to contempt, and his blood leapt up again. But inwardly he still knew that, even if Hayes had been completely sober, he would not have fought him.

Tarrant turned toward the intruder. "You get out of here," he said.

"Get out of here? I'll see you to hell first—I'll . . ."

Eric Rauch, who had not been in the office, came running up the stairs. He glanced about the group, bewildered, and turned to Vance. "What's up?" he asked. Bunty shouted back: "He's taken my girl and he won't fight me for her," and there was another snicker among the lookers-on. It was manifest that sympathy was veering away from Vance.

Vance felt Rauch's luminous eyes rest curiously and not unkindly on his white face with the burning welt. Rauch smiled a little and put his hand on Hayes's arm. "If you'll step this way," he said, with a faint wink at the spectators, "I'll take you down to my private office, and you can tell me what it's all about." He drew Hayes across the threshold, with a quick sign to the office boy to follow. But Hayes had already collapsed—the tears were running down his face, and he was putting his arm about Rauch's neck as the door closed on them.

Tarrant turned back to his private room. His hand on the door he paused to say to Vance: "I don't care for any explanation. But you understand, of course, that if this sort of thing happens again . . . I can't have . . ."

"Oh, of course not," Vance stammered, half dazed.

In a few moments Rauch came back, unconcerned, and lighting a cigarette. His eloquent eyes rested again on Vance. "You must have been reading the Russians lately," he said with his soft incisiveness. He nodded and passed on to his desk.

Vance sat down at his, and began to write furiously. But he was merely making meaningless scratches on the paper. These people had of course realized that Hayes was half drunk, and would no doubt think he had been unwilling to fight him at a disadvantage. And on the whole, they would regard this as being to his credit. But Vance knew that the real reason was different: he had refused to fight Hayes because he had read his letter. And that was something he would never be able to explain.

On his desk lay a bundle of galleys—the proofs of "Coleridge Today." He spread them out before him and tried to set to work revising. An hour ago each word, each syllable, would have been subjected to the most searching scrutiny; but now the page danced meaninglessly before him. . . . Suddenly he laid down his pen. Something of dominating importance had steadied his shaking nerves. What had Eric Rauch meant when he said: "You must have been reading the Russians lately"? Who *were* "the Russians," and how was it that Vance had never read or even heard of them? At the mere thought, his mind felt firm ground under it again, and Bunty Hayes and his bluster were swept away like chaff on the wind.

"I'll find out who they are before night," Vance resolved, and settled down again to his work.

BOOK V

⚓ XXIV ⚓

Tarrant, that evening, got home late and out of humor. His lateness ought in reason to have annoyed his wife, for they were off to Eaglewood the next day for Christmas, and many holiday questions were still unsettled; but she met him with her vague short-sighted smile and the air of one whom nothing in the world can annoy.

At dinner she ascribed his sulkiness and taciturnity to strained nerves and the effort not to betray himself before the maid. The first number of the *New Hour*—they had accepted Frenside's rechristening—was to appear on the second of January, and the intervening week was a bad time for readjustments. No wonder the editor was on edge.

Over coffee and his cigar he broke out. What did she suppose? That damned protégé of Frenside's—that Middle-Western yahoo . . . Weston, yes . . . had been turning the office into a beer garden. . . . Yes, this very afternoon. Outrageous . . . Why, a drunken fellow came in and tried to fight him . . . and, well, the fact was Weston funked it . . . luckily, or they might have had the police there . . . and the other man would have made mincemeat of him. . . . Disgusting business . . . he'd told Weston what he thought of it. . . . Over a woman, of course . . .

"A woman?" Halo echoed, startled. "Why, he's only just married, isn't he?" Well—there you had it, her husband's shrug emphasized. He was that sort, was Frenside's little pet. . . . Messing about with women before his honeymoon was over . . . The cigar drew less well than usual; Tarrant stood up and paced the floor angrily. Disgusting . . . he wouldn't have it, he repeated. Good mind to sack the fool on the spot . . . a coward too, that was the worst of it. He threw the cigar into the fire, and groped nervously for another. . . .

Halo, leaning back in her deep armchair, looked up at him with indolent curiosity. "Lewis, aren't you just simply overworked—overwrought?" she suggested.

"Just simply—?"

"I mean haven't you let your nerves get the better of you? You look dead beat." She made a friendly gesture toward the opposite armchair. "Sit down and light your cigar. Who told you this preposterous yarn anyhow?"

"Preposterous yarn?" He paled with anger, and she saw her mistake. "No one told me—no one had to. I was there. In the front row—saw the ruffian slap Weston's face, and Weston turn the other cheek. Precisely."

Halo mused, perplexed but still unperturbed. "But the fact that the ruffian was drunk—isn't that the reason?"

"Why Weston wouldn't fight?"

"Not in your office, at any rate. Put yourself in his place."

But Tarrant knew of few places worthy to put himself in. "Thank you, my dear. I don't happen to have lowdown blackguards trying to fight me."

"I should have thought any man might, accidentally." She paused and reflected. "Anyhow, it doesn't seem to have bothered young Weston much," she let drop with a retrospective smile.

Through Tarrant's fresh cloud of cigar smoke she saw his suspicious flush. "I don't know how much it bothered him; but he looked pretty thoroughly ashamed of himself."

"He got over it quickly then. He'd forgotten all about it when he was here just now."

Tarrant swung round in surprise, and she continued, in the tone of leisurely narrative: "About an hour ago. He dashed in on his way to the train, staggering under his mother-in-law's Christmas bundles. He'd called on very particular business. You'll never guess . . ."

"Why should I?" Tarrant growled.

"Try—"

He answered by another shrug—this time of indifference.

"Well, he wanted to borrow Tolstoy and Dostoyevsky. He'd never heard of them till today. Or of Tchehov or the moderns, of course . . . It appears someone in the office said something about 'the Russians,' and as soon as he'd finished his work he rushed to the public library; but it was closed, so he came here. Rather sweet of him, I thought. He didn't say how d'ye do, or any of the useless things. He just said: 'Who are the Russians? I want to read them. Have you got them?' And went off with his arms full." She sank back in her cushions, and closed her lids on the picture. The fire crackled companionably, and Tarrant's cigar smoke wove its soothing cloud about their silence. Even with her eyes shut she could guess that something was slowly breaking down the hard crust of his resentment. Expediency . . . uncertainty . . . it didn't matter. . . . After an interval he said, more to himself than her: "Well, I suppose he *was* right not to let that blackguard raise hell in the office. . . . Only it goes against me when a man seems to show the white feather. . . ."

"Ah, but *you* . . ." his wife murmured; and opened her eyes to meet his gratified smile.

But his face was not the one on which her gaze rested. Her vision was turned inward. There had happened to her, suddenly, what may happen at any stage, however late, in the acquaintance, even the intimacy, between two people: she had seen Vance Weston that afternoon—really, literally seen him—for the first time. Before that, her glance—curious, then interested, then admiring—had merely brushed him with a glowworm spark. She had caught, as it were, glimpses of him in the blur of himself; rifts and gleams; a bit here, a bit there, of the outward accidents of his appearance. Now, all at once, she possessed him as a whole, seemed to discern behind his fluid features the power which had built them. Uneven, untrue to itself, as his face appeared, with its queer mixture of maturity and boyishness, instability and power, she suddenly beheld it in the something which harmonized these contradictions and bound him together like a strong outline. Was that perhaps what genius was? And this boy with the tumbled brown hair, the resolute lines of brow and nose, the brooding impulsive lips and the strident untutored voice—was this the way genius was cut? . . . Her heart missed a beat, as if it had paused with her mind to consider him. "It's like seeing him dead," she thought—so entirely had his face been stripped to the essentials. And she reminded herself, with a shiver, that one never forgot a single lineament of a face one had seen dead. . . . "It's more than I bargained for," she murmured, and then: "Coward!"

She pulled herself up to the surface of her eyes, and gave her husband back his smile.

The first number of the *New Hour* made a hit. The New York publishing world rang with the figures of its sale; and the crown of its success was "Unclaimed," the quiet story by the young author no one had heard of. A war story too—fatal handicap! But everyone agreed that it sounded a new note. The public was fed up with new notes, yet dared not praise anything without applying that epithet to it (so Frenside explained). "But it *is* a new note; I saw it at once when he brought me the thing," Tarrant grumbled, adding impatiently: "If it depended on you to give a new author a start—!"

"Where's my lantern?" Frenside mocked; but the sting of his mockery was submerged in the warm tide of praise which met Tarrant wherever he went. He was acutely proud of his first editorial achievement, and his gratified pride transformed him in his wife's eyes. "I've always known he was cleverer than anybody else—all he needed was a chance to show it," she thought, her hungry imagination clutching at every substitute for belief in him. Yet in an inner fold of her heart something whispered: "How much I would rather believe in him against everybody!"

Tarrant had said one day, in a burst of satisfaction: "I think you ought to invite that Weston boy here; we ought to have a party for the *New Hour's* first birthday. People are beginning to ask about him; they're already wondering about the Pulsifer Prize—" and Halo, rousing herself from an indolence she could hardly explain, had echoed: "Oh, if you think so—certainly." In reality, she had relegated the thought of Vance to the back of her mind. After all, it was her husband who had resuscitated *The Hour*, not Vance Weston. But that was the way of the world: people fastened on one good thing in a review—a new review especially— and talked as if that were the principal, if not the only, reason for its popularity. Whereas the real credit belonged to the editor, the guiding and selecting mind, in this case to the man who had discovered Vance Weston and made him known, as he would in future discover and make known many others. Halo flamed with impatience at the public's obtuseness. . . .

"Oh, but of course you must . . . you must let me introduce him. . . . Of course he won't think anything of the kind. . . ." Mrs. Tarrant, slim and animated in her black dress, with lacy wings floating with the motions of her arms, moved away from the hearth, where she had been standing beside an exaggeratedly tall young woman whose little head drooped sideways from a long throat, and whose lids were cast down in deprecation on the rich glitter of her gold brocade.

"Oh, Halo, no . . . I don't know . . . Won't he think . . . ? I do want to be so utterly aloof and impartial. . . ."

"Well, but you will, my dear. You don't suppose every young writer who's introduced to you in the course of the winter will imagine you're sampling him for the Pulsifer Prize?"

"How absurd, Halo! When of course it's *all* in the hands of the committee. . . . But I do so want to preserve my complete serenity, my utter detachment. . . ." Mrs. Pulsifer flung the words after her in a series of staccato cries.

Halo laughed, and moved through the groups of guests scattered about her library to the corner where Vance Weston, his back to the company, stood in absorbed contemplation of the bookshelves. Until he had entered the room a few minutes earlier she had not seen him since he had come to borrow her Tolstoy and Dostoyevsky, and now, in the noise and sparkle of her first evening party for the *New Hour*, he had become once more an exterior, episodical figure, not the being whose soul had touched hers that other evening. She even reflected, as she approached him: "He's shorter than I remembered; his shoulders are too heavy . . . he gets into fights about women. . . ." as if retouching an idealized portrait abruptly confronted with the reality.

"Vance," she said, and he turned with a start of surprise, as though he had imagined himself alone. Halo smiled: "This isn't the Willows, you know—I mean," she hurried on, fearing he might misinterpret the allusion, "you're at a party, and lots of the people here want to know you; first of all, Mrs. Pulsifer."

"Mrs. Pulsifer—?" he echoed, his eyes coming back from a long way off and resting on his hostess in slow recognition.

"The prize-giver. Over there, in the gold-coloured dress. Come—poor Jet's not alarming; she's alarmed."

"Alarmed?"

Halo slipped her arm through his. "Frightfully shy, really. Isn't it funny? She's in terror lest every author who's introduced to her should ask for the prize—yet she wants them all introduced!"

"But isn't the prize given by a committee?"

"Yes. Only she likes to look the candidates over. Come!"

It amused her to introduce Vance to people. It was the first time she had seen him in a worldly setting, and she was interested in watching the effect he produced—especially the effect on Mrs. Pulsifer. On the whole, giving parties for the *New Hour* might turn out to be great fun. She was only sorry that her young lion, in his evening clothes, looked unexpectedly heavy and common. . . .

Vance hung back. "What's she like?" he asked, as if his decision depended on that.

"Like? I don't know. . . ." Halo hesitated. "You see, she's not an actual person: she's a symptom. That's what Frenny and I call the people who are everything in turn. They catch things from another kind that we call germ-carriers, people who get every new literary and artistic disease and hand it on. But come: she's awfully nice, really."

Vance still hesitated. "Do you think I'll like her?" he asked oddly; and Halo laughed and wrinkled her short-sighted eyes. "Does one have to—at parties?"

"I don't know, I've never been to a party before—like this."

"Well, the important thing is that she should like you."

"Why?"

She gave a slight shrug, and at that moment the golden

lady swayed across the room and came up to them. "He
hates the very idea, Halo—I knew he would!" she cried.

"Vance, this is Mrs. Pulsifer. Jet, be good to him—he's
my particular friend. Take her over to that quiet corner under the Buddha, Vance, and tell her how you write your
stories." She swept away to her other guests, and Vance
found himself seated on a divan in a dim recess, with this
long golden woman, half frightened and half forthcoming,
and swaying toward him like a wind-swept branch. For a
moment he had been annoyed at his hostess's request. As
soon as he had entered he had gone straight back to the
shelves from which, a few weeks earlier, Halo had taken
down Tolstoy and Dostoyevsky. Near them, he remembered
noticing, were the Gogols, and there was one, "The Cloak,"
which he heard the fellows at the Cocoanut Tree talking
about ("All Tolstoy and Tchehov came out of 'The Cloak,'"
the advanced ones said. Well, he must read "The Cloak"
then—) As soon as his eyes lit on that shelf he forgot where
he was, and that there were other people about. He stood
running his hands along the backs of the volumes in the
happy agitation produced by the sight of unexplored bookshelves; and then Mrs. Tarrant came and spoilt it all. . . .

But now a new wave of sensation swept over him. The
nearness of this strange Mrs. Pulsifer, her small feverish
face, the careless splendour of her dress, the perfume it gave
out, had caught his restless imagination. She interested and
excited him as part of the unfamiliar setting which he had
hardly noticed on his arrival because the books had thrust
themselves between, but which now stole on him with the
magic of low lights, half tints, easy greetings, allusive
phrases, young women made for leisure and luxury, young
men moving among them lightly and familiarly. The atmosphere was new to Vance—and this woman, neither young
nor old, beautiful nor ugly, but curious, remote, like a picture or a statue come down from some storied palace wall,

seemed to embody everything in the scene that was unintelligible and captivating.

"Oh, but I'm sure you oughtn't," she murmured, drooping away but leaving her eyes close to his.

"Oughtn't what?" he stammered, entangled in his confusion.

"To tell me how you write your stories; or anything at
all about them. Halo's so reckless—she doesn't stop to consider. And of course I'm burning to know. But people might
think . . . you see, I simply *must* preserve my aloofness,
my entire impartiality . . . or they'd say I was interfering.
. . . And I'm sure I shall never like another story as much
as yours. Oh, Mr. Weston, it's a dreadful responsibility," she
wailed.

Vance was watching her curiously. He noticed the way
her wandering eyes were set guardedly under a small contracted brow ("as if they were peering out of prison," he
thought, "and reckoning up the chances of escape"). The
idea amused him, and he had to rouse himself to answer:
"You mean giving the prize is a responsibility? But you
don't, do you? I thought there was a committee?"

"Of course, of course, but that's the reason. If it should
be suspected that I tried to influence them . . . and yet I
do so worship what you write!" She swayed nearer, enveloping him in a golden network of smiles and shimmers, imparting in confidential murmurs common-places that might
have been published on the housetops, telling him what a
burden her money was, how much she needed sympathy,
how few people she could talk to as she was talking to him,
how the moment she had read the first lines of "Unclaimed"
she had felt that *there* was someone who would understand
her—and how she envied his heroine for being able, even at
the cost of her last penny, to be herself, to proclaim her love
openly, to starve herself in order to build a monument to
the man who had never known she loved him. "How you do

know women!" she murmured, swaying and gazing and retreating. "How in the world did you ever guess . . . ? Several of my friends have told me your Tullia was my living
portrait. . . . But I mustn't talk of that now. Won't you
come and see me some day? Yes—that would be better. I'm
so alone, Mr. Weston—I do so need advice and encouragement! Sometimes I wish I'd never undertaken this prize
business; but wealth has its duties, hasn't it?"

She had rambled on for a long time, yet not long
enough to satisfy his curiosity, when suddenly she started
back. "Oh, but I mustn't keep you any longer. . . . Why,
there's Fynes over there staring at us!" she exclaimed in agitation. "He's one of our committee, you know. And he never
goes to evening parties—not respectable ones, I mean. I
daresay he's come here just to look you over. . . ." She stood
up nervously.

"Tristram Fynes? Who wrote *The Corner Grocery?*"
Vance interrupted with a shock of excitement.

"Yes, over there. That dreary little man by the door.
You think him so wonderful?"

"It's a big book."

"Oh, I daresay, but the people are so dreadfully unsym-
pathetic. I suppose you'll call me very old-fashioned; but I
don't think our novelists ought to rob us of all hope, all belief. . . . But come, everybody's waiting to talk to you.
Fynes sees that, and he hates it. Oh, I do hope I haven't
spoilt your chance of the prize!" She held out her hand.
"You *will* come to see me, won't you? Yes—at six some day.
Will you come tomorrow?" she insisted, and drew him after
her across the room.

Vance, in following, had his eyes on the small dreary
man by the door. Of the many recent novels he had devoured very few had struck him as really important; and of
these *The Corner Grocery* was easily first. Among dozens of
paltry books pushed into notoriety it was the only one enti-

tled to such distinction. Readers all over the country had
felt its evident sincerity, and its title had become the pro-
verbial epithet of the smalltown atmosphere. It did not fully
satisfy Vance; he thought the writer left untouched most of
the deeper things the theme implied; if he himself had been
able to write such a book he would have written it differently. But it was fearless, honest, preternaturally alive; and
these qualities, which to Vance seemed the foundation of
the rest, were those he most longed to acquire. "First stand
your people on their feet," Frenside had once enjoined him;
"there'll be time enough afterward to tell us where they
went." If only Tristram Fynes should be moved to say that
the people in "Unclaimed" stood on their feet!

Vance's heart thumped furiously as Mrs. Pulsifer
paused near the great man. If it should really turn out that
Fynes had read "Unclaimed," and was here because of it!

"Oh, Mr. Fynes—what a surprise! I didn't know you
ever condescended . . . Oh, but you mustn't say you're
going—not before I've introduced Mr. Weston! Vance Weston; yes; who wrote "Unclaimed." He's simply dying to talk
to you about . . ."

Mr. Fynes's compressed lips snapped open. "About *The
Corner Grocery*, eh? Well, there's a good deal to be said
about it that hasn't been said yet," he rejoined energetically,
fixing his eyes on Vance. "You're one of the new reviewers,
aren't you? Do 'The Cocoanut Tree' in the *New Hour?* Yes—
I believe I saw something of yours the other day. Well, see
here; this is no place for a serious talk, but I'd be glad if
you'd come round some day and just let me tell you exactly
what I want said about *The Corner Grocery*. . . . Much
the best way, you know. The book's a big book; no doubt
about that. What I want people told is *why* it's big. . . .
Come round tomorrow, will you? I'm going to cut it
now. . . ."

He vanished, and Vance stood dazed. But not for long.

Others claimed his attention, people who wanted to talk to him not about themselves but about "Unclaimed." The room was not crowded; there were probably not more than thirty guests in the library and the dining room beyond, into which they wandered in quest of sandwiches and cocktails, coming back refreshment in hand, or lingering about the dining table. But to Vance the scene was so new that he seemed to be in a dense throng; and the fact of being in it not as an observer, but as the centre of attention and curiosity, filled him with the same heady excitement as when he had tossed off his first shellful of champagne.

These easy affable people wanted to know him and talk to him because he had written "Unclaimed," because they had even heard (some of them) of his other story, that old thing Tarrant had fished out of a back number and spoke of republishing; they wanted to know what else he had written, what he was doing now, when he was going to start in on a novel, when he would have enough short stories for a volume, whether he had thought up any new subjects lately, whether he found it easier to write in a big city or in his own quiet surroundings at home, whether Nature inspired him or he had to be with people to get a stimulus, what his best working hours were, whether he could force himself to write so many hours a day, whether he didn't find that regular work led to routine, whether he didn't think a real artist must always be a law unto himself (this from the two or three of the younger women), and whether he found he could dictate, or had to type out his own things. . . .

Vance had never before been confronted with so many exciting and stimulating questions. At first he tried to answer each in turn, going into the matter as fully as he felt it deserved, and seizing by the way on the new ideas it developed; but by the time he had said, with his slow shy drawl: "Why, I guess I haven't got far enough yet to have worked out any regular rules, but I seem to find . . ." or: "Well,

sometimes I feel as if I had to have a lot of new faces and
sights to start me going, and then again other times . . ." he
noticed that his questioners either lost interest, or else, obey-
ing some rule of behaviour unknown to him, felt they ought
to give way to others with other riddles to propound. The
result was that he had soon run the whole gauntlet of introductions, and found himself at a little table in the dining
room, voraciously consuming cocktails and foie gras, and
surrounded at last by familiar faces—as though he had
swum through a bright tossing sea to a shore where old
friends awaited him. Frenside was there, gruffly smoking
and sipping, Eric Rauch, glossy and vivid in evening
clothes, and Mrs. Spear, white-haired and affectionately
wistful, murmuring: "How wonderful, Vance! To think the
Willows should have led to this . . ." while Halo, flitting
by, paused to introduce a new arrival, or to say, with a hand
on his shoulder: "How does it feel to be It?"

Best of all was it, when everyone had gone but a few
familiars, to draw up to the library fire, replenished with
crackling logs, and listen to Tarrant and Rauch discussing
the future of the *New Hour*, Frenside dropping his comments into the rifts of the talk, and Mrs. Spear saying, from
the drowsy depths of her armchair: "But you simply mustn't
do what they tell you, Vance—you must just drop *everything* and give yourself up to your novel. What's it to be
called? *Loot*—ah, there's a whole panorama in that! Lewis,
you must really give him his head; you mustn't tie him
down to dates. Let him have all the time he wants. Remember, the Spirit bloweth where it listeth . . . and genius *is*
the Spirit, isn't it, Frenside?"

It was past one in the morning when Vance sprang to
his feet in comic anguish. "Oh, say, what about my last train
home?" They all laughed, and Tarrant said, glancing at his
watch: "No hurry, my boy—it left an hour ago, and there's
no other till six-thirty," whereat the group about the fire

vanished from Vance's eyes, displaced by Laura Lou's white
face peering through her window into the icy darkness. . . .
"What a place to live in, anyhow!" he thought, exasperated
at being thus forced back into reality; and when the party
finally broke up he accepted Eric Rauch's invitation to go on
with him to "The Loafers' Club," an all-night affair where
they could talk and drink till the dismal hour when the first
train started for Paul's Landing. After all, it wasn't Vance's
fault if he had to live in the wilderness, and the minute he'd
cleared off that Hayes debt he was going to bring Laura
Lou back to New York, where there were people a fellow
could talk to, and who understood what he was trying for.
It filled him with sudden despair to think that of all he had
heard and said that evening not a syllable would mean anything to his wife.

⊰ XXV ⊱

AT THE "Loafers'" Vance had felt the relief of a familiar atmosphere. In the low-ceilinged noisy room he found several of the fellows to whom Rauch had introduced him at the Cocoanut Tree, and with them the sculptress girl, Rebecca Stram, in a dirty yellow sweater and a cloud of smoke. They all hailed him joyfully, the Stram girl besought him anew to sit for his bust, and the talk rambled on, much as it did in his father's office at Euphoria on idle winter afternoons, go as you please, leaning back with your feet up and developing what you had in your mind while the others smoked and swung their legs and listened: all as easy and intelligible as could be.

Yet that was not the impression that lasted. What Vance carried back to Paul's Landing was his bewildering adventure at the Tarrants', where everybody talked and nobody listened, or said anything particularly worth hearing, if you thought it over—but where the look of the rooms and the people had something harmonious and long-related, suggesting a mysterious intelligence between persons and things, an atmosphere as heavy with the Past as that of the library at the Willows.

Vance couldn't, for the moment, define it more clearly; but it was something impossible to shake off, close and haunting as a scent or a cadence, like the perfume in Mrs. Pulsifer's clothes, or her curious unfinished ejaculations. It made him want to lie and stare at the sky and dream, or else start up and write poetry; not a big sweeping thing, such as he had dreamed of by the winter ocean, but the wistful fragments that used to chant in his brain during his solitary sessions at the Willows. Yes . . . poetry: that was what was stirring and murmuring in him again.

When these impulses came they were overmastering. As he walked through the still-torpid town and out to Mrs. Tracy's, lines and images rose in his glowing mind like sea gods out of a summer sea. He had forgotten where he was, or to whom he was returning. The morning was gray and cold, and when he got out of the town he started on a run, and reached the house out of breath. At the door he was met by Laura Lou, wide-eyed and trembling a little, but forcing a smile of welcome. "Oh, Vanny—" He caught her to him, and cried out: "Give me some coffee quick, darling, and fix it up so I won't be bothered for the rest of the day, can't you? I've got to write a poem straight off . . . a long one . . . before the light fades."

"Light fades? Why, it's early morning," she rejoined with bewildered eyes.

"Yes, but not that light," he said, loosening her arms and smiling at her as if she were a remote memory, and not a sentient creature on his breast.

Mrs. Tracy emerged from the kitchen. "I'll get your coffee for you. I guess you'll need it, after one of your nights," she said severely. "Laura Lou, you better go straight up now and try and get a little sleep," she added in the same tone to her daughter.

They had not understood; they would never understand, these women. Mrs. Tracy, he was sure, was recalling that other night, his night of dissipation with Upton after the ball game; and Laura Lou perhaps had the same suspicion, though she would never own to it. And he knew he could never make either of them understand that what he was drunk with now was poetry. . . . Mrs. Tracy brought his coffee into the dining room (piping hot, he had to admit); then she poked up the fire, and left him at his writing table. His head dropped between his hands, and he murmured to himself: "Gold upon gold, like trumpets in the sunrise. . . ." It had sounded glorious as he crooned it over, drowsing in the train; but now he was not so sure. . . . When Mrs. Tracy, four hours later, came in to set the table for the midday dinner he started up out of a deep sleep on the springless divan. "No—she's more beautiful than that. . . ." he stammered; and his mother-in-law admonished him, as she set down the plates: "Well, I guess you better not say anything more about that; and I'll hold my tongue if you do."

Vance stared and pushed back his rumpled hair. "It was somebody—in a poem. . . ." he said; and Mrs. Tracy responded with her mirthless laugh: "That what they call it in New York? I guess you better go up and get washed now," she added; and looking at the blank sheets scattered over his desk, Vance saw that he must have fallen asleep directly after she had left him, without writing a line of his poem.

He had no difficulty in reassuring Laura Lou. She saw that, as one of the staff of the *New Hour*, he had to be present at the Tarrants' party; he even coaxed a laugh from her about his having missed his train. She wanted to know where he had gone after leaving the Tarrants', and whether he wasn't worn out, waiting around so long in the station; and he said evasively, no, he hadn't minded, feeling that the mention of the "Loafers'" would only unsettle her again. His own mind was unsettled enough. He was tormented with the poem he wanted to write, and exasperated at the thought of being chained up to his next monthly article (they had to be ready a month ahead), and then to a short story, and eventually to a novel, none of which, at the moment, he felt the least desire to write. How could he ever have been fool enough to run his head into such a noose? He remembered Frenside's warning, and cursed himself for not having heeded it. What he earned at the *New Hour* (supposing he were able to fulfill his contract) wasn't enough to keep him and his wife, if ever they had to leave Paul's Landing—and to leave Paul's Landing had become his overmastering desire. He wanted, worse than ever, to be back in New York, back among all those fellows he could talk to. He wanted to be able to spend an evening at the Tarrants'—or at the "Loafers'," for that matter—without being confronted at dawn by two haggard women who thought themselves magnanimous because they didn't cross-examine him like a truant schoolboy. He wanted to see whom he pleased, go where he chose, write what he wanted —be free, free, free, in body as well as mind, yes, and in heart as well as soul. That was the worst of it: if life went on like this much longer his love for Laura Lou would fade to a pitying fondness, and then there would be no meaning in anything.

The afternoon trailed on. Vance could not write; the poem had vanished like a puff of mist. He sat staring at the paper, and smoking one cigarette after another. Suddenly he remembered that he had promised, that very afternoon, to call on Mrs. Pulsifer and on Tristram Fynes. And here he sat in Mrs. Tracy's dining room, looking out on her frozen garden patch and the cold purple of the hills, and doing nothing and seeing no light ahead. Toward dusk he was seized with the impulse to sprint down to the station, jump into the first train for New York, and pay his two visits. Then he remembered that city people were always full of engagements, and could not be found without an appointment—or might be annoyed if a fellow barged in when he wasn't expected. Besides, he didn't particularly want to see either Fynes or the Pulsifer woman—what he really wanted was to breathe the atmosphere they breathed. But that was another difference that Laura Lou would never understand. . . .

The next morning was his regular day at the office. But an obscure reluctance kept him from going back to New York. When he got there Eric Rauch would ask him for his next article, of which he hadn't written the first line, the subject of which he hadn't yet chosen. And Tarrant would call him in to his sanctum, and want to know if they couldn't announce the title of his next short story while "Unclaimed" was fresh in people's minds. And he hadn't even settled on a subject for his story either—there were so many to choose from, and none that he felt ready to tackle. Poetry . . . poetry was what he was full of now. . . .

He got up early from Laura Lou's side, flung open the window, and leaned out quaffing the wintry gold and scarlet of the sunrise. The sky looked immeasurably far-off, pure and cold above the hills; but against their edge the gold and scarlet bubbled up in plumy clouds like the down from a fabulous bird's breast. What had the city to give compared with that? Vance recalled the summer sunrise seen from Thundertop with Halo Spear. Then he had stood so high that he had seen the new day flood the earth below him in all its folds and depths and dimmest penetralia; and beauty had brimmed his soul with the same splendour. But now he could only look out through the narrow opening of a cottage window to a patch of currant bushes and a squat range of hills behind which the sun seemed imprisoned—as he himself was imprisoned by fate. Fate? Nonsense—by his own headlong folly. Only, when the sirens sang, could a fellow help listening? And how could he distinguish between the eternal beauty and its false images, the brief creatures it lit up in passing? Something whispered: "Create the eternal beauty yourself—then you'll know . . ." and he shut the

window and turned back into the low-ceilinged room where
his life belonged.

But life was not always such a baffled business. The
second night after Vance's return there was a belated snow-
fall, and the next morning when he opened the shutters he
looked out on a world of white ablaze under a spring sun. It
was a Saturday, thank heaven, and there could be no question of going to the office. For forty-eight hours he and
Laura Lou could range as they willed through this new
world. The winter, so far, had been harsh but almost snow-
less; now, in early March, with the smell of buds in the air,
Vance was seeing for the first time the magic of a snowstorm on the Hudson. If only they could climb to Thundertop! Was it possible, he wondered? The snow was not so
deep, after all; it would be melting soon, under such a sun.
What did Laura Lou think? She thought as he did: anything that seemed possible to him always seemed so to her.
She had never before regarded a snowstorm as something to
be admired, but merely as an opportunity for fun; staying
away from school, sleighing, snowballing, and coasting. But
now that he pointed out its beauties he could see she was
ashamed of having looked upon them as created for her
own amusement—as if she had stripped the hangings from
a sanctuary to dress herself up in. Vance was touched by her
compliance, her passionate eagerness to see what he saw,
hear what he heard—and then, in spite of himself, irritated
by her inability to be more than his echo. But today the
glory was so searching and miraculous that he was sure she
must feel it. "Come, wrap up warm and we'll take some hot
coffee and sandwiches, and see how high we can scramble
up the mountain." Mrs. Tracy had gone off to spend a night
with Upton, and they had the freedom of the little house,
and felt like lovers honeymooning again. Laura Lou filled
the thermos with boiling coffee, made some sandwiches

with the cold meat Mrs. Tracy had left for dinner, and got into her rubber boots and her thickest coat. Vance wanted to hire their neighbour's cutter; but Laura Lou was frightened lest her mother should hear of this extravagance, so they set out on foot, laughing and swinging their joined hands like schoolchildren. The snow was soft—too soft for easy walking. But Vance's feet were winged, as they had been when he first saw the sea; and Laura Lou sprang on after him, exulting and admiring. "Oh, Vanny—do look! Isn't it just like powdered sugar? Or one of those lovely Christmas cards with the stuff that sparkles?" Luckily he hardly heard her, saw only the radiant oval of her face under the shaggy knitted cap pulled down over crimson eartips.

The snow clung downy to the hemlocks, rolled blinding white over meadow and pasture, gloomed indigo blue on the edges of the forest, flashed with prismatic lights where a half-caught brook fringed it with icicles. And bordering the lane, as they climbed, how each shoot of bracken, each bramble and dry branch glittered and quivered with white fire! How the blue air, purified by all the whiteness, soared over them on invisible wings! How the far-off sky curved a clear dome above an earth with all its sins and uglinesses blotted out, an earth renewed, redeemed in some great final absolution!

A man passed in a sleigh and offered them a lift. He was going to a farm up Thundertop way; and presently they were gliding by the gateposts of Eaglewood, and Vance remembered how he had passed them for the first time with Miss Spear, motoring up the mountain in the summer dawn. The sight of the padlocked gates, the snow-choked drive, the hemlocks trailing white branches with sapphire shadows, swept him back into that world to which Halo Spear had given him the key: the world of beauty, poetry, knowledge, of all the marvels now forever shut off from him. He was glad when they mounted higher, and the man, turning in at a farmyard, left them to scramble on alone. . . . "Better make the most of it—there'll be a thaw by night!" he called back, his runners cutting black grooves in the whiteness.

They climbed on, laughing and chattering. It was so good to look at Laura Lou, and feel her warm hand in his, that Vance, as was his way when he was enjoying anything she could share, glowed with a sense of well-being. At length their ascent brought them to a deserted shed standing on a sunny ledge by the roadside. There was some hay on its dry floor, and in this shelter they unpacked their lunch, and comforted themselves with hot coffee. Laura Lou, curling up against the hay in the warmest corner, tossed off her cap, and Vance, stretched out at her feet, watched the sun turn her hair to golden filigree, and her lips to jewels. "Happy?" he queried; and her eyes rained down acquiescence. . . .

He had never spoken to her of Bunty Hayes' visit; she had never spoken to him of the letter he had picked up and read. She had doubtless answered it, or in some way made the truth known to Hayes; that was probably the cause of the scene in the office. . . . Vance, as he looked up at her, was obscurely troubled by the thought that behind that low round forehead with its straying curls there lurked a whole hidden world. This little creature, who seemed as transparent as a crystal cup (his little cup, he had once called her) —this Laura Lou, like all her kind, was a painted veil over the unknown. And to her no doubt he was the same; and she knew infinitely less of him than he of her, if only because there was so much more to know. As he lay and brooded on these mysteries he wondered if this were not the moment to speak. He was not in the least sorry for what they had done to Bunty Hayes. In that respect neither Vance nor Laura Lou had been at fault; the pressure of des-

tiny had been too strong for them. But the way they had
treated him since was not pleasant to remember. Vance had
never been able to get that poor love letter out of his head;
and he wanted to find out if Laura Lou remembered it too.
If he could have been sure that her silence was due to the
same feeling as his, and not to some mean instinct of con-
cealment, it would have drawn them so much closer. . . .
But as he continued to lie there and to drink her drowsy
smile, he felt in himself the same reluctance that he suspected in her . . . a reluctance to mar the perfect hour.
Why not suffer the episode to bury itself? There were things
in the lives of the most decent people that left raw edges,
that gave you the feeling you had when you'd abandoned a
wounded bird in a thicket. . . .

"Come along!" Vance cried, jumping up. "I'd like to get
to the next ridge, wouldn't you? We'd see all the world from
there. . . . Let's try." And she sprang to her feet echoing
joyfully: "Yes—let's!"

After that the day seemed to rush by on silver wings.
Such sparkling tumultuous hours, sunlit, shadow-flecked,
whirling past like the spray of racing waves. . . . Vance
could hardly believe it when the twilight shut in without a
warning, the twilight with its bleak shadows and the death-
like pallor of unlit snow. . . .

Not till then did it occur to him that Laura Lou must
be dreadfully tired. He ought to have thought of it before.
He was dismayed to see how high they had climbed; but as
they set out on the long descent her gay voice kept on assur-
ing him that, no, she was feeling first-rate, that she'd loved
every minute of it, she had, really . . . and, oh, Vanny,
look, there was the new moon: did he see it? Like a dia-
mond brooch, up in the branches there—and over their
right shoulders too! What luck! . . . Her tone reassured
him, and he laughed and kissed her, slipping his arm about

her to help her down the endless windings. It was dark
night when they reached the cottage, cold and hungry.
Vance fumbled under the mat for the key and pushed her
into the passage. How black the inside of the house was,
and how cold! It had been fun, having the place all to themselves that morning; but now even Mrs. Tracy's dry disapproval would have been bearable, for the sake of a fire and
supper.

Vance struck a match and reached for the hall lamp. As
he turned back after lighting it he saw on the floor a telegram which had been thrust under the door in their absence. Laura Lou bent to pick it up. "I guess it's from
Mother, to say what train she'll be back by." She opened the
telegram, and stood looking at it with a puzzled frown.
Then she read aloud: " 'Dreadfully upset not seeing you
yesterday what happened waited till nine must see you
count on you same hour Monday. Please telegraph. Jet.'
What a funny name!" she commented.

Vance put his hand out hastily. "Say—I guess that's
mine."

"Who's it from?"

"Oh, just somebody I had an appointment with. I guess
I forgot." She looked relieved, and he added: "Say—it's
colder than blazes. I guess I forgot to make up the fire too,
before we went out." He laughed at his own joke as he drew
her into the kitchen. "There—you sit down and I'll fix things
up in no time."

He pushed her into Mrs. Tracy's rocking chair, lit the
lamp, raked out the stove, shook in coal and kindlings, and
rummaged for milk, while she leaned back and watched
him with dusky burning eyes. She looked little and frail in
the faint light, and the returning heat brought out on her
cheekbones those scarlet spots which made the hollows underneath so wan. Why was it that whenever she and Vance
attempted to do anything jolly together she got tired? That

she seemed fated never to keep step with him? He poured out the milk and brought it to her. "Here—swallow this down quick. The matter with you is, you're hungry," he tried to jolly her; but she shook her head, and the smile on her gaunt little face turned into a grimace of weariness. "I guess I'm just tired—" Always the same wistful refrain! "She's sick," Vance thought with sudden terror. Aloud he said: "Wait till I heat the milk up; then maybe it'll tempt you." He thought with a shiver of the cold bed upstairs, their fireless room, the time it would take to warm the house —and where on earth could he find a brick to heat and put at her feet when he got her undressed? He warmed the milk, pressed it to her lips again—but she pushed it away with feverish hands, and the eyes she lifted were dark with a sort of animal fright. "Vanny—I'm so tired. Darling, carry me upstairs!" She wound her arms about his neck, and her cheek burned on his. . . . Halfway up she clutched him closer, and he felt her whisper in his ear. "It wasn't a woman who telegraphed you, Vanny?" "Woman? Hell no! The idea!" he lied back, stumbling up the steps, pressing her tight, and shrinking from the touch of her tears. . . .

He had had the vision of a big poem up there on the mountain—yes, he knew it was big. Line after line had sprung up like great snow eagles challenging the sun, soaring in inaccessible glory: he had only to lie back and wait, and one by one they planed down and shut their wings in his breast. And now, stumbling up the stairs in the darkness with this poor child, getting her undressed, trying to find something warm to wrap her feet in, wondering why her eyes were so fixed, her cheeks so scarlet, wondering how you felt a pulse, how you knew if anybody had fever . . . all the while, with another sense, he watched the crystal splinters of his poem melt away one after another, as the spring icicles were melting from the roof.

≈ XXVI ≈

MRS. TRACY was not expected back till the following evening, and for twenty-four hours Vance struggled alone against the dark mystery of illness. As he watched through the night beside Laura Lou, watched her burning face and hollow eyes, and sought to quiet her tossings and soothe her incessant cough, he tried to recall what had been done for him during his own illness. He too had been consumed with fever day and night, week after week; and his mother and sisters had been always there, with cooling drinks, soft touches, ingenious ways of easing his misery—and here he sat by his wife, his hands all thumbs, his shoes creaking, his brain in a fog, unable to imagine what he ought to do for her.

At one moment her eyes, which had clung to his so anxiously, always asking for something he could not guess, suddenly became the eyes of a stranger. She looked at him in terror, and sitting up thrust him back. "Oh, go away—go away! You shan't take Vanny from me . . . I say you shan't!" For a while she rambled on, battling against the obduracy of some invisible presence; then she sank back, and tears of weakness forced their way through the lids she had shut against her husband . . . Vance threw himself down by her and held her in beseeching arms. "Laura Lou . . . Laura Lou . . . Vanny's here; love, it's Vanny holding you. . . ." With passionate murmurs he smoothed the hair from her forehead, and gradually her contracted face relaxed, and she opened her lids, and tried to smile. "Is it you, Vanny? Don't go . . . you'll never leave me any more, will you?" . . . She dozed off on his shoulder for a few minutes before the cough woke her again. . . .

When morning came she refused to touch the milk he had warmed, and lay tossing and coughing in parched misery. What was it? Bronchitis? His heart sank: what was it people did for bronchitis? There was no telephone, and no nearby neighbour except an old deaf woman who would probably not be of much use—even if Vance could absent himself long enough to summon her. He decided to run across to the deaf woman's house, and bribe her grandson, a lazy fellow who was not on good terms with Mrs. Tracy, to bicycle to Paul's Landing for a doctor; but whenever he tried to creep out of the room his shoes creaked or a board cried, and Laura Lou started up. "Don't leave me, Vanny— you mustn't leave me . . ." and the heavy hours dragged on . . . Vance rummaged out an old bottle of cough mixture, and gave her some; but it did not relieve her, and the hands she wound about his neck grew drier and more burning. It was as if the fever were visibly consuming her, so small and shrunken had her restless body become. As he sat there and watched it was her turn to become a stranger: this haggard changeling was not the tender creature whom he loved. This discovery of the frail limits of personality, of the transformation of what seemed closest and most fixed in the flux of life, dragged his brain down into a labyrinth of conjecture. What was she, this being so beloved and so unknown? Something in her craved for him and clung to him, yet when he tried to reach that something it was not there. Unknown forces possessed her, she was wandering in ways he could not follow. . . . Now and then he got up and replenished the stove; now and then he wet a handkerchief with cologne water and put it on her forehead, or clumsily shook up her pillows. . . . But he did it all automatically, as if he

too were elsewhere, in ways as lonely as those she walked.
. . . Was this why we were all so fundamentally alone? Because, as each might blend with another in blissful fusion,
so, at any moment, the empty eyes of a stranger might meet
us under familiar brows? But then, where was the real pri-
mordial personality, each man's indestructible inmost self?
Where did it hide, what was it made of, what laws controlled it? What *was* the Vance Weston who must remain
himself though sickness and sorrow and ruin destroyed the
familiar surface of his being? Or was there no such unchangeable nucleus? Would he and Laura Lou and all their
kind flow back finally into that vast impersonal Divinity
which had loomed in his boyish dreams? . . . But, oh,
those little hands with twining fingers, the deep-lashed eyes,
the hollows under the cheekbones—those were Laura Lou's
and no other's, they belonged to the body he worshipped,
whose lovely secrets were his. . . .

He started up with blinking eyes. The room was dark—
the fire out. Had he fallen asleep in trying to soothe his wife
to rest? He became dimly conscious of someone's having
come in; someone who groped about, struck a match, and
held a candle in his face. "For God's sake, Vance! Why are
you here in the dark? What's happened to my child?" Mrs.
Tracy cried; and Vance, stumbling to his feet, brushed back
his hair and stared at her.

But she had no time to deal with him. In a trice she had
lit the lamp, revived the fire, thrust a thermometer between
Laura Lou's lips, and piled more blankets on her. "What is
she taking? What does the doctor say?" she whispered over
her shoulder.

"She hasn't seen the doctor."

"Not seen him? You mean he hasn't been?"

"No."

"How long's she been like this?"

"Since last night."

"Last night? And she's seen no doctor? When did you go for him?" She drew closer, deserting her daughter to approach her fierce whisper to his ear.

"I didn't go. She wouldn't let me leave her. . . ."

The withering twitch of Mrs. Tracy's lips simulated a laugh. "I guess it'd be luckier for her if you'd leave her and never come back. And now," she added scornfully, "go and get the doctor as quick as you can; and don't show yourself here without him. It's pneumonia. . . ."

Five anxious days passed before Vance could think of his writing or of the office. Mrs. Tracy had given him to understand that he'd better go back to work, for all the use he was to her or Laura Lou: cluttering up the house, and no more help to anybody than a wooden Indian. . . . But it seemed part of his expiation to sit there and let her say such things. He suspected that, though she railed at him for being in the way, it was a relief to have him there, to be scolded and found fault with; besides, now and then there was something for him to do: coals to carry up, provisions or medicines to fetch, tasks not requiring much quickness of wit or hand. . . . He knew that Mrs. Tracy was justified in blaming him for Laura Lou's illness. The doctor said he had been crazy to drag her up the mountain through the snow, and expose her to the night air when her strength was lowered by fatigue. She hadn't much stamina anyway; and the long climb had affected her heart. The doctor took Vance aside to tell him that this sort of thing mustn't happen again; and Vance saw Mrs. Tracy gloating over the admonishment. Well, let her . . . he deserved it.

During those days it seemed to him that he had at last grown from a boy into a man. He was not quick in practical matters; such lessons came to him slowly; but this one sank deep. He was frightened to think how completely, when

Beauty called, that celestial Beauty which haunted earth and sky, and the deeps of his soul, he forgot everything else, and rushed after the voice unheeding. When that happened, his two worlds were merged in one, or rather the world of daily duties vanished under a more overwhelming reality. But this would no longer be so. He would school himself to keep the two apart. . . .

At length, when Laura Lou, propped against her pillows, first looked at him with reassured eyes, he decided to go to New York. He arrived empty-handed at the office, for he had not been able to write a line in the interval. He hoped to see Eric Rauch first and explain to him; but Rauch was out, and Vance was told that Mr. Tarrant was expecting him. Rauch was pliant and understanding; but his chief, to Vance, was a riddle. You could never tell if he was going to turn his nervous brilliant smile on you or meet you with a face of stone. He greeted Vance with a surprise in which the latter scented irony, and when told of Laura Lou's illness uttered the proper sentiments and at once jerked back to business. "Too bad . . . too bad . . . yes, of course. . . . My wife would have been glad to do anything . . . Well, now the anxiety's over I hope you'll take hold again. So much time's been lost that you really owe it to us . . ." and so on. Vance listened in silence. What could he say? At length he began: "You wouldn't care to have me change 'round and write some poetry for you?" Tarrant's face expressed a mixture of dismay and resentment. Poetry? Good God, everybody wanted to write poetry for them: magazine poetry was the easiest thing on earth to turn out. And here was a fellow who could do something else; who had a real gift as a short-story writer; as a novelist, perhaps—and wanting to throw away a chance like that to join the anonymous crowd in the Poets' Corner! Really, now, didn't Weston understand? He was bound to them; bound to do a certain thing; had signed a contract to that effect. Contracts weren't one-sided affairs, after all. . . . Tarrant's frown relaxed, and he laid his hand on his contributor's shoulder. "See here; you've had a bad shake-up. It's liable to happen to any of us. Only, once a fellow's formed the habit of work he keeps straight at it . . . through everything. . . ." Tarrant straightened his shoulders, as though discreetly offering himself as an object lesson. "Now then, Weston, better get back home as quick as you can, and tie up to your next short story. If "Unclaimed" doesn't pull off the Pulsifer Prize, who knows but you've got something up your sleeve that will? I understand that Fynes asked you for an article on *The Corner Grocery*. The sale of his book has fallen off lately, and he counts on us to buck it up. If you'd made a hit with the article it would have given you a big boost for the prize. But I've had to turn Rauch onto it because there was no time to wait. So you can put that out of your mind anyhow, and just tackle your story," Tarrant ended on a note of affability.

"All right," Vance mumbled, glad to be gone.

He had a couple of hours to spare before his train, and began to wander through the streets, as he had during his first dark days in New York. Then he had been unknown and starving; now he had a name, had friends, a roof over his head, and a wife who adored him; yet his inner solitude was deeper than ever. Was the fault his, or was it latent in this dreadful system of forcing talent, trying to squeeze every drop out of it before it was ripe; the principle of the quick turnover applied to brains as it was to real estate? As he walked, the old dream of the New York novel recurred to him: the jostling crowds, the swarm of motors, the huge arrogant masses of masonry, roused his imagination, and he thought to himself: "Tarrant's right; what a fool I was to talk poetry to him!" He stood on a corner of Fifth Avenue while the motors crawled up and down in endless procession, and looking into one slowly moving carriage after another he wondered what sort of a life each of these women (they were almost all women) led, where they were going, what they were thinking of, what other lives were interwoven with theirs. Oh, to have a year to dream of it all, without putting pen to paper! But even a year would not be enough; what he needed was to immerse himself in life without so much as remembering that it must some day bring him in a return, to live as carelessly as all these women rolling past him in their motors. . . .

Mrs. Pulsifer—she was that kind, he supposed. The thought reminded him of her telegram. He hadn't answered it because he hadn't known what to say. But now that he was in town, why not try to see her? Funny woman—she'd signed the wire "Jet," as if he and she were old friends! Lucky she had such a queer name; if she'd been called Mabel, or any real woman's name, he'd never have heard the end of it from Laura Lou. . . . He remembered her address: she lived only a few streets off, he had plenty of time to call before catching his train. She'd be out, probably; but then he could write and say he'd been. . . . He reached the street and identified the number as that of an impressive wide-fronted house, the kind he had often curiously gazed at in wandering about the city, but never imagined himself entering. He rang the bell, and instantly, as if he had been expected, the heavy double door of glass and wrought iron flew open, and a tall young man in a dark coat with silver buttons barred the threshold.

Mrs. Pulsifer? No—she wasn't in, the young man said in surprise, as if Vance had asked something almost too ridiculous to be worth answering. But as he spoke, at the far end of a perspective of marble and dusky rugs and majestic stairway Vance saw a figure flit forward and hesitate. "Oh, Mr. Weston—it *is* Mr. Weston? Why, I *am* out, really . . . I'm due at the other end of nowhere at this very instant. . . ." Mrs. Pulsifer stood before him, wrapped in furs, her long jade earrings making her face narrower and more anxious than ever under the swathings of her close little hat. "But do come in all the same—just for a minute, won't you?" Her tone was half aggrieved, half entreating, she seemed to want him to say yes, yet not to forget that she had just cause for resentment.

Vance was looking curiously about him; at that moment the house interested him more than its owner. "We'll go upstairs—you really don't mind walking?" she queried, implying that of course there was a lift if he did; and he followed her across the many-coloured paving of the hall, up the wide staircase with its ornate rail of steel and gilding, across another hall and through a great room with shadowy hangings full of figures and trees and colonnaded architecture. Vance had never been in a house so big and splendid, never even imagined one. From the room of the tapestries they passed to another, all in dark wood, with pictures on the panels, and great gilt standards bearing lights; and finally came to a small circular apartment where there were forced flowers in porcelain bowls, more pictures, books, and low wide armchairs covered with dove-coloured silk. Vance gazed at it all, enchanted. "Do you live here all alone?" he asked.

She looked at him in surprise. "Do I—? Why, of course, yes. How funny of you! What did you think—?"

"I thought maybe the house was divided up into apartments, it's so big."

"Well, it might be," she admitted, sighing. "Sometimes I wish it were. It's horribly lonely, having it all to myself." She sighed again. "I *hate* big houses, don't you?"

His captivated eyes were still scanning the long vista of rooms. "No; I think they're great—when they're like this . . . all the space and the height and the quietness. . . ."

She gave a little conscious laugh and instantly adopted his view. "Oh, you like it? I'm so glad; because, you see, these big rooms were really rather my doing. I insisted on the architect's carrying out my own ideas—giving me all the elbowroom I wanted. They have so little imagination." The tall young man with the silver buttons presented himself, as if noiselessly summoned, and she dropped her furs on his arm, said: "Yes—tea, I think; and I'm at home to no one," tossed off her hat, and sank into one of the dove-coloured chairs. The tall young man closed the door behind him, and shut Vance and his hostess into flower-scented privacy. Mrs. Pulsifer turned her anxious eyes on her visitor. "I suppose you were horrified at my telegraphing?"

"Horrified; no, why?"

"I was afraid you thought I oughtn't to ask you to come here at all, because of that wretched prize; that you were afraid of what people might think. . . . But I really wanted most desperately to see you about Fynes. You see, practically he has the casting vote; the others just cringe to him. And I knew he'd told you to come and see him about an article or something, and was very huffy because you didn't; and I wanted to warn you, and to beg you to do whatever he asks. And when you didn't answer and didn't come I was perfectly miserable. . . . I know I'm a goose, I know what you'll think. . . . But I can't help it; I do so want you to get the prize," she said, suddenly leaning forward and laying her hand on his.

Her touch startled him, for he was still absorbed in contemplation of the room. "Oh, that's ever so kind of you," he stammered, feeling he ought to take her hand; but it had already slipped from him, and she had drawn back with one of her uncertain movements. "It's all wrong, I know," she insisted. "I oughtn't to care about it, I oughtn't to have any opinion; you'd think ever so much better of me if I stood aloof and let the committee decide." For a moment a wistful smile gave her thin face the contour of youth. "But the first moment I saw you I felt . . ." She stood up, moving away with her long step. "Should you like to see the rooms? Do you care for pictures?"

Yes, Vance said, he'd like first-rate to look round. He explained eagerly that he'd seen hardly any pictures, and wanted to get hold of some good books on the history of painting . . . maybe she could lend him some? But he was checked by the perception that Mrs. Pulsifer was no longer listening, and that this was not the sort of thing she wanted to hear. He was dimly aware that he had missed his chance, that had he imprisoned her hand the prize would have been his. "Rauch would never have let her go," he thought, half amused. But she was too unlike the other women with whom he had exchanged easy caresses. She seemed blood-less, immaterial, as if she were a part of her splendid and unfamiliar setting, and might at any moment recede into one of the great gilt frames at which he stood gazing. She poured out a glib patter about the pictures, *her* pictures; her Constable, *her* Rembrandt, *her* Ver Meer, other names he didn't catch in his excitement; and then led him to another room to show him her "moderns," bewildering things with unknown names, but all alluded to in the same proprietary tone, as if the artists, whoever they were, had worked, like her architect, only for her and under her direction. Some painters, not represented on her walls, she spoke of with contempt, said she wouldn't have them at any price though other people fought for them—she was determined to be herself, to be independent, no matter how hard people tried to influence her. Didn't he think she was right, she chal-lenged him? Her nervous chatter disturbed his enjoyment of the pictures, and prevented the isolation of soul in which great impressions reached him. What a pity, he thought! His heart was beating and murmuring with new harmonies; but perhaps another day, when he got to know her better, and they felt more at ease with each other, he could ask her to let him come back. And he thought how different it would have been if the woman at his side had been Halo Tarrant, who always made him see beautiful things more clearly instead of blurring them.

"Ah—here's tea. But you'd rather have a cocktail?" Mrs. Pulsifer said. They had returned to the circular room; by the fire stood a table with cups of thin porcelain around a shining urn. Vance said he'd rather have tea. No one had ever offered it to him at that hour, and it amused him to watch her slim hands moving over the tray, shaking the tea into the teapot, regulating the flame of the urn. It reminded him of a scene in an English novel he had read at the Willows. He began to think of his own novel again, and had to rouse himself to hear what Mrs. Pulsifer was saying—something hurried and confused about being lonely, and hating her riches because they shut her off from the only people she cared to see . . . and worshipping genius, and wondering if he wouldn't promise to be her great great friend, and come often to see her, and tell her all her faults, and let her talk to him about herself—which, it seemed to Vance, was just what she had been doing for the last hour. . . . He mumbled that he was ever so grateful, and would be glad if she'd let him come back for another look at the pictures; but she said if it was only to see the pictures that he wanted to come he was like everybody else, and didn't care for her but for her house, and what she wanted was a friend who would feel the same about her if she lived in a hovel; but she supposed she wasn't clever enough to interest the only kind of people who interested her, and must just make the best of this dreadful loneliness that her money seemed to condemn her to. . . . Her eyes filled, and for a moment she seemed to break her unreality and become human. "Oh, don't say that—you mustn't, you know—" he began, putting down his cup and moving nearer; but as he did so he caught sight of a clock over her shoulder, and exclaimed: "God, I've only just got time to catch my train—Sorry . . . I've got to run for it. . . ." Her face changed again, narrowing into distrust and resentment. Why did he have to catch that particular train? Weren't there plenty of others? She forced a smile to add that people always made excuses like that when they were bored with you, and she supposed she'd bored him . . . or else why wouldn't he stay? But Vance remembered a promise to get back with a new tonic for Laura Lou. No, he couldn't, he said; there was no train till much later, and he had his work. . . . "Ah, your work; how I envy people with work, work like yours, I mean. . . ." Her face softened, she left her hand in his. "You'll really come again soon, won't you? You'll come next week? You shall have the pictures all to yourself; I'll hide away, and you won't even see me," she assured him laughingly; and he thanked her and fled.

By the time he reached Paul's Landing the whole episode had faded into unreality. Were there houses like that, women like that, pictures like that? The chief impression that remained was that she had said he could come back and see the pictures. . . .

Mrs. Tracy was waiting on the threshold, and he handed her the tonic with the satisfaction he felt when he had managed not to forget an errand. How was Laura Lou? Had the day been good? Pretty good—yes; but she was a little tired. He'd better not go up: she was sleeping. He turned in to the dining room and went over to his desk, his mind full of things he wanted to put down while they were hot. But Mrs. Tracy followed, and after straightening the plates on the dinner table came and stood by the desk. "There was someone called to see you," she said.

"Someone—who?"

"Bunty Hayes."

The blood rushed to Vance's forehead. Hayes—the cheek of the fellow's having followed him here! "I'll have to fight it out with him after all," he thought.

"He's been after me already, at the office. He says he wants to fight me."

Mrs. Tracy smiled coldly. "He didn't want to fight you today. What he wanted was his money."

Vance's anger exploded. "His money? I'm doing all I can to earn it for him. If I could do it quicker I would."

"That's what I told him," she agreed, still coldly.

"Well, did he go away after that?"

Mrs. Tracy hesitated, and wiped her wasted hands on her apron. "Not right off."

"Why—what else did he want?"

"To see Laura Lou."

"Laura Lou? The fellow's impudence!" Vance laughed indignantly.

"He wasn't impudent. He was sorry she was so sick. I could see how bad he felt."

Vance found nothing to say. The remembrance of the crumpled letter on the floor of his wife's room shot through him with the same pang as before.

"Well, I've got to get to work," he said.

❧ XXVII ❧

LAURA LOU's convalescence was slow, her illness expensive. Upton, appealed to by Mrs. Tracy, said all his savings had gone into buying a Ford, and he could do nothing for them for the present. Vance knew that his mother-in-law expected his family to come to his aid. She ascribed Laura Lou's illness to his imprudence, and felt that, since his endless scribbling brought in so little, he ought to get help from home. But Vance could not bring himself to ask for money, and his reports of Laura Lou's illness produced only letters of sympathy from his mother and grandmother, and knitted bed jackets from the girls. His father wrote that times were bad in real estate, and offered again to try and get him a job on the *Free Speaker* if he would come back to live at Euphoria. And there the matter ended.

At odds with himself, he ground out a dull article on "The New Poetry," the result of random reading among the works of the Cocoanut Tree poets; but it satisfied neither him nor the poets. He tried to make a plan for *Loot*, but it crumbled to nothing. He was too ignorant of that tumultuous metropolitan world to picture it except through other eyes. If he could have lived in it for a while, if somebody like Mrs. Tarrant had let him into its secrets, perhaps he could have made a book of it; but anything he did unaided would have to be borrowed from other books. Besides, he did not want to denounce or to show up, as most of the "society" novelists did, but to take apart the works of the ma-

chine, and find out what all those people behind the splendid house fronts signified in the general scheme of things.
Until he understood that, he couldn't write about them. He
brought his difficulty to Eric Rauch. "Unless I can think
their thoughts it's no use," he said. Rauch looked puzzled,
and seemed to regard the difficulty as an imaginary one.
"Funny to me you can't get hold of a subject," he said; and
Vance rejoined: "Oh, but I can—hundreds; they swarm.
Only they're all subjects I don't know enough about to
tackle them." "Well, I guess you're in the doldrums," Rauch
commented; and the talk ended.

One day someone related in Vance's presence a tragic
episode which had happened in a group of strolling actors.
The picturesqueness of it seized on his imagination, and he
tried to bring it to life; but here again he lacked familiarity
with the conditions, and his ardour flagged. Fellows at the
Cocoanut Tree talked a lot about working up a subject,
about documentation and so forth; but Vance obscurely felt
that he could not go out on purpose to hunt for local colour,
and that inspiration must come to him in other ways. Perhaps a talk with a man like Tristram Fynes would given him
his clue. He wrote and asked Fynes for an appointment; but
he received no answer to his letter.

Mrs. Pulsifer did write again. She asked why he hadn't
been back to see her, and suggested his coming to dine, giving him the choice of two evenings. The letter reached him
on the day when he had taken his watch and his evening
clothes to a pawnbroker. He wrote that he couldn't come to
dine, but would call some afternoon; and she wired naming
the next day. When he presented himself he found the great
drawing rooms empty, and while he waited he wandered
from one to another, gazing and dreaming. Art had hitherto
figured in his mind as something apart from life, inapplica-
ble to its daily uses; something classified, catalogued, and
buried in museums. Here for the first time it became a
breathing presence, he saw its relation to life, and caught a

glimpse of the use of riches and leisure—advanced even to the assumption that it might be the task of one class to have these things and preserve them, to live like a priestly caste isolated for the purpose. The stuffed dove on the gilt basket, he thought, reverting again to his old symbol of the mysterious utility of the useless. . . . Mrs. Pulsifer's arrival interrupted his musings, and gave him a surprised sense of the incongruity between the treasures and their custodian.

She looked worried and excited; drew him at once into the circular sitting room, and impetuously accused him of being sorry she'd come back, because now he'd have to talk to her instead of looking at the pictures. Vance had no conversational parries; he could only have kissed her or questioned her about her possessions; the latter course he saw would be displeasing, and he felt no temptation to the former, for she had a cold, and her face, in the spring light, looked sallow and elderly. "I do like wandering about this house first-rate," he confessed.

"Well, then, why don't you come oftener? I know I'm not clever; I can't talk to you; but if you'd come and dine I'd have just a few of the right people; brilliant people—Frenside, and Lewis and Halo Tarrant, and Sibelius, from the Metropolitan, who'd tell you ever so much more than I can about my pictures." She became pathetic in her self-effacement, and when she repeated: "Why won't you come? Why do you always refuse?" he lost his head, and stammered: "I . . . no. . . . I can't—I can't dine with you."

"You mean you've got more amusing things to do?" she insinuated; and he answered: "Lord, no, not that. It's—I'm too poor," he finally blurted out.

There was a silence.

"Too poor—?" she echoed, with an uncomprehending look.

He laughed. "For one thing I've got no evening clothes. I've had to pawn them."

Mrs. Pulsifer, who was sitting near him, and leaning

forward in her solicitous way, involuntarily drew back. "Oh—" she faltered, and he divined that her embarrassment was greater than his. The discovery somehow put him at his ease.

"Oh, you don't need to look so frightened. It's a thing that happens to people," he joked. She murmured: "I'm so sorry," and her lips seemed shaping themselves for the expression of further sympathy. She leaned nearer again, and he saw she was feverishly wondering what she ought to say. Her helplessness touched him; in her place he would have known so well! She seemed a creature whose impulses of pity had become atrophied, and who was vainly trying to give him a sign of human feeling across the desert waste of her vast possessions. "I'm so sorry," she began again, in a whisper, as if her voice was unable to bridge the distance. Vance stood up and took a few steps across the room. If she *was* sorry, really—as sorry as all that. . . . He stopped in front of her, and began to speak in a low confused voice. "Fact is, I'm down and out—oh just temporarily, of course; I've had unexpected expenses. . . ." He paused, wondering desperately why he had ever begun. Mrs. Pulsifer sat before him without moving. Even her eyes were motionless, and her startled hands. He wondered if no one had ever spoken to her of such a thing as poverty. "Look here," he broke out, "if you really believe in me, will you lend me two thousand dollars?"

His question echoed through the room as if he had shouted it. A slight tremor passed over Mrs. Pulsifer's face; then her immobility became rigid. The situation clearly had no parallel in her experience, and she felt herself pitifully unequal to it. The fact exasperated Vance. It was all wrong that these people, the chosen custodians of knowledge and beauty, should be so stupid, so unfitted for their task. He hung before her irresolute, angry with himself and her. "I'd better go," he muttered at length.

She looked up, disconcerted. "Oh, no . . . please don't. I'm so sorry. . . ."

The meaningless repetition irritated him. "I don't suppose you ever before met a fellow who was dead broke, did you? I suppose that young man who opens the door has orders not to let them in," he jeered, flushed with his own humiliation.

She grew pale, and her hands moved uneasily. "I—oh, you don't understand; you don't. I try to . . . to live up to my responsibilities. . . . These things . . . I have advisers . . . a most efficient staff who deal with them. . . . Every case is—is conscientiously investigated." She seemed to be quoting a social service report.

"Oh, I'm not a case," Vance interrupted drily. "I thought you acted as if you wanted me for a friend—that's all."

"I did—I do. I only mean. . . ." She lifted horrified eyes to his. "You see, there's the prize. . . . If anyone knew that . . . that you'd come to me for assistance . . . that I. . . ."

"Oh, damn the prize! Excuse me; I'm sorry for my blunder. There are times when a man sees a big ditch in front of him and doesn't know how he's going to get across. I'm that man—and I spoke without thinking."

Her eyes, still on his, grew moist with tears. "It's so dreadful—your being in such trouble. I had no idea. . . ." She glanced about her, almost furtively, as if the efficient staff who dealt with her "cases" might be listening behind a screen. "I do want to help you if I can," she went on, hardly above a whisper. "If you'll give me time I . . . I think I could arrange . . . but of course it would have to be quite privately. . . ."

He softened at the sight of her distress. "You're very kind. But I guess we won't talk of it anymore. I've been tired and worried and I started thinking out loud."

"But it's so wrong, so cruel, that you, with your genius, should have such worries. I don't understand." She drew her brows together in anxious conjecture. "I thought there was such a demand for what you write, and that you had a permanent job in the *New Hour*."

"Yes, I have. But they're just starting and can't pay much. And I'm pledged to give them whatever I write. But I'd have pulled through all right if other things hadn't gone wrong. And I will anyhow." He held his hand out. "You've helped me a lot, just letting me look at those pictures. Thank you for it. Good-bye."

The decision of his manner seemed to communicate itself to her, and she stood up also, pale and almost beautiful under the stress of an unknown emotion. "No, no, not good-bye, I do want to help you—I want you to tell me what it is that's wrong. . . . I know young men are sometimes foolish." She laid on his arm a bejewelled hand of which one ring would have bought his freedom.

Vance gave an impatient laugh. "Foolish? Is that what you people call not having enough money to keep alive on? What's wrong with me is that my wife's been desperately sick . . . sick for weeks. That costs."

There was a silence. Mrs. Pulsifer's hand slipped away. She drew back a step and slowly repeated: "Your wife? You mean to say you're married?" Vance made a gesture of assent.

"But I don't understand. You never told me. . . ."

"Didn't I? Maybe I didn't."

She continued to look at him uncertainly. "How could I know? I never thought . . . you never spoke. . . . But perhaps," she faltered, a curious light of expectancy in her tired eyes, "it's because your marriage is—unhappy?"

Vance coloured hotly. "God, no! I'm only unhappy because I can't do all I want for her." He thought afterward that he had never loved Laura Lou as he did at that moment.

"Oh. . . . I see. . . ." he heard Mrs. Pulsifer murmur; and he was vaguely conscious of the fading of the light from her eyes.

"Well, good-bye," he repeated. She seemed about to speak, to make some sign to detain him; but her narrowed lips let pass only a faint echo of his good-bye. It drifted mournfully after him as he walked down the endless perspective of tapestried and gilded emptiness to the hall below, where the tall young man in dark clothes and silver buttons was waiting with a perfectly matched twin to throw back the double doors. Vance wondered ironically whether they added to their other mysterious duties that of investigating Mrs. Pulsifer's cases; but he knew that his own, at any rate, would never be brought up for examination.

One of the fellows at the Cocoanut Tree gave him the name of a moneylender; and a few days later he had a thousand dollars in his pocket. He told Mrs. Tracy he had enough to pay off Hayes, and asked for his address. She gave it without comment, and Vance, thankful to avoid explanations, returned to New York the next day to discharge his debt. He had no idea how he was going to meet the interest on the loan; but he put that out of his mind with the ease of an inexperienced borrower.

The address led to a narrow office building in an uptown street, where, across the front of an upper floor, he read: "STORECRAFT," and underneath: "Supplies Taste and saves Money." He was admitted to a small room with roughcast walls, a sham Marie Laurencin, slender marquetry chairs, and a silvered mannequin in a Spanish shawl. There he waited till a fluffy-headed girl in a sports suit introduced him to an inner office, where Bunty Hayes, throned at a desk, was explaining to another girl: "Chanel, six almond-green Engadines: Vionnet, duplicate order apricot charmeuse pyjamas. . . ." He broke off and sat staring. "Patou, six pastel-blue Rivieras—" he went on automatically; then, with a change of tone: "All right, Gladys; we'll finish up later." The girl vanished, and he turned to Vance. "Say, I didn't see it was you, first off."

"Maybe you're too busy," Vance began.

"No, but I was expecting a fellow with a new style of bust-restrainer. Never mind; sit down." He pushed a chair forward. His manner was curt and businesslike, but not unfriendly; and Vance felt less at ease than if he had not been met with anathemas.

"You're on a new job," he said tentatively.

Bunty Hayes leaned back, swung around in his swivel chair, and thrust out his legs, displaying perfectly creased trousers. He had grown stouter, and had large yellow horn spectacles and carefully varnished hair. "Why, yes," he said. "Fact is, there's more in it. Folks want to tour in the holidays; but they want to shop all the year round, and they all want to shop in New York. Hundred and fifty million of 'em do. Storecraft's the answer to that. Here: seen one of our cards? We're going to move to Fifth Avenue next year. If you want to *do* big, you got to *see* big. That's my motto. See here, now; you live in the suburbs: well, we're the commuter's Providence. Supply you with everything you like, from your marketing to a picture gallery. We're going to have an art guild next year: buy your old masters for you, and all you got to do is to drive the hooks into your parlour wall and invite the neighbours."

Vance had not seated himself. He drew out the money and laid it on the desk. "Here's what we owe you," he said.

"Oh, hell—" said Hayes. The two men faced each other uneasily. At length Hayes nodded and said: "A'right," and put his hand out toward the money. "Who'll I make the re-

ceipt out to?" he asked, evidently not knowing what to say
next. Vance said to Mrs. Tracy, and stood with his hands in
his pockets leaning against the door. Hayes wrote the re-
ceipt rapidly, blotted and handed it to Vance. "Well, that's
over," he remarked with an attempt at ease. Vance put the
paper in his pocket. As he was turning to go Hayes stood
up, and began, in an embarrassed voice: "See here—"

"Yes?"

"I—your wife was sick when I called the other day. I
was real sorry. Wish you'd tell her."

"Sure," said Vance, nodding and swinging out of the
door. On the stairs, it came over him that he had behaved
like an oaf, and he was half minded to turn back and tell
Hayes— Tell him what? He didn't know. But he vaguely
felt there was a score between them which the money, after
all, hadn't wiped out. . . .

He had never yet spoken to Laura Lou about Hayes.
On his return that evening, when he went to her room, he
made up his mind to do so. The room looked pleasant.
There was a fire in the stove and a bunch of spring flowers
on the table. Laura Lou's bed was neatly made, and she lay
on the old steamer chair which he had brought up from the
porch. Mrs. Tracy was below, preparing supper, and the
house, sometimes so dreary and repellent to him, seemed
peaceful and homelike. Laura Lou's face lit up at his entrance. "Here—I brought you these. They're good and
juicy," he said, pulling a couple of oranges out of his overcoat pockets. He bent to kiss her, and she pressed her cheek
against his. "Oh, they're beauties, Vanney; but you oughtn't
to have spent all that money."

He sat down beside her, laughed, and said: "I've spent
a lot more; I've paid off what was owing to Hayes."

She flushed a tender rose colour. "Oh, Vanny! The
whole of it? Isn't that great?" Her hands tightened in his.

"Mother'll be crazy glad. But it's such a lot of money; how in the world did you manage?"

"Oh I . . . I fixed it up. It was easy enough. I got an advance."

The vague answer seemed to satisfy her, and she rested her head against his shoulder and stroked the oranges with her free hand. "Well, that's just great. I guess they must think the world of you at the office," she said placidly.

Vance held her to him. After a pause he said: "I always felt sorry for the fellow, somehow."

Through her deep lashes she looked up, as though wondering a little. "Well, you don't have to any longer, do you?"

Vance felt as if she had moved away from him; but in reality her light body was pressed more closely to his. "Why, I don't know," he said, "I guess we didn't act any too square to him, apart from the money. I wish now we'd given him warning . . . or something . . ."

She gave a little wriggle of contentment. "Well, yes, I wish we had too; but I guess it was safer, the way we did it." For her, at least, the old score had been completely wiped out. He wondered, as he clasped her, if anyone would ever feel about the deep invisible things as he did.

To stifle conjecture he bent down and kissed her lids shut, one ofter the other. That funny lonely woman in the big house, who had imagined he was unhappily married . . . !

Next morning the expressman deposited at the door a big basket with the "Storecraft" label, full of perfumed grapefruit and polished mandarins and boxes of Californian delicacies.

❧ XXVIII ❧

Vance stopped short. It was three years since he had seen the Willows.

June sunlight lay on the weed-grown lawn. Turrets and balconies showed in uncertain glimpses through layer on layer of overlapping lilac fringes. A breath of sweetness, which would have been imperceptible but for the million of calyxes exhaling it, enveloped the old house as faintly but pervasively as the colour of the wistaria flowers. As he stood there other perfumes stole to him: the purple burden of lilacs, the warm drip of white laburnums, and that haunting syringa smell which was like the noise of bees on a thundery day. On the fluctuations of the breeze they came now from one corner, now another, of the deserted shrubberies, way-laying Vance with their loveliness. But inside the house was that magical room, and all the shadowy power of the past.

He had not been near the Willows since the day when the late Mr. Lorburn had accused him of stealing the books. The place lay on the farther side of Paul's Landing, and his daily tramp to and from Mrs. Tracy's took him nowhere near it. He had been forbidden to return there, and if he disobeyed it might cost his mother-in-law her job. Yet there were days when he could hardly trust himself not to scramble over the gate and try for a loose shutter or a broken latch. Those unused books, row on row in the darkness, drew him unbearably; so he walked in other directions.

Mrs. Tracy, some days earlier, had been seized with inflammatory rheumatism. Laura Lou had to wait on her and do the cooking and washing; besides, she had never got back her strength since her illness, and it would have been imprudent to expose her to the cold of an uninhabited house. For two weeks the Willows remained unvisited; and the thought was misery to Mrs. Tracy, who was sure another caretaker would supersede her. Laura Lou said: "Mother, it's too silly not to send Vanny," and Vance added jocosely: "Even if I *had* stolen those books, it would be too risky trying it on again." Mrs. Tracy, turning her face from him, said: "The keys are under the pincushion in the upper right-hand drawer. . . ." And there he stood.

Laura Lou had charged him not to forget what he was there for. He was to open windows and shutters, air the rooms thoroughly, and make sure that no harm had come to the house since Mrs. Tracy's last visit. The two women prudently refrained from laying other duties on him: for the present the house must go undusted. "Just you tell him to take a good look round, so't that hired man'll see somebody's got his eye on him, and then come straight back here," was Mrs. Tracy's injunction to her daughter; who interpreted it: "Darling, all you got to do is to walk round, and tell her everything's all right."

Vance decided to begin by a general inspection. He passed from room to room, letting light and warmth into one melancholy penumbra after another, wakening the ghosts in old mirrors, watching the live gold of the sun reanimate the dead gold of picture frames and candelabra. Under the high ceilings of the bedrooms, with their carved bedsteads and beruffled dressing tables, he had now and then an elusive sense of life, of someone slipping through doors just ahead, of a whisper of sandals across flowered carpets, as if his approach had dispersed a lingering congress of memories. In Miss Lorburn's dressing room he paused before the ornate toilet set with the porcelain swan in a nest of rushes. "She dreamed of Lohengrin, and saw a baby in the bulrushes." Lorry Spear's comment came back to him. Funny—he'd never seen Lorry Spear since that day; the fellow owed him ten dollars, too. Vance wondered what had become of him. . . . In the circular boudoir, with the upholstered blue satin armchairs and those gay lithographs of peasants dancing and grape-gathering, he lingered again, trying to imagine the lady in her youth, when the rooms were bright and dustless, and she wore one of those ruffled dresses looped with camellias. . . . "And she ended reading Coleridge all alone. . . ."

He sat down in a blue armchair and closed his eyes. If he should open them on the young Elinor—pale and eager, the dark braids looped along her cheeks! As he sat there, Halo Tarrant's face substituted itself for the other. Slim and dark-braided, with flowing draperies and sandalled feet, she leaned in the window, looking out through the wistaria fringes for something, for someone. . . . Vance stood up, brushing away the vision. Weren't we all like Elinor Lorburn, looking out, watching for what never came? Ah, but there were the books—the books that had sufficed her, after all! He moved away, as if with her hand in his—that shy compelling virgin hand—moved through the rooms, down passages and stairs, and across the patterned parquet of the drawing rooms to the library. He reached out to open the shutters, and as he did so Miss Lorburn's hand slipped from his, and he knew that when he turned she would no longer be beside him, young and wistful, but withdrawn into her frame above the mantelpiece, the mature resigned woman with the chalk lights on forehead and lappets. The woman who read Coleridge alone. . . .

An orderly hand had effaced the traces of his former passage. The books he had taken down were back in their places, the furniture had been straightened. But on the fringed table cover of green velvet the Coleridge still lay open at "Kubla Khan," the gold-rimmed spectacles across the page. A touch of Halo's piety. . . .

In the three-year interval much else had happened. Vance had read and studied, new avenues of knowledge had opened to him, linking together many unrelated facts, and Miss Lorburn's library was now less interesting in itself than because of the sad woman who had lived there. Sad, but not shrunken. He looked up at her, and she looked down with her large full-orbed eyes, the eyes of one who has renounced but not repined. . . . What a subject, if he could do it! He dropped again into the highbacked armchair where he had sat on that first day. "This is the Past—if only I could get back into it. . . ." She must have been lovely when she was young, with a sharp austere loveliness like Halo's; her long thin hands full of gifts for someone, or else stretched out empty to receive. No one, apparently, had wanted to give her anything, or to receive what she offered; yet instead of withering she had ripened. Her books, and some inner source of life, had kept her warm—he wondered how? And suddenly a queer idea came to him: the idea that Halo Tarrant knew. Was the fancy suggested by some resemblance in their features, or a likeness in expression, something about the eyes and hands? Halo had those same hands, long, like her face, and opening wide when she held them out to you, as if ready to receive or give, while her eyes questioned which it was to be. Yet Halo was married, had presumably fulfilled her destiny. . . . And so, perhaps, had the other woman in her different way. That was what explained the likeness—or else made it all the more obscure. . . . The afternoon shadows wheeled unnoticed across the lawn. Vance continued to sit motionless, letting the secret forces move within him. Whenever he could surrender to his creative fervour it always ended by carrying him to the mysterious point where effort ceased, and he seemed just to have to hold his breath and watch.

He watched. . . .

When he got home, Laura Lou said why'd he been gone so long, and her mother was fretting, and would he go upstairs right away and tell her everything was all right? He stared at her out of his dream, as if she had spoken an unknown language. "Oh, yes—all right . . . everything's all right. . . ." That night he sat up late, writing, writing. . . .

Mrs. Tracy's recovery was slow, and she got into the habit of entrusting to Vance the weekly inspection of the Willows. The new owner, old Miss Louisa Lorburn, never came, never asked questions; and the Spear family, since Halo's marriage, were either in New York, or too busy with weekend parties at Eaglewood to think of policing the Willows. Sometimes Laura Lou went with Vance, accompanied by the woman who helped with the Tracys' washing: they left Vance in the library, and Laura Lou sang out to him to join her when the cleaning was over. On other days he went by himself; and before long the keys were in his pocket instead of being under Mrs. Tracy's pincushion. . . .

During those long summer hours in the library he was conscious, for the first time, of a sort of equilibrium between the rush of his words and images and the subject they were to clothe. At first he did not write regularly; he was feeling his way. Much of his time was spent in a state of rich passivity; but the inner travail never ceased. . . . On the days when he had to report at the office he seemed to be walking in his sleep. New York had become a shadow, a mirage, the fermenting activities of his comrades of the Cocoanut Tree as meaningless as dancing to which one cannot hear the music. A subtle transposition had situated his only reality in that silent room among the books. He told Rauch he had started a novel, and on his next visit he was uncomfortably aware of editorial curiosity and impatience; but as yet he could show nothing to satisfy them. "I guess the book'll be called *Instead*," he merely stated; on which Rauch remarked: "Well, it don't sound exactly incandescent. . . ." Vance drew a breath of relief when, toward the end of the month, he learned that the Tarrants were starting for London and Paris to pick up new stuff for the review. . . .

Rauch had said the title didn't sound incandescent. Well, the book, if it was ever written, wouldn't be incandescent either. Vance was more and more conscious of some deep-seated difference that cut him off from the circumambient literary "brightness," or rather left him unsatisfied by it. Perhaps he could have written like those other clever fellows whose novels and stories he devoured as they appeared. He was quick at picking up tricks of language and technique; and his reading had taught him what Frenside had meant by saying he was at the sedulous age. Ape these fellows— yes, he knew he could! He'd tried his hand at it, not always quite consciously; but though he was sometimes rather pleased with the result he always ended by feeling that it wasn't his natural way of representing things. These brilliant verbal gymnastics—or the staccato enumeration of a series of physical aspects and sensations—they all left him with the sense of an immense emptiness underneath, just where, in his own vision of the world, the deep forces stirred and wove men's fate. If he couldn't express that in his books he'd rather chuck it, and try real estate or reporting. . . . Some of the novels people talked about most excitedly—*Price of Meat*, say, already in its seventieth thousand, or *Egg Omelette*, which had owed its start to pulpit denunciations and the quarrel of a Prize Committee over its exact degree of indecency—well, he had begun both books with enthusiasm, as their authors appeared to have; and then, at a certain point, had felt the hollowness underfoot, and said to himself: "No, life's not like that, people are not like that. The real stuff is way down, not on the surface."

When he got hold of *Faust* at the Willows, and came to the part about the mysterious Mothers, moving in subterranean depths among the primal forms of life, he shouted out: "That's it—the fellows that write those books are all Motherless!" And Laura Lou, hurrying down duster in hand, rushed in exclaiming: "Oh, Vanny, I thought there were burglars!"

He got into the way of going oftener and oftener to the Willows. He knew that he risked little in doing so. The Tarrants were in Europe, and nobody else was likely to bother him. If he could have carried off the books he wanted the temptation would have been less great; but even so he would have been drawn back by the contrast between the house at Paul's Landing, where there was neither beauty nor privacy nor peace and this tranquil solitude. On his second visit he brought with him a supply of paper and notebooks. They remained on Miss Lorburn's table, beside her Coleridge; and the temptation to return was doubled by the knowledge that he would always find them there, not tidied away or mixed up by interfering hands, but orderly and receptive, as he had left them. As soon as he was seated at the table his mind became clear and free, accidental preoccupations fell from it, and he was face to face with his vision.

To explain his daily absences he told Laura Lou that he was needed at the office. Tarrant, he mentioned, had been called to Europe on business, and they were shorthanded. . . . A few months ago he would have been ashamed of deceiving her; now, since her illness, prevarication seemed wiser as well as safe. She mustn't be worried . . . she wouldn't understand. . . . He was beginning to see that there might be advantages in a wife who didn't understand. . . .

Curiously enough, since he had settled down to this view his tenderness for her had increased. It was as though at first he had expected too much of her, and of himself in his relation to her. Since her illness he had learnt to know her better, had found her limitations easier to accept; and now that his intellectual hunger was appeased she satisfied the rest of his nature. The fact that he had so nearly lost her made her more precious, more vividly present to him; he felt in her a new quality which not only enchanted his senses but fed his imagination—if indeed there were any dividing line between the two. For Laura Lou seemed to belong equally to his body and soul—it was only his intelligence that she left unsatisfied. Into the world of his mind, with its consuming curiosities, its fervid joys, she would never enter—would never even discover that it existed. Sometimes, when a new idea grew in him like a passion, he ached to share it with her, but not for long. He had never known that kind of companionship, had just guessed at it through the groping wonder of his first talks with Halo Spear, when every word she spoke was a clue to new discoveries. He knew now that he and she might have walked those flaming ramparts together; but the path he had chosen was on a lower level. And he was happy there, after all; intellectual solitude was too old a habit to weigh on him. . . .

Meanwhile the tale called *Instead* was taking shape. It began by a description of the Willows, and was to deal with the mysterious substitution of one value for another in a soul which had somehow found peace. The beginning went quickly; he had only to let the spirit of the place work in him, the picture shape itself under his attentive pen. And this justified his daily escape to the Willows—he had to do the novel as quickly as he could to pay off the interest on his loan. . . .

One day he put his pen down, dismayed to find that—as so often before—he did not know his subject well enough to go on. His mind wandered back to his first sight of the Willows, when he had come there with Laura Lou and

Upton. He had recalled, then, waking in the night years before at Euphoria, as a little boy, and hearing the bell of the
Roman Catholic church toll the hour. That solemn re-
verberation, like the note of Joshua's trumpet, had made the
walls of the present fall, and the little boy had reached back
for the first time into the past. His first sight of the Willows
had renewed that far-off impression; he had felt that the old
house was full of muffled reverberations which his hand
might set going if he could find the rope. . . . Since then
the years had passed, and he had learned many things. His
hand was nearer the rope—he was "warm," as the children
said. But when he tried to evoke the Elinor Lorburn who
had waltzed in the ballroom and wreathed her hair with
flowers before her tilted toilet mirror the dumb walls remained dumb . . . he could not wake them. . . .

The meagreness of his inherited experience, the way it
had been torn off violently from everything which had gone
before, again struck him with a pang of impoverishment.
On the Fourth of July, at Advance and then at Euphoria,
the orators of the day (and Grandpa Scrimser foremost
among them) had been much given to dilating on the price-
less qualities the pioneers had brought with them into the
wilderness. To Vance it sometimes seemed that they had
left the rarest of all behind. . . .

He fancied he heard a step in the shadows and glanced
up from his writing. "Vance!" Halo Tarrant exclaimed. She
was standing there, in the doorway of the drawing room,
with a look so amazed that Vance, jumping to his feet, lost
his own sense of surprise in the shock of hers. "Why I
thought you were in Europe!" he said.

"I was to have been." She coloured slightly. "And then,
at the last minute, I didn't go." She moved a step nearer.
"You hadn't heard I was at Eaglewood?"

"No. I didn't know."

She smiled a little. "Well, I didn't know you were at the

Willows. But just now, in passing the gate, I saw it was open—" (Oh, curse it, Vance thought—how could he have forgotten the padlock?) "and as I knew it wasn't Mrs. Tracy's day I came in to see who was here."

Her eyes were fixed on him with a looked which seemed to call for an explanation, and he mumbled: "Mrs. Tracy's been sick. . . ."

"I know; I'm sorry. And you're replacing her?"

"There was no one else. At first I came only on Saturdays, just to see that things were all right. Then—" he lifted his head, and returned her look, "then the books pulled me back. I couldn't help it. And I got in the way of coming oftener."

"I see. Very often?"

"Every day, I guess. But they don't know it at home," he added hastily.

"I know that too," she said, and, in answer to his glance of interrogation: "I've just come from there. I heard Mrs. Tracy was ill, and I looked in to see if there was anything I could do." She went on, a gleam of irony beneath her lashes: "Laura Lou seemed to think you were in New York."

The blood rose to Vance's face and burned its way slowly to his temples. "I . . . she's been sick too. . . . I knew she'd just get fretting if she thought I came here often . . . like this. . . ."

Halo Tarrant stood before him pale and grave as a young judge; he felt that his fate trembled in the balance. "She'll despise me for it, too," he thought, with a pang which blotted out his other apprehensions. She made no answer, but presently she said: "I hadn't seen Laura Lou for a year. How very beautiful she's grown."

Vance, in his surprise, could produce only an inarticulate murmur. There was no answer in his vocabulary to such amenities, especially when they were unexpected; and he stood abashed and awkward. At length he faltered out: "I guess you think I oughtn't to be here at all."

"Well, I won't betray you," she rejoined, still gravely. For a moment or two neither spoke; then she moved toward the table, and resting her long hand on it (yes, he thought, it was certainly like the hands in the picture), she bent over his manuscript. "You do your work here?"

"Yes. Down home there's no place but the dining room. And they're always coming in and disturbing me."

Mrs. Tarrant tossed off her hat, and seated herself in the carven armchair. The severity of her gaze had softened. Vance leaned with folded arms in the window recess. From where he stood her head, with its closely folded hair and thin cheeks, was just below that of the portrait, and though the eyes were different he felt again the subtle resemblance between the two women. "You do look like her!" he exclaimed.

She glanced up, narrowing her short-sighted eyes. "Like poor Cousin Elinor? I suppose you and she are getting to be great friends, aren't you?"

"Yes." He laid his hand on the page at her elbow. "This is about her."

"About Elinor?"

He nodded excitedly. "I'm writing her life—trying to."

His visitor looked at him with astonishment. "Her life— Elinor Lorburn's?"

"I mean, the way I imagine it. How things were in the days when this house was built. I don't know how to explain . . . but I think I see a big subject for a novel— different from the things the other fellows are trying for. What interests me would be to get back into the minds of the people who lived in these places—to try and see what we came out of. Till I do I'll never understand why we are what we are. . . ." He paused, breathless with the attempt to formulate his problem. "But I guess it won't do," he began again. "I don't know enough about those old times. I think there are good things in what I've done, though . . . the beginning's good, anyway. See here," he broke out, "I wish you'd let me read it to you; will you?"

Hesitations and scruples had fallen from him. He forgot that he had been found where he had no right to be, and the probable consequences—forgot the possibility of Halo Tarrant's disapproval, was hardly aware of her presence even, save as a listener to what he thirsted to have heard. She nodded and leaned back in her chair; and gathering up the sheets he began.

His elocution was probably not much better than when he had recited his poems to her on Thundertop. But he did not think of that till he had started; and after the first paragraph he was swept on by the new emotion of watching his vision take shape in another mind. Such a thing had never happened to him, and before he had read a page he was vibrating with the sense of her exquisite participation. What his imagination had engendered was unfolding and ripening in hers; whatever her final judgment was, it would be as if his own mind had judged him.

As his self-possession returned, the enjoyment of her actual presence was added to the intellectual excitement. Everything about her seemed to be listening and understanding, from the attentive droop of her lids to the repressed eagerness of her lips and the hands folded quietly on her knee. When he had ended he turned away abruptly, as though she might see even the heart thumping in his throat. He threw the manuscript down, and his self-confidence crumbled.

Mrs. Tarrant did not speak. She merely unclasped her hands, and then laid one over the other again, without otherwise moving. To Vance the silence seemed abysmal. He turned back and almost shouted at her: "Well, it's no earthly good, is it?"

She looked up. "It's going to be by far the best thing you've done." Her voice sounded rich with restrained emotion. "I can't tell you how strange the feeling is—all those dull familiar things with their meaning given back to them. . . ."

"Oh, is that what I've done? You see—you *do* see?"

"Of course—I see with your eyes, and with mine too. That's the strangeness—and the beauty. Oh, Vance, how did you do it? I'm so glad!" She stood up and drew nearer. It was as if achievement were shining down on him. "You must go on—you must give up everything to finish this." He nodded, speechless, and she stood looking about the shadowy room. "And of course you must do your work here. You've made this place yours, you know. And you must be quiet and undisturbed. I'll arrange it for you." She sat down again, leaning toward him across the table. "But this is only a beginning; tell me how you mean to go on."

⇜ XXIX ⇝

HALO TARRANT's eleventh-hour decision not to sail with her husband was due to a trifling domestic quarrel; so most people would no doubt have called it—though she sometimes wondered how it was possible, in any given case, to say in advance what would turn out trifling and what ominous in the world of sentiment.

She had, or imagined she had, been looking forward eagerly to the trip; to the interesting people they would see, the excitement of playing even a small part in the literary world of London and Paris, and all the inducements which change offers to the young and the unsatisfied. Then, suddenly, a link had snapped in the chain holding her to Tarrant, and they stood miles apart, hardly visible to each other.

Queer that life should be at the mercy of such accidents! But in this case circumstances had been tending for some time to unsettle her husband's moral atmosphere, which was not at best a stable one. The *New Hour* was not taking hold as they had hoped. Subscriptions were not increasing. That, they were told, was natural: the first year of a new periodical is always critical. More disquieting was the fact that book shops and newsstands were not sending in heavier orders. There had even been a falling off in the sale of the last numbers, and the editorial programme for the rest of the year was hardly brilliant enough to revive the demand. The situation was not unusual; but that was precisely what made it mortifying to Tarrant. Halo had already learned that in her husband's scheme of life half successes were almost worse than failures. He had taken hold of the moribund journal and put new life into it; and if it were to languish again in his hands—if somebody else's failure were to become *his*—the situation would be much more humiliating (and more difficult for his vanity to account for) than if he had started a new enterprise and not made it a success.

Frenside, at this juncture, had the happy thought of suggesting that Tarrant should go over to London and Paris and look about him: personal contact with editors and authors abroad might lead, he thought, to something interesting. Tarrant, always exhilarated by any new plan, at once became buoyant and masterful. He declared he had always thought he ought to go; he was glad that, for once, his wife and Frenside had come round to his view. He was prepared, Halo knew, to face a pecuniary loss on the review for the first year or two, but not a loss of prestige. Being his review, it must be brilliant or vanish: a slow decline would be unbearable. But he was confident that great things would result from this journey, and that he would come home with a glittering list of contributors.

Whenever his faith in himself returned, his wife's revived with it, and the two hurried joyfully through their preparations. But on the evening before they were to sail Tarrant came home in a different humour. He and Halo were alone, and when they returned to the library after dinner he broke out at once: "Well, we're dished this time; I don't see that there's much use in sailing."

Halo roused herself out of her happy preoccupation. Hurry, confusion, sudden preparations of any sort, always amused and stimulated her; but they made Lewis nervous—and so did the mere reaction from optimism. She had learned to allow for that, and only echoed absently: "No use sailing?" while her real self remained absorbed in luggage labels, passports and deck chairs. At length her husband's silence told her that something more was expected of her, and still absently she added: "Why?"

As if her delay had reached to the extreme limit of his patience, his answer sprang back: "The Pulsifer Prize. That fool Weston has gone and lost it."

Halo shook off her travel dream with a start. What on earth, she wondered, could have set Lewis fretting about the Pulsifer Prize? But what was the use of wondering? She supposed that, after two or three years of marriage, there were times when most husbands seemed to their wives like harmless lunatics (when it wasn't the other way round, or perhaps reciprocal), and she answered, in a tone of good-humoured reminder: "Lost it? How could he, when it's not given until next November?"

Tarrant, with a shrug, threw himself back wearily in his chair, and she remembered, too late, that there was nothing he so loathed as being humoured. "My dear," he said, "what's the sense of that sort of talk? You're not really as simple as all that: you know perfectly well that the prize is given the minute Jet Pulsifer takes a shine to one of the candidates. And she had taken a shine to that silly ass."

Halo's indifference was giving way to a sense of counter-irritation. Where would he go to dig up his next grievance, she wondered? And just as she ought to be writing out the labels—! "Oh, if that's all—" The whole subject of the Pulsifer Prize, with its half-confessed background of wire-pulling and influencing, was particularly distasteful to her, and she was really thankful there was no time to deal with it.

"All?" Tarrant echoed. "It's everything. She fell for Weston the minute she laid eyes on him—that evening at the party here. It was rather what we'd planned the thing for—you remember? And she's been awfully nice to him ever since . . . seeing him very often, and encouraging him a good deal, I imagine. You know what she is."

Halo murmured reluctantly: "Well—?"

"Well, what does the infernal fool do? Goes there the other day and holds her up for a loan."

"A loan?"

"A loan. And how much, do you suppose? The exact amount of the prize. Two thousand dollars—not a copper less!" Tarrant started up angrily and began to pace the floor. "She sent for me today; I never saw a woman so upset. She says he talked as if he were merely asking for an advance— as if his getting the prize was a sure thing, and she might as well hand the cash over at once, as long as he was bound to get it."

Thoughts of luggage labels and deck chairs vanished from Halo's mind. Into their place there stole a cold insidious dread of what was coming, of what her husband was going to say, and she was going to feel about it. "Nonsense, Lewis," she exclaimed. "I don't believe he ever said anything like that."

Tarrant laughed. "We all know you think he can't do wrong. But I suppose you'll admit he did ask for the money, if she says so?"

Halo pondered. She had forgotten herself and Tarrant in the shock of a new distress. "Poor fellow—I wonder why he wanted it so badly."

"Well, I own I'm less interested in that. What I care about is that he's fairly dished us, and that we were banking on the prize to give us a boost at the end of the year. With a new review it would have made a lot of difference. But the idea of considering *us* is the last that would enter his head."

"I suppose it is, if he wanted the money as much as that; and he must have, to dream of asking Jet Pulsifer."

"Oh, I don't know. I daresay it's rather in his line. That kind of man, when he sees a woman's gone on him . . ."

"He's not that kind of man!" Halo exclaimed. She also stood up, trembling with an unaccountable dismay. "What reason did he give—didn't she tell you?"

"Oh, the usual one, I believe. Hard up—wife ill, or

something—they always tell the same story. To think the fool had only to sit tight and let her go on admiring him!"

There was a long silence. Tarrant stopped his nervous pacing and returned to his armchair, throwing himself into it with a groan of impatience. "That prize was ours!"

"Ours?"

"Well—isn't he our discovery?" He laughed. "Yours, if you prefer. You're welcome to it. I hold no brief for black-mailers."

She looked at him with astonishment. He had suddenly crowded Vance Weston out of her mind and taken posses-sion of its centre himself. "Blackmailers?" she repeated. She said the word over slowly, once or twice. Then: "But, Lewis, if he's that, what are we? What's the *New Hour?*"

Tarrant threw back his handsome head and returned her look with faintly raised brows of interrogation, and a glance which declared resignedly: "Ah, now I give up!"

"What are we," his wife went on, "who knew what Jet was, and put the boy in her way, and worked up her imagi-nation about him, all to . . ." She broke off, vexed with her own exaggerated emotion, yet unable to control it.

Tarrant's tone, in contrast, grew profoundly quiet. "All to—what?"

"Steal the prize for our paper."

He looked at her, still with arched ironic brows. "That's what you call it? Stealing?"

"Don't you? We began to throw that boy in Jet's way months ago—began in this very house, and at your sugges-tion." (Oh, of course, he interjected, he knew she'd end by putting all the blame on him.) "No, I don't," Halo contin-ued. "I keep my share; and it's a big one. But I see now that we ought both to be ashamed—far more ashamed than Vance. And I *am*—I'm revolted. If that's the way literature is produced, it had better cease altogether. If it has to be shoved down people's throats like Beauty Products and patent collar buttons it shows our people don't really want it; that's all!"

Tarrant leaned back, and stretched his hand out for a cigar. "Did you ever really think they did?"

Her colour rose. "I suppose I didn't think at all—I just rushed ahead with the crowd. But now . . ."

"Well—now?"

"Now it seems to me there's only one thing we can do to save our souls—we must lend the boy that money."

Tarrant paused attentively in the lighting of his cigar. "We—?"

"You," she corrected herself, crimsoning. Something, perhaps involuntary, in the inflexion of his voice seemed to imply that, where there was a question of bestowing money, the plural pronoun could hardly be current between them. But his next retort brushed aside the implication.

"We—I? Lend him the money? What on earth are you talking about? He gets us into a damned mess, and we reward him for it?" She was silent. "Is that your idea of it?" he insisted.

She murmured with a shrug: "I suppose it's your idea of my idea."

"Ah, and what *is* yours, if I've misinterpreted it?"

"That the fault is all ours, and that we ought to expiate."

"Expiate!" He smiled. "You talk like an old-fashioned Russian novel. . . ." He paused a moment, and then added: "I had no idea you were such an idealist. . . . Well, it's getting late," he continued, standing up with a shake of his long body. "I've got to throw some last things into my trunk, and we'll postpone this discussion till we're on board."

Halo felt a sudden blur before her eyes. "Lewis!" she exclaimed.

He turned back, irritated, impatient to make an end, and as the two stood looking at each other Halo saw, in a

revealing flash, how immeasurably far apart they were—
had always been, perhaps. It was as if she had been walking
in her sleep, and had now abruptly opened her eyes on the
edge of a sheer drop. Yet what was there in this paltry
wrangle to throw such a glare into the depths?

Tarrant stood waiting. He looked drawn, tired, exasperated. It was no time for reasonable explanations; he
hated tactlessness, and she was being tactless. Yet speak she
must—speak (she said to herself) before they were so far
apart that he was out of hearing. . . .

"Well?" he repeated.

"Lewis . . . you're not going to understand. . . ."

"Understand what?"

"Why I say what I'm going to say—"

"Lord! How portentous! What are you going to say?"

"That our talk has made me feel I want to be by myself
for a while—away from you, I mean. . . ."

"Oh, is that all? All right. I'm off to bed this minute," he
said, strangling a yawn.

"I don't mean that. I mean . . . I'd rather not sail with
you tomorrow."

"Not sail?" He swung round and mustered her incredulously. "What in God's name are you driving at now?"

"Just what I say. I'd rather not go. . . ."

He leaned in the doorway, waiting. She said nothing
more, and he broke into the thin laugh which often preceded his outbursts of anger. "May I ask what all the fuss is
about anyhow?"

She gave back his look almost timidly. She had not
known she meant to say just those words till they were uttered; but now she knew it was her inmost self which had
said them, and she could not take back what was spoken.
Yet how was she to explain? "Because I . . . because I feel
I want to be alone for a while. . . ."

"That's why you're not going?"

"I don't feel as if—I could. . . ."

"You're not serious, are you?"

"Yes. I'm serious."

There was another silence. She saw that he was baffled and mortified, and yet too proud to argue with her or entreat her.

"Oh, all right—if you say so," he muttered. Then, after a pause: "All the same, though, I'm curious to know why."

She hesitated, still caught in the hopeless difficulty of finding words. "It's because . . . I suddenly see that we feel too differently about things, and I want to have time to think . . . to go away and think by myself. . . ."

Tarrant's lips narrowed, and his cold eyes seemed to draw closer together. "If you mean that we feel differently about lending Vance Weston money, we certainly do. I rather wonder, though, that you should pick that out as a grievance. I should have thought you might have remembered that as a rule I'm not backward about lending money."

There was a long pause. Halo leaned against the chair from which she had risen, and the eyes resting on her husband filled with tears. Her resentment had died at the very moment when he had found the taunt most calculated to quicken it. She would have given the world if he had not said those particular words, because they laid bare to her the corner of his mind where old grudges and rancours were stored, the corner into which she had always refused to look. But now that the words were spoken she felt only pity for him—and for herself. It seemed to her that he and she merited equally such humiliation as the moment involved. "Oh, Lewis," she began, "please don't. . . ."

"I don't want to—all I want is to make myself clear."

"You have," she murmured. She straightened herself and took a step back. He still leaned in the door and looked at her.

"All right," he said, again with his thin laugh. "Then we may call the matter settled?"

She made no answer, and after waiting a moment he went out of the room. When the door had closed she sat down and leaned back in her chair with closed eyes.

To justify her appearance at Eaglewood on the day when she was supposed to be sailing with her husband, Halo told her parents that at the last minute she had decided he would do his job better without her. Dragging a wife about on such a hurried expedition—what a nuisance! Of course he couldn't tell her so; but his beautifully simulated distress, when she had announced her decision, had shown her how relieved he felt. "You know how he is: never so polite as when he wishes you were dead and buried," she reminded her father and mother; and smilingly watched their incredulity melt into reassurance. It was easy now to reassure the Spears! Since their own wants were provided for they had grown less exacting for others. With a comforting word or two you could put Mr. Spear's mind to rest about the treatment of live bait, or Mrs. Spear's about the future of democracy. And so with the case of their daughter. Mrs. Spear, who still needed to be told at intervals that all was right with the world, instantly seized on the idea that Halo had given up sailing because she had "hopes" again— at last!—had perhaps been advised by the doctor . . . though the poor child, after her previous disappointments, was naturally reticent. And Mr. Spear smoked his good cigars, and said, well, no doubt his daughter knew her business better than they did, and he rather admired the way the modern young people had of respecting each other's independence. Halo knew that her parents were enchanted to have her to themselves; Tarrant rather intimidated them, and it was easier to praise him behind his back than to humour him to his face. The easy happy-go-lucky quarrelsome atmosphere of Eaglewood was always chilled by his presence; and there were so many of their friends whom he regarded as bores or cranks, and whom they couldn't invite when he was there. . . .

Halo did not care what her parents thought of her sham reasons, as long as they feigned to accept them; she was too busy examining the real ones. She knew that she had at last emerged into the bald light of day from the mist of illusion she had tried to create about her marriage. That talk with Lewis had been a turning point: the inevitable stocktaking. Never again would she see him save as he was; but she would also, as inevitably, see herself as chained to him for life.

The fact that he had reminded her of her obligation would make it perpetually present to her. The new carpets at Eaglewood, the Spear flat in New York, Mrs. Spear's black velvet, Mr. Spear's cigars, the funds for Lorry's theatrical enterprise—these were the links of her chain. They held her as tight as if divorce had never existed. For she knew now that all Lewis's generosity (yes, yes, he *was* generous!) had proceeded not from the heart but from the head. He wanted her; she suited him; he had bought her. It was no more romantic than that. And being a gentleman, he punctiliously paid the annual tax on his acquisition, and would continue to as long as she continued to suit him. And it was her business to go on suiting him, since, the day she ceased to, the Spear household would fall to pieces. . . .

The idea frightened her, and as soon as he was safely at sea she began to think how to conciliate him. Everything seemed easy when he was not there. His cold unreasonableness always silenced her at the moment, and then stung her to resistance; but she could make her submission in writing because, escape being impossible, common sense warned her to make the best of her fate. And something higher than common sense whispered that, after all, she was only paying her dues. . . .

She sent him, by the next steamer, a simple friendly letter, telling him that she knew she'd been stupid, but she'd been feeling dreadfully nervous and overtired, and he must forgive her, and not think of their disagreement. It was really providential, she added, that she hadn't gone with him, because the doctor found she was rather rundown and anaemic, and badly in need of a rest, and she would just have been a drag on him, and unable to keep up the pace. But to show she was forgiven he must send her long cable letters with all his news and the review's. . . .

She had written that her not going with him had been providential; but how true it was she did not dream till she heard those first chapters of Vance Weston's.

Under his touch the familiar setting of the Willows became steeped in poetry. It was his embodiment of the Past: that strange and overwhelming element had entered into his imagination in the guise of these funny turrets and balconies, turgid upholsteries and dangling crystals. Suddenly lifted out of a boundless contiguity of Euphorias, his mind struck root deep down in accumulated layers of experience, in centuries of struggle, passion, and aspiration—so that this absurd house, the joke of Halo's childhood, was to him the very emblem of man's long effort, was Chartres, the Parthenon, the Pyramids.

It was extraordinary, how this new vision of it reanimated the dusty scene. Countless details that Halo had taken for granted, or dismissed as negligible, were now ripe with meaning. The mere discovery that there were people who had been born and died in the same house was romance and poetry to Vance. It gave to all these anonymous particles a relief and a substance she had never guessed in them. And the fact that she could help him in his magical evocation, provide him with countless necessary details about these people who were so near yet so remote, so trivial yet so significant, could tell him how they spoke and felt and lived and died, made her feel of use again in the world.

Every day at the same hour she came back to the Willows to meet him, so that there should be no break in his inspiration. Ah, now, indeed, the *New Hour* was to have its masterpiece!

⚜ XXX ⚜

MRS. TRACY had recovered. The keys of the Willows were safely back in her drawer, and she and Laura Lou began again going to the house on stated days. On those days Vance usually stayed at home to write in the stuffy little dining room; or, if the stuffiness was too oppressive, wandered off up the mountain, past the gates of Eaglewood, past the highest-lying farms, to the open ridges below Thundertop.

Mrs. Tracy's day was Saturday. On her first return to the Willows she apparently discovered nothing unusual or out of order; if she had, Vance would certainly have heard of it. She had never thrown off the worry of having to entrust the keys to him, and had manifestly expected to find books dislodged and cigarette ends lying about, if nothing worse.

"I told Mother you'd be ever so careful," Laura Lou reported afterward with a little smile of triumph; and Vance, pushing his manuscript aside, smiled back absently: "After the scare I had in that house—!"

He was not afraid of scares now. He knew that on the days when he went to the Willows he was still supposed by his wife and mother-in-law to be "at the office." And so, technically, he was. After all, he had simply transferred his papers from a precarious desk corner at the *New Hour* to the sanctuary of Miss Lorburn's library. He no longer needed Mrs. Tracy's keys (those damned keys!) for Halo Tarrant had her own, and was always there before him. He did not remember how that tacit arrangement had been established, nor at whose suggestion he and she, when the afternoon's work was over, invariably restored every book to its place, locked up the manuscript in a cupboard below the bookshelves, and buried their cigarette ends in the border outside of the window. On the day when Mrs. Tarrant had first surprised him in the library Vance had confessed that his wife and mother-in-law did not know of his coming to the Willows to work, and had told her his reasons for keeping his visits secret. She had understood in a flash—when did she not?—and all their subsequent precautions had grown out of that brief avowal, without any comment or question that he could remember.

That was one of her rare qualities, to him perhaps the rarest: the way she took things for granted, didn't forever come harping back on them. That, and her not asking questions—personal questions. In the world of Euphoria and the Tracys the women did nothing but ask questions. They never stopped asking questions. The only things that seemed to interest them unfailingly were the things a man might conceivably want to keep to himself. They had noses like shooting dogs for those particular things, whatever they were; a good part of the time a man spent away from his women had to be devoted to inventing prevarications as to how he spent it. If a fellow had only strolled down to the station to see the Chicago express come in, he would invent something else from the mere force of habit. . . . With Mrs. Tarrant it was different. She had a way of dashing straight at the essentials. And anyhow, she didn't seem to care how Vance spent his time when he was away from her, an indifference as surprising to him in a woman friend as in wife or sweetheart. No one had ever cross-questioned him more searchingly than his own sisters; yet here was a woman with whom he was on terms of fraternal intimacy—who shared with him almost daily the long hushed midsummer after-

noons, yet seemed interested only in the hours they lived together in fervid intellectual communion. The truth was that,
both as Halo Spear and as Halo Tarrant, she had always appeared to Vance less as a simple human creature than as the
mysterious custodian of the unknown, a being who held the
keys of knowledge and could render it accessible and lovely
to him. The first day she had found him at work on his new
tale she had plunged into his enchanted world with him,
and there they met again each afternoon. She had entered
instantly into his idea of evoking the old house and its
dwellers, and as he advanced in his task she was there at
each turn, her hands full of treasure, like a disciple bringing
refreshment to an artist too engrossed to leave his work.
Only it was he who was the disciple, not she: he who, at
each stage, had something new to learn of her. He had
brought his fresh untouched imagination to the study of the
old house and the lives led in it—a subject which to her had
seemed too near to be interesting, but to him was remote
and poetic as the Crusades or the wars of Alexander. And he
saw that, as she supplied him with the quaint homely details
of that past, she was fascinated by the way in which they
were absorbed into his vision, woven into his design. "I
don't see how you can feel as those people must have felt. I
suppose it's because they're already history to you. . . .
Don't forget that Alida" (Elinor Lorburn had become Alida
Thorpe) "would always have had her handkerchief in her
hand: with a wide lace edge, like the one I brought down
from Eaglewood to show you yesterday. . . . It's important, because it made them use their hands differently.
. . . And their minds too, perhaps . . . like the old gentlemen I remember when I was a child, who always carried
their hat and gloves into the drawing room when they
called. And her wedding dress" (for their Alida was to have
had the hope of marriage) "would, I think, have been like
my great-great-grandmother's: India mull, embroidered at

Madras, and brought back on one of her grandfather's merchantmen. For of course all their finery would have been stored away for generations in those old chests we found in the attic. Elinor really was an epitome of six or seven generations—the last chapter of a long slowly moving story."

"Ah—slowly moving! That's it! If I could get the pace the way you seem to give it to me when you tell me all those things . . ."

He leaned his elbows on the scattered pages and stared at her across the table. The long folds of the green velvet table cover drooped to the floor between them, and from her shadowy place above the mantel Miss Lorburn looked down meditatively on the young pair who were trying to call her back to life. Halo Tarrant, facing him, her dark hair parted on her temples, her thin face full of shadowy hollows, seemed in the shuttered summer light, almost as ghostly as Miss Lorburn. "I wonder—" Vance broke out, laying down his pen to look at her. "Have you had to give up things too . . . ?"

"Give up things . . . ?"

"I mean: a vision of life."

"Oh, *that*—!" She gave a faint laugh. "Who doesn't? Luckily one can recapture it sometimes—in another form." She pointed to the manuscript. "That's exactly your theme, isn't it?"

He nodded. The allusion sent him back to his work. He did not know why he had strayed from it to ask her that question—the first personal question he had ever put to her. But there were moments when the shape of her face, the curves of her hair and brows, reminded him so startlingly of the thwarted lady above the mantel that the comparison sent a pang through him. And then Mrs. Tarrant would burst into banter and laughter, would flame with youthful contradictions and enthusiasms, and he would wonder how he could have seen in her any resemblance to the sad spinster who had leaned on winter evenings on the green velvet table, reading Coleridge.

"Yes—but it was *Coleridge;* don't forget that! It wasn't *The Saints' Rest* or *The Book of Martyrs.*" That had been one of Halo's first admonitions. Vance was not to make a predestined old maid or a pious recluse out of his Alida. She must be a creature apt for love, but somehow caught in the cruel taboos and inhibitions of her day, and breaking through them too late to find compensation except under another guise: the guise of poetry, dreams, visions. . . . That was how they saw her.

His work had always been engrossing to Vance—something he was driven to by an irresistible force. But hitherto it had been laborious, thankless, full of pitfalls and perplexities, as much a weariness as a joy, and always undertaken tentatively, hazardously, with a dread lest the rich fields through which it beckoned should turn into a waterless desert. Now he felt at ease with his subject, assurance grew in him as he advanced. For beside him was that other consciousness which seemed an extension of his own, in which every inspiration, as it came, instantly rooted and flowered, and every mistake withered and dropped out of sight. He was tasting for the first time the creator's supreme joy, the reflection of his creation in a responsive intelligence; and young as he was, and used to snatching what came to him as recklessly as a boy breaking the buds from a fruit tree, he was yet deeply aware of the peculiar quality of this experience.

"That about the handkerchief always in her hand— that's the kind of thing that gives me the pace. . . ." He leaned back, rumpling his hair and looking straight ahead of him into his dream. He had been reading aloud the afternoon's work, and Halo, as her way was, sat silent, letting the impression of the reading penetrate her.

"You see, from the first day I set foot in this house I got that sense of continuity that we folks have missed out of our lives—out where I live, anyway—and it gave me the idea of a different rhythm, a different time beat: a movement without jerks and breaks, flowing down from ever so far off in the hills, bearing ships to the sea. . . . I don't say one method's better than another; only I see this is mine . . . for the subjects I want to do, anyhow. . . . And so even a handkerchief in a woman's hand counts. . . ."

She nodded: "Of course."

"And those are the things I never could have found out if you hadn't told me."

"Oh, yes, you would. . . . You were destined to. . . ."

"I guess I was destined to *you*," he rejoined, half laughing.

She echoed the laugh; then she pushed back her chair with a sigh. "It's late—I must be going. But you're all right now; you've got all the material you need, and you know what to do with it. I'm glad to go away feeling certain of that."

Still deep in his dream, he protested: "But you're not going away? It's not late, really; and there are two or three things more . . ."

She stood up with a gesture of negation. "Oh, you'll have to write me about those, or drop in some day when you come to New York—"

He sat crouched over the table, his chin sunk in his locked hands, and stared up uncomprehendingly. "Write to you? What do you mean? Can't you come back tomorrow?"

"No, nor the next day. Our holiday's over, Vance—didn't you know?"

"Over—why?"

"Because my husband's arriving; I'm going back to New York to join him."

The words fell on his excited brain like little blows

from some deadly instrument. At first he hardly felt them—
then his head reeled with the shock, and for a moment he
found no word to say.

"But you're all right now; I mean the book's all right—
you can see your way ahead; can't you, Vance?"

He still looked up at her incredulously. "I can't see anything but you."

"Oh—" she murmured, and sat down once more, facing
him across the familiar table. "Well, no wonder: we've
looked at each other like this nearly every day for two
months now. . . ."

Vance was not listening. He had reached the same degree of absorption which, the day he had met Laura Lou in
the rubberneck car, had made it impossible to fix his attention on what she was saying. He sat looking at Halo Tarrant
with a concentration as remote as possible from that April
ecstasy, yet as intense. "I feel as if I'd never looked at you
before," he blundered out.

"I don't believe you ever did!" she said. Her lips began
a smile; then they became grave, and her slow colour
mounted. She sat motionless, giving him back his gaze so
steadfastly that hers seemed to enter into his eyes and slip
down their long windings to his very soul. She dropped her
lids after a while, and made a motion to rise again. "But
you'll know me now, won't you, the next time we meet?"

He made no answer. Her banter hung in a meaningless
dazzle somewhere outside of him; all his real self was
within, centred in the effort of holding her image fast, of
tracing it, line by line, curve by curve, with the passionate
hands of memory. She who had seemed to him but a disembodied intelligence was now stealing into every vein and
fibre like wine, like wind, like all the seed-bearing currents
of spring. He looked at her hands, which lay folded before
her on the table, and wondered what their hidden palms

were like, and the dimpled recess of her inner arm at the elbow. "No, I've never known you," he repeated stupidly.

"Oh, but we've been . . . but we've been. . . ." She broke off, and began again, in a more decided tone: "Your book has reached a point now when it will be all the better for you to go on with it alone. A writer oughtn't to get too dependent on anybody's advice. If I've been able to help you . . ."

"Oh, curse the book," he broke in, burying his face in his hands. The tears choked in his throat and burnt his close-pressed eyeballs. He hadn't known—why hadn't he known? —that it would be like this. . . . The room grew still. He heard a fly bang against the window and drop to the sill from the shock of its own impact. Outside was the confused murmur of the summer afternoon. Presently Mrs. Tarrant moved. She walked around the table, he felt the stir of her nearness, her hand rested on his shoulder. "Vance—don't. Remember, you've got your job; and you belong to it."

He did not move lest he should lose the shock of her light touch running through him like his blood. But to himself he groaned: "It's always the same way with you, you fool. You see only one thing at a time, and get into a frenzy about that, and nine times out of ten it's not the real thing you're chasing after but only something your brain has faked up."

Mrs. Tarrant went on in the same even tone. "Vance, are you listening to me? You must listen. Of course you must go on with your work here. You mustn't be disturbed —and you must have this atmosphere about you; I'll see to that—I'll arrange it." Still he did not answer; did not drop his hands or turn his head when he heard a slight click on the table at his elbow. "See, Vance, I'm leaving you the keys. Don't forget them. You can return them to me in New York when you bring me the finished book."

He did not move. She too was silent for a moment; then her hand was withdrawn. "Come—we must say good-bye, Vance."

He dropped his hands and leaned back, looking up at her. "I never thought about its ending," he muttered.

"But it isn't ending; why should it? You must stick to your job and carry it through; and then, when it's done, you'll be coming back regularly to the office—and I shall see you often, I hope. . . ."

"Not like this."

"This had been good, hasn't it? But when your book's done, that will be lots better; that will be the best that could happen. . . ."

"I don't care a curse about the book."

She stood looking down at him, and a faint smile stole to her lips. "You ought to, if you say we've done it together."

Again the tone of banter! She was determined to force that tone on him then. She was teasing him, ridiculing him, condescending to him from the height of all her superiorities: age, experience, education, worldy situation; and he, this raw boy, had sat there, forgetting these differences, and imagining that because he had suddenly discovered what she was to him, he could hope to be as much to her! He ached with the blow to his vanity, and a fierce pride forced him to feel no other ache. If she thought of him as a blundering boy, to be pitied and joked with, to hell with dreams and ambitions, and all he had believed himself to be!

"I guess I don't know how to talk," he grumbled out. "Better tie up to my writing—that your idea?"

She sat down beside him again, and while he covered his eyes from the glare of his own blunder he heard her, on another plane of consciousness, with other ears, as it were—heard her talking to him reasonably, wisely, urgently of his work, of the opportunities ahead of him, of what he was jus-

tified in hoping, of what his effort and ambition ought to
be: all in an affectionate "older friend" voice, a voice so cool
and measured that every syllable fell with a little hiss on the
red-hot surface of his humiliation.

"You know how I've always believed in you, Vance.
Oh, but that's nothing . . . I'm nobody. But my husband
believes in you too . . . believed in you from the first, before I'd read anything of yours; he's proved his belief, hasn't
he? And Frenside—Frenside, who's never pleased, never
satisfied . . . And when they see what you've done now
they'll feel they were justified—I know they will. . . .
Vance, you know artists always have these fits of discouragement . . . often just when they've done their best; it's
the reaction after successful effort. And this *is* your best so
far, oh, so much your best! I'm sure something still bigger
and better will follow; but meanwhile, dear boy, for your
soul's sake you must believe in this, you must believe in
yourself. . . ."

For his soul's sake he could not have looked up or
changed his attitude. Her friendly compassion crushed him
to earth, her incomprehension held him there. "If she'd only
go," he thought, "if only it was over. . . ."

The stillness was broken by the scraping of her pushed-
back chair. He felt a stir of air as she moved, and heard,
through interlocked hands, her footfall sink into the bottomless silence of the old house. A door closed. She had gone; it
was over. . . .

❧ XXXI ❧

VANCE CONTINUED to sit there. He had imagined he had
suffered on the day when he had seen his grandfather down
by the river with Floss Delaney: poor simpleton! That was a
wound to his raw senses. He had escaped from it by writing
it out and selling it to an editor. But now there was not a
vein of his body, not a cell of his brain, not a dream or a
vision of his soul, that was not hurt, disabled. . . . This
woman who had kindled in him the light by which he lived
had sat there complacently telling him that she believed in
his work, that her husband and old Frenside believed in it
. . . and had thought she was leaving him comforted!

But did she really think so? Or was all she had said only
a protective disguise, the conscientious effort to repress
emotions corresponding to his own? He had an idea she
would be very conscientious, full of scruples he wasn't sure
he wholly understood. For if she hadn't cared as much as he
did, why should she have devoted all those hours to helping
him? If it was just for the good of the *New Hour,* she was
indeed the ideal wife for an editor! But no: those afternoons
had been as full for her as for him. What was that phrase
she had pointed out, in the volume of Keats's *Letters* she
had given him—about loading every rift with gold? That
was what they had done to their hours together: both of
them.

Suddenly, as he sat brooding, he heard a door open:

then, after a moment's delay, a step coming through the empty rooms. The carpets muffled it, the stealing twilight seemed to envelop it; but it was hers, hers surely—who else would have business there? She was returning, coming back to say all the things that were surging in his heart. . . . He sat still, not daring to look up.

The step drew nearer, reached the threshold, clicked on the parquet of the library. He started up and saw Mrs. Tracy. In the faint light her face looked so drawn and wretched that he thought she had been taken ill again, and went toward her hurriedly.

"Why, what's the matter?"

"Matter? It *is* a woman you come to meet here then!" She had reached the table, and with a quick pounce picked up a glove which lay there. "That's what you call your literary work, is it?" she triumphed venomously.

Vance stood silent. His mind was still so charged with ardent and agonizing thoughts that he could not grasp what she was saying. What was she talking about, what was she trying to insinuate, what had she come for? Once more he caught in her face the gleam of animosity he had been conscious of, just below the surface, ever since he had gone with Upton to the ball game.

"Well, haven't you got anything to say? No, I don't suppose you have!" Mrs. Tracy taunted him.

"I don't know what you expect me to say. I don't know what you're talking about. That glove is Mrs. Tarrant's—she left here only a few minutes ago."

Mrs. Tracy's sallow face grew sallower. He saw that she was unprepared for the answer and not wholly inclined to believe it. "Mrs. Tarrant—what was she doing here?"

"She came to see me."

"And what were you doing here?"

"Writing, as you see."

Mrs. Tracy was silent for a moment, her eyes fixed incredulously on the piled-up pages before her. "I'd like to know who it is lets you in," she said at length.

"Why, Mrs. Tarrant let me in today, of course."

"Today! Maybe she did. I'm not talking only about today. It's not the only day you've been here."

Vance hesitated. He had expected to silence his mother-in-law, and dispel her suspicions, by naming Mrs. Tarrant—one of the few persons who had the undisputed right to come and go in that house. But it would be a different matter, he instantly felt, to let Mrs. Tracy associate Halo's name with the frequent and clandestine visits of which she evidently suspected him. He was convinced now that she had come on purpose to surprise him, as the result of information received; and he was never ready-witted in emergencies.

"Well, I don't know's I need ask who lets you in," she pursued. "You had plenty of time to have duplicate keys made while I was sick."

"Certainly I had—if it had occurred to me to do anything so low-down."

"Low-down? I guess it isn't that would have prevented you, if you'd been set on coming here, whether it was to steal books or to meet women . . . maybe both . . ." she flung back, trembling.

Her agitation had a steadying effect on Vance. "Why not both, as you say?" he rejoined impartially, beginning to gather up his papers. He was sure she was not there without a definite purpose, and it was obviously safer to leave the burden of explanation on her shoulders. After all, he had nothing to reproach himself with but the venial wrong of concealing from Laura Lou that he did his writing at the Willows, and not at the *New Hour* office. He had been slaving all summer to pay off the money Mrs. Tracy had accepted from Bunty Hayes, and the women had better leave him alone, or he'd know why. . . . Silently he crammed his papers into their usual storing-place and walked toward the door.

Mrs. Tracy stepped in front of him. "Where are you going?"

"Home."

"Home? It's a place you don't often trouble. Why don't you do your writing there—if it's writing you say you come here for?"

"Because I'm never left alone," he said, his anger rising again. Mrs. Tracy saw her chance and laughed. "Not with the right woman, you mean?"

Vance halted in front of her. After all, if there was a scene coming—and he saw she was not to be cheated out of it—better have it out here than wait and risk Laura Lou's being drawn in. "What is it you're driving at? I can't answer till I know," he said sullenly.

"Well, answer me this, then. Who's the woman you come here to meet?"

The blood rose to his face. "Nonsense. I told you Mrs. Tarrant came here today. You'd better give me her glove and I'll take it back to her."

Mrs. Tracy paid no attention to this. She hesitated a moment; then she said: "You haven't answered my question yet. It's no good beating round the bush. The neighbours all know about what's been going on here. Laura Lou's had a letter warning her. You say, what am I driving at? Well, I'm here to find out what you propose to do, now we've caught you. That's plain enough, isn't it?" She flung the words out in a kind of shrill monotone, as if she had learned them from someone else and were afraid of not getting them in the right order.

Vance was speechless. His mind had seized on one phrase: "Laura Lou's had a letter," and he turned sick with an unformed apprehension. "What nonsense are you talking? What kind of letter? I've got nothing to hide and nothing to explain. If you have the letter with you, you'd better let me see it, and if I can find the sneak who wrote it I'll go and break his neck."

Mrs. Tracy laughed. "Well, you'll have some trouble doing that, I guess. But the letter isn't here—it's locked up at home. It's done enough harm to my poor child already—"

"Who wrote it?" Vance interrupted.

"It's not signed."

"I thought as much. That kind never is. And you've come here to spy on me on the strength of a rag of paper with God knows what anonymous slander on it?" He took his hat up again, and as he did so, his eye lit on the keys which Halo, in leaving, had laid beside him. They were no good to him now; he would never use them again, never come back here without her. He would take them back to Eaglewood this very night, with the glove. . . .

He put them in his pocket and turned again to his mother-in-law. "I come here to work, not to meet women." This sounded impressive, and in a way was true—yet he didn't care for the ring of it. He cleared his throat, and began again: "If you'll give me Mrs. Tarrant's glove I'll send it back."

For all answer Mrs. Tracy opened her handbag (it was the very one the bridal couple had bought for her on their return to Paul's Landing), and put the glove in it, snapping shut the imitation ivory clasp.

"See here—give me that glove," Vance burst out; then crimsoned at his blunder. Mrs. Tracy tucked the bag under her arm. "I'll see to returning it," she said.

He affected indifference. "Oh, very well—" There was a pause, and then he added. "If that's all, I'll be off."

Mrs. Tracy, however, continued to oppose him from the threshold. "It's not all—nothing like. I guess it's for me to decide about that."

Vance waited a moment: angry as he was, he had the

sense to want to check Mrs. Tracy's recriminations. "If there's anything else to be said, I guess it's for Laura Lou to say it. I'm going back home now to give her the chance," he declared.

Mrs. Tracy raised her hand in agitation. "No, Vance—no! You won't do that. The letter's half killed her, anyway. And you know she can't stand anything that excites and worries her. . . ." She paused a moment, and added with a certain dignity: "That's why I came here—it was to spare her."

Vance pondered. "Was it her idea that you should come?"

"No, she doesn't even know I'm here. I told her we'd have to take steps to find out—but she was so upset she wouldn't listen. My child's a nervous wreck, Vance. That's what you've made of her."

"If I've made her a nervous wreck, is it your idea that it's going to quiet her if you go back and report—as you apparently mean to do—that I come here to meet other women?"

The reasoning of this was a little too close for Mrs. Tracy's flurried brain. She considered it for a while, and then said: "I didn't come here to go back and report to her."

Vance looked at her in astonishment. "Then what on earth did you come for? Your imagination is so worked up against me that all my denials wouldn't convince you—I see that. But if Laura Lou's to be left out of the question—"

His mother-in-law moved nearer to him, with a look of appeal in her face that made it human again. "It all depends on you, Vance."

"Well, you don't suppose—"

"I don't suppose you want to hurt Laura Lou more than you can help—any more than I do," she continued, with an effort at persuasiveness. "And what I'm here for is to ask you to spare her . . . give her a chance . . . before it's too late. . . ." She lifted her hands entreatingly. "For God's sake, Vance, let her go without a fight. It's her chance now, and I mean she shall take it; but if you'll let it be easy for her, I'll let it be easy for you—on my sacred word. Vance . . . See here; I've got you where I can make my own terms with you . . . I've got my proofs . . . I've got the whip hand of as they say . . ." She broke off, and went on in an altered voice: "But that's not the way I want to talk to you, Vance. I just want to say: Why not recognize it's all been a failure and a mistake from the first, and set my child free before it's too late?"

"Too late for what?"

"For her to get back her health—to enjoy her youth as she ought to. . . ."

Vance's brain was still so confused with the shock of Mrs. Tarrant's abrupt leave-taking that this fresh assault on his emotions left him dazed. Mrs. Tracy hated him; had always hated him. He had long been carelessly aware of that, and had instantly seen how eagerly she must have caught at this chance of getting the whip hand of him, as she called it; of finding herself justified in all her disappointments and resentments. But he had not suspected that she might have a more practical object in mind, that what she wanted was not to injure him but to free Laura Lou. It was dull of him, no doubt, it was incomprehensible even, that, having lived all his life in a world of painless divorce, where a change of mate was often a mere step in social advancement, it should never have occurred to him that he and Laura Lou could part. But though he had often chafed at the bondage of his unconsidered marriage, though he had long since ceased to think of his wife as the companion of his inner life, and had stooped to subterfuges to escape her fond solicitude . . . yet now her mother's proposal filled him with speechless wrath. He and Laura Lou divorced! . . . He turned to Mrs. Tracy. "Are you talking seriously?"

Of course she was, she said. Wouldn't he try and understand her and listen to her, and not get all worked up, and make her so nervous she couldn't get out what she had to say . . . ?

"*Have* to say?" he interrupted. "Who obliges you? You say Laura Lou doesn't know you're here."

Mrs. Tracy's embarrassment increased. When Vance flew out at her like that, she said, she couldn't keep her wits together; and what was to be gained by making a fuss, anyhow? She was determined, whatever he said, that her child should be free to make a fresh start, and get back her health and spirits. . . . She talked on and on in the same half scared yet obstinate tone. They'd been married too young, she said; that had always been her chief objection to the match. And Vance with no fixed prospects . . . or not enough to support a wife on, anyhow . . . and his parents doing nothing . . . and Laura Lou's health so delicate, and her lungs threatened since that crazy climb up the mountain in the snow, and no way, as far as her mother knew, for her to get to a mild climate for the winter, as the doctor said she ought to, if she was to get her lungs healed. . . . Mrs. Tracy paused, breathless and drawn. "It all depends on you, Vance," she began again, still panting a little. "You've got your own life—your own ambitions. I don't say but what you'll go a great way yet, and maybe get onto a big newspaper job some day. But meantime, how are you going to get ahead with a sick wife on your hands—and your own family not doing anything to help? . . . Let her go, Vance; I say it in your own interest as well as hers; for pity's sake, let her go. Think what it would be to you to be free yourself."

He stood with bent head, her last words resounding

strangely in his ears. "Think what it would be to be free yourself." He had not thought of that.

"Let her go—go where?"

South, Mrs. Tracy hurriedly explained—to California somewhere. That was what the doctor said. She'd worked it all out with Upton. Upton had had the offer of a job in a big California nursery, and he would make up his mind to take it if his mother would go out and keep house for him; and Mrs. Tracy would sell the little place at Paul's Landing for whatever it would bring, if only they could get Laura Lou away before the cold weather. . . . And out there, in some of those western states, folks said you could get a divorce as easy as you get a cake of yeast at the grocer's. Just walk in and ask for it; and nothing said against either party . . . no question about other women or anything . . . so that if Vance wanted to marry again he'd have a clean slate . . . absolutely. . . . "Oh, Vance, if you only would—if you'd only agree to part as friends, and let my child have her chance!" Mrs. Tracy broke off in a spasm of dry sobbing.

Vance did not afterward recall how the discussion ended. He only knew that dusk had fallen when he and Mrs. Tracy at length left the house. As they turned down the lane they saw the lights of the high road, and the illuminated trolleys jogging by. Mrs. Tracy got into one and disappeared.

Vance sat down under a road lamp and pulled a scrap of paper from his pocket. He wrote on it: "I don't want these; I'll never go back there," wrapped the keys in the paper, and addressed it to Mrs. Tarrant. Then he caught the next trolley, and was carried as far as it went in the direction of Eaglewood. He meant to walk up there and leave the keys for her; after that he would see. The late August night was hushed but not oppressive; the stars already seemed to hang higher than in midsummer, as if receding to autumn altitudes; as he climbed there was a stir of air in the upper branches. The walk might help to clear the confusion from his brain; at any rate, it was out of the question to follow Mrs. Tracy home. First of all he had to be by himself, and in the open. . . .

The Eaglewood gate was unlatched, and he walked along the drive to the house. It lay low and spreading under mysterious tree shadows, and he thought of the day when he had been caught asleep in the broken-down motor, and brought there, a bewildered culprit, by the scandalized Jacob. Every step was thick with memories which in the making had worn no special look of happiness, but were now steeped in it. He remembered how ashamed and angry he had been when Jacob had shoved him into the hall among those unknown people. . . .

Through the canopy of foliage one or two lights peeped from the upper panes, but the lower floor was dark, the shutters were not closed. Perhaps everybody was still out. Silence and night seemed stealing unnoticed into the empty rooms, and Vance would have liked to open one of the windows and enter too. . . . But as he stood on the lawn, a little way off, a light appeared in one of the drawing room windows, and he heard a few chords struck on the piano, and voices rising and falling. Without looking to see who was in the room he hurried back into the shade of the drive, and dropped the keys into the letter box by the front door. They were all strangers to him, those people—he did not belong up there, in the light and music and ease, any more than he did in the dismal Tracy house below. He walked away heavy with that sense of inexorable solitude which sometimes oppresses young hearts. From all the glorious worlds he could imagine he seemed equally shut out. . . .

Where did he belong then? Why, with himself! The idea came like a flash of light. What did he want with other people's worlds when he would create universes of his own? What he wanted was independence, freedom, solitude—and they cost less than houses and furniture, and much less than human ties. Mrs. Tracy's words came back to him: "Think what it would be to you to be free yourself."

Out in the lane again, he continued to climb. Through pearly clouds the moon of late summer climbed with him, lighting the way capriciously, as it had been lit by Halo's motor lamps that morning before daylight when they had mounted to Thundertop. He had been free then, the world had lain before him in all its conquerable glory. And a few months of discouragement and the unexpected sight of a fresh face had annihilated everything, and reduced him to the poor thing he now was. He walked and walked, unconscious of the way, driven by the need of being alone and far from the realities to which he must so soon come back. At length he threw himself down on a ledge from which he could catch a first twist of the moon-silvered Hudson, remote and embosomed in midnight forest.

"Think what it would be to you to be free." That was what they were offering him . . . the return to that other world, the world he had looked down on from Thundertop.

He tried to clear his mind of anger and confusion and look at his case dispassionately. The Tracy case was plain enough; from the first, very likely, Mrs. Tracy had been bent on getting rid of him, on giving Laura Lou what she called her chance. But she was not a woman of initiative, and would probably have ended by resigning herself if some persistent influence had not pushed her forward. Upton's—? Vance shrugged away the thought of Upton . . . Hayes, of course! The blood rushed to his forehead. He could hear Bunty Hayes rehearsing the scene with Mrs. Tracy. Very likely they had cooked up the anonymous letter between them. And now they were going to turn him out like a boarder whose room was wanted . . . that was about the way they looked at it. . . . "Nothing easier . . . slick as a button . . ." Hayes would say. . . .

Well, why not?

He lay there, stretched out on the ledge, and looked down into the nocturnal depths. In the contemplation of that widespread beauty calmer thoughts came back, little things fell away. . . . What had he been able to do for Laura Lou? What had she done for him? The tie between them had so quickly become a habit, an aquiescence, nothing more. Perhaps Laura Lou had been conscious of that too, perhaps she too had chafed and longed for freedom—or simply for relief from worry, for material well-being, a home of her own—all that he could never give her. His eyes filled. . . . What was there to prevent their both trying again?

He could not find the answer to this question. He had never heard of any reason why married people shouldn't agree to part and begin life again if they wanted to . . . only he could not picture its happening to himself and Laura Lou. Whenever he tried to, it was as if a million delicate tendrils, of which he was unconscious when he and she were together, tightened about his heart and held it fast to hers, in a strange bondage closer than that of love or desire. He lay and lay there, and tried to puzzle it out, but in vain. His last conclusion was: "Of course if she really wants to be free, she shall be—" and for an instant his soul blazed again with the rekindled light of opportunity. . . . After that, worn out, he fell asleep on his ledge. . . .

It was broad daylight when he woke up, aching and hungry. His watch had stopped, but from the position of the sun he judged it must be after eight o'clock. His first craving was that of a ravenous boy—for a cup of Mrs. Tracy's hot coffee. What was all the fuss about, anyhow? How different things looked by daylight, with the same old sun lighting up the same old daily road of duty. There was the office, there was his wife—and, oh hallelujah, there was his work!

He sprang down from rock to rock, reached the road, and hurried homeward.

When he got to Mrs. Tracy's door he ran up the steps calling out Laura Lou's name. What nonsense it all seemed now, that ranting scene of last night! But to his astonishment the door was locked. He called again, shook the handle, banged on the panel—but no one answered. He walked around to the back of the house, expecting to find his mother-in-law among the currant bushes. "Laura Lou is sound asleep still, I suppose?" he would begin jokingly. But there was no one among the vegetables either, and the door of the back porch was also locked. Vance stepped back and threw a handful of pebbles at his wife's window, calling out to her again. Again there was no answer.

He returned to the front door, shook and rattled it without result, and finally, disheartened, sat down on the doorstep and wondered. . . .

All the way down the mountain conciliatory phrases, jokes, words of endearment had crowded to his lips—anything to smooth the way back to the old life. And now he was confronted by this silent hostile house, which seemed to know nothing of him, but stared down from blank forbidding windows as if on an intruder.

An intruder? Was it possible that he was already that? By God, no! His smouldering wrath against Mrs. Tracy blazed up again. It was all her doing, whatever had happened. She wouldn't rest till she had separated him from Laura Lou. . . . He was beginning to feel a sort of terror at the silent house and the unknown behind it. He saw the son of a neighbour walking down the lane, and stood up and hailed him. "See here—I'm just home, and I guess I'm locked out. Seen my womenfolk round anywhere?" he asked facetiously.

Yes, the youth said, he had; he'd met them up the lane. They were going to see if they could get Dixon's team to

take them to the station, they told him; he guessed they
were taking some baggage with them, for a stay. . . . He
grinned and loafed on, and Vance stood and looked after
him without moving. It had all been planned in advance,
then; they were going to the city—going straight to Bunty
Hayes, no doubt! He would have secured rooms for them,
where they could stay till they started for California. . . .

Vance walked dizzily back to the porch. It was true,
then—it had really happened, this thing which was still in-
conceivable to him. He stood there staring about him like a
man walking out of sleep; and as he did so, he noticed a
suitcase and two or three insecurely tied bundles in a corner
of the porch. They had already packed, then; they would
come back presently to pick up their belongings.

It was all as queer and telescopic as things piled up in a
nightmare. Yesterday morning this house had been his home
and Laura Lou's—now it was shut, empty, unrelated to
them. That phase of its existence and theirs was over. . . .
His eye lit casually on the suitcase, and he recognized it as
the one which had accompanied him and Laura Lou on
their honeymoon. He sat down beside it on the floor of the
porch, and recalled how he had unpacked it on the beach
on their wedding day and pulled out their sticky oozing
wedding breakfast. And how Laura Lou had had her first
taste of champagne out of a seashell! And it had been his
first taste, too—only he had got out of the way remembering
that. . . .

His eyes filled, and he was overcome by the sudden
boyish craving to see something belonging to her and touch
it. It seemed to him now that he and she had really parted
long ago; that the laughing child who had helped him to
unpack the lunch from that suitcase had for months past
been farther from him than there were miles between Paul's
Landing and California. He had not meant it to be so; had
not been aware that it was so—but now it came over him

that perhaps, for Laura Lou, the knot had long since been untied, that the anonymous letter had been a pretext long waited for, perhaps provoked. At the thought, the physical sense of her stole back on him; it was clinging and potent, like the perfume of a garden in June. Vance bent over the suitcase, and hardly knowing what he did, pushed open the lock and lifted the lid. Her poor little possessions had been crammed in carelessly and in haste, and on top, flattened out and disjointed, lay the old stuffed dove from the gilt basket he had sent to her mother.

The sight caught him by the throat. He knelt for a long time, clutching the limp moth-eaten bird in both hands. He had not thought of the dove for ages—but he remembered now having noticed that she had fastened it by a wire above the little looking glass on her chest of drawers. It had hung there, a little crooked, with one wing limp, ever since they had come back from their honeymoon.

He had hardly noticed it; but she had remembered, in the haste and grief of her going, to unfasten it from its perch and cram it into her bursting suitcase. "But if she feels like that, why is she going?" The thought rushed through him like a burst of warm rain in spring, softening, vivifying. He was afraid of nothing now, with the old stuffed dove in his hand! He stood up, pressing it to him, as the wheels of Dixon's carryall halted before the gate.

BOOK VI

❧ XXXII ❦

"UNDER A waning moon the little fleet stood out from Pondi-cherry . . ."

Vance sat lost in his vision. The phrase had murmured in his brain all day. Pondicherry—where was it? He didn't even know. Memories of the movies furnished the vague ex-oticism of the scene: clustered palms, arcaded houses, dusky women with baskets of tropical fruit. But lower than this surface picture, of which the cinema had robbed him, the true Pondicherry—*his*—hung before him like a mirage, re-mote, rare and undefiled. . . . Pondicherry! What a name! Its magic syllables concealed the subject of his new tale, as flower petals curve over the budding fruit. . . . He saw a harbour lit by a heavy red moon, the dusty cobblestones of the quay, a low blue-white house with a terrace over the water. . . .

"Vance *Weston*—wake up, for the Lord's sake! Don't look as if you were trying to listen in at a gas pump. . . ."

He roused himself to the fact that he was in Rebecca Stram's studio, perched on a shaky platform, and leaning sideways in the attitude the sculptress had imposed on him. . . . "I must have been asleep. . . ." he mumbled.

The studio was an attic, self-consciously naked and un-tidy. Somebody had started to paint maps of the four quar-ters of the globe on the bare walls, but had got bored after Africa, and the fourth quarter was replaced by a gigantic Cubist conundrum which looked like a railway junction

367

after a collision between excursion trains but was cryptically labelled: "Tea and Toast for One."

A large black stove stood out from one wall, and about it were gathered, that December afternoon, a group of young men as self-consciously shabby as the room. The only exception was Eric Rauch, whose dapperness of dress seemed proof against Bohemian influences, and who smoked cigarettes undauntedly among a scornful cluster of pipes. He, and everybody else, knew that he was there only on sufferance, because he was one of the *New Hour* fellows, and might come in useful any day, and because Vance Weston, the literary hero of the hour, belonged—worse luck!—to the *New Hour*. Eric Rauch, in spite of his little volume of esoteric poetry, was regarded as a Philistine by the group about Rebecca's stove, the fellows who wrote for the newest literary reviews and the latest experimental theatres. But they knew it was all in the day's work for Rebecca to portray the last successful novelist, and as poor Weston was owned by the *New Hour*, they had to suffer Rauch as his bear leader.

Above the stove they were discussing *This Globe*, Gratz Blemer's new novel, and Vance, roused out of his dream of Pondicherry, indolently listened. At first these literary symposia had interested and stimulated him; he felt as if he could not get enough of the cryptic wisdom distilled by these young men. But after ten or fifteen sittings to Rebecca, about whose stove they were given to congregating, he had gone the round of their wisdom, and come back still hungry.

He knew exactly, beforehand, what they were going to say about *This Globe*, and was bewildered and discouraged because he did not see how they could possibly admire it as much as they professed to if they also admired *Instead*. And of that fact there could be no doubt. *Instead* had taken as much with the Cocoanut Tree crowd as with what they contemptuously called the parlour critics. It was one of those privileged books which somehow contrive to insinuate themselves between the barriers of coterie and category, and are as likely to be found in the hands of the commuter hurrying to his office as of the wild-haired young men in gaudy pullovers theorizing in the void about Rebecca's stove.

Rebecca Stram, clothed to the chin in dirty linen, stepped back with screwed-up eyes, gave a dab at the clay, and sighed: "If you'd only fall in love with me I'd make a big thing out of this. . . ."

Vance heard her, but drew a mask of vacancy over his face. Love—falling in love! Were there any words in the language as hateful to him, or as void of meaning? His love, he thought, was like his art—something with a significance so different from the current one that when the word was spoken before him a door flew shut in his soul, closing him in with his own groping ardours. Love! Did he love Laura Lou—had he ever loved her? What other name could he give to the upwelling emotion which had flung him back in her arms when she had driven up to the door that day in Dixon's carryall? It was over a year since then; and he did not yet understand why the passion which had shaken him that day to the roots of his being had not transformed and renewed both their lives. The mere thought that she was leaving him—and leaving him because he had unwittingly wounded, neglected her—had opened an abyss at his feet. That was what life would be to him without her: a dark pit into which he felt himself crashing headlong, like falling in an aeroplane at night. . . . It hadn't taken five minutes to break up Mrs. Tracy's plan, win back Laura Lou, and laugh away all the bogies bred of solitude and jealousy—poor child, she'd actually been jealous of him! And he had been young enough (a year ago) to imagine that one can refashion life in five minutes—remould it, as that man Fitzgerald

said, nearer to the heart's desire! . . . God—the vain longing of the soul of man for something different, when everything in human relations is so eternally alike, unchanging
and unchangeable!

They had broken up at Paul's Landing. Mrs. Tracy,
embittered and resentful, had sold the house and gone to
California with Upton. But Laura Lou had remained, reconciled, enraptured, and Vance had brought her to New
York to live. . . . Could anything be more different, to all
appearances? And yet, in a week, he had known that everything was going to be exactly the same—and that the centre
and source of all the sameness were Laura Lou and her own
little unchangeable self. . . .

"What you feel about Blemer's book" (one of the fellows was haranguing between pipe-puffings) "is that it's so
gorgeously discontinuous, like life—" (life discontinuous?
Oh, God! Vance thought.) "Not a succession of scenes fitting into each other with the damned dead logic of a picture
puzzle, but a drunken orgy of unrelatedness. . . ."

"Not like Fynes, eh?" (Vance thought: "Last year Tristram Fynes was their idol," and shivered a little for his own
future.) "Poor old Fynes," another of them took it up;
"sounded as if he's struck a new note because he made his
people talk in the vernacular. Nothing else new about *him*—
might have worked up his method out of Zola. Probably
did."

"Zola—who's he?" somebody yawned.

"Oh, I dunno. The French Thackeray, I guess."

"See here, fellows, who's read Thackeray, anyhow?"

"Nobody since Lytton Strachey, I guess."

"Well, anyway, *This Globe* is one great big book. Eh,
Vance, that the way you see it?"

Vance roused himself and looked at the speaker. "Not
the way I see life. Life's continuous."

"Gee! I guess you're confusing life with Rebecca. Let

him get down and stretch his legs a minute, Becka, or he'll be writing books like *The Corner Grocery*."

Under shelter of the general laugh Vance shifted his position and lit a cigarette. "Oh, well—" Rebecca Stram grumbled, laying down her modelling tool and taking a light from his match.

"Life continuous—continuous? Why, it's a series of jumps in the dark. That's Mendel's law, anyhow," another budding critic took up the argument.

"Gee! Who's Mendel? Another new novelist?"

"Mendel? No. He's the guy that invented the principle of economy of labour. That's what Mendelism is, isn't it?"

"Well, I'm shattered! Why, you morons, Mendel was the Victorian fellow that found out about Nature's proceeding by jumps. He worked it out that she's a regular kangaroo. Before that all the Darwins and people thought she planned things out beforehand, like a careful mother—or the plot of a Fynes novel."

Fynes had become their recognized butt, and this was greeted by another laugh. Rebecca threw herself full length on the broken-springed divan, grumbling: "Well, it's too dark to go on. When'll you come back, Vance—tomorrow?"

Vance hesitated. Laura Lou was beginning to object to the number of sittings—beginning, he fancied, to suspect that they were a pretext; just as, under her mother's persuasion, she had suspected that his work at the Willows was a pretext for meeting Mrs. Tarrant. Oh, hell—to give one big shake and be free! "Yes, tomorrow," he rang out resolutely, as if Laura Lou could hear him, and resent his challenge. . . . When the sittings began he had begged her to accompany him to the studio. "When the Stram girl sees you she'll do you and not me," he had joked; and the glow of gratified vanity had flown to her cheeks. But she had gone with him, and nobody had noticed her—neither Rebecca nor any of the young men. The merely beautiful was not in demand in

Rebecca's crowd—was in fact hardly visible to them. Or
rather, they had forced beauty into a new formula, into
which Laura Lou's obvious loveliness did not fit. And when
she had murmured: "Why, you don't *say* . . ." or: "See
here, I guess you're quizzing me," her conversational moves
were at an end, and she could only sit, lovely and unperceived, in a cloud of disappointment. She never went back
to Rebecca's.

Eric Rauch walked away with Vance, and as they
reached the street Vance's bruised soul spoke out. "Hearing
those fellows talk I don't see what they can find in my
book."

"Why, they have a good time reading it. They crack
their teeth over their own conundrums, and now and then
they just indulge in the luxury of lying back and reading a
real book."

"But they believed in Fynes last year."

"Sure. And they believed in you till Gratz Blemer came
along. What you've got to do now is to go Blemer one better
—do your big New York novel in his style," Rauch ended
with a laugh, as their ways parted.

Vance was going home; but he felt within himself a
dammed-up flood of talk, and as he reached Washington
Square it occured to him that Frenside lived nearby, and
might sometimes be found at that hour. Vance did not often
see Frenside nowadays. The latter seldom came to the *New
Hour*, and Vance as seldom went to Mrs. Tarrant's, where
the old critic was most often to be met. Vance's relation
with the Tarrants had shrunk—by his own choice—to business intercourse with Tarrant at the office. Some native
clumsiness had made it impossible for him, after he came to
New York, to work out a manner, an attitude, toward Halo
Tarrant. Other fellows knew how; took that sort of thing in
their stride; but he couldn't. The art of social transitions was
still a mystery to him. He remembered once hearing his

grandmother (rebuked by Mrs. Weston for bad management and extravagance) say plaintively: "Why, daughter, I presume I can go without—*but I can't economize.*" Vance understood that: morally and materially, he had never known how to economize. But he could go without—at least he supposed he could. . . .

Halo, who had heard of their arrival in New York from her husband, had written a friendly little note to Laura Lou, asking her and Vance to lunch; and Laura Lou, after a visible struggle between her irrepressible jealousy and the determination to prove to Vance that she had never been jealous (how could he have thought so, darling?)—Laura Lou had decided that they must accept.

They did, and the result was disastrous. From the first moment everything had bewildered Laura Lou and roused her inarticulate resentment. She was used to Halo—didn't care a straw what *she* thought of anybody or anything. . . . Hadn't she seen her, for years, coming and going at the Willows? They were distant cousins too—Halo needn't have reminded her of that in her note! But she had never seen Mrs. Tarrant in this setting of New York luxury and elegance; she had never met Tarrant, who at once struck her as heartless and sardonic; she had never seen people like the other guests, men young and elderly, all on a footing of intimacy with their hosts, and talking carelessly, allusively, easily, of people and things that Laura Lou had never heard of. . . . She did not confess a word of this to Vance; she did not have to. Her face was like a clear pool reflecting every change in a shifting sky. He could measure, partly from his own memories, partly from his knowledge of her, the impact of every allusion, every unexpected gesture or turn of phrase of the people about her. The mere way in which the lunch was served was something to marvel at and be resented—didn't he know? ("Caviar? That what you call it— that nasty gray stuff that smelt like motor grease? No, I didn't touch it. . . . When I watched you eating it I thought you'd be sick, sure. . . ." and so on.) For the rest, she took the adventure as something completely matter-of-course and not worth discussing, and remained coldly surprised, faintly ironic, and indifferent. *Is that all?* her attitude seemed to say. But how well he knew what was under it!

Since then he had never been back to Mrs. Tarrant's. What was the use? Not to see her at all was less of a privation seeing her like that. . . . She had sent him, a few days later, a note asking how the novel was getting on, and when he was coming to read the next chapters to her; and he had not answered. He did not know how to excuse himself from going to see her, and was resolved to avoid the torment of renewing their friendship. So the months passed, and they did not meet. . . .

He cared only for his work now, or so he told himself. It was his one refuge from material and moral conditions so stifling and embittering that but for that other world to escape to he would have borrowed a revolver and made an end. . . . But his work too was becoming a perplexity. By the time he had finished *Instead* forty subjects were storming at the gates of his imagination and clamouring for embodiment. But his first encounter with the perplexing contradictory theories of the different literary groups to which the success of his book introduced him, all the wild currents and whirlpools of critical opinion in New York, had shaken his faith in himself; not in his powers of exposition and expression, which seemed to grow more secure with every page he wrote, but in his choice of a theme, a point of view, what the politicians called a "platform." It had never before occurred to him that the artist needed any, except that to which his invisible roots struck down, in the depths ruled by The Mothers; but these fellows with their dogmas and paradoxes, their contradictory pronouncements and condemnations, though all they said seemed so on the surface, excited his imagination and yet unsettled it. "What I need is a good talk with somebody outside of it all," he thought, his mind instinctively turning to Halo Tarrant; but it turned from her again abruptly, and he concluded: "A talk with a man—much older, and with a bigger range. Somebody who'll listen to me, anyhow—" for that was what his contemporaries would never do.

He read "In" on the dingy card under Frenside's doorbell, and ran upstairs to his door. Frenside, in a haze of pipe smoke, let him in, and Vance found himself in a small shabby room. A green-shaded lamp made a studious circle of light on a big table untidily stacked with books and reviews, and an old steamer chair with a rug on it was drawn up to a smouldering fire. Frenside looked surprised, and then said: "Glad you've come," and signed to Vance to take the seat opposite him. "Well, how are you standing your success?" he enquired, settling down into his deck chair.

"Oh, I don't think much about what's done," Vance answered. "It's the thing ahead that bothers me." He paused, and then asked: "Can I talk to you?" and the other pushed out his thorny eyebrows and answered: "Try."

"Well—it's this way. I'm not a bit like that fellow in the hymn. One step isn't enough for me. And I can't seem to see beyond; I'm in a fog that gets thicker and thicker."

Frenside leaned back with half-closed lids and seemed to take counsel of his pipe. "Creative or doctrinal?"

Vance smiled. "Oh, chiefly doctrinal, I guess."

"Well, that's not mortal. Out with your symptoms." And Vance began.

It was his first opportunity for a quiet talk with Frenside, and he saw at once that there was nothing to fear if one really had something to say to him. Vance had plenty to say; the difficulty was that he did not quite know where to begin. But before he had done floundering Frenside had taken the words out of his mouth and was formulating his problem for him, clearly, concisely. He did not harangue him, but put a series of questions and helped Vance to answer them, so that even when Frenside was talking Vance seemed to be listening to himself.

"Yes—it's a bad time for a creator of any sort to be born, in this after-war welter, with its new recipe for immortality every morning. And I suppose, for one thing, you're torn between the demands of your publishers, who want another *Instead,* and your own impulse, which is to do something quite different—outside it, beyond it, away from it. And when you add to that all the critics (I believe they call themselves) knocking down their own standards once a day, and building up others to suit their purblind necessities —God, yes, it's a tough old vocation that will force its way through that yelping crowd, and I don't wonder a youngster like you is dazed by it."

Vance listened attentively. "I'm not dazed, though, not exactly. I said I couldn't see around me and outside of me. But there's a steady light somewhere inside of me. . . ."

"Yes, I believe there is," Frenside nodded. He drew at his pipe, crossed one leg over another, and finally said: "I'd have given a gold mine to have that light, at your age."

The blood rushed to Vance's forehead. "Oh, but you—"

"No, not that. But I'm straying from the subject: which is, plainly, what had you better do next?"

"Well, yes, that's so."

"And the obvious answer: 'Follow your impulse,' is no use when you have a hundred impulses tugging at you from the inside, and all that clatter of contradictory opinion from the outside, eh?" Frenside considered again. "The trouble with you is that you're suffering from the self-distrust produced by success. Nothing is as disintegrating as success: one blurb on a book jacket can destroy a man's soul more surely than the *Quarterly* killed Keats. And to young fellows

like you, after you've made your first hit, the world is all one
vast blurb. Well, you've got to stuff cotton in your ears and
go ahead. . . ."

"Ahead, you say? But where? Well, Nature abhors a
void, and to fill it she's wasteful—wildly wasteful. In the abstract, my advice would be: follow her example. Be as
wasteful as she is. Her darlings always are. Chase after one
impulse and another; try your hand at this and that; let your
masterpieces die off by the dozen without seeing the light
. . . But what's the use of such talk nowadays? Besides,
you've got to earn your living, haven't you? Well, that's not
a bad thing either. You don't want to risk getting lost in the
forest of dreams. It happens. And if you once went to sleep
under the deadly Tree of Alternatives you might never wake
up again. So—" He paused, relit his pipe, and blinked at
Vance meditatively.

"As far as I can see, one trouble is this. The thing
you've just done (yes, I've read it; Halo made me) well, it's
a pretty thing, exquisite, in fact, and a surprise, a novelty
nowadays, as its popularity has proved. But it's a thing that
leads nowhere. An evocation—an emanation—something
you wrought with enchantments, eh? Well, now take hold
of life as it lies around you; you remember Goethe: 'Wherever you take hold of it, it's interesting'? So it is—but only in
proportion as *you* are. There's the catch. The artist has got
to feed his offspring out of his own tissue. Enrich that, day
and night—perpetually. How? . . . Ah, my dear fellow,
that's the question! What does the tortoise stand on . . . ?"

Vance sat silent. Perhaps his adviser was right. Perhaps
the only really fruitful field for the artist was his own day,
his own town or country, a field into which he could plunge
both hands and pluck up his subjects with their live roots.
Instead had charmed his readers by its difference—charmed
them because they were unconsciously tired of incoherence
and brutality; but the spell would soon break because, as

Frenside said, his tale had been an "emanation," not a reality. He had given very little of what Frenside called his "tissue" to its making. And now his thoughts reverted to *Loot*, the old theme which had haunted him since his first days in New York—it seemed a century ago—and his imagination instantly set to work on it.

"I suppose you go out a good deal these days—see a good many people? A novelist ought to, at one time or another," Frenside continued. "Manners are your true material, after all."

Vance hesitated. "I don't go out much." He could not add that Laura Lou made it impossible; but he said, with equal truth: "Fact is, I can't afford it. I mean, the time—or the money either . . ."

"The money?" Frenside looked surprised. "Why, you ought to be raking in royalties by now. I don't suppose you got much out of the *New Hour* for your serial? No, I thought not. The highbrow papers can't pay. But the book; why it's been out three or four months, hasn't it? It was a good deal talked about while it was coming out in the review, and you ought to have had a handsome sum on the advance sales, and another instalment after three months. I understand that's the regular arrangement for fiction—I wish it was for book-reviewing," he added mournfully.

Vance was glad of the opening; but for Frenside's question he would never have had the courage to mention his material difficulties, though it was partly with that object that he had called. But he felt the friendliness under the old man's gruff interrogations, and his anxiety burst from him. No, he said, he'd had no such privileges. The publishers, Dreck and Saltzer, to whom Tarrant had bound him for three years for all book publication, had been visibly disappointed by *Instead*. They didn't think the subject would take, and even if it did, they said the book was too short for big sales. There's nothing a publisher so hates to handle as a book—especially a novel—that doesn't fit into the regulation measures. *Instead* was only forty-five thousand words long, and Mr. Dreck told Vance he didn't know a meaner length. He'd rather have an elephant to handle like *Ulysses* or *American Tragedy*, than a mouthful like that. When readers have paid their money they like to sit down to a square meal. An oyster cocktail won't satisfy 'em. They want their money's worth; and that's at least a hundred thousand. And if you try charging 'em less, they say: "Hell, what's wrong with the book for it to sell so cheap? Not an hour's reading in it, most likely." So Dreck and Saltzer had halved the percentage previously agreed on, on the plea that the book wasn't a novel anyhow—nothing under ninety thousand is; and there had been no advance royalties, and there would be no payment at all till June. Of course, they said, if Vance had pulled off the Pulsifer Prize it would have been different. As it was, there was nothing in it for them, and they took the book only to oblige Tarrant.

Frenside listened attentively. When Vance had ended, he said: "From a business point of view I suppose they were right—before the book came out. But now? It's had a big sale, or so they say in their advertisements; and they wouldn't keep on advertising it if it hadn't. Can't you ask them to make you an advance, even if it's not in the bond?"

Vance reddened as he said that he had asked and been turned down. The publishers claimed that they were advertising the book at a dead loss, that the sales hadn't been much bigger than they had expected; but that they "believed" in Vance's future, and were ready to risk some money on it—a pure speculation, they declared. So they really couldn't do more.

Frenside gave a contemptuous wave of his pipe. "That's what the small publishers call 'business,' and why they never get to be big ones. Pity you're tied up to them. However—" He paused, and Vance felt that he was being

searchingly scrutinized from under those jutting brows.
"And you'd be glad of a loan, I gather? Have you—put the
matter before Tarrant?"

"Oh, no—I couldn't," Vance interrupted in a thick
voice.

Frenside nodded, as if that were not wholly a surprise.
"See here, young fellow, I believe you've got the stuff in
you, and I'd like to help you. I'm never very flush myself; I
daresay my appearance and my surroundings make that
fairly obvious. But if a hundred would be any good—"

He made a motion to pull himself up out of his chair;
but Vance raised a hand to check him. A hundred dollars—
any good? God . . . his mouth watered . . . But somehow
he didn't want to take the money; didn't want their inspirit-
ing talk to end in the awkwardness of pocketing a cheque;
didn't, above all, want to overshadow the possibility of future talks by an obligation he might be unable to meet. He
must keep this spiritual sanctuary clear of the moneylenders'
booths.

"Thank you," he stammered. "But no, honest, I couldn't
. . . I mean, I guess I can make out. . . ." He stood up,
and looked Frenside in the eyes. "When I get the chance to
talk to you I'd rather it was about my work. Nothing else
matters, after all. . . ."

Frenside rose also. "Well, I've got to pack you off now
and get into harness myself." He pointed to the papers on
his desk. "But come back when you can," he added. "And
wait a minute—let me give you a cocktail . . . I daresay
you can operate the shaker better than I can. . . . Here's to
your next."

⤞ XXXIII ⤝

VANCE WALKED away with a conquering step. Frenside had set his blood circulating. "I believe you've got the stuff in you"—when a man like Frenside said it, all the depths cried out in answer. "*Loot—Loot—Loot*—a big American novel; that's what I've got to do," Vance sang, almost shouted to himself, as he trudged homeward in the dusk.

He had spoken the plain truth when he told Frenside that nothing mattered but his work. When that possessed him it swept away all material miseries, poverty, debt, the uncertainty of the future, the dull dissatisfactions of the present. He felt that he could go without food, money, happiness—even happiness—as long as the might within drove him along the creative way. . . . "That's a man to talk to," he thought, tingling with the glow of Frenside's rude sincerity. He was dead right, too, about a thing like *Instead* being a sideshow, about the necessity of coming to grips with reality, with the life about him. Vance brushed aside the vision of his East Indian novel—the result of a casual glance at a captivating book called *The French in India*—and said to himself: "He's right, again, when he says I ought to go into society, see more people, study—what's the word he used? —manners. I read too much, and don't brush up against enough people. If I'm going to write *Loot* I've got to get my store clothes out of pawn." He laughed at the idea. . . .

His dream was cut short by the vision of Laura Lou waiting for him in the dismal bedroom of the place where they boarded. They had begun life in New York in a decent rooming house, recommended by Vance's old friend, the manager of Friendship House. It was clean, hygienic, not too dear; in fact, would have suited them exactly if, as cold weather came on, Laura Lou's colds had not so often prevented her going out for her meals. She tried preparing their food on an electric cooker, but the dishes she produced were unpalatable and indigestible, and the woman who kept the house objected to the mess that resulted. So they had moved to their present quarters, far over on the West Side, in a leprous brownstone survival of an earlier world. When Vance entered the greasy hall a smell of canned soup and stale coffee told him that dinner had begun. "I do wish Laura Lou would go down without waiting for me," he thought impatiently; but she never would, and on the days when he was late, and she had to eat her food cold, she always ended up with a sick headache. He reflected with a grin, as he sprang up the stairs, that the people he was going to describe in *Loot*—the dress-clothes people—were at that hour still dawdling over tea and cocktails, as he and Mrs. Pulsifer had done, in that circular panelled room with the flowers and the dove-coloured armchairs, to which he had never again been admitted. . . . Dinner, in that world, was two or three hours off, down the vista of a brilliant night. . . .

In the letter rack Vance found some letters, and pocketed them without a glance. He guessed at once what they were: offers from editors and publishers tempted by the success of *Instead* and making proposals which, hard up as he was, he would have to refuse. Neither Tarrant nor the publishers Tarrant had imposed on him would consent to let him off his bargain, or to increase by a dollar the contracts made with him. He couldn't see what there was "in it" for them; his indifference to his own work, once it was finished and he had turned to something else, made him underrate

the prestige that *Instead* had conferred on the *New Hour,*
and he ascribed to editorial obstinacy Tarrant's natural desire to make the best of his opportunity. For another two
years every line that Vance wrote was tariffed in advance
and belonged to the *New Hour,* and then to Dreck and
Saltzer. Yet write he must, without a pause, or he and Laura
Lou would starve. For himself he would have preferred
starvation; but for Laura Lou he must at least provide such
sustenance as Mrs. Hubbard's table offered. Mrs. Hubbard,
his landlady (for obvious reasons called "Mother" by her
boarders), was very particular about the character and an-
tecedents of the guests she received; the latter understood
that the social fastidiousness entailed by her being the
widow of a southern colonel made it impossible for her to
be equally particular as to the food she provided. "If I have
to overlook a blemish I'd ruther it was in the mutton than in
the *moràl* of the ladies and gentlemen I receive in my home
—in the late Colonel Hubbard's home," said Mrs. Hubbard,
who was persuaded that *"moràl,"* a word she often used,
was French for morals. The late colonel had been vice-
consul in a French colonial port, and Mrs. Hubbard prided
herself on her French.

Vance, springing upstairs, pushed open the door of the
room into which he and Laura Lou and their humble possessions (including the fetish dove) were crowded. "Hullo,"
he flung ahead of him gaily. "Sorry I'm late; I've been working out a big new idea for a novel."

As he spoke he remembered how often of late he had
given the same reason for his unpunctuality, and how slight
a spark of interest it roused in her. Did she believe him,
even? Very likely not. She was becoming more and more resentful of the hours he devoted to Rebecca Stram; unless,
indeed, she suspected him of using the sculptress as a
screen, and secretly giving his time to "that woman"—who
to her was still, and perhaps always would be, Halo Tarrant.

For whatever cause, he saw at a glance that she nursed a grievance, a fact confirmed by her not replying to his remark. It was always a proof of resentment in Laura Lou to ignore what he said, and meet each of his conversational attempts by a totally irrelevant reply.

"The dinner bell rang ever so long ago," she said, rising listlessly from her rocking chair.

"I could smell that fact as soon as I opened the front door," he returned, his eagerness driven back on itself by her indifference. "Just let me wash my hands—" and he began to throw down on the floor a pile of linen stacked in the washbasin.

"Oh don't, Vance—it's the laundry, just come home," she exclaimed, stooping to pick up the scattered garments. "And this floor's so dirty—"

"Well, you've got a closet to keep things in," he retorted, exasperated, as he always was, by her growing inertia, her way of letting their clothes lie about and accumulate in the cramped untidy room, rather than take the trouble of putting them where they belonged. But he was always ashamed of himself when he spoke to her impatiently, and to efface his retort he added, while he dried his hands: "Been out any this afternoon, old lady?"

"No."

"Why not? A little walk would have done you good."

"I didn't feel like walking."

It was their eternal daily dialogue. Why didn't she ever feel like walking? In the early days she used to spring up the hillsides with him like a young deer—but now, day after day, she just sat in her chair, and rocked and brooded. He suspected her of thinking—not unnaturally—that in a city there was no object in going out unless you had money for shopping or the movies. She had never said so—she never complained of their lack of money; but she could not understand what else there was to do in a place like New York.

"Then you've stuck indoors again all day and not spoken to a human being? I hate your being always alone like that," he said, dashing the brush irritably through his hair.

"I wasn't alone." She paused, and then brought out: "Not this afternoon, at least. I had a visitor."

"A visitor? Well, that's good." He supposed it was one of Mrs. Hubbard's other "guests," though he knew that Laura Lou did not encourage their neighbourly advances, partly through shyness, partly, he suspected, through some fierce instinct of self-protection, the desire to keep him and their two lives absolutely to herself.

"Come along down. . . . Who was it?" he continued absently, passing his arm through hers.

She stood still. "It was Mrs. Tarrant."

He stopped short also, in astonishment. "Mrs. Tarrant? She came to see you?"

"Yes."

"Was the parlour empty? Could you see her there?" he questioned, evoking in a flash the strange unlikely scene, and the possibility of Mrs. Hubbard's other ladies watchfully clustered about the unknown visitor.

"I don't know. I sent word by the girl I was sick—and the first thing I knew she came up here."

"*Here*—Mrs. Tarrant did?" Vance stood gazing about him, as if brutally awakened to the sight of the room, its blistered faded paper with patches of a different design, their scanty possessions untidily tossed about, the slovenly intimacies of bed and washstand and night table.

"Well, why shouldn't she? I didn't ask her to."

"I only meant, I should have thought you'd rather have seen her downstairs."

Laura Lou's lips narrowed. "I'd rather not have seen her at all." When she spoke in that tone, between those level lips, the likeness to her mother, which had already peeped out at him now and again, suddenly took possession of her whole face. Vance looked at her attentively. It was no doubt because she had grown thinner in the last months, and lost her colour, that the resemblance affirmed itself in this startling way. Vance remembered what his grandmother had said about Mrs. Tracy's prettiness and her pink silk flounces, when, on her bridal tour, she had visited her western relatives at Advance. He was chilled by the sense of life perpetually slipping by, and leaving its stealthy disfigurement on spirit and flesh. . . . What was the use of anything, with this decrepitude at the core?

"I didn't ask her to come up," Laura Lou repeated querulously.

"Oh, well, no matter. . . . What did she come for?"

"To ask us to a party."

"A party—?"

"She wants to give you a party. She says lots of people are crazy to see you. She said I oughtn't to keep you so shut up. . . . She asked me to pick an evening. . . ." There was a curious ring of gratified pride under the affected indifference of Laura Lou's voice.

"Well, did you?" Vance asked ironically.

"I said she'd better see you. I said I didn't care about parties, but I'd never kept you from going." She paused, and added rigidly: "I told her there was no use coming here to see you because you were always out."

Vance received this in silence. What was there to say? Mrs. Tarrant had come to invite them to a party—had delivered her invitation in that room! Did she really think parties were a panacea for such a plight as theirs? Or had she been moved by another impulse which had been checked on her lips by Laura Lou's manifest hostility? The dreary ironic light of failure lay on everything, as it had on that far-off day at Euphoria when Vance, recovering from his fever, had poured out his bitterness in his first tale. Perhaps life

would never again be bearable to him except as material for
his art. In itself it seemed persistently ugly and uncontrollable, a horror one could neither escape from nor master
—as if one should be forever battling in the dark with a
grimacing idiot.

"See here—there'll be nothing left to eat if we don't go
down," he reminded his wife.

"I don't want anything. I'm not hungry. Besides, it's too
late . . . you're always too late. . . ."

At that he snatched up his hat and coat in sudden
anger. The likeness to Mrs. Tracy was not in his wife's face
alone. "Oh, all right. Just as you like. I'm hungry, if you're
not. If dinner's over I'll go out and get a bite somewhere."

"You better," she rejoined, in the same lifeless tone; and
without looking back at her he flung the door shut and ran
downstairs and out of the house.

In the first chophouse that he passed he found a table,
ordered sausage and potatoes, with a cup of coffee, and devoured them ravenously. He was still young enough for
anger and grief to make him hungry. . . . There was no
one he knew in the place, and after he had satisfied his
hunger he pulled out his letters and glanced over them. As
he had expected, they were all on literary business. One important publisher, who wanted his next novel, asked him to
call and see if, in the course of a talk, they could not devise
some plan of adjustment with Dreck and Saltzer. Though
Vance had no hope of this he was encouraged by the ur-
gency of the request. How easy it would have been, he
thought, to work his way through his two remaining years of
bondage if only Laura Lou had not weighed down every
endeavour—if only he had been free and alone! But there
was no use in going through that weary round again. He
had had the chance of freeing himself and had refused it.
How could a fellow tell beforehand where each act would
lead, and what would be the next to grow out of it? Perhaps

they were right, those chaps at Rebecca Stram's, who said it was all a blind labyrinth, a disconnected muddle. . . .

The despair of youth overcame him. He felt a sudden loss of faith in himself, in his powers, in the intrinsic interest of things, in his capacity to drag through these next two years of poverty, drudgery, and mental hunger.

He asked the waitress if he could telephone. She said yes, and led him to the back of the room. He looked up a number and rang. . . . Suddenly he heard an answering voice, and repeated the number. "Yes," the voice said. He stammered: "I want to speak to Mrs. Tarrant," and the same voice, with a note of reproach, came back: "Why, Vance, don't you know me? Yes . . . I'm here. . . . Yes, come . . . come at once . . . do." He hung up, and turned back dizzily to the door. She was there, she was so close that he seemed to feel her light touch on his shoulder. . . . And she had been there, so near to him, all these months, and he had never once tried to see her. It seemed incredible, preposterous, the very core and centre of his folly. Why had he gone on starving when the banquet was spread and within his reach?

At the door of the Tarrants' apartment house his morbid sensitiveness to the visible world and its implications produced in him an abrupt change of view. It was long since he had entered one of those quiet commodious buildings, where everything bespoke conditions so different from those which imprisoned him. He recalled with compunction his outburst against Laura Lou. No wonder she had resented Mrs. Tarrant's visit—no wonder any advance from people living in ease and amenity seemed to the poor child like a deliberate condescension. Poor Laura Lou! If he could have given her a little cottage in a pleasant suburb, something of her own to be proud of and fuss over, it might have altered everything . . . As he stepped into the panelled lift and swung up to the top story he felt a gnawing anger

against the unfairness of life, the cruelty of social conditions. He no longer remembered that when he had called up
Mrs. Tarrant the thought of her had been a means of escape
from his misery, that he had yielded to the urgent need of
talking over his new book with her, and plunging once more
into the healing springs of her sympathy. Now that he was
on her threshold he felt only the blind desire to punish her
—punish her for her tactless intrusion on his wife, for living
as she lived, for being what she was, for not leaving him
and Laura Lou alone to live and to be as they were doomed
to, with or without her interference. . . .

The door opened on the softly lit anteroom. A maid
took his hat and coat, and said: "This way;" and there she
sat, by the fire in the library, alone. She wore something
dark and lacy, through which her upper arms showed; and
the sober book-lined room, with its shaded lamps, and a few
lilylike crimson flowers in a tall jar, seemed a part of her,
the necessary background to her aloof and reticent grace.
Vance recalled the room in which he had left Laura Lou,
and at the same moment, joined to that evocation, came the
vision of this woman turning from him, with a careless
pleasantry, in that other room at the Willows where he had
cast his soul at her feet. . . . No, there could be no common meeting ground for him and Halo Tarrant; the conditions of life divided them too sharply. Material well-being,
security from hunger and debt, made people callous and unfeeling, perhaps without any fault of their own. But he had
been right in deciding not to see her again, and wrong in
yielding to the impulse which had led him to her tonight.

"Vance—how glad I am!" she said, rising and holding
out her two hands in the old friendly way.

He stood near the door, bound hand and foot in coils of
awkwardness and resentment. "You went to see my wife
today," he began, and stopped, not knowing how to go on.

Mrs. Tarrant raised her eyebrows slightly. "Yes. It was

so long since I'd had any news of either of you. I thought she was not looking well the day she lunched here . . . and I wanted to see if there was anything I could do. . . ."

"No. There's nothing you can do."

He felt the surprise and pain in her eyes without daring to meet them. "I'm sorry," she rejoined simply. "But I'm glad you've come this evening. Sit down, won't you, Vance? I'm all alone—Lewis is at a man's dinner, and I thought I'd snatch a quiet evening with my books."

Vance still hung in the middle of the wide space between the door and the fireplace. "I guess I won't interrupt you then," he said, still at a loss for his next phrase.

"Interrupt me? How can you say that? You know I've wanted a talk with you for a long time."

"No, I didn't know . . . I mean . . ." He broke off suddenly. "My wife wasn't well when you called. You oughtn't to have gone up into her room without her asking you," he blurted out.

"Vance!"

"Can't you see how people feel," he continued passionately, "when somebody like you, coming out of this—" he took in the room with a gesture of reproach, "when you come into the kind of place we have to live in, and try to pretend that there can ever be anything in common between our lives and yours?"

Mrs. Tarrant, resting one hand on the back of her chair, still gazed at him in perplexity. "Vance—I don't understand. Did Laura Lou object to my visit?"

"She felt about it the way I do. We know you mean to be kind. But it's no use. We don't belong to your kind of people—never will. And it just complicates things for me if you . . ." He checked himself, conscious that he was betraying what he had meant to conceal.

"I see," she murmured in a low voice. There was an interval of silence; then she said: "I'm sorry to have done anything stupid. You know I'm impulsive, and not used to standing on ceremony. I went to see Laura Lou because I wanted to have news of you both, and because I particularly want you to come here some evening to meet a few people who really care for your book, and would talk to you intelligently about it. You ought to see more people of that sort—give them a chance to know you and talk with you. It would stimulate you, I'm sure, and be good for your work."

Vance felt his colour rising. It was difficult to reply in a spirit of animosity to words so simple and kindly. But the suggestion of the evening party recalled Laura Lou's resentment.

"Thank you—but that's no use either. Evening parties, I mean. They're not for people like us. . . ."

She did not answer immediately; then she said: "Won't you sit down, Vance? I hoped you'd come for a long talk. . . ."

He replied, without noticing her request: "I came to say we're much obliged to you for thinking of us, but it's no use your bothering—really no use."

She moved nearer and laid her hand on his. "Vance—what's wrong? What has happened? How can you speak to a friend of 'bothering' about you? If you don't want to meet people, I won't invite them; but that seems no reason why you and I shouldn't talk together sometimes in the old way. Perhaps you haven't missed our talks as much as I have—perhaps they didn't count as much in your life as they did in mine. . . ."

She paused, and suddenly he flung up his hands and hid his face in them. "Not count—not count in my life?"

He felt her fingers gently slipped through his, drawing his hands down so that his face was uncovered to her scrutiny and his eyes were forced to look into hers. "Not count . . . not count?" He stared at her through a blur of tears.

"They did, Vance? I'm so glad. Then why try to deny it? Why shouldn't we just go back to where we were before? I'm sure you've got lots to tell me about your new plans. . . ."

He snatched his hands away and hid his face again, struggling to choke back his sobs. What would she think— what would she suppose? But it was no use fighting against the surge of joy and agony that caught him and shook him like a young tree in a spring gale. He stammered out: "I'm a fool. . . . You mustn't mind me. . . . I've been through hell lately. . . . Just let me sit here a little while without talking, till I get used to you again. . . ." and without a word she went back to her chair and sat there silently, the shaded lamplight on her quiet head.

≫ XXXIV ≪

IT WAS long past midnight when he cautiously pushed open his door on Mrs. Hubbard's third story. The light from a street lamp, shining through the shutterless window, showed him Laura Lou in bed, asleep or pretending to be; and he undressed as noiselessly as he could and lay down beside her. He was used to her ways now: he knew she would not begin questioning him till the next morning, and he lay there, his arms crossed under his head, staring up at the cracked and blotched ceiling, and reliving with feverish vividness the hours he had spent with Halo Tarrant. He did not mean to tell Laura Lou where he had been; to do so would only grieve her. Besides, she would never believe him when he told her that all those hours had been spent in talk: the absorbing, illuminating, inexhaustible exchange of confidences and ideas. Laura Lou could not imagine what anybody could have to say that would take that length of time. . . . And Vance himself could hardly believe that this woman, without whom life was so lame and incomplete a business, this woman whom he had so missed and longed for, and thought he hated, could have calmed his vehemence, cast a spell over his throbbing senses, and kept him with her, enriched and satisfied, by the mere magic of her attentive understanding. . . .

He had told her everything—tumbled out all his distresses and anxieties, the misery of his marriage, the material cares that made his work so difficult, his secret resent-

393

ment of what had appeared to him her hardness and indifference when they had parted at the Willows. Nothing
had been farther from his intention than to speak to her in
this way: he had sought her out as the one confidante of his
literary projects, had imagined that pride and loyalty forbade any personal confession. But once his reserve had
broken down there rushed through the breach all the accumulated distress of the long months since he had seen her.
The exquisite solace of confessing everything effaced all
scruples and reserves. He was as powerless as ever to conceal his soul from her . . . and with every word he felt her
understanding reaching out to him, soothing the way for
what he had to tell. Instead of the resistance against which
he was always instinctively arming himself, which made
him involuntarily deform every phrase to fit it to a mind so
different from his own that there was not one point where
they dovetailed, or even touched—instead of that he felt the
relief of knowing that his clumsiest word, his lamest statement, would be smoothed out, set upright, and drawn in
across the threshold of a perpetually welcoming mind. . . .

And then, when he began to talk about his work ("the
only thing worthwhile," he passionately repeated)—ah,
then it seemed as if they were in the library of the Willows
again, in the green summer twilight, while he read and she
listened, taking in his meaning with every line of lids and
lips, and the quietness of that head supported statuelike on
her smooth bare arm. . . . It was curious, though, how
some substitution of values of which she held the secret
caused this spiritual communion to bring them nearer than
the embraces he had hungered for at the Willows. Or perhaps his recoil from the idea of combining physical endearments with such a communion was due to Laura Lou's persistent suspicion. He would have to dissociate sensual passion from all that had debased and cheapened it before it
could blend with his vision of this woman who had under-

stood and pitied him. . . . Next morning, when the questioning began, Vance told his wife that he had stopped in at
the "Loafers'," and stayed late talking about his book with a
lot of fellows. "And that Stram woman, I suppose?" she suggested; and he retorted, plunging his angry face into the
basin: "Oh, yes, and half the vaudeville stage of New York."
Laura Lou was brushing her hair before the looking glass.
He caught the reflection of the small pale oval, the reddened lids, the ripe lips crumpled up with distress, and turning to her he passed his wet hand through her hair, tum-
bling it forward over her eyes. "You little goose, you . . ."
She caught his hand and flung herself against him. "I don't
care a single scrap, darling, as long as you didn't go and see
Mrs. Tarrant," she whispered, her lips on his. "Oh, hell," he
laughed, jerking away from her to finish his dressing. . . .

He had given Mrs. Tarrant a rough outline of *Loot*, and
had been troubled, for a moment, by her hesitation, her reluctance to express an opinion. She thought the subject too
big for him—was that it? No, not too big . . . she had confidence in his range . . . and she agreed with Frenside that
he must above all not attempt another *Instead*. That had
been a radiant accident; it would be disastrous to try to repeat it. When he murmured: "Pondicherry," and spoke of
the vision the word evoked, she shook her head, and said:
"The publishers would jump at it; but take care!" No, Frenside was right; he must try his hand now at reality, the reality that lay about him. For the novelist, fantasy was a sterile
bloom, after all. Only (she wondered) was he sufficiently
familiar with the kind of life he was going to describe?
Vance laughed and said that Frenside had put the same
question. He ought to go out more, Frenside said, rub up
against New York in its various phases, especially the social
ones—oh, none of your damned documentation, that corpse-
dissecting, as Frenside called it—Vance must just let himself

live, go about among people, let the place and the people
work themselves into his pores. . . . Excellent advice, but
not so easy, when a fellow . . .

Here she interrupted him, leaning forward with her
drawn-up scrutinizing gaze. "Vance, what is it? What's
wrong? Why do you persist in burying yourself instead of
taking advantage of your success?"

"Well, I guess it's because I'm not used to society, for
one thing. . . ."

"Don't think of it as 'society,' but just as a few friendly
people who admire your work and want to know you. . . .
Come here and see them," she urged; and when he confessed that he had no evening clothes she laughed, and
asked if he supposed she meant to invite him to formal en-
tertainments, and if he didn't know that Frenside never
could be coaxed out on tailcoat occasions? Later, she added,
when Vance had got more used to it all, he must go to some
of the big shows too—the opera, musical parties, millionaire
dinners, the whole stupid round—just to see how "the other
half lived"; but meanwhile all she suggested was that he
should not cut himself off from the small group of the cultivated and intelligent, who might stimulate him and enlarge
his point of view—not, at least, she added, if he meant to go
on writing novels. . . .

Of course he agreed with her; of course he said he
would come on whatever evening she named. The mere
sound of her voice made the creative ardour beat in him,
and when she asked him if he couldn't soon bring her his
first chapter he answered joyfully that she should have it before the end of the week. . . .

After breakfast he hurried off to Lambart & Co., the
publishers whose letter he had received the previous day. In
the inner office where the great Mr. Lambart himself
awaited him he heard fresh praises of *Instead,* and the hope

that he was already starting "on another just like it; it's what
your public wants of you, Mr. Weston"; and finally the crucial question: "Will you leave it to us to see if we can come
to an understanding with Dreck and Saltzer? Between ourselves (and quite confidentially, of course) their financial
situation isn't sound enough to let them give their authors a
chance. They can't advertise properly, they can't—" Oh, yes,
Vance interrupted; he knew all that. The trouble was that
his contract with them was tied up with his *New Hour* contract . . . and he didn't see . . .

The publisher smiled the faint secret smile of initiation.
That was just it: the *New Hour* wasn't in any too healthy a
state either. There too there might be something to be done:
negotiations . . . If Mr. Weston would simply authorize
him to act. . . .

Vance hardly heard the suggestion. The statement with
regard to the *New Hour*, coming to him with a shock of
surprise, suddenly recalled the look on Mrs. Tarrant's face
when, the night before, he had blurted out that he was imprisoned by his contract with her husband. She had not answered; had not spoken at all: but her eager eyes and lips
seemed drawn back, immobilized, and for the only time in
their talk he felt between them an impenetrable barrier.
. . . It was that, then! She knew the review was in a bad
way, but pride, or perhaps loyalty to her husband, forbade
her to admit it. She had merely said, after a moment: "The
two years that are left will soon be over; then you'll be
free . . ." with a smile which seemed half ironic and half
sympathizing. And they had passed on to other matters.

Yes, Vance said, rousing himself to answer Mr. Lambart, yes, of course he would authorize any attempt to buy
him off . . . only, he added, Tarrant was a queer-tempered
fellow . . . you never knew . . . The publisher's smile
flicked Tarrant away like a straw. "Gifted amateur . . .
They can't edit reviews . . ." He promised to let Vance

know the result as soon as possible. "And now about the next novel," he said, a ring of possessorship in his voice. The terms proposed (a third in advance, if Mr. Weston chose) made Vance's blood drum in his ears; but there was a change of tone when he began to outline *Loot*. A big novel of modern New York? What—*another?* Tempting subject, yes—tremendous canvas—but there'd been so many of them! The public was fed up with skyscrapers and niggers and bootleggers and actresses. Fed up equally with Harlem and with the opera, with Greenwich Village and the pluto-crats. What they wanted was something refined—something to appeal to the heart. Couldn't Mr. Weston see that by the way his own book had been received? Why not follow up the success of *Instead* by another novel just like it? The quaintness of the story—so to speak—had taken everybody's fancy. Why not leave the New York show to fellows like Fynes, and the new man Gratz Blemer, who couldn't either of them do anything else, didn't even suspect there was any-thing else to do? This Gratz Blemer: taking three hundred thousand words to tell the story of a streetwalker and a bootblack, and then calling it *This Globe!* Why, you could get round the real globe nowadays a good deal quicker than you could dig your way through that book! No, no, the pub-lisher said—if Mr. Weston would just listen to *him*, and rely on his long experience . . . Well, would he think it over, anyhow? A book just like *Instead*, only about forty thousand words longer. If *Instead* had a blemish, it was being what the dry-goods stores called an "outsize"; the public did like to get what they were used to. . . . And if a novelist had had the luck to hit on something new that they took a shine to, it was sheer suicide not to give them more of it. . . .

It was an odd sensation for Vance, after so many months of seclusion, to find himself again in the harmonious setting of the Tarrants' library, with friendly faces pressing about him and adulation filling the air like a shower of perfumed petals. . . . There were fewer people than at his former party at Mrs. Tarrant's; there was no Mrs. Pulsifer, there were no ladies in gold brocade to startle and captivate. The men were mostly in day clothes, the few women in simple half-transparent dresses such as Mrs. Tarrant had worn that other evening when he had called her up and found her alone over the fire. Those women dressed like that when they were sitting at home alone in the evening! The fact impressed Vance more than all Mrs. Pulsifer's brocades and jewels—made the distance seem greater between the world of Mrs. Hubbard's third story and that in which a sort of quiet beauty and order were an accepted part of life.

Vance had tried to induce Laura Lou to come with him, but had not been altogether sorry when he failed. He had not forgotten their disastrous lunch at the Tarrants', and he told himself that he hated to see his wife at a disadvantage among people who seemed blind to her beauty, and conscious only of her lack of small talk. But in fact it was only in her absence that he was really himself. Every situation in which she figured instantly became full of pitfalls. The Vance Weston who was her husband was a nervous, self-conscious, and sometimes defiant young man, whereas the other, the real one, was disposed to take things easily, to meet people halfway, and to forget himself completely in the pursuit of any subject that interested him. And here at the Tarrants', as always, the air was full of such subjects, and of a cordiality which instantly broke down his lingering resentments. He felt this even in Tarrant's handshake on the threshold. Tarrant, at the office, was an enigma to Vance. What he had heard of the difficulties of the *New Hour* had prepared him to find them reflected in his host's manner; but apparently among these people business concerns were left behind after business hours, and Tarrant had never been so friendly and fraternal. He detained Vance for a few moments in talk about the new book ("my wife tells me it's really on the stocks"), and then effaced himself, declaring: "But it's the author of *Instead* that people want to see; come along to my wife, and she'll introduce you."

Halo, at the farther end of the library, was talking to a short, heavily built young man with a head cropped like a German *Bursche*, whom she introduced as Gratz Blemer. Blemer was blunt but affable. "I guess we can't read each other—anyway, you'll never flounder through a morass like my last book—but I'm glad of the chance of a talk. Writing's always a mannerism; talk's the only real thing, isn't it?" He spoke with a slight German accent, oiled by Jewish gutturals, and Vance, while attracted by his good-nature and simplicity, wondered for the thousandth time why American novels were so seldom written by Americans. He would have liked to go off into a corner with Blemer and put a series of questions about his theory of his art; but other people came up. There was little O'Fallery, whose short story, "Limp Collars," had taken the Pulsifer Prize on which Tarrant had counted for Vance; Frenside, gruffly benevolent, Rebecca Stram (who was exhibiting Vance's bust in the clay at a show of "Tomorrowists" got up by that enterprising industry, "Storecraft"), and others, men and women, unknown to Vance, or known only by reputation, but all sounding the same note of admiring interest and intelligent comprehension. . . .

Comprehension? At the moment it seemed so; yet as the hours passed, and the opportunity came for one after another to capture the new novelist, and start a literary conversation of which he was himself the glowing centre, Vance felt, again and again, how random praise can isolate and discourage. All that made his work worthwhile, all that made the force of his vocation, was apparently invisible or incomprehensible to others. He longed to learn more about this mysterious craft, the instruments of which some passing divinity had carelessly dropped into his hands, leaving him to puzzle out their use; but the intelligent and admiring people to whom he strove to communicate his curiosities seemed unable to follow him. "Oh, you're too modest," one cordial critic assured him; and another: "I suppose when you start a story you don't always know yourself how it's going to end. . . ." Not know how it's going to end! Then these people had never heard that footfall of Destiny which, for Vance, seemed to ring out in the first page of all the great novels, as compelling as the knock of Macbeth's gates, as secret as the opening measures of the Fifth Symphony? Gratz Blemer, even, whom he managed to corner later in the evening, and whose book gave him so great a sense of easy power—Gratz Blemer, good-natured and evidently ready to be communicative, twisted a cigar between his thick lips, stared at the ceiling, and returned from it to say: "Novel-writing? Why, I don't know. You have a story you want to tell, and instead of buttonholing a fellow and pouring it out—which is the only natural way—you shut yourself up and reel it off on a Remington, and send it to the publisher, so that more fellows can hear it. That's the only difference, I guess—that and the cash returns," he added with a well-fed chuckle.

"Yes, but—" Vance gasped, disheartened.

"Well, what?"

"I mean, how does the thing germinate, spread itself above and below the surface? There's something so treelike, so preordained. . . . I came across something in Blake the other day that made me think of it: 'Man is born like a garden ready planted and sown. This world is too poor to produce one seed.' That just hints at the mystery . . . but I can't make it all out—can you?"

Blemer gave his jovial laugh. "Never tried to," he said, reaching with a plump hairy hand for a passing cocktail.

And after a moment he added good-naturedly: "See here, young man, don't you go and read the Prophets and get self-conscious about your work, or you'll take to writing fifty pages about a crack in the ceiling—and then the Cocoanut Tree'll grovel before you, but your sales'll go down with a rush." No, evidently Blemer did not know how or why he wrote his novels, and could not even conceive the existence of the problems which were Vance's passion and despair. . . . The footfall of Destiny would never keep him from his sleep . . . and yet he had written a good book.

But if Vance was disappointed by his talks with the literary lights, he was stimulated by the atmosphere at the Tarrants', by the flattering notice of these enviable people who spoke freely and familiarly of so many things he was aching to know about, who took for granted that you had seen the last play at the Yiddish Theatre, had heard the new Stravinsky symphony, had visited the Tcheko-Slovakian painters' show, and were eager to discuss the Tomorrowists' coming exhibition, at which they all knew that Vance's bust by Rebecca Stram was to be shown.

The air was electrical, if not with ideas at least with phrases and allusions which led up to them. To Vance the background of education and travel implied by this quick flashing back and forth of names, anecdotes, references to unseen places, unheard-of people, works of art, books, plays, was intoxicating in its manifold suggestions. Even more so, perhaps, was the sense of the unhampered lives of the people who seemed so easily able to satisfy all their curiosities—people who took as a matter of course even the noble range of books in the Tarrant library, the deep easy chairs, the skilfully disposed lamps and flowers, and the music which, toward the end of the evening, a dreaming hand drew from the Steinway in its shadowy corner. As in every one of his brief contacts with this world, Vance felt a million currents of beauty and vitality pouring through him.

If the life of a great city had such plastic and pictorial qualities, why not seize on them? Why not make the most of his popularity with these people who had so many ways of feeding his imagination? Before the party broke up he had accepted a dozen invitations to dine, to sup, to hear new music or look at old pictures. What a world it was going to be to dig into and then write about!

❧ XXXV ❧

"STORECRAFT" HAD lodged itself on the summit of a corner building in Fifth Avenue, with a "roof patio" (the newest architectural hybrid) surrounded by showrooms and a cabaret. This fresh stage in its development was to be inaugurated by the Tomorrowist Show, and when Vance and Laura Lou shot up to the patio in the crowded lift the rooms were already beginning to fill with the people whose only interest in exhibitions is to visit them on their opening day.

Laura Lou, at the last moment, had decided to accompany her husband. The day was radiant, and treacherously warm for March, and she had put on a little blue hat, of the same blue as the one she had worn that fatal day in the rubberneck car, and a coat with a collar of fluffy amber fur. Between cerulean hat brim and blond fur her face looked as tender as a wild rose, and the shadow of fatigue under her eyes turned them to burning sapphire. Vance looked at her in wonder. What did she do with all this loveliness in their everyday life? It seemed to appear suddenly, on particular occasions, as if she had pulled it out of the trunk under their bed with her "good" coat; and he knew it would vanish again as quickly, leaving her the pale heavy-eyed ghost of her old self. Some inner stimulus, now almost lacking in her life, seemed required to feed that precarious beauty. He noticed how people turned their heads as she entered the gallery, as they had done in the fashionable restaurant, and at the theatre, on their wedding journey. Masculine pride flushed through him, and he slipped his arm possessively in hers. "Take me right to where it is," she enjoined him with a little air of power, as if instantly conscious of his feeling.

They worked their way into the second room, and there, aloft on a central pedestal, Vance caught a half glimpse of himself as embodied in the clay of Rebecca Stram. The conspicuous placing of the bust astonished him—he hadn't supposed that Rebecca's artistic standing, even in her own little group, was of such importance.

"Gee—for a beginner they've given her a good place," he said to his wife.

"Oh, Vanny, it isn't her—it's *you*!"

He laughed a little sheepishly, in genuine surprise. He had forgotten that for anyone but himself and Laura Lou his features could be of interest.

"Shucks," he growled self-consciously.

"Why, just look! We can't get up to it—I can't see it, even!" she exulted.

The bust was in fact enclosed in a dense circle of people, some few of whom were looking at it, while the greater number hung on the vibrant accents of a showily dressed man whose robust back was turned to Vance and Laura Lou.

"Know him? Know Vance Weston?" they heard Bunty Hayes ring out in megaphone tones. "Why, I should *say* so. Ever since he was a little kiddie. Why, him and me were raised together, way down on the Hudson River, as the old song says. Born out West?" (This is evident response to the comment of one of his auditors.) "That's so—Illinois, I guess it was, or maybe Arizona. But he came east as a little fellow, to live with his mother's relatives—don't I remember the day he arrived? Why, I met him when he stepped off the train. Even then you could see the little genius in him. 'Bunty,' he says to me, 'where's the public library?' (First

thing!). 'I want to consult the *Encyclopaedia Britannica*,' he
says. Couldn't ha' been more'n sixteen, I guess—thinking of
his writing even then! Well, I was on a newspaper in those
days myself, and I walked him right round to the office, and
I said: 'What you want to study isn't encyclopaedias, it's
Life.' And I guess, if I do say so, that was the turning point
in his career; and I claim it was my advice and help that
landed him where he is today: at the head of the world's
fiction writers, and in the place of honour at 'Storecraft's'
first art exhibit. Proud of it? Well, I guess I've got a right to
be. . . ."

He swung suddenly round, mustering the crowd with
an eye trained to the estimation of numbers; and his glance
met Vance's. The latter expected to see signs of discomfiture
on the orator's compact countenance; but he did not yet
know Bunty Hayes. The showman's eye instantly lit up, and
he elbowed his way toward Vance with extended hand.

"Well, ladies and gentlemen, I see it's time for me to
pack up my goods and step down off the platform. Here's
the great man himself. Now, then, Mr. Weston, step up here
and give your admirers the chance to compare the living
features with the artist's inspiration!"

Vance stood paralysed with rage; but he had no time to
express it, for friends and acquaintances were pressing
about him, and Bunty Hayes was swept aside by their approach. Vance found himself the centre of a throng of people, all eager to say a word, all determined to have one in
return; and his only conscious desire was to be rid of it all,
and of them, and let his rage against Hayes take breath. He
managed to mumble his wife's name to the first comers, but
presently her hand slipped from his arm, and he saw her
drawn away by a tall sable-draped figure whose back he
recognized as Mrs. Pulsifer's. Mrs. Pulsifer and Laura Lou—
he wished there had been time to be furious at that too! But
perhaps it was better to laugh at it—to laugh even at Bunty

Hayes, whose showman's instinct so confidently triumphed over every personal awkwardness. "Why," Vance thought, "if I was to collar him now and give him the licking he deserves, he'd use *that* to advertise 'Storecraft.' No wonder he gets on, and 'Storecraft' too." And instantly he began to weave the whole scene into *Loot,* his heart beating excitedly as he felt himself swept along on the strong current of the human comedy. . . . If only he could tell Halo Tarrant, he thought! He turned, and there she stood beside him, with Frenside.

"Yes, we've come. I hate these performances; but I wanted to see you battling with the waves, and I made Frenny come too." How fine and slender and aloof she managed to look among them all, and how his blood instantly caught step with hers! "Well, this is fame—how do you like it?" she bantered him.

He shrugged. "I guess it's a good page for *Loot.*"

She nodded delightedly. "You see I was right! I told you you must see it all. But where's Laura Lou? Surely she was with you a minute ago?"

"Yes. But she's gone."

"Gone?"

"With Mrs. Pulsifer. I think they're in the other room."

Their eyes met, and Mrs. Tarrant laughed. "I've noticed signs of uneasiness in Jet lately. She realizes that she made a bad mistake last year about your short story, and I hear she now talks of founding a First Novel prize. She's probably telling Laura Lou all about it."

Vance laughed too; and then they turned together to the bust, which Mrs. Tarrant had not yet seen. She studied it thoughtfully for a long time; then, as other visitors crowded her away, she turned back to Vance. "I didn't think that Stram girl had it in her. She *has* caught a glimpse of you, Vance—a glimpse of what you're going to be. Don't you think so, Frenny?"

"Well, I'm sorry to think that our young friend's going to have a goitre," said Frenside gloomily.

"Oh, dear—what a pity you can't like anything that isn't photographic! Artistically, you know," she explained to Vance, "Frenny's never got beyond the enlarged photograph of the 'eighties, when people used to have their dear ones done twice the size of life, with the whiskers touched up in crayon."

Vance echoed her laugh. He echoed it because certain inflexions of her voice were always laughter-provoking to him, and he would have thought anything funny if her eyes and her dimple had told him it was. But in reality he did think the bust queer, and had never understood why Rebecca had given him a swollen throat, and big lumps on his forehead, as if he'd been in a fight and got the worst of it. And he remembered too, with a pang, the colossal photograph which Grandma Scrimser had had made of Grandpa after his death, with the hyacinthine curls and low-necked collar of his prime, a photograph which the family had all thought so "speaking" that even Mrs. Weston dared not grumble at the expense. . . . Still, Vance, since then, had had a glimpse of other standards, and as he studied through Halo's eyes the rough clay head with tumbled hair and heavy brooding forehead he began to see that under her surface mannerisms Rebecca Stram had reached down to his inner self, that the image seemed, as Halo said, to body forth what he was trying to be.

"It oughtn't to have been done till after I've pulled off *Loot*," he said, trying to hide his satisfaction under a joke.

"Oh, but it's a proof that you will pull it off," Halo rejoined; and then other people came up to them both, and swept them apart. He found her again at last, seated alone in a corner, and as he sat down beside her she said: "Who was that ridiculous man who was bragging about having known you when you were a boy?"

Vance's dormant indignation against Bunty Hayes flamed up again. "Oh, he's the manager of 'Storecraft.' He was just doing a blurb for the show."

"Obviously. But where on earth did you know him?"

Vance hesitated. "I ran across him at Paul's Landing. He used to go round with Upton Tracy."

"Oh, I see." She made a little grimace and rose to her feet. "Well, I'm going. I only came here to see you. I mean Rebecca's *you*," she corrected herself with a smile.

"Not yours?" he asked, flushing.

"No, I'd rather see him some evening quietly at home. When are you going to bring me your next chapters?"

"Any time," he stammered, whirling with the joy of it; and she named a date which he of course accepted, as he would have accepted any other, at the cost of breaking no matter what other engagements. His head was light and dizzy with anticipation as he watched her vanish with Frenside in the throng.

When he roused himself from the spell he remembered that Laura Lou was somewhere in the gallery. He went back to look for her, but she was nowhere to be found, and at last he concluded, though half incredulously, that she must have gone off with Mrs. Pulsifer. It was very unlike her—but he had discovered that Laura Lou was often unlike herself, and that he really knew next to nothing of the secret springs of her actions and emotions. He did not think of this for long; his heart and brain were still full of the thought of Mrs. Tarrant. He was to see her again in two days: "a quiet evening," she had said. That meant, he and she alone under the lamp, in that still meditative room which was like no other that he knew: a room of which the very walls seemed to think. And they would sit there alone together, while the logs crackled and fell, and he would read his new stuff to her, and she would sit motionless and silent, her chin on her lifted hand, her long arm modelled by the lamplight; and even while his eyes were on the page he would see her hand and arm, and her nearness would burn itself at the same time into his body and brain.

He slipped out of the gallery and found himself below in the street. The weather had changed, it had grown very cold, and the skyscrapers flung down a rough wind into the tunnel-like thoroughfares at their base. Vance remembered the March snowstorm on the Hudson, which had come after just such a mild spell; and that led him to wonder if Laura Lou had got safely home before the change. Her pretty coat with the blond fur was only a summer garment, put on because it was her best; and she mustn't catch another cold, he reflected. But his mind was too full of excited thoughts for that one to dominate it. He was at once too happy and too anxious to dwell for long on anything; and he turned westward and struck into the park, to try to walk his jostling ideas into order.

The encounter with Bunty Hayes had disgusted him profoundly. That kind of slovenly good-nature was merely a caricature of the superficial tolerance, the moral apathy, of most of the people he came in contact with. Nothing mattered to any of them except to get on, to shove a way through and crowd out the others. There was Hayes, a man who had reason to hate him—or thought so—who loved his wife, and must therefore be jealous of him, and yet in whom the primitive emotions were so worn down by the perpetual effort to get on, to gain an inch or two in the daily struggle, that they could be silenced at will whenever it was to his interest. As Vance tramped on against the stinging wind his anger subsided also, but for a different reason. Hayes, the human fact, was being gradually absorbed, transubstantiated, into the stuff of his book; was turning from a vulgar contemptible man into a grotesque symbol of the national futility. . . . And then Vance began to examine his own case. He had not complied, he had tried to stand on his feet,

to defend his intellectual integrity. And where was he?
What was he? The flattered and envied author of the newest craze, a successful first novel; yet in himself an unhappy
powerless creature, poor, hungry, in debt, the bewildered
bondslave of the people he despised, the people who sacrifice everything and everybody to getting on.

And in thus summing up his case he had left out the
central void: the blank enigma of his marriage. He could
hardly remember now the gleams of joy which Laura Lou's
presence had shed on their early days. He had imagined
that she shared all his ideas, whereas she was merely the
sounding board of his young exuberance. Now the delusions
and raptures were all gone. If he and she could have had a
house of their own, instead of having to live in one room,
how often would he have sought her out? All that remained
of his flaming dream was a cold half-impatient pity. He supposed, vaguely, that the real meaning of marriage, the need
that upheld it as an institution in spite of all revolts and
ironies, was man's primitive craving for a home, children, a
moral anchorage. Marriage had brought him none of these.
What sense was there in living in one room with an idle
childless woman whom he had long since forgotten though
she was always there? He despised himself for yielding to
their enforced propinquity, and giving her what her soft endearments asked as carelessly as if she had been the casual
companion of a night.

He sat on a bench in the park and revolved these world-
old riddles till the cold drew him to his feet, and he turned
homeward, heavy and confused as when he had started.

Laura Lou must have got back long before him. She
would be waiting at home, perhaps resenting the fact of his
not having stayed with her at the gallery. He swung along
impatiently, trying to put out of his mind the secret well of
joy that fed him: the thought of the quiet evening with Mrs.
Tarrant and his book. . . . Since he had rung her up that

evening, more than a month ago, he had been with her perilously often, meeting her at dinners, at informal studio parties, sometimes going with her to the theatre or to a symphony concert. To be with her nearly every day, to share with her all his artistic and intellectual joys, to carry to her every new experience, every question, every curiosity, had become an irresistible need. She had drawn him back to the frank footing of friendship, and skilfully kept him there. But they had not yet had another long evening alone by the lamp, and now he felt that he must pour out his whole soul to her or have no peace.

Laura Lou was huddled up close to the radiator, which gave out but little warmth on Mrs. Hubbard's third floor. She had tossed her hat and coat on the bed, and wrapped her stooping shoulders in the bedquilt.

"Well," Vance said, with hollow gaiety, "where the devil did you run away to? I hunted for you all over the place."

She lifted a face in which triumph struggled with resentment. He saw that for some reason she was annoyed with him, yet for another pleased. "Oh, I got tired staying round there with all those strange people; and I couldn't bear to look any longer at that hateful thing."

"What hateful thing?"

"That awful bust. How could you let them show such a thing? It made me sick to see it."

"Didn't you like it? It's been a good deal admired," he muttered, piqued by her tone.

"Why, Vanny, can't you see they're only laughing at you when they tell you that?"

"Who's 'they'?"

"Why, all your fashionable friends. That Mrs. Pulsifer, for instance. And even *she* wasn't sure. She said: 'Do you suppose we *ought* to admire it, Mrs. Weston?' And when I said: 'I never saw anything so awful,' I could see she was kind of relieved. Oh, Vanny," she continued, her face brightening, "I think you ought to see more of her. She says she was the first one to recognize your talent, and she wanted ever so much to help you, but she never sees you any more because you won't go with anybody but those Tarrants."

His blood leapt up. "Nonsense—that fool of a woman! The biggest humbug . . ."

"It's not humbug to say you always go with the Tarrants. . . . You never left her at the gallery. . . ."

"He's my employer. I've told you a hundred times . . ." His voice rose angrily, but he checked himself, resolved not to let her draw him into another wrangle over that threadbare grievance. She might think what she pleased— explaining anything to her was useless. To divert her attention he questioned ironically: "I suppose you talked me over with Hayes too?"

Her colour rose quickly, painting her cheekbones with the familiar feverish patches. "I never talk you over with anybody—not the way you mean."

"Well, you did talk with Hayes, didn't you?"

She looked at her husband half furtively, half in resentment. "He was almost the only person I knew in the place. Of course I talked with him. I didn't know you wouldn't want me to."

Vance was silent. Since the reconciliation at Paul's Landing he had never spoken to his wife of Hayes. At that time, in answer to his brief questioning, she had sobbingly admitted that Hayes was ready to marry her if he, Vance, didn't want her any longer. Hayes, it appeared, had arranged it all with Mrs. Tracy, and Laura Lou had been on the point of acquiescing because she was convinced that her husband no longer loved her and had been unfaithful to her with "that other woman."

Feeling her then so soft and surrendered on his breast, seeing her despair, and conscious of his own shortcomings, Vance had brushed aside these negligible intrigues, and sworn to her that they would begin a new life together. And from that day he had never questioned her about Hayes, had purposely avoided pronouncing his name. He had the feeling that the tie between himself and Laura Lou was even then too frail to stand the slightest strain. . . . But now the instinct of self-protection stirred him to cruelty; he, who was never cruel, desired to hurt his wife. "Do you see Hayes often? Does he come here? He's just the kind to sneak round after you when he knows I'm at the office. . . ." How stupid the words sounded when he had spoken them! How little bearing they had on the intrinsic flaw in his relation with Laura Lou!

She hesitated a moment; then she said simply: "I've never talked with him but once since we've been here, one day when I met him in the street."

"Oh, that's all right; I didn't mean—I'm no gaoler: you can see him here at the house all you want to," he grumbled, irresolute and half ashamed.

"When I spoke to him just now at the gallery," she continued, "all I did was to thank him for the lovely things he said about you when we first came in."

"The lovely—?" Vance echoed, forgetting, in his blank amazement, what had gone before.

She looked surprised. "Why, didn't you think what he said about you was lovely?" She smiled a little; her tone was confident and yet conciliatory. "Sometimes I think you don't realize you're celebrated, Vanny. He said you were—he told all those people so. I thought what he said was fine."

For a moment Vance thought she must be making fun of him, avenging herself by this clumsy pleasantry for his supposed neglect. But she was incapable of irony; he saw that she had really taken Hayes's oratory as a tribute to her husband's genius.

"What he said of me—that blithering rubbish? It was an insult, that's all! And that heap of lies; blowing that way before all those people about having known me since I was a kid! Good God—you didn't thank him for making an everlasting fool of me?"

Her lower lip began to tremble, and a mist of distress dimmed her face. "Nothing I ever do is right. I didn't know you didn't even want me to speak to him when we met."

"I've told you you can speak to him as much as you like. What beats me is your not seeing that he was publicly holding me up to ridicule."

Her mouth grew narrow and vindictive. "I thought the bust did that. I was grateful to him for doing the best he could so that people would look at you and not at the bust."

"Oh, God," Vance groaned. He turned away, and began to fumble with the papers on the rickety little table between bed and window where he had to do his writing. He had meant to buckle down to a hard evening's work, to get his chapters into final shape before submitting them to Mrs. Tarrant. But Laura Lou had a genius for putting him into a mood which made work or meditation equally impossible. . . . As he stood there sullenly, with his back to her, he heard a low sound like a child's whimper, and turned around, irritated with himself and with her.

"Oh, see here, child! Don't cry—what's the use? I didn't mean . . . all I meant was . . ."

"You hurt me *so*," she sobbed.

"Nonsense, Laura Lou. Listen . . . Don't be a goose. . . ." He caught her to him and felt the fever on her lips. Pressed each to each, they clung fast, groping for one another through the troubled channels of the blood.

❧ XXXVI ❧

AFTER VANCE had finished reading, Halo Tarrant sat silent. The library was very still. Only one lamp was lit, on a low table near Vance's armchair; the rest of the room hung remote and shadowy about them, except when a dart of flame from the hearth woke up a row of books here and there, or made the flanks of a bronze vase glitter like a wet rock.

Vance's heart was beating hurriedly. His voice was hoarse with excitement; he could not have read any longer without breaking down. In his agitation he did not dare to lift his eyes to his listener's, but sat fumbling mechanically among the pages on his knee. Since the first paragraph he had been more and more certain that her verdict would be unfavourable.

"Well—?" he questioned at length, with an uneasy laugh. He could hardly endure the interval that elapsed before she answered. His throat was parched, and little prickles ran all over his skin. He felt as if she would never speak.

"I think you ought to take more time over it," she said. "The canvas is much bigger than you're used to—and the subject is so new. There are things in it that I like very much; but there are bits that seem incomplete, undigested. . . . I'm sure you can do the book; but you must give yourself time . . . lots of time. Can't you put it away for a few months and turn to something else?"

Her verdict was exactly what he had expected, yet it filled him with unreasonable discouragement. She always lit instantly on the flaws of which he himself was half conscious, even in the heat of composition, the flaws he hoped she would overlook, but knew in advance that she would detect; and for this reason he lost his critical independence in her presence, and swung uneasily between elation and despondency.

"Yes, I know. It's a failure," he muttered.

"How can you tell, when only a few chapters are written? And in them there's so much that's good. That first impression of the heartless overwhelmingness of New York—it's been done so often, but no one has seen it and felt it exactly as you have. . . . And the opening scene in the little western town—all that's good too, except that perhaps—" she paused, lifting her eyes doubtfully to his, "perhaps when you did that part you'd been reading *The Corner Grocery* a little too attentively," she concluded with her hesitating smile.

He smiled too: it felt like a dry contraction of the muscles. "Too much of the sedulous ape, you mean?"

"Well, you seem to be struggling against crosscurrents of influence. But you'll work out of them when you really get into your subject."

"Trouble is it's not my subject," he broke in nervously; but she continued: "Not yet, perhaps; but it will be if you'll only give yourself more time." He looked up and met her scrutinizing eyes. "You look terribly tired, Vance. Can't you drop the book for a few months?"

She made the suggestion gently, appealingly, in her most tranquil and compassionate voice. Yes, he thought, stirred by sudden exasperation: that was the way with people to whom material ease was as much a matter of course as the air they breathed. It was always an unwholesome business for the rich and poor to mix; the poor ought to keep to their own kind.

"Drop it?" he echoed with a laugh. "Well, that wouldn't

be exactly easy. Your husband has agreed to let me off my monthly article so that I can keep all my time for the novel; and now you advise me to drop the novel! What I've got to do is to finish it as quickly as I can, and let it take its chance. I'm doomed to write potboilers—if ever I can learn the trick!"

She paled a little. He saw that his words had hurt her, and he was glad they had. She continued to look at him earnestly, with her narrowed wistful gaze.

"You never *will* learn the trick; I'm not afraid for you."

He laughed again—she was preposterous! "Oh, well, I didn't come here to talk business," he said irritably. "What I wanted was your opinion—now I've got it. And as it's exactly the same as mine I'd throw the book into the fire if I could."

She received this in silence, sitting quite still, as her way was when she was turning over anything in her mind. "Vance," she said abruptly, "when you brought me these last chapters you didn't feel like that about them. You had faith in them an hour ago. You mustn't let my chance suggestions influence you; no artist should care so much for what people say. . . ."

He jumped up, the pages on his knee scattering to the floor. "Care what people say? I don't care a damn what people say. . . . It's only what you say," he broke out with sudden vehemence.

A little flash of light ran over her face: her only way of blushing was this luminous glow on her pallor. "But that's even more unreasonable . . ." she began.

"Oh, God, what's reason got to do with it? You've been the breath of life to me all these months. If you cut off a fellow's oxygen he collapses. . . . Don't talk to me about not caring what you say! There'd be nothing left to me then."

The silence of the dusky room seemed to receive and

reverberate his words as the shadows caught and intensified the wavering gleams of the fire. Vance leaned against the mantel and stared down with blind eyes at the scattered pages of his manuscript. For a while—a long while, it seemed to him—Mrs. Tarrant did not move or look up.

"There'd be your genius left to you," she said, still motionless in her corner.

He laughed. "I sometimes think my genius is a phantasm we've manufactured between us. When I'm not with you I don't believe in it—I don't believe in anything when I'm not with you."

"Oh, Vance, don't—don't blaspheme!"

"Blaspheme! The only blasphemy would be to say that you're not the whole earth to me!"

Still she did not move; and her immobility held him spellbound on the hearth. "That's too much to be to anyone," he heard her murmur, and immediately afterward: "All I've wanted was to help you with your books. . . ."

"My books? My books?" He moved a step or two nearer to her, and then stood checked again by her immobility. "What do you suppose books are made of?" he cried. "Paper and ink, or the marrow of a man's bones and the blood of his brain? But you're *in* my books, you're part of them, whether you want to be or not, whether you believe in them or despise them, whether you believe in me or despise me; and you're in me, in my body and blood, just as you're in my books, and just as fatally. It's done now and you can't get away from me, you can't undo what you've done: you're the thoughts I think, and the visions I see, and the air I breathe, and the food I eat—and everything, everything, in the earth and over it. . . ."

He broke off, startled by his own outburst. He who was in general so tongue-tied, to whom eloquence came only with the pen, what power had driven this rush of words from him? Some fiery fusion of his whole being, the height-

ening and merging of every faculty, seemed to have un-
loosed his tongue. And it was all as he had said. He and his
art and this woman were one, indissolubly one in a passionate mutual understanding. He and she understood each
other—didn't she know it?—with their intelligences and
their emotions, with their eyes, their hands, their lips. Ah,
her lips! All he could see now was the shape of her lips, that
mouth haunted by all the smiles that had ever played over
it, as if they were gathered up in her like shut flowerbuds.

"Didn't you know—didn't you know?" he stammered.

She had risen and stood a little way off from him.
"About you—?"

"About you and me. There's no difference. *Is* there any
difference?"

He moved closer and caught her hands in his. They lay
there like birds with their wings folded; birds that are
frightened, and then suddenly lie still, with little subsiding
palpitations. He was trying to see her face, to trace it line by
line. "One of your eyebrows is a little higher than the
other—I never noticed it before!" he cried exultantly, as if
he had made an earthshaking discovery. She laughed a little
and slipped her hands out of his.

"Oh, stop exploring me—you frighten me," she murmured.

"Frighten you? I mean to. And you frighten me. It's because we're so close . . . leaning over into the gulfs of each
other. . . . Don't you like it, don't you *want* it? Don't you
see there's no difference anymore between you and me?"

She drew away from him. "My poor Vance—I see only
what is. It's my curse."

His heart fell with a thump. All of a sudden she seemed
hopelessly far away, spectral and cold. Inexperienced as he
was, he knew this was no clever feint, that she was not playing with him. There was a fearless directness in her voice.

"You mean to tell me," he cried, "that you're all right?

That your life is full enough without me?" She made no answer, and he burst out: "I shouldn't believe you if you did!"

The exclamation brought a faint smile to her lips. "I won't then. What would be the use? And what difference would it make? I'm here—you're *there*. It's not our nearness to each other that frightens me; it's the leagues and leagues between—that is, when you begin to talk like this. . . ."

"Haven't you always known I was going to talk like this?" he interrupted her.

"I suppose I have . . . but I hoped it wouldn't be for a long time. . . ."

"Well, it's been a long time since I began to love you." Again she was silent. "You remember Thundertop?"

"Oh, Vance—even then?"

"Even before, I guess. The first time I read poetry or looked at a sunset you must have been mixed up with it. I didn't have to wait to see you."

She had sunk back into her armchair and sat there with her hands over her eyes. He wanted to snatch them away, to kiss her on the lids and lips; but there hung between them the faint awe of her presence. She was the woman his arms longed for, but she was also the goddess, the miracle, the unattainable being who haunted the peaks of his imagination.

"She's sorry for me, that's all," he thought bitterly.

Other fellows, he felt, would have known how to break through the barrier; he had no such arts, and probably no experience of life would instruct him. There was an absoluteness in his love which benumbed him, now that his exaltation had fallen. It had always seemed to him that on the pinnacles there was just room to kneel and be mute.

Halo Tarrant dropped her hands and looked up at him between narrowed lids. She was excessively pale; her face looked haggard, almost old. "Oh, Vance," she murmured, "take care. . . ."

"Take care?"

"Not to spoil something perfect. This free friendship. It's been so—exquisite."

The blood rushed back to his heart, and his eyes were blurred with happy tears. They choked in his throat, and he stood looking at her with a kind of desperate joy.

"I've never once called you by your name, even," he stammered out.

"Well, call me by it now," she answered, still smiling. She stood up and moved toward him. "Friends do that, don't they? But we can't go beyond friendship—"

"This has got nothing to do with friendship."

"Oh, what a mistake, Vance! It includes friendship—" She spoke very low, as if what she had to say were difficult; but her eyes did not leave him. "It includes everything," she said.

"Well, then—if it does?"

"Only, what we've got to do is to choose—take what we may, and leave the rest."

"Never, never! I can't leave it." He was looking at her almost sternly. "Can you?" he challenged her.

"Yes," she said, facing him resolutely.

"Ah—then you don't care!"

"Call it that, then. At least I've cared for our friendship. . . ."

"Friendship! Friendship! If that means seeing you for a few minutes every now and then, and talking to you this way, with half the room between us, when what I want is nothing else than all of you—all your time, all your thoughts, all yourself—then I don't give a curse for your friendship."

She said nothing, and his words were flung back at him from the dead wall of her silence. He didn't give a curse for her friendship! He had said that! When her friendship had been all of life to him, the breath of his nostrils, the sight of his eyes—well, and it was true nevertheless that he wanted no more of it, or rather that it had ceased to exist for him, and that henceforth she must be the world's length away from him, or else in his arms.

"You don't understand—I want to kiss you," he stammered, looking at her with desperate eyes.

"That's why I say—we can't go on."

"Can't—why?"

She hesitated, and he saw that the hand resting on the back of her chair trembled a little.

"Because you don't want to?" he burst out.

"Because I won't take a lover while I have a husband—or while my lover has a wife," she said precipitately.

Vance stood motionless. A moment before his thoughts had enveloped her in a million caressing touches, soul had seemed to clasp soul as body would presently embrace body, the distance between them had vanished in the hallucinating fusion of sight and touch. There had been no other world than that which the quiet room built in about them, no human beings in it but themselves. And now, abruptly thrust across the plane on which they stood, the other crowded grimacing world had pushed itself in, and between them stood Laura Lou and the sordid boarding house room, the moneylenders and the unfinished book, Mrs. Hubbard and the washing bills, and the account that Laura Lou was always running up at the druggist's . . .

"And because I can't leave my husband—any more than you can leave your wife. . . ."

He was not sure if it was Halo who had completed the sentence, or if it was the echo of his own thought.

Leave Laura Lou? No, of course he couldn't. What nonsense! There was nobody else to look after her. He had chosen to have it so—and it was so. His world had closed in on him again, he was handcuffed and chained to it. He felt like a man in a railway smash who has come suddenly back to consciousness and finds himself pinned down under a dead weight. The sluggish current of reality was forcing itself once more into his veins, and he was faint with agony.

From a long way off he seemed to hear her saying: "This mustn't be the end, Vance. Someday . . . ?

(Oh, yes—someday!)

"I *have* been able to help you, haven't I? . . . and I want, I do so want to go on . . ."

(What were women made of? He wondered.)

"You'll promise me, won't you?"

(Oh, he'd promise anything, if only a rescue party would come along and hoist up this dead weight off his chest. Couldn't she *see* what he was suffering . . . ?)

"Yes, *I'll* promise."

(You had to be everlastingly promising things to women . . . even with your life blood running out of you, they'd make you promise. . . .)

"Well, good-bye."

"Good-bye, Vance."

He turned to go, and heard a little exclamation behind him. He looked back from the doorway and saw that she had stooped down and was gathering up the sheets of manuscript he had left scattered about the floor.

He came back, stammering: "Here . . . don't you trouble . . . I'll do it . . ." and knelt down on the floor beside her. The pages seemed innumerable; they had fluttered away on all sides, he had to reach out right and left to recover them. One had even flown over the brass fender onto the hearth. Yet in a second they were all gathered up again: there were no normal time measures in this world of fever.

She held out the pages she had put together; his hand touched hers as he took them. Then he turned away and the door shut on him. That was over.

❧ XXXVII ❦

VANCE STOOD in the street and looked up into the night sky. The star-strewn darkness, though blotched with the city's profaning flare, recalled that other sky he had looked up at from the beach, when he had crept out at dawn from his wife's side.

The sea—he had never seen it since! Could he get to it now? he wondered. Its infinite tides seemed to be breaking over him; its sound was in his breast. The craving to stand on that beach swept over him again, vehement, uncontrollable, surging up from the depths which held the source of things. He stood staring at his vision till it mastered him. He must see the sea again, must see it this very night. One in the morning . . . a March morning. But he must get there somehow; get there before dawn, waylay the miracle. . . .

He made his way across to the Pennsylvania Station, and asked about trains. There was one just going out: he found himself in it as it began to move. The haste of getting in and the mystery of gliding out so easily into darkness and the unknown reduced his private tumult to something like peace. He recalled the same sensation, humbling yet satisfying, when he had gone out on the morning after his wedding, and felt so awed yet safe in the sight of the immensities. . . . The train passed on between islands of masonry and endless streets strung with lights, then through the hush of dimly glimpsed trees and pastures; it stopped at sleepy stations, pulled out again, groped on in dreamlike confusion

425

under a black sky full of stars. At last a little station stood out dark against pallid sandhills . . . and Vance, alone on the platform, watched the train clank on again uncertainly, as if groping out a new trail for itself. Then he turned and began to grope for his own way. A worn-off slip of moon hung in the west, powerless against the immensity of darkness; but when he reached the last line of dunes they were edged with a trembling of light which gradually widened out into the vast pallor of the Atlantic.

There it was at last: the sea at night, a windy March night tossing black cloud trails across the stars and shaking down their rainy glitter onto the hurried undulations of the waves. The wind was cold, but Vance did not feel it. The old affinity woke in him, the sense of some deep complementary power moving those endless surges as it swayed his listening self. He dropped down on the beach and lay there, letting the night and the sea sweep through him on the wings of the passionate gale. He felt like a speck in those vast elemental hands, yet sure of himself and his future as a seed being swept to the cleft where it belonged. And after a while he ceased to feel anything except that he was obscurely, infinitesimally a part of this great nocturnal splendour. . . .

At five in the morning, through dying lights and dead streets, he made his way back to Mrs. Hubbard's. All the glory had vanished; his brain was sick with the forced inrush of reality. A last glimpse of the impossible swept through him. Halo had said: "Because I will never leave my husband for my lover . . ." and that meant—what else could it mean?—that she would have come to him if there had been no obstacle between them. For one moment it seemed almost enough to feel that there, out of his sight but in his soul, the great reaches of her love lay tossing and silvering. . . . But as he drew near his own door the ugliness

of the present blotted out the vision. At the corner of Sixth
Avenue a half-tipsy girl solicited him. At Mrs. Hubbard's
door, a gaunt cat shot out of the area. That was his world,
his street, his house. . . . He knew now that he and she
would never be free, either of them. She would never come
to him; it was all a fading blur of unreality. . . . He put his
key into the lock, and went upstairs with the feet of an old
man.

The next day Laura Lou was in bed with one of her feverish colds. She had caught a chill the day of the "Storecraft" show, in her thin summer coat. These colds were frequent with her now, and each seemed to leave her a little
weaker. Vance did not dare to send for the doctor again; he
had been several times lately, and there had been no money
to pay him. Vance did what he could to make her comfortable, and explained to Mrs. Hubbard—whose manner, as
the weeks passed, though still oppressively ladylike, had
grown more distant—the food must be carried up, milk
heated, the cough mixture measured out. Then, having put
a quarter into the hand of the dishevelled Swedish servant
girl, who seldom understood his instructions and never carried them out, he took his way to the office.

There had been no word from Lambart & Co., the publishers who had been so confident about detaching him from
Dreck and Saltzer; probably the subject of his novel had
made them lukewarm. In his letter box he found a letter
from his grandmother; there was no time to read it then, but
the sight of her writing brought up a vision of Euphoria, of
the comfortable Maplewood Avenue house, the safety and
decency of home. What if he were to accept his father's suggestion and take Laura Lou out there to live? If he took on
a newspaper job, and wrote no novels or literary articles, he
supposed his contracts with Dreck and Saltzer and the *New*

Hour would lapse of themselves. He would simply go back to being the old Vance Weston again, and it would be as if the New York one had never existed. . . .

At the office he found neither Tarrant nor Eric Rauch. He had brought his work with him, and installed himself at his desk with the idea of going over his last chapters, and at least trying to eliminate the resemblances to *The Corner Grocery*. But the sight of the pages suddenly evoked the library where he had sat the night before with Halo Tarrant, and the floor on which he and she had knelt together to pick up the scattered sheets. The paper burned with her touch. He shut his eyes and pushed it aside. . . . Euphoria was the only way out. . . .

He opened his grandmother's letter. She always wrote affectionately, and the careless freedom of her phrases would call her up to him in the flesh, with her velvety voice and heavy rambling body. The livest person he'd ever known, he thought, smiling. Then he read: "Vance, child, I'm coming to New York—be there next week with Saidie Toler . . ." (she always wrote of her daughters by their full names) . . . "I guess you're not as surprised as I am; and I feel as if God Himself must be a little mite surprised too . . ." She went on to explain that, since Grandpa's death, she had been able to give more time to spiritual things, and had been rewarded by the invitation to preach in various churches, not only at Euphoria, New Swedenborg, and Swedenville, but way beyond Chicago, at big places like Dakin and Lakeshore—only she didn't call it preaching (he could be sure of that!) but "Meeting God"; didn't he think that was a good phrase? Her "Meeting God" talks had been published in *Spirit Life,* and the paper's circulation had gone up so much that they'd already contracted with her for another series; and suddenly she'd got an invitation from a group of intellectual people in New York, who called themselves "The Seekers"—a beautiful

name, wasn't it? It appeared they'd come across some of her
talk in *Spirit Life*, and been so much struck that they
wanted her to come over to New York for a week, and speak
in private houses, and give the "Seekers" a chance to submit
their personal doubts and difficulties to her. ("You know,"
she added, dropping into her old humorous tone, "it's holiday work telling other folks what's wrong with them.") Of
course, she said, she couldn't help but see God's hand in all
this, and when *Spirit Life* offered to pay her fare and Saidie's out and back she telegraphed to the "Seekers" that
she'd come at once—and Vance needn't trouble about her,
because she and Saidie were going to stay with a Mrs. Lotus
Mennenkoop, a lovely woman who lived at Bronxville and
was one of the "Seekers"—but of course she must see her
boy as soon as she arrived, and get acquainted with her new
granddaughter; and would Vance be sure and call her up
right off at Mrs. Mennenkoop's?

Vance stared at the big wavering script, so like his
grandmother's ungirt frame. For the "Seekers" he cared not
a fig; but the springs of boyhood welled up in him at the
prospect of seeing Mrs. Scrimser. She was the only human
being he had really loved in the days when his universe was
enclosed in the few miles between Euphoria and Crampton;
the others, parents, sisters even, were just the more or less
comfortable furniture of life; but his grandmother's soul and
his had touched. . . . He thought himself back onto the
porch at Crampton, smelt the neglected lilacs, heard the
jangle of the Euphoria trolley, and his grandmother saying:
"Don't a day like this make you feel as if you could get to
God right through that blue up there?" He remembered
having answered, rather petulantly, that he didn't feel as if
anything would take him near God; but now he was at least
nearer to understanding what she had meant. Perhaps what
she called "God" was the same as what he called "The
Mothers"—that mysterious Sea of Being of which the dark

reaches swayed and rumoured in his soul . . . perhaps one
symbol was as good as another to figure the imperceptible
point where the fleeting human consciousness touches In-
finity. . . .

Curious, that this should happen just as he was facing
the idea of going back to Euphoria. His grandmother's letter, the prospect of seeing her in a few days, made the return home appear easier and more natural. As soon as she
and Laura Lou had met he would decide. . . . He was sure
those two would take a liking to each other.

Mrs. Scrimser bade him call her up at six on the day
when she was to arrive, and he hoped to persuade her to
come down that very morning to see Laura Lou, who was
still too feverish to leave her bed. Laura Lou was excited
and happy at the prospect of the visit; he saw from her
eagerness how much she had felt the enforced solitude of
her life in New York. "I guess maybe she'll go round with
me a little when I'm better," she said with her drawn smile.

"Why, I'd go round with you myself if you wanted me
to," Vance rejoined, with conscious hypocrisy; but she said
evasively: "Why, how can you, with all your work?"

The day came, and Vance was waiting at the office to
call up Mrs. Mennenkoop's flat when he was told that Mrs.
Spear was on the telephone. It was some time since he had
seen Mrs. Spear, and he wondered, somewhat nervously, if
she could be the bearer of a message from her daughter.
The blood began to buzz in his ears, and he could hardly
catch the words which tumbled out excitedly from the receiver. But presently, to his surprise, he heard his grandmother's name. "Only think, Vance, of my not knowing that
Mrs. Scrimser—the *great* Mrs. Scrimser—was your grandmother! She's just told me so herself, over the telephone.
. . . Why, yes—didn't you know? She's coming to speak in
our drawing room this very evening. . . . Of course you
knew I was one of the 'Seekers'? No—you didn't?" Mrs.

Spear was always genuinely surprised when she found that anything concerning herself or her family had not been trumpeted about by rumour. "Why, yes—it's my *life,* Vance, my only real life . . . so marvellous . . . and now I'm to have the privilege of having this wonderful being under my roof. . . . You must be with us, of course; you and Laura Lou. . . . Your grandmother wanted me to tell you not to go out to Bronxville: she'd rather meet you here. Her train was late; there's barely time for her to take a rest and withdraw into herself—you know they always do, before a meeting. . . . So she wants you to come here early instead. She says she's sure you'll understand. . . ."

The announcement filled Vance with astonishment. He had had glimpses of some of Mrs. Spear's hobbies and enthusiasms, and had heard others humorously reported by Halo—but the idea of any connection between the Spear milieu and his grandmother was so unexpected that he began to wonder if, all unconsciously, he had spent his youth with an illustrious woman. Mrs. Spear was in touch with the newest that New York was thinking and saying; Frenside's decomposing irony was her daily fare; clever and cultivated people of all kinds frequented her house; she was always on the track of the new movements. Did the "Seekers" then represent a movement important enough to attract those whose lead she followed? And was his grandmother actually the prophetess of a new faith? He recalled the religion he had himself "invented" in his boyhood—the creed whose originality had crumbled away with his first glimpse of the old philosophies—and wondered if his grandmother had stumbled on the revelation he had missed. It was all so confounding that he hardly found voice to stammer out his thanks, and his excuses for Laura Lou. . . . And the Tarrants, he wondered—would they be there? And what did Halo think of the "Seekers"? Above all, what would she think of Mrs. Scrimser?

He had not wished to see Halo again—not for some time, not till the storm in him should subside. Had she been right when she had warned him the other night not to "spoil something perfect"? In his unsatisfied anguish, he had half believed her; but in the interval he had come to know that this anguish was worth all the rest. Friendship—love? How vain such restricting words now seemed! In reality, his feeling for her included friendship, passion, love, desire, whatever thought or emotion, craving of sight and touch, a woman can excite in a man. All were merged in a rich deep communion; it was the element in which everything else in him lived. "All thoughts, all motions, all delights, Whatever stirs this mortal frame—" the poet whom Elinor Lorburn loved had summed it up long ago. . . .

When he got to Mrs. Spear's the maid showed him into a little study. The room was so small that it made his grandmother, who was waiting there, seem immense, like a great spreading idol. But she managed to get to her feet; her arms engulfed him; he sank into her warmth as into a tepid sea. If he'd been a child he would have burst out crying, she smelt so like home and the Mapledale Avenue soap!

"Oh, Vanny, Vanny—my little Vance . . . this *is* God's Hand," she said, and hugged him.

He thought, with a quick recoil: "She wouldn't have dragged God in that way, in old times—" and suddenly heard an emotional murmur at his back, and became aware that his grandmother, as she clasped him, had seen Mrs. Spear enter the room.

Vance's recoil was only momentary; yet the impression left a faint smirch on the freshness of Mrs. Scrimser's spontaneity. She had become a prophetess now, conscious of her audience.

"Dear Mrs. Scrimser, you'll forgive me? I felt I must see the meeting between you two!" Mrs. Spear sighed out with eloquent eyes and a hand affectionately extended to Vance.

But already there were sounds of arrival in the hall; the sense of the little apartment becoming more and more packed with people; the door of the study opening to admit Saidie Toler, straight and colourless as usual, and accompanied by a large battered blonde, Mrs. Lotus Mennenkoop, who declared emotionally that she must see Vance before the speaker took her place on the platform. . . .

The two little drawing rooms had been thrown into one, and they were already crowded when Vance slipped in at the back. Before him, rank on rank, the packed heads of the "Seekers" stretched up to an improvised platform, with wax lights and a table covered with old brocade. Vance did not recognize many people; most of those present seemed to belong to other regions of Mrs. Spear's rambling activities. But he was sure they were representative of their kind; Mrs. Spear was not the woman to have anything but the newest, even in religion. This world of spiritual investigation was unfamiliar to him; there were no "Seekers" in the Tarrant group, much less at the Cocoanut Tree or Rebecca Stram's. The audience seemed mainly composed of elderly men with beards and gold-rimmed glasses, pallid youths, and ladies of indeterminate age, in black silk or Greek draperies. He was surprised to see among them Mrs. Pulsifer, with Tarrant at her side, and in another part of the room the sleek heads and jewelled arms of a cluster of smart young women who belonged to the Tarrant set. Such a mixture was unexpected, and still more so the earnest and attentive expression of the fashionable members of the audience, who appeared to have come in good faith, and not to scoff, as he had feared.

Vance forgot to wonder if Halo Tarrant were in the room; forgot everything but his passionate curiosity to see what impression his grandmother would make on an audience so strangely blent, and so new to her. Whoever they were, he knew the "Seekers" would test Mrs. Scrimser by standards other and more searching than those of Euphoria, or even of Dakin and Lakeshore; and his heart was up in arms to defend her.

And now here she was, in the soft illumination of the little platform. As he gazed at her across the fervent backs of the "Seekers" she seemed to him to have grown still larger. Saidie Toler, seated at one elbow, looked like a shadow, Mrs. Mennenkoop, at the other, like a shrivelled virgin. Womanhood, vast and dominant, billowed out between them.

Mrs. Scrimser rose to her feet. Mrs. Lotus Mennenkoop had spoken a few words of introduction; phrases about a "new message," "our spiritual leader," "the foremost exponent of the new psychical ethics," had drifted by unheeded; the "Seekers" wanted Mrs. Scrimser.

She swayed to them across the table and began. "Meet God," she said, spacing her syllables impressively; then she paused. Her voice sounded richer, more resonant than ever; but Vance's unaccustomed ear was shocked by her intonation. Had she always had those hideous drawling gutturals?

"Meet God—that's what I want all you dear people here with me this evening to do . . . I presume some of you know *about* God already; and all of you at least know *of* Him," she urged, caressing her italics. She paused again, reaching out toward her audience. "The way we know about folks in the next street." ("New Yorkers don't," her grandson reflected.) "Or the way we know of famous people in the past: great heroes or splendid noble-hearted women. That's not the way I want you to know about God. I want you to know Him Himself—to get acquainted with Him, the way you would if He was living in the house next door, and you sent round to borrow the lawn mower. I want you to get to know Him so well that you're always borrowing, and He's always lending; so that finally you don't

hardly know what belongs to you and what belongs to Him
—and I guess maybe He don't either. That's the reason I say
to you all: *Meet God!* Because, oh, you dear beloved people
sitting here listening to me, I've met Him; and I know what
it's like!"

She stood silent, her face illumined, as Vance had seen
it when she looked up to the sky from the porch at Crampton. She was certainly a beautiful old woman, he thought;
and he felt that the people about him thought so too. But
what did they make of her exordium? They were silent; he
felt that their judgment was suspended. But there was the
hideous slur of her pronunciation, blurring and soiling every
word. . . .

She was hurrying on now, swept along on the full flood
of revelation, pleading with them to see what to her was so
plain, so divinely visible. The point was, she argued, that
God wasn't just here or there, in lecture halls, in churches,
and on the lips of preachers. He wasn't even just up in the
sky, as holy people used to think. They knew now that the
marvellous star-jewelled heavens were just atoms, like all
the rest of the universe . . . all those wonderful stars that
people in old times used to believe were the crowns of the
angels! They knew now that God was a million times
greater and bigger than all that, because He was in men's
souls; He was always creating, but also He was always
being created. The quaint old idea of the Mass, of the priest
turning bread into God, that seemed to enlightened modern
minds so ignorant and barbarous, had something in it after-
all, if you looked at it as the symbol of the wonderful fact
that man is always creating God; that wherever a great
thought is born, or a noble act performed, there God is created. *That* is the real Eucharist, the real remaking of Divinity. If you knew God, you knew that: you knew you had in
your soul the power to make Him . . . that every one of us,
in the old Bible phrase, may be a priest after the Order of

Melchizedek. . . . Talk of the equality of man with man! Why, we'd got way past that. The new Revelation wasn't going to rest till it had taught the equality of man with God. . . .

But how, she pressed on, was this wonderful equality, this God-making, to be achieved? Why, in the simplest way in the world: just by loving enough. Love was Christ's law; and Christ was just one of the great God-makers. And what she wanted of everybody was to be like Christ: to *be* Christ. What the world needed was Christs by the million—for the millions. What it needed was a standardized God. No caste religions any more! No limited God for the privileged and cultured, no priesthood, no preaching for rich pew-owners. Why, you could all of you go home now and be your own Christ, and make your own God, just by the simple recipe of loving enough. You didn't even have to . . .

The flood of words poured on and on over Vance's bent head. He did not want to look at her now: her prophetic gestures, her persuasive smiles, repelled him. Her intonations were unctuous, benedictory; she had become identified with her apostolic rôle. Behind the swaying surging prophetess he still felt the rich-hearted woman in whose warmth his childhood had unfolded; it was bitter to him that the people about him would never know her as she really was. He was already prepared to hate them for smiling at her rambling periods. He could have smiled at them himself if his heart had been less sore; but no one else should do so. He looked about him suspiciously, trembling to detect derision; but he saw only a somewhat blank expectancy. It was all very well, the faces about him seemed to say; but they had heard that kind of thing before. Something else must surely be coming. This inspired teacher was going to tell them the secret they yearned for. But apparently there was no other secret; nothing came but a crescendo of adjurations to love everybody and everything, to be all love, all Christ-likeness, all God-creativeness. . . .

Mrs. Scrimser paused. The room was pervaded by the peculiar sense of uncertainty of an audience which has lost touch with the speaker. The silence seemed to ask: What next? Vance knew. Though he had never before heard his grandmother speak in public he had often gone with her to the meetings which she frequented in her incessant quest for new religious sensations, and he knew the exact moment at which the orator's appeal, having reached its culmination, held itself ready for an emotional response. It was the moment when here and there someone stood up and gasped out devout ejaculations; when a hymn burst spontaneously from hundreds of throats; when the listeners fell on their knees in audible prayer.

Nothing of all this happened. Mrs. Scrimser stood motionless. The weight of her heavy body bearing on her outspread palms, as she rested them on the table before her, she watched for the tide of emotion to rise. It did not rise, but the audience did. There was an uncomfortable lull, followed by a discreet rustling of chairs. A "very beautiful," launched by Mrs. Spear from the platform, drifted languidly down the room. A very few of the more determined "Seekers" pressed back against the tide to Mrs. Scrimser; the others, somewhat too hastily, poured through the doors of the dining room toward the glimpse of a buffet supper. . . . As Vance passed out, he caught sight of Mr. Spear's alert head between two retreating backs, and heard him say in his thin crackling voice: "Isn't there some mistake about this? Seems to me I've met Mrs. Scrimser's God before—and Mrs. Scrimser too."

⚹ XXXVIII ⚹

THE NEXT morning Vance went early to Mrs. Mennenkoop's.
He wanted to see his grandmother before she began to be
besieged by the prophets and seers who had been such a
trial to Mrs. Weston when the Scrimsers came to live under
her roof. All night he had lain awake, torn between his disil-
lusionment and his wrath against those who had shared it.
. . . Those damned unsatisfied people who always had to
have some new sensation to batten on! Why had they
dragged his grandmother out of Euphoria, where she belonged, persuaded her that New York was in need of her,
that she had a "message" for them, as her jargon called it?
Such wrath as he had felt against the rich after Mrs. Pulsifer's rebuff now blazed up in him against these ridiculous
"Seekers"—seekers of new sensations, new catchwords, new
fads to take up or to turn to ridicule! At Euphoria Mrs.
Scrimser had her place in the social order. She was more
persuasive than the ministers of the rival churches, better
educated than their congregations. She had an authority
which no one questioned—except Mrs. Weston, who saw no
sense in telling people how to run their lives when you
couldn't manage your own hired girl.

Here in New York everything was different—and
Vance himself, in the interval, had grown different. The
world had come to have a perspective for him, and Euphoria was a hardly perceptible dot far off between two
narrowing lines. But in proportion as he understood this,

438

and suffered for his grandmother, his tenderness for her increased. It became defensive and fierce; he would have jumped at the chance of doing battle for her against all the Frensides and Spears. After all, wasn't his own case precisely hers? He too was the raw product of a Middle-Western town, trying to do something beyond his powers, to tell the world about things he wasn't really familiar with; his pride winced at the exactness of the analogy, and it moved him to acuter sympathy. If only he could persuade his grandmother to give up this crazy crusade; to go back to Euphoria, and take him and Laura Lou with her! He made up his mind, on the way out to Bronxville, that he would propose to her to break her lecturing engagements and go back at once.

His aunt Saidie Toler, who received him, did not share his apprehensions. She said she had never seen her mother more inspired than on the previous evening. Evidently New York audiences were less responsive at first than those in the western cities where Mrs. Scrimser had hitherto spoken; but Mrs. Mennenkoop had prepared them for that. She thought quite a number of converts would seek out Mrs. Scrimser in the course of the day, and was sure that in Brooklyn, where that evening's meeting was to be held, there would be more of an emotional surrender. . . .

Vance had always hated his aunt Saidie's jargon. She reminded him of a salesman retailing goods, and repeating automatically what was on their labels. . . . He wanted to know if he couldn't go in and see his grandmother; but Mrs. Toler said there was somebody with her on business: a man who organized lecture tours. He wanted to take Mrs. Scrimser right through the country, he said. . . . He'd answer for it that upstate she'd get the response she was accustomed to. . . . In New York it was a fashion to sit back and pretend you knew everything.

Vance's heart sank. He asked if he couldn't go in at

once, while the man was there—and at the same moment a
door opened, and Mrs. Scrimser came out into the hall. "I
thought I heard my boy's voice," she said, coming to him
with open arms. She begged him to step in and see the gentleman who had called about a lecture tour—he had made a
very interesting proposal. Vance followed her, and found
himself being named to Bunty Hayes, who held out his
hand with undiminished cordiality. "Why, yes," he said,
with an explanatory glance between grandmother and grandson, " 'Storecraft' aims to handle all the human interests. We
can't leave out religion, any more'n we could art or plumbing. And the minute I heard about this grand new religious
movement of Mrs. Scrimser's, I said: 'That's exactly our line
of goods, and there's nobody but "Storecraft" can do it justice.' If only she'd of got in touch with me before she came
to New York I'd of had her addressing three thousand human people in Steinway Hall instead of trying to get a kick
out of a few society highbrows from Park Avenue."

Vance stood silent between the two. His grandmother
looked more aged in the morning light. In spite of her increasing bulk she seemed smaller: as if Fate had already
traced on her, in deep lines and folds, her future diminu-
tion. But Bunty Hayes's flesh was taut and hard; he shone
with a high varnish of prosperity. And he looked at Vance
with a bright unwinking cordiality, as if their encounter
were merely a happy incident in an old friendship. "On'y to
think she's your grandmother; seems as if you'd got a corner
in celebrity in your family," he said.

"Oh, Vanny's our *real* celebrity," Mrs. Scrimser murmured, her tired eyes filling as they rested on her grandson.

"Well, I guess there's enough of it to go round," Hayes
encouraged them both. "What I say is . . ."

Mrs. Scrimser's gaze was still caressing Vance. She took
his hand. "I guess he'll be lecturing all over the United
States before long," she said.

"Well, when he does, 'Storecraft' 'll be all ready to handle him too—we'll feature you both on the same program," Mr. Hayes joked back.

Mrs. Scrimser answered humorously that she guessed that would depend on how well "Storecraft" handled *her*; and he challenged her to take a good look round and see if any other concern was prepared to do it better. It was agreed that she was to think over his proposition and give him an answer the next day; and thereupon he took his leave.

Mrs. Scrimser, when they were alone, held her grandson fast for a minute saying only: "Vanny boy, Mapledale Avenue's been like the grave since you went away," and he felt the contagion of her tenderness and a great longing to lay his cares in those capacious arms. She asked about Laura Lou, and why Vance hadn't brought her the night before, or today; and when he said she was ill in bed, exclaimed reproachfully at his not telling her sooner, and said she would go straight down to Mrs. Hubbard's after lunch. She began to question Vance about how they lived, and whether Laura Lou was comfortable and well looked after, and if the food was nourishing, and he was satisfied with the doctor; and gradually he was drawn into confessing his financial difficulties, and the impossibility of giving his wife such a home as she ought to have. Mrs. Scrimser's ideas of money were even vaguer than her grandson's, but her sympathy was the more ardent because she could not understand why a successful novelist, who knew all the publishers and critics in New York, shouldn't be making a big income. She was indignant at such injustice; but she implored Vance not to worry, since the "Storecraft" offer would enable her to help him and Laura Lou as soon as she'd paid back what she owed his father. From her confused explanations Vance gathered that Mr. Scrimser's long illness, and his widow's unlimited hospitality, had been a heavy strain on Mr. Weston, who, besides having to support his family-in-law, had been crippled by one or two unlucky gambles in real estate. Vance guessed that Mrs. Scrimser's attention had finally been called to these facts (no doubt by his mother), and that in a tardy rush of self-reproach she had resolved to wipe out her debt. It was not religious zeal alone which had started her on her lecturing tour. In the West, she told Vance, she had spoken without pay; but now that she understood her pecuniary obligations she was impatient to make money by her lectures. No one was more scrupulously anxious not to be a burden on others; the difficulty was that for her, to whom no fellow creature could ever be a burden, it was an effort to remember that she might be one herself. Vance was moved by the candour and humility of her avowal. He too knew what it felt like to be dragged down from the empyrean just as the gates of light were swinging open; how happy it would have made him to relieve this old dreamer of her cares, and leave her to pursue her vision! "I daresay when she came here she thought I'd be able to help her out," he reflected bitterly, and regretted that he had mentioned his own troubles. But Mrs. Scrimser's optimism was irrepressible; already she was planning, with the proceeds of her tour, to hire a little house in Euphoria and take Vance and Laura Lou to live with her. "Saidie Toler'll take all the housekeeping bothers off our hands, and you can do your writing, and I'll go on speaking in public if God's got any more use for me; and in the good clean prairie air Laura Lou'll get all the poison of New York out of her in no time." Her face was as radiant as if she were enumerating the foundations of the Heavenly City.

"Don't you think you and Laura Lou could be happy, making your home with me?" she pleaded.

Yes, Vance said, he was sure they could; it was long since his eyes had rested on anything as soothing as the vision of that little house. "I'd have a big kitchen table, six feet long, for my writing," he mused voluptuously; and then roused himself to his grandmother's summary of the "Store-craft" offer for a three months' tour, for which she was to be featured as: "God's Confidant, Mrs. Loraine Scrimser," who was to "tell the world about her New Religion."

"You see, Vanny, Saidie Toler's been all over the figures with him, and she says I ought to clear twenty or thirty thousand dollars. And perhaps that would be only a begin-ning. . . ." Her face glowed with tenderness, and Vance, trembling a little, took her large warm hand and pressed it against his cheek.

"Why, Van darling, don't—don't cry! You mustn't! I guess your troubles are all over now."

He sat silent, holding her hand. How could he tell her what was in his mind? Perhaps the inertness of his hand be-trayed the lack of response in his thoughts; for she ques-tioned him with eyes softened by perplexity. "Maybe you don't care for the way he's featured me?" she suggested tim-idly. "I guess you could find something more striking yourself—only I wouldn't want to bother you." He shook his head, and she went on, still more timidly: "Or is it the way I was received last night among those fashionable people? Don't suppose I didn't see it, Vanny; I was a failure; I know it as well as you do. My message didn't get over to them . . . it was a terrible disappointment to me. But Mrs. Men-nenkoop says that in that set they're dreadfully inexperi-enced in the spiritual life . . . infants wailing in the dark . . . and that maybe what I gave them was too startling, too new. . . ."

"Oh, no, that's not it," Vance interrupted with sudden vehemence. "It was *not* new to them—that's the trouble."

"Not new—?" Her hand began to tremble in his, and she drew back a little. "Do you mean to say, Vanny, that every profound and personal spiritual adventure is *not* new, is *not* different. . . ?"

"No, it's not. That's the point. Lots of people have thought they'd had spiritual adventures that were personal to them, and then, if they've taken the time to study, to look into the religious experiences of the past—"

"But what does the past matter? What I bring is a forward-looking faith, a new revelation—something God's given to *me*."

"No, it's not," Vance repeated vehemently. He felt now that he must speak out, at whatever cost to her feelings and his. "Those people last night were mostly well-educated, cultivated—some of the men were students of theology, scholars. They were there because they take an intellectual interest in religious ideas. . . ." He hurried on, trying to explain that, to such an audience, there was no novelty in what Mrs. Scrimser had to say, that her "revelation" belonged to a long-classified category of religious emotionalism. People had thought for centuries that God had given them a particular message, he went on. But supposing any direct access to the Divine to be possible, it was one of the great services of the organized churches to have maintained an authorized channel of communication between the Deity and men, and not to recognize any other.

"But, Vanny, that's the way the old tyrannical religions talked. All that's got nothing to do with the modern world. What people want nowadays is a new religion—"

Well, he interrupted her, if that was it, what she called her religion wasn't new; it had been in the air for centuries; and anyhow, even if it had been new, that was no particular recommendation. The greatest proof of the validity of a religion was its age, its duration, its having stood through centuries of change, as something that people had to have, couldn't in any age get on without. Couldn't she feel the beauty of continuity in the spiritual world, when the other was being pulled down and rebuilt every morning? Couldn't she see that, ninety-nine times out of a hundred, it was sheer ignorance and illiteracy that made people call things new—that even in the brick-and-mortar world that was being forever pulled down and rebuilt, the old materials and the old conceptions had to be used again in the rebuilding? Who wanted a new religion, anyhow, when the old one was there, so little exhausted or even understood, in all its age-long beauty?

He pressed on, so possessed by his subject that the words came of themselves, as they had when he had poured out his soul to Halo Tarrant: all unconsciously, he had yielded again to the boyish hope that his grandmother would be able to follow his reasoning.

She listened with bent head, and then lifted a face humbled yet admiring. "Yes, yes, I see what you mean, Vanny," she began eagerly—and even as she spoke he remembered that she had always said that, had always believed that she saw what people meant; but whereas in his boyhood he had retorted brutally: "No, you don't!" now he only mumbled: "Oh, well, I don't know that it matters so much about seeing. . . ."

Her face lit up. "No; that's it. Feeling's everything, isn't it, dear?"

"Well, I didn't mean that, either. I only meant—"

She raised her tired eyes and fixed them on his. "You meant that I'd better not try any more of my talks on your clever literary friends? But I don't intend to, Vanny; I'm sure you're right. My message is for the plain folks who want to be told how to get to God. . . . I know they'll come to me in their hundreds. I don't mean to give up or lose courage because I can't reach the hearts of a few super-cultivated intellectuals. . . . All that doesn't matter, as long as I can make money enough for us all to live on—does it?"

Vance got up and bent over to kiss her. He could not tell her at the moment that what he really wanted was to make her give up her lecturing tour altogether. Their talk had carried him back to the old days when she had been his only listener, had understood him with her heart if not with her mind; he could not bear, just then, to say anything that would bring the anxious humbled look into her eyes. He must be off, he explained, he had to hurry down to the office; but he promised to be waiting for her when she called after lunch to see Laura Lou.

He knew it was only a postponement: he had already decided that he could not live on his grandmother's earnings. Everything in his life seemed a postponement nowadays: morally as well as materially he was living from hand to mouth. But his intelligence still refused to bow to expediency; it was impossible for him to think of living on the money which Mrs. Scrimser's own ignorance was prepared to extract from that of others. His long hours of study and meditation at the Willows had made any kind of intellectual imposture seem the lowest form of dishonesty.

His grandmother's hour with Laura Lou nearly undermined his resolution. Seeing them thus—Laura Lou in one of her strange moments of loveliness, her head resting contentedly against the pillows, her willing hand yielded to Mrs. Scrimser's, and the latter settled in the rocking chair by the bed, her great person giving out an aura of good-humour and reassurance—it seemed to Vance that nothing mattered except that these two should understand each other. If only the conditions had been reversed, and he had been able to provide a home for his grandmother! He saw all his difficulties solved; Laura Lou soothed and sustained, the housekeeping somehow managed, and he himself with a free corner in which to go on undisturbed with his work. . . . This was precisely what Mrs. Scrimser and "Storecraft" were offering him; and the irony of the contrast burnt itself into him. He made up his mind to see that very day the publisher who had made him such tempting proposals. Per-

haps there was still some hope of readjustment with the
New Hour and Dreck and Saltzer.

On the way downstairs Mrs. Scrimser laid her hand on
his arm. "Is there anywhere that I can speak to you for a
minute alone, Vanny?"

He pushed open the parlour door and found its desert
spaces untenanted. Mrs. Scrimser seated herself on one of
the antimacassared sofas and drew him down beside her.
She looked at him tenderly, and before she spoke he knew
what she was going to say. "You think Laura Lou looks
sick?" he broke out. "She was a little excited at seeing you—
I guess it sent her temperature up. But she's all right,
really. . . ."

"Who looks after her when you're at the office?" his
grandmother asked.

"Well—the hired girl goes up every now and then. And
Mrs. Hubbard—that's our landlady—has been very nice to
her . . . until just lately. . . ."

"Just lately?"

He reddened. "Well, I've been behindhand about
paying—I suppose that's the reason."

"Vanny, you must take that child away from here."

He gave an impatient laugh. "Take her away? Where
to? To begin with, she wouldn't go anywhere without
me. . . ."

She looked at him gravely. "You must go with her then.
Young eyes don't recognize sickness the way old ones do.
. . . No, dear, I don't want to frighten you; she'll get well;
she just wants nursing and feeding—and comforting, I
guess. Isn't she fretting about you and your affairs? Maybe
thinking she's a burden to you? Poor child—I thought so.
. . . Well, Vanny, all that's got to stop. It *must* stop!" She
stood up with sudden resolution. "I'll send for that 'Storecraft' man—I could see they were anxious to get me; he was
fairly scared that I'd fall into the hands of another manager.

I'll see him tonight, Vanny; I'll get a good big advance out of him. . . . Saidie Toler'll manage that for me . . . you'll see!"

She stood beaming on him with such ample reassurance that his resolution wavered. Wasn't she right, after all? What business was it of his if (in perfect good faith, he was sure) she chose to sell her hazy rhetoric to audiences more ignorant than herself? After all, it was probable that her teaching could do only good . . . why try it by standards of intellectual integrity that none of her hearers would think of applying? He was frightened by her tone in speaking of Laura Lou; he knew that, unless he could raise a little money at once, he and his wife could not stay on at Mrs. Hubbard's; and to his grandmother's question as to where he intended to take Laura Lou he could find no answer.

"See here, Vanny, don't you look so discouraged. You'll see, I'll pull it off in the big towns upstate. And then—"

"No, no," he broke out uncontrollably. "You don't understand me; you must listen. I can't take your money—no matter how much of it you make. I want you to give up lecturing; to give it up at once. I want you to go back home now—tomorrow. Don't you see, Granny, we can't either of us live on money that isn't honestly got?"

Mrs. Scrimser stood listening with a face of gentle bewilderment. He felt the uselessness of his words; no argument of that sort could penetrate through the close armour of her conviction. Under her genuine personal humility there was a spiritual pride, the sense of a "call," of the direct mandate of the Unseen. The word "honestly" had not even caught her attention, and she evidently attributed Vance's scruples to the pride of a young man unwilling to be helped out of money difficulties by an old woman. He did not know what to say next; and for a minute or two they stood and faced each other in an embarrassed silence. Then he saw a tremor cross her face, followed by a look of painful enlightenment.

"Vanny," she said, laying her hand on his shoulder, "perhaps, as you say, I haven't understood what you meant. But you've got to tell me. Is it because you're afraid I'll hurt your reputation—a foolish old woman going about telling people about things she doesn't half understand? I know that's the way it struck you and your fashionable friends last night—and maybe you don't want them to go round saying: 'Who'd ever have thought that old evangelist woman with her Salvation Army talk was Vance Weston's grandmother —the *novelist's* grandmother?'" She paused, and let her eyes rest on his. "That it, Vanny? You see I'm not so stupid, after all." She smiled a little, and drew him closer. "If you do feel that, sonny, I guess I'll have to give up after all."

Vance could find no reply. The words choked in his throat. "It's not that—how could you . . . ?" he mumbled, answering her embrace. She groped in a big silk bag, drew out a crumpled handkerchief, and wiped her spectacles. When she had put them back, she plunged again into the deeper recesses of her reticule, and finally produced a hundred-dollar bill. She smoothed it out and pressed it into her grandson's hand. "No, it's not for you—it's for Laura Lou. And you can let her take it, Vanny"—a whimsical twinkle crept into her eyes—"because I didn't earn a dollar of it lecturing. I made every cent baking gingerbread for charity sales last winter—and see here, Vanny, it's twice the work it is coaxing folks back to Jesus. . . ."

❧ XXXIX ❧

VANCE HAD not seen Lewis Tarrant for a long time. Tarrant was at the office less often than formerly; the practical administration of the *New Hour* was entrusted to Eric Rauch, who ran it according to his own ideas save when his chief, unexpectedly turning up, upset existing arrangements and substituted new plans of his own. This state of things did not escape the notice of the small staff. It was rumoured that Tarrant was losing interest—then again that he was absorbed in the writing of a novel; it was agreed that, in any case, something was wrong with his nerves. Handling Tarrant had always been a gingerly business; Rauch was the only man supple enough to restore his good-humour without yielding to him; and even Rauch (as he told Vance) never knew beforehand whether he was going to pull it off or not. "The trouble is, he's got enough ideas to run a dozen reviews; and he wants to apply them all to this one poor rag." The result was that the rag was drooping; and as soon as an enterprise gave the least sign of failure it was Tarrant's instinct to disclaim all responsibility for it.

His frequent absences had been a relief to Vance. When the two did meet, though usually it was only to exchange a few words, Vance felt unhappy in the other's presence. To any one less simplehearted it might have been easier to despise the husband of the woman he worshipped than to be on friendly terms with him; but his opinion of Tarrant added to Vance's general distress of mind. It made him utterly wretched to think of Halo Tarrant's life being

spent with a man for whom she must feel the same contempt that Tarrant excited in him; and since his last talk
with her—since she had uttered that "I won't take a lover
while I have a husband" which still filled him with its poi-
gnant music—his feeling for her husband had hardened to
hatred. His own grievance against Tarrant played little part
in this, except insofar as it showed him the kind of man she
was chained to; but he wondered bitterly how she could
consider the tie binding. In his own case it was different; he
was bound to Laura Lou by her helplessness and his own
folly, and the bond seemed to him so sacred that he had at
once acknowledged the force of Halo's argument. He knew
he could not abandon his wife for the woman he loved; he
owned the impossibility and bowed to it. But Halo's case
was different. Tarrant was not an object of pity; and what
other feeling could hold her to him?

It was a strange and desperate coil, but one on which
his immediate domestic problem left him no time to brood.
He was still determined to do all he could to prevent his
grandmother from continuing her lecturing tour; even if he
could not prevail with her, and she did continue it, he was
determined that his wife and he should not live on her earnings. Whatever the alternative might be—and all seemed
hopeless—that resolve was fixed in him.

As soon as his grandmother had gone he decided to
look up the publisher who had made him such urgent proposals. He carried the hundred dollars up to Laura Lou, and
let his heart be warmed for an instant by her cry of surprise,
and the assurance that she'd never seen anybody as lovely
as his grandmother; then he hurried off on his errand. But at
the door he ran into a messenger from the *New Hour*, with
a line from Rauch saying that Tarrant wished to see him
about something important. "Better come along as quick as
you can," a postscript added; and Vance unwillingly turned
toward the office.

He had not realized till that moment how deeply distasteful it would be to him to see Tarrant again. He had no time to wonder what the object of the summons might be; the mere physical reluctance to stand in the man's presence overcame all conjecture, filled him to the throat with disgust at being at his orders. "That's got to end too," he thought— and then it occurred to him that the Mr. Lambart's negotiations might have been successful, and that Tarrant, as conscious as himself of the friction between them, had decided to give him his release.

This carried him to the office on lighter feet, and he entered the editorial retreat with a feeling almost of reassurance. It would be hateful, being near Tarrant, seeing him, hearing him—but the ordeal would doubtless soon be over.

Tarrant looked up quickly from his desk: it was one of the days when his face was like a perfectly symmetrical but shuttered housefront. "Sit down," he sighed; and then: "Look here, Weston, I'm afraid you'll have to move to some place where I can reach you by telephone. It's the devil and all trying to get at you; and your hours at the office are so irregular—"

Vance's heart sank. That dry even voice was even more detestable to listen to than he had expected. He hardly knew which part of Tarrant's challenge to answer first; but finally he said, ineffectively: "I can work better away from the office." This was not true, for he did most of his writing there; but he was too bewildered to remember it.

Tarrant smiled drily. "Well, that remains to be seen. It's so long since any of your script has been visible here that I've no means of knowing how much of the new book you've turned out."

Vance's blood was up. "I don't understand. It was with your consent that I dropped the monthly articles to give all my time to my novel—"

"Oh, just so," Tarrant interrupted suavely. "And I presume you've got along with it fairly well, as I understand you've been negotiating privately to sell it to Lambart."

"It was Lambart who came to me. He offered to fix it up with Dreck and Saltzer. The price I had contracted for with them is so much below what I understand I have a right to expect that I couldn't afford to refuse."

"Refuse what? Are you under the impression that you can sell the same book twice over, to two different publishers? You signed a contract some time ago with Dreck and Saltzer for all your literary output for four years—and that contract has over two years more to run. Dreck and Saltzer have asked me for an explanation because it was through me that the *New Hour* was able to put you in the way of securing a publisher. They're not used to this way of doing business; neither am I, I confess."

Vance was silent. The blood was beating angrily in his temples; but, put thus baldly, he could not but feel that his action seemed underhand, if not actually dishonourable. Of course he ought not to have concealed from Tarrant and his publishers that he had authorized Lambart to negotiate for him. He saw clearly that what he had done was open to misconstruction; but his personal antagonism toward Tarrant robbed him of his self-control. "The price I was to get from Dreck and Saltzer wasn't a living wage—"

Tarrant leaned back in his chair, and drummed on the desk with long impatient fingers. His hands were bloodless but delicately muscular: he wore a dark red seal ring on his left fourth finger. With those fingers he had pushed back his wife's hair from the temples, where Vance had so often watched the pulses beat . . . had traced the little blue veins that netted them. . . . Vance's eyes were blurred with rage.

"Why did you sign the contract if you weren't satisfied with it?" Tarrant continued, in his carefully restrained voice. It was evident that he was very angry, but that the crude

expression of his wrath would have given him no more pleasure than an unskilful stroke gives a good tennis player. His
very quietness increased Vance's sense of inferiority.

"I signed because I was a beginner, because I had
to. . . ."

Tarrant paused and stretched his hand toward a cigarette. "Well, you're a beginner still . . . you've got to remember that. . . . You missed the Pulsifer Prize for your
short story: for that blunder you'll agree we're not responsi-
ble; but it did us a lot more harm than it did you. We were
counting on the prize to give you a boost, to make you a
more valuable asset, as it were. And there was every reason
to think you would have got it if you hadn't tried to extract
the money out of Mrs. Pulsifer in advance." Vance crimsoned, and stammered out: "Oh, see here—"; but Tarrant
ignored the interruption. "After that you dropped doing the
monthly articles you'd contracted to supply us with, in order
to have more time for this new novel. In short, as far as the
New Hour is concerned, ever since the serial publication of
Instead came to an end we've been, so to speak, keeping
you as a luxury." He paused, lit the cigarette, and proffered
the box to Vance, who waved it impatiently aside. "Oh, you
understand; we accepted the situation willingly. It has always been our policy to make allowances for the artistic
temperament—to give our contributors a free hand. But we
rather expect a square deal in return. If any of our authors
are dissatisfied we prefer to hear of it from themselves; and
so do Dreck and Saltzer. We don't care to find out from out-
siders that the books promised to us—and of which the
serial rights are partly paid in advance—are being hawked
about in other publishers' offices without our knowledge.
That sort of thing does no good to an author—and a lot of
harm to us." He ended his statement with a slight cough,
and paused for Vance's answer.

Vance was trembling with anger and mortification. He

knew that Tarrant had made out a case for himself, and yet that whatever wrong he, Vance, had done in the matter, came out of the initial wrong perpetrated against him by his editor and publisher. But he could not find words in which to put all this consecutively and convincingly. The allusion to his attempt to borrow money from Mrs. Pulsifer, the discovery of her having betrayed the fact, were so sickening that he hardly noticed Tarrant's cynical avowal that, but for this, they could have captured the prize for him. His head was whirling with confused arguments, but he had sense enough left to reflect: "I mustn't let go of myself. . . . I must try and look as cool as he does. . . ."

Finally he said: "You say you and Dreck and Saltzer want to be fair to your authors. Well, the contract you advised me to make with them wasn't a fair one. *Instead* was a success, and they've wriggled out of paying the royalties they'd agreed on on the ground that they've lost money on the book because it's not a full-length novel."

"But didn't your contract with them specify that the scale of royalties that you accepted applied only to a full-length novel?"

"Well, I suppose it did. I guess I didn't read it very carefully. But they must have made a lot more money on *Instead* than they expected."

Tarrant leaned back in his chair and laid his fingertips together, with the gently argumentative air of one who reasons with the unreasonable. "My dear Weston," he began; and Vance winced at the apostrophe. All authors, Tarrant went on—young authors, that is—thought there was nothing easier than to decide exactly how much money their editors and publishers were making out of them. And they always worked out the account to their own disadvantage—naturally. In reality it wasn't as simple as that, and editors and publishers often stood to lose the very sums the authors accused them of raking in. A book might have a lot of fuss

made about it in a small circle—*Instead* was just such a case
—and yet you couldn't get the big public to buy it. And unluckily it was only the favour of the big public that made a
book pay. As a matter of fact, *Instead* was a loss to Dreck
and Saltzer. If Weston would write another book just like it,
but of the proper length, very likely they'd make up their
deficit on that; a highbrow success on a first book often
helped the sales of the next, provided it was the right
length. Dreck and Saltzer knew this, and though they were
actually out of pocket they were ready to have another try.
. . . Publishing was just one long gamble. . . . And perhaps it wasn't unfair to remind Weston that, both to the
New Hour and to Dreck and Saltzer, he'd so far been, from
the business point of view, rather a heavy load to carry. . . .

Vance had controlled himself by a violent effort of the
will; but at this summing-up of the case he broke out. "Well,
I daresay I have—but why not let me off our contract, if it's
been as much of a disappointment to you as to me?"

Tarrant's slow blood rose to his cheeks. "I'm curious to
know why you consider yourself disappointed."

"Why, for the reasons I've told you. My articles haven't
been a success—I know that as well as you. But my book
has, and under our agreement it's brought me no more than
if it had been a failure. I can't live, and keep my wife alive,
on the salary you give me, and if you'll let me off I can earn
three times the money tomorrow."

Tarrant was silent. He began to drum again on the
desk, and the dull red of anger still coloured his pale skin.
"My dear fellow, you've had plenty of opportunities to complain to me of our contract, and it never seems to have occurred to you to do so till that pirate Lambart came along.
Even then, if you'd come straight to me and stated your
case frankly, I don't say . . . But I'm not in the habit of letting my contributors be bribed away behind my back, and

neither are Dreck and Saltzer. You signed a contract with us, and that contract holds."

"Why do you want it to hold?"

Tarrant continued his nervous drumming. "That's our own business."

"Well, if you won't answer, I'll answer for you. It's because I've given you one success at a bargain, and you feel you may miss another if you set me free. And it pays you to hang on to me on that chance."

. Tarrant's lips moved slowly before his answer became audible. "Yes—I suppose that's the view · certain people might take. . . . It's one that doesn't enter into our way of doing business. Besides, before knowing whether the chance you speak of was worth gambling on, as you assert, I should have had to see the book you're at work on now; it doesn't always happen that beginners follow up a first success with a second. Rather the other way round."

"Then why won't you let me go?"

Tarrant, instead of replying, lit another cigarette, puffed at it for a moment, and then said: "By the way, is your manuscript here?"

"Yes."

"I should like to have a look at it . . . only for an hour or two. So far I haven't much idea of what it's about."

Vance pulled the manuscript out of his pocket. "If you do like it, will you let me off?" he repeated doggedly.

"No, certainly not. I shall ask you to make an effort to give us something more satisfactory, as I have every right to."

There was another pause. The air between the two men seemed to Vance to become suddenly rarefied, as if nothing intervened to deflect the swift currents of their antagonism.

"You won't like it," Vance insisted with white lips.

"I daresay not. No doubt you've seen to that."

The sneer struck Vance like a blow. He felt powerless with wrath and humiliation.

"It's no use your reading it anyhow," he exclaimed, no longer knowing what he was saying. He leaned across the desk, snatched up the pages, and tore them to bits before Tarrant's astonished eyes. He could not stop tearing—it seemed as if the bits would never be small enough to ensure the complete annihilation of his work.

He was conscious that Tarrant, after the first shock of surprise, was watching him with a sort of cold disgust; and also that, when the work of destruction was over, their relative situations would be exactly what they had been before. But this cool appreciation of the case was far below the surface of his emotions. He could not resist the sombre physical satisfaction of destroying under that man's eyes what he had made. . . .

The last scrap dropped to the floor, and Tarrant said quietly: "I'm afraid now you'll have to send round and get the copy you have at home."

"I've no other copy," Vance retorted.

"That's a pity. You've given yourself a lot of unnecessary work—and I'm damned if I see why. What's the sense of having to begin the thing all over again?"

"I shall never begin it over again."

"Well, if you weren't satisfied with it, or thought it wouldn't suit our purpose, I daresay you're right. But in that case I'll have to ask you to buckle down and turn out something else in the shortest possible time. We've been a good many months now without getting any return for our money. . . ."

"I shall never write anything for you again," said Vance slowly.

Tarrant did not speak for a moment or two. His colour had faded to its usual ivory-like sallowness, and the furrow deepened between his ironically lifted eyebrows. He had the immense advantage over his antagonist that anger made him cold instead of hot.

"Never? You'd better think that over, hadn't you? You understand, of course, that your not writing for us won't set you free to write for anybody else till the four years are over."

Vance looked at him with something of the other's own chill contempt. His wrath had dropped; he felt only immeasurably repelled.

"You mean, then," he said, "that even if I don't write another line for you you'll hold onto me?"

"I'm afraid you've left me no alternative," Tarrant answered coldly. He rang the bell on his desk, and said to the office boy who appeared: "Clear up those papers, will you?"

In the street Vance drew a long breath. He did not know what would happen next—could not see a fraction of an inch into the future. But in destroying the first chapters of *Loot* he felt as if he had torn the claws of an incubus out of his flesh. He had no idea that he had hated the book so much—or was it only Tarrant he was hating when he thought of it? He flung on, flushed, defiant. He felt like a balloonist who has thrown out all his ballast: extraordinarily light and irresponsible, he bounded up toward the zenith. . . .

As he turned the corner of his street he came upon a pedlar beating his horse. Horses were rare nowadays in New York streets, pedlars almost obsolete; but in this forgotten district both were still occasionally to be seen. . . . Vance stopped and looked at the load and the horse. The load was not very heavy: the horse was thin but not incapable of effort. He was not struggling against an overload, but simply balking, thrusting his shabby forelegs obstinately against the asphalt. Unknown to his driver, something was offending or torturing him somewhere—he had the lifted lip and wild-rolling eye of a horse in pictures of battlefields. And the human fool stood there stupidly belabouring him. . . . Vance's anger leapt up. "Here, you damned fool, let that horse alone, will you. . . ."

The man, astonished and then furious, cursed back copiously in Italian and struck the horse again. "Ah, that's it, is it?" Vance shouted. He caught the man by the arm, and remembering his Dante, cried out joyously: *"Lasciate ogni speranza!"* as he fell on him. The tussle was brief. He struck the whip out of the pedlar's hand, punched him in the face, and then, seeing the loafers assembling, and a policeman in the distance, suddenly remembered that it was Tarrant he had been thrashing, and shamefacedly darted away down the street to the shelter of Mrs. Hubbard's door.

❧ XL ❧

It was one of Tarrant's accomplishments to be able to go imperturbably through a scene where his advantage depended on his keeping his temper; but it was one of his weaknesses to collapse afterward, his overtaxed self-control abandoning him to womanish tremors, damp hands, and brittle nerves.

When he turned up that evening, his wife knew at once that he was in the throes of one of these reactions. Something had gone wrong again at the office. Of late, on such occasions, he had taken to seeking comfort in the society of Mrs. Pulsifer. Halo knew this and was faintly amused. She knew also that he was losing interest in the *New Hour* because it had not succeeded as he had hoped, and that he had begun to write a novel—probably under Mrs. Pulsifer's inspiration. An important Pulsifer Prize for First Novels was to be added to the one already established for the Best Short Story; and it was like Tarrant, to whom the money was utterly indifferent, to be tempted to compete for the sake of publicity. His restless vanity could never find sufficient pasturage, and as the years passed without the name of Lewis Tarrant becoming a household word on two continents (or even figuring in the English *Who's Who*), his wife noticed that his appetite for praise grew coarser.

All this Halo marked with the lucid second sight of married experience. As long as she had continued to be fond of her husband she had seen him incompletely and confusedly; but under the X ray of her settled indifference every muscle and articulation had become visible. At times she was almost frightened by the accuracy with which she could calculate the movements of his mind and plot out his inevitable course of action. Because really she no longer cared to do so. . . . She would have been glad enough to impart the unneeded gift to Mrs. Pulsifer; and one day when Mrs. Spear, after various tentative approaches, had put a maternal arm about her and asked ever so gently: "Darling, has it never occurred to you that Lewis is being seen about rather too much with Jet Pulsifer?" Halo had burst into hysterical laughter, and caught her bewildered parent to her bosom. . . .

But no. There was no escape that way. Lewis still needed her, and she knew it. Mrs. Pulsifer ministered to his thirsting egotism, but Halo managed his life for him, and that was even more important. Some day, perhaps . . . But she shook off the insinuating vision. Penny by penny, hour by hour, she was still paying back the debt she had assumed when she found out that, all through his courtship, her family had been secretly and shamelessly borrowing from him. And since then the debt had gone on increasing much faster than she could possibly reduce it. The comfort he had given to Mr. and Mrs. Spear since he had become their son-in-law, the peace and security assured to them by his lavish allowance—how many years of wifely devotion and fidelity would it take to wipe out such a score?

Musing fruitlessly on these things she sat alone, waiting for her husband to join her and go in to dinner. She had refused several invitations for that evening, thinking that Lewis would probably dine out (as he did nowadays on most nights), and hoping rather absurdly that Vance Weston might come in and see her. . . .

The poor boy must have calmed down by this time; it would be safe to see him; and she was eager to hear more of

the novel. Her sympathy with him, she told herself again
and again, was all intellectual; she was passionately in love
with his mind. It was a pity that he had not understood this;
had tried to mix up "the other thing" with their intellectual
ardours. And yet—no, certainly, she did not want him to
make love to her; but would it not have mortified her to be
treated forever like a disembodied intelligence? She had to
confess to herself that she could not wish undone that foolish scene of the other evening . . . that the incident in it
she most obstinately remembered with his despairing boy's
cry: "I want to kiss you. . . ."

Oh, but what folly! Of course, if she was really to help
him with his work, all those other ideas must be put aside
and forgotten. And she did so want to help him; it was her
greatest longing, the need of her blood. The thought of it
fed her lonely hours, filled her empty life—or nearly filled it.
And she hoped he would feel the same longing, the same
urgent necessity, and would come back to her soon for more
companionship, more encouragement. . . . Perhaps she
had not encouraged him enough, that last evening, about
his work, that is. It was well to remember that authors, even
the least fatuous and the most intelligent of them, were nervous, irritable, self-conscious: the slightest unfavourable
criticism flayed them alive. In that respect certainly (she
smiled) Tarrant seemed qualified to join the brotherhood.
But poor Vance's sensitiveness was of a different kind, the
result of inexperience and humility. Under it she always felt
an inarticulate awareness of his powers; his doubts, she was
sure, concerned only his aptitude for giving those powers
full expression. She could almost picture him, in some glorious phase of future achievement, flinging down his pen to
cry out like a great predecessor: "My God, but this is
genius—!"

She was thus softly pondering, in a mood of moral beatitude, when Tarrant turned up with his usual nervous: "I'm

not late, am I? Well, put off dinner a few minutes, will
you?" And now here he was again, fresh from his dressing
room, brushed, glossy, physically renovated, but nervously
on edge and obviously in need of consolation. . . . Good-
bye to her moral beatitude!

Since their one quarrel about Vance Weston—the quarrel which had resulted in Halo's deciding not to accompany
her husband to Europe—the young man's name had seldom
figured in their talk. The unexpected success of *Instead* had
been balm to Tarrant's editorial vanity, and Halo had not
suspected that there had been a subsequent difference between the two men till the evening, a few months previously, when Vance had told her of his asking Tarrant to
raise his salary or annul their contract. She had suffered bitterly on hearing of this, but she had suffered in silence. She
could not give Vance the clandestine help she would have
wished to; she had neither money of her own, nor means of
raising any. And she knew it would only injure him if she
betrayed his confession and appealed to her husband's generosity. Tarrant had no generosity of that kind; he would
simply have said: "I suppose he's been trying to borrow of
you now, after failing to pull it off with Mrs. Pulsifer"; and
if he had said that she thought she would have got up and
walked out of his house—forever.

No; that was not the way to help Vance. Her only intervention on his behalf had been a failure. All she could do
was to hold her tongue, and do what she could to contribute
to the success of his new book. It flattered her (far more
than she knew) to feel that in that way she really could be
of use to him. To be his Muse, his inspiration—then there
really was some meaning in the stale old image! She knew
she had had a real share in the making of *Instead*, and she
wore the secret knowledge like a jewel. . . .

"Well?—" she questioned her husband, when they had

returned to the library after dinner. She knew it was necessary for his digestion (an uncertain function) that he should
unburden himself of the grievance she read in every look
and intonation. And sometimes, when she rendered him this
service, she felt as impersonal as a sick nurse smoothing out
a fractious invalid.

Tarrant gave his short retrospective laugh—like the
scratch of a match throwing back a brief flare on his grievance. "Oh, it's only your protégé again—"

She felt a little shiver of apprehension. Usually a cool
harmony reigned between Tarrant and herself. Since the
day of her great outburst, when she had refused to accompany him to Europe, she had carefully avoided anything approaching a disagreement. She had learned her lesson that
day; and futile wrangles were humiliating to her. But whenever Vance Weston's name was pronounced between them
the air seemed to become electric. Was it her husband's
fault or hers? She was always on the alert to defend Vance,
she hardly knew from what. Or was it herself she was
defending . . . ?

"What protégé?" she asked carelessly.

"I didn't know you had more than one. Weston, of
course—yes, he's been treating me to another of his scenes.
Really, the fellow's not housebroken. And a sneak too . . .
can't run straight. . . ."

"Lewis!"

"Dirty sneak. He's after more money, as usual, and he's
been trying to get Lambart to buy his book from Dreck and
Saltzer without first consulting me. Buy up our double contract with him . . . behind my back! But women can never
see the enormity of these things. . . ."

He paused, and stirred his coffee angrily. "I daresay
you see nothing in it," he challenged her.

Halo's heart had subsided to a more regular measure. It

was not what she had feared . . . she was ashamed to think how much! She assured herself hastily that her fears had been for Vance, and not for herself. If he had lost his head and betrayed his feeling for her to her husband it would have meant ruin for him. She knew the deadly patience of Tarrant's retaliations.

"Of course," Tarrant continued, "things aren't done that way between men. But the fact is I know only one woman who has a man's sensitiveness in money matters"—he paused—"and that is Jet Pulsifer. . . ." He brought the name out with a touch of defiance which amused his wife.

"Oh, yes," she murmured, with increasing relief.

"You don't see anything in it yourself?" he insisted.

"I see what I always have—that your contract's not fair to Vance; I've told you so before."

"That's neither here nor there—"

"Surely it's very much *here*, if the poor boy's in want of money."

"Ah, he's been whining to you again about money, has he?"

She shook her head and her eyes filled with tears. She remembered the uselessness of her previous intervention in Vance's behalf, and wondered again by what curious coincidence it happened that his name always brought to a climax the latent tension between herself and Tarrant.

"Look here, Halo—I can see you still think I've treated him badly."

"I think you've treated him—indifferently. What you call business is essentially an affair of indifference, isn't it? It's designed to exclude the emotions."

"Do you want me to be emotional about Weston?"

"I want you to be generous, Lewis—as you know how to be. . . ." She paused to let this take effect. "He's young and unhappy and bewildered. Perhaps he did make a mistake in going to Lambart about his book without telling you." (Tarrant snorted.) "But surely you can afford to over-look that. He's given the *New Hour* one good book—and I believe he's going to give you another. This last novel is a very fine thing—"

Tarrant shifted his position slightly, and looked at his wife. "Ah—so you've read it, then?" he said, a sudden jealous edge in his voice.

"The first chapters—yes."

"Well, there are no more first chapters—or last ones, either." He saw her startled movement, and laughed. "When I refused to let the young gentleman off his bargain he tore up the manuscript before my eyes and said he'd never write another line for any of us. Good old-fashioned melodrama, eh?" He waited, and then added with a touch of flatness: "He swore he had no other copy—but I wouldn't trust him about that."

Halo sat speechless. The scene had evidently been more violent than she had imagined. She knew Tarrant's faculty for provoking violent scenes—his cool incisiveness cutting into the soul like a white-hot blade into flesh. The pound of flesh nearest the heart—that was what he always exacted. And she knew too that Vance had spoken the truth: to her also he had said that he had no duplicate of those first chapters. He still kept to his boyish habit of scribbling the pages with his own hand, and usually did not trouble to type them out till the book he was doing was well advanced. The mechanical labour of copying his own work was hateful to him, and he had never been able to pay for having it done. In the first months Laura Lou had tried to act as amanuensis; but she found his writing hard to decipher, her spelling drove him frantic, and she had nearly destroyed his Remington. Since her illness there had been no question of her continuing to render these doubtful services. The doctor said that stooping over was bad for her, and the manuscripts piled themselves up uncopied, in spite of Halo's frequent protests.

Why, she thought, had she not insisted on typing his work for him herself? But it was too late now; she could only try to swallow back the useless tears.

"Well, what do you think of that?" Tarrant insisted. It always annoyed him to have his climaxes fall flat, and he behaved like a conscientious actor whose careless partner had missed the cue. "You don't seem to have heard what I've been saying," he insisted.

"Oh, yes. And I'm sorry—dreadfully sorry."

"Well, that's not much use." She saw that he was reaching the moment of reaction. It was the moment when, after he had produced his effect, brought out and aired his grievance, his taut nerves gave way, and he secretly asked himself what to do next, like a naughty child after a tantrum. The hour always came when he had to pay for the irresistible enjoyment of making somebody angry and unhappy, and there was something at once ludicrous in his surprise when it arrived, and slightly pitiful in his distress. "These things take it out of me," he said, and drew his handkerchief across his damp forehead.

Usually Halo had some murmur of reassurance ready; but on this occasion none came. Vance had destroyed his manuscript—those pages in which she had indeed found things to criticise, but so much more to praise! She remembered now only what was admirable in them, and felt helplessly indignant at the cruelty which had driven him to such an act.

"The fact is, I'm not used to treating with people of that kind," Tarrant went on, with rising self-pity.

"No—you're not!" she retorted, carried away by sudden indignation. "It's your only excuse," she added ironically.

He stopped short, and looked at her with the injured eyes of a child who had expected compassion and gets a box on the ear.

"You've destroyed a fine thing—a great thing, perhaps. It's an act of vandalism, as much as slashing a picture or breaking a statue—things people get arrested for," she continued recklessly.

"I—I? Destroyed—? But, Halo, you haven't even been listening. You think I tore up the manuscript? It was that damned fool who—"

"Yes, because you hurt him, wounded his pride as an artist. You don't know what it is to respect other people's work, the creation of their souls. . . . You don't know anything about anything, unless it happens to yourself!"

She saw the beads of perspiration come out again on his forehead, and while he felt for his handkerchief she knew he was anxiously asking himself how he was to go through another painful discussion so soon after the previous one. Usually he required twenty-four hours to recover after he had given somebody hell—and here was his own wife, who knew better than anyone else how sensitive he was, how heavily he had to pay for every nervous strain, and who was ruthlessly forcing him into a second scene before he had recovered from the first!

But Halo felt no pity. The sight of her husband's discomfiture only exasperated her. Often and often she had helped him back to self-esteem after one of his collapses; to do so was almost as necessary to her pride as to his, as long as they were to go on living together. But she was far past such considerations now, and pushed on without heeding. "You've destroyed something rare . . . something beautiful. . . ." She could only uselessly go over the same words.

Suddenly Tarrant's face became attentive. "You thought as well of the book as all that?"

"I thought great things of it—" The only thing that relieved her indignation was to rub into him the value of what he had lost. He should at least feel it commercially, if there was no other way of making him suffer.

He was looking at her rather shamefacedly. "Really, you might have dropped a hint of all this before. . . ."

"I read the chapters only a little while ago; and Vance

didn't want me to form an opinion till he'd got on further, or to say anything about it."

"Saying anything about it hardly applies to telling me— your husband, and his editor."

"I've no doubt he would have shown it to you if you'd asked him."

"I did ask him, just now; and his answer was to tear the thing up." There was a long pause, during which the two opponents rested rather helplessly on their resentment. Halo was still too angry to speak, and her husband, she knew, was beginning to ask himself if he had made a mistake—if there were times when even the satisfaction of bullying someone who depended on one had better be foregone. He said sullenly: "After all, it only means the loss of the time it'll take him to rewrite the thing. I don't believe there were more than sixty pages."

"Creative writers can't rewrite themselves. It would be mental torture if they could . . . and they can't."

"Oh, well, we'll see."

"Do you mean to say he told you he'd try?"

"Lord, no. On the contrary. He said he'd never write another line for us. . . . But of course he will—he'll have to. He belongs to the review for another two years, as I reminded him."

Halo pondered. At length she said, in a quieter tone: "You can't make him write if he doesn't choose to."

"I can threaten him with a lawsuit."

"Oh, Lewis—"

"Well, what about it? Here's a fellow who's destroyed something beautiful—pricelessly beautiful. You tell me artists can't do the same thing twice over. Well, that makes it unique. And that unique thing that he's destroyed belonged to me—belonged to the *New Hour,* and to Dreck and Saltzer. As I told him, it was partly paid for already—and how's he going to make it up to us now, I ask you? I could see the young ass had never even thought of that."

Halo suddenly felt ashamed of her own impotent anger. She could have rendered Vance no worse service than by harping to her husband on his blunder. For the sake of satisfying a burst of temper as useless as Tarrant's she had risked what little hope there was of bringing him around to a kindlier view. But it was almost impossible for her to be adroit and patient when she dealt with anything near to her heart. Then generosity and frankness were her only weapons—and they were about as availing as bows and arrows against a machine-gun. At length she said: "I can understand Dreck and Saltzer taking this stand—I suppose, from a business point of view, it's all right. But with you it's so different, isn't it? Fellow artists surely ought to look at the question from the same angle. Vance is terribly poor . . . his wife is ill . . . in some respects his collaboration hasn't been of much use to the review, and I should think you'd be glad, if the *New Hour* can't afford to raise his pay, to let him off his bargain, and get Dreck and Saltzer to do the same. What harm can it do either of you? And at any rate you'll have given him the chance of trying his luck elsewhere. . . . I daresay he was stupid, and even rude, in his talk with you—he's got no tact, no cleverness of that kind—but you, who've got all the social experience he lacks, you ought to be generous . . . you can afford to be. . . ." Her lips were so parched that she had to stop. To go on talking like that was like chewing sawdust. And when she paused she understood in a flash the extent of her miscalculation. It is too easy to think that vain people are always stupid—and this was the mistake she had made. Yet she ought to have known that her husband, though he was vain, was not stupid . . . or at least not always so; and that flattery administered at the wrong time will not deceive even those who most thirst for it. Tarrant stood up and looked down on her with a faintly ironic smile.

"What you really think," he said, "is that I'm a fool—but I'm not quite as an egregious one as all that. I leave that superiority to your young friend. Besides," he added, "I ought not to forget that you've never understood anything about business. It was the only gift your fairy godmothers left out. I'm awfully obliged for your advice; but really, in matters of this kind, you must leave me to deal with our contributors myself. . . ."

BOOK VII

⊱ XLI ⊰

THE SUMMER light lay so rightly on the lawn and trees of the Willows that Halo Tarrant understood more clearly than ever before the spell the place had cast on Vance Weston.

She had gone there to take a look, for the first time in months. The present owner, the old and infirm Miss Lorburn, sat in her house in Stuyvesant Square and fretted about her inability to keep an eye on the place; she always said what a pity it was that poor Tom hadn't left it to poor Halo instead of to her. Miss Lorburn's world was peopled with friends and relatives who seemed to her best described by the epithet "poor"; what with one thing or another, she thought them all objects of pity. It was only of herself, old, heavy, with blurred eyes, joints knotted by rheumatism, legs bloated by varicose veins, and her *good* ear beginning to go, that she never spoke with compassion. She merely said it was a pity poor Halo would have to wait so long for the Willows . . . not that it would be much use to the poor child when she did get it, if the value of property at Paul's Landing continued to decline at its present rate.

Since Mrs. Tracy's departure for California the Willows, for the first time, had been entrusted to hands unconnected with its past, and as Miss Lorburn feared the new caretakers might not treat poor Elinor's possessions with proper reverence it behoved Halo to see that everything was in order.

As she walked along the drive she was assailed by memories so remote that she felt like an old woman—as old

475

as the Elinor Lorburn of the portrait above the mantel or
the purblind cripple in Stuyvesant Square. "I almost wonder
I'm not on crutches," she mused; so heavily did the weight
of the past hang on her feet and her mind.

The place wore its old look of having waited there
quietly for her, with a sort of brooding certainty of her return—not changing, not impatient, not discouraged, but just
standing there, house, turf, and trees, the house yearly losing more of its paint, the wistaria adding more clusters to
the thousands mercifully veiling the angles and brackets it
had been meant to adorn. As she looked about her she understood for the first time how, in what seemed the gro-
tesqueness of discarded fashion, Vance's impatient genius
had caught the poetry of the past. For him the place had
symbolized continuity, that great nutritive element of which
no one had ever told him, of which neither Art nor Nature
had been able to speak to him, since nothing in his training
had prepared him for their teaching. Yet, blind puppy,
groping embryo as he was, he had plunged instantly into
that underlying deep when the Willows had given him a
glimpse of it.

Halo had purposely avoided the new caretakers' day.
She wanted the place to herself; there were ghosts of her
own there now. . . . She felt her way in among the familiar
obscurities. That looming darkness on her right was the high
Venetian cabinet in the hall; this spectral conclave on which
a pale starlight twinkled down was the group of shrouded
armchairs in confabulation under the prisms of the drawing
room chandelier. Capricious rays, slanting through the shutters, seemed to pick out particular objects for her attention,
like searchlights groping for landmarks over a night landscape. She fancied the inanimate things assisted in the
search, beckoning to the light, and whispering: *Here, here!*
in their wistful striving for reanimation. There was no
amount of psychic sensibility one could not read into the
walls and furniture of an old empty house. . . .

Her own youth was in it everywhere, hanging in faded shreds like the worn silk of the curtains—her youth, already far-off and faded, though she was now only twenty-eight! As she stood in the library she recalled her first meeting with Vance Weston—how she had strolled in on one of her perfunctory visits and surprised an unknown youth in Elinor Lorburn's armchair, his hair swept back untidily from a brooding forehead, his eyes bent on a book; and how, at her approach, he had lifted those eyes, without surprise or embarrassment, but with a deep inward look she was always to remember, and had asked eagerly: "Who wrote this?" How like Vance! It was always so with him. No time for preambles—always dashing straight to the vital matter, whether it were the authorship of "Kubla Khan," or the desperate longing to kiss her. . . . She shut her eyes a moment, and listened to that cry: "You don't understand—I want to kiss you!" He thought she didn't understand—so much the better. . . .

In those early days, for all her maternal airs with him, she had been as young, as inexperienced as he was. She knew a good deal about art and literature, but next to nothing about life, though she thought herself a past mistress in its management. Her familiarity with pecuniary makeshifts, with the evasions and plausibilities of people muddling along on insufficient means, bluffing, borrowing, dodging their creditors, entertaining celebrities and neglecting to pay the milkman and the butcher—all these expedients had given her a precocious competence which she mistook for experience. They had also called forth a natural ardour for probity and fair dealing which she must have inherited from one of the straitlaced old Lorburns on the panelled walls at Eaglewood. Side by side with it burned an equally fierce ardour for living—for the beauty of the visible world, its sunrises and moon births, and the glories with which man's labours have embellished it. Never was a girl more in love with the whole adventure of living, and less equipped to hold her own in it, than the Halo Spear who had come upon Vance Weston that afternoon.

In love in the human way too? Yes, that she had been equally ready for—only it seemed beset with difficulties. Hers was one of the undifferentiated natures which ask that all the faculties shall share in its adventures; she must love with eyes, ears, soul, imagination—must feel every sense and thought impregnated together. And either the young men who pleased her eye chilled her imagination, or else the responsive intelligences were inadequately housed. She wanted a companion on the flaming ramparts; and New York had so far failed to find her one.

Lewis Tarrant came the nearest. He was agreeable to look at; she liked his lounging height, the sharp thinness and delicate bony structure of his face, and she was impressed by the critical aloofness of mind, which unbent only for her. Her wavering impulses sought in him a rectitude on which she could lean. He had a real love of books, a calm culti-vated interest in art; his mind was like a chilly moonlit re-flection of her own. She nearly loved him—but not quite. And then, just as she had decided that he could never walk the ramparts with her, came the discovery that her family, certain of the marriage, had accepted one or two discreet loans—and the final shock of learning that it was Lewis who had found the missing Americana from the Willows and bought them back in time to avert a scandal. . . .

Well, what of all that? Hadn't she always known what her family were like—long since suspected the worst of her brother? Why had she not washed her hands of them and gone her own way in the modern manner? She could not; partly from pride, but much more from attachment, from a sort of grateful tenderness. She had been happy, after all, in that muddling happy-go-lucky household. Her parents had a gipsylike charm, and they were always affectionate and responsive. The life of the mind, even the life of the spirit, had been enthusiatically cultivated in spite of minor moral shortcomings. If she loved poetry, if she knew more than most girls about history and art, about all the accumulated wonders peopling her eager intelligence, she owed it to daily intercourse with minds like her own, to the poetry evenings by the fire at Eaglewood, when Mrs. Spear would rush out to placate an aggrieved tradesman, and come back unperturbed to "The Garden of Proserpine" or "The Eve of St. Agnes"; to those thrifty wanderings in Europe, when they vegetated in cheap Italian pensions or lived on sunshine and olives through a long winter at Malaga, but wherever they went, it was always hand in hand with beauty.

Desert such parents in their extremity? It was unthinkable to a girl who loved their romantic responsiveness as much as she raged against their incurable dishonesty. Lewis Tarrant had been immensely generous—was she going to let herself be outdone by him? Some day—if she inherited the Willows, and a little of Cousin Tom's money—she might be able to pay him back, and start fair again. But meanwhile, what could she do but marry him? And at the thought of his generosity she began to glow with tenderness, and to mistake her tenderness for love. On this tidal wave of delusion —and after the news that her cousin Tom had disinherited her—she was swept into the dull backwater of her marriage. . . .

She had not seen Vance since the destruction of the manuscript. After a sleepless night—a night of dry misery and crazy unreal plans—she had telegraphed him: "Have you gone mad? Is there really no other copy? Come this evening after nine. I must see you." The day dragged by. She did not see Tarrant again before he departed for the office. She had nothing further to say to him, and was afraid of making another blunder if the subject of Vance came up. If she had not foolishly reproached her husband for destroying a masterpiece he might have been glad to let Vance off his bargain—but now she knew he would exact his pound of flesh. In what form? she wondered. She was not clear about the legal aspects of the case, but she knew Tarrant would move cautiously and make certain of his rights in advance. The meaningless hours crawled on. Her husband was dining at Mrs. Pulsifer's—a big affair for some foreign critic who had been imported to receive a university degree. She was sure of her evening alone with Vance. But the hours passed, the evening came, and he did not come with it, and he sent no message. She sat waiting for him till after midnight; then she heard the click of her husband's latchkey and hurried away to her room to avoid meeting him. When she looked at herself in the glass as she undressed she saw a ravaged face and eyes swollen with crying. She had wept unconsciously as she sat there alone and waited.

The next day and the next Vance made no sign; it was not until the third that a note came. "I am going away from New York. My wife is sick, and we are moving out to the country. I couldn't come the other night. There isn't any other copy; but then you never cared for it much, and I guess I can do better. Vance."

Not a word of tenderness or of regret. But the phrases had the desperate ring of the broken words he had jerked out that evening in the library. It was never his way to waste words over the irremediable. And, as far as he and she were concerned, she saw now that the case was irremediable. How could she have asked him to come back to her house? The breach with her husband made that impossible. And now he was going away from New York, he did not even tell her where. It was all useless, hopeless—whatever she might have been to him, or done for him, the time was past, the opportunity missed. . . .

After waiting a day or two she had sent for Frenside, and told him as much of the story as concerned her share in Vance's work, and the intellectual side of their friendship.

When she came to the destruction of the manuscript, and to her husband's attitude in the matter, Frenside, who had listened musingly over his pipe, gave a short laugh. "Well, my dear, you have made a mess of it!" She was too much humiliated to protest. "But what can I do now?" she merely asked, and was not unprepared for the "Nothing!" he flung back.

"Oh, Frenny, but I *must—*"

He shrugged her protest away. "And you know," he went on, "it's not such a bad thing for a young novelist with a demoralizing success behind him to tear up a manuscript or two. Chances are they wouldn't have been much good— just the backwash of the other. He's done the right thing to go off into the country and tackle a new job in new surroundings—without even you to advise him."

She winced, but Frenside's sarcasm was always salutary. "But he can't afford to wait," she said. "He's starving— and with that poor little ill wife. How can I persuade Lewis to let him off his bargain? His only hope is to get an advance from Lambart on his unwritten book, so that he can go off and work quietly, without this dreadful anxiety about money. But I can't make Lewis feel as I do about it. . . ."

Frenside contemplated his pipe in silence. "Tarrant's writing a novel himself, isn't he? What about—?"

She felt a little shock of apprehension. "Oh, I don't know. He's so secretive. He's never asked me to look at it, and I don't dare suggest . . ."

Frenside looked at her shrewdly. "Dare—suggest— insist. Get him to let you see what he's done; tell him it's a darned sight better than any of Weston's stuff. If he can be got to believe that—and you ought to know how to make him—he may stop bothering about Weston."

She remained silent while Frenside got up to go. "Look here, my child; get him to read his book to you, and try to think it's a masterpiece. Perhaps it is." But seek as she would she could find no answering pleasantry. She sat helpless, benumbed, while her old friend emptied his pipe, pushed it into his pocket, and reached out for his stick. But as he got to the door she started up and broke out, with a little sob: "All the help I wanted to give him has turned to harm. Oh, Frenny, how am I going to bear it?" Frenside limped back to her and laid his hand for a moment on her shoulder. Then he took off his glasses to give her one deep look. "Bravely," he said, and turned to go.

All that had happened three months ago; and she was glad now that she had said what she had to Frenside, and also that he had guessed what she left unsaid. It made her world less lonely to think of that solitary spark of understanding burning in another mind like a little light in an isolated house. But that was the only help he had been able to give. As far as she could bring herself to do so, she followed his advice with respect to Tarrant. But though she refrained from all further reference to Vance, and behaved to her husband as though the bitter scene between them had never happened, she found it impossible to question him about his work. When she tried to do so her throat grew dry, and every phrase she thought of sounded false and hollow. Some premonition told her that his novel would be an amateurish performance, and that if it were she would not be able to conceal her real opinion of it. For days she tried to think of a method of approaching the subject, of flattering his hypersensitive need of praise without running the subsequent risk of wounding it; but she found no way. "I know he can't write a good novel—and if it's bad he'll find out at once that I think it is. . . . What he wants is an audience like Jet Pulsifer. . . ." She smiled a little at the picture of their two ravenous vanities pressing reciprocal praises on each other; yet even now it wounded her to think that the man she had chosen was perhaps really made for Mrs. Pulsifer. . . .

⇲ XLII ⇱

JUST OUTSIDE the cottage window an apple branch crossed
the pane. For a long time Vance had sat there, seeing neither it nor anything else, in the kind of bodily and spiritual
blindness lately frequent with him; and now suddenly, in
the teeming autumn sunlight, there the branch was, the
centre of his vision.

It was a warped unsightly branch on a neglected tree,
but so charged with life, so glittering with fruit, that it
looked like a dead stick set with rubies. The sky behind was
of the densest autumnal blue, a solid fact of a sky. Against it
the shrunken rusty leaves lay like gilt bronze, each fruit
carved in some hard rare substance. It might have been the
very Golden Bough he had been reading about in one of
the books he had carried off when he and Laura Lou left
New York.

Whatever happened to Vance on the plane of practical
living, in the muddled world where bills must be paid, food
provided, sick or helpless people looked after, there still
came to him this mute swinging wide of the secret doors.
He never knew when or how it would happen: it sometimes
seemed that he was no more than the latch which an unseen
hand raised to throw open the gates of Heaven. . . .

And here he was, inside! No mere latch, after all, but
the very king for whom the gates had been lifted up. . . .
It was utterly improbable, inexplicable, yet the deepest part
of him always took it for granted, and troubled no more

over the how and why than a child let loose in an unknown
garden. In truth it was the only human experience that was
perfectly intelligible to him, though he was so powerless to
account for it. . . .

As usual with him now, the sudden seeing of the apple
branch coincided with the intensely detailed inner vision of
a new book. In the early days that flash of mysterious light
used to blot out everything else; but with the growing mastery of his craft he noticed, on the contrary, that when the
gates swung open the illumination fell on his daily foreground as well as on the heavenly distances. Mental confusion ceased for him from the moment when the inner lucidity declared itself, and this sense of developing power gave
him a feeling of security, of an inviolable calm in the heart
of turmoil. . . .

The quarrel with Tarrant had ended vaguely, lamely,
as business disputes most often do. Vance was beginning to
understand that only intellectual differences, battles waged
in the abstract for absolute ends, can have heroic conclu-
sions. The tearing-up of his manuscript had been the result
of a passionate impulse, but it had neither bettered his situation nor made it appreciably worse. Eric Rauch told him
that Tarrant would never have let him off anyhow: "it
wasn't his way." Rauch advised Vance to rewrite the lost
chapters, and was genuinely surprised to hear him pro-
nounce this an impossiblity. Rauch's own conception of the
products of the creative arts was as purely businesslike (in
spite of his volume of poems) as if they had been standardized like motor parts. But Vance could only say that the
book was gone past recovery. . . .

Finally it was agreed that Tarrant should give him time
to write another novel, and that the *New Hour* should
meanwhile continue his slender salary. Soon afterward the
first instalment of the royalties on *Instead* fell due. It was
slightly above Dreck and Saltzer's expectations, and Vance

was able to pay back half of the money he had borrowed, and to clear off the interest and his other debts. He had thought long and painfully over the future after his last talk with his grandmother, and had finally concluded that he would leave to Laura Lou the decision as to her future and his. He refrained from telling her of Mrs. Scrimser's offer, and of his resolve not to share the money she hoped to make on her lecturing tour. To speak of this might raise hopes that he would have to disappoint without being able to make his wife see why. The alternatives he put before her were the offer of a home with his family, or the possibility of her joining Mrs. Tracy and Upton in California. It went hard with him to suggest the latter, for it meant the avowal of his failure to make her happy or comfortable. But he said to himself, with a gambler's shrug: "If she chooses to go to her mother it will mean she wants to be free—and if she does, I ought to let her." He still did not understand why he resented this idea instead of welcoming it, or how much there was of memory, and how much of mere pride, in his dogged determination to keep her with him as long as she was willing.

Hardly less distasteful was the idea of going back to his family. The offer had been renewed by Mr. Weston, who, though his ill-advised speculations had checked his career in real estate, was ready to take his son and his son's wife into his house, and find a job for Vance (he thought there would still be a chance on the *Free Speaker*). But Vance's few hours with his grandmother had put Euphoria before him in merciless perspective. In every allusion, every turn of her speech, every image that came to her, he saw how far he had travelled from Mapledale Avenue. With cruel precision he evoked the mental atmosphere of the place; the slangy dingy days at the *Free Speaker*, the family evenings about the pink-throated gramophone; and he knew he could not face it. Yet he was determined not to let Laura Lou suspect his reluctance. His business was to do his best for her, and perhaps, according to her lights, his best was this. He put the case for Mapledale Avenue first, without betraying his own feelings; he even exaggerated the advantages of his father's offer. But, to his surprise, Laura Lou rejected it. She was never good at giving reasons or analysing her instinctive reluctances, and he suspected that the fear of hurting his feelings benumbed her. But she seemed to feel that he ought to be near New York, and not have to go back to newspaper work, at least not at Euphoria. . . . "I know you'd be doing it just for me," she tried to explain.

"Well, we've got to live," he rejoined, not unkindly; and she said, in her disjointed way: "If we were somewhere where I could cook . . . and nobody interfere. . . ." If they had a home of their own! He knew that was what she meant. But he said, still more gently: "See here, Laura Lou, till I can give you a place where nobody'll interfere, how about going out to your mother and Upton? You know that climate—"

She flushed, this time with pleasure; then her eyes grew dusky, as they did when she was troubled. "But I guess California'd be a good way farther from your work than Euphoria even; and we'd have more expenses. . . ." She looked at him with a little practical smile. Oh, Lord—how was he to tell her? Yes, he said, he supposed he'd have to stick on here in New York, on his job; what he meant was—"For me to go out alone?" she completed, and added immediately: "Oh, Vanny, it isn't what you *want*, is it? You're not trying to tell me it would be easier for you if I went back to Mother? If that's it, I'd rather you. . . ." She ended desperately: "If we could only find some little place where I could do the cooking . . ." and as he kissed away her tears he swore he would find a way, if she was really sure she didn't want to leave him. . . . "I'd mend for you too, better than I have," she sobbed out, rapturous and repentant; and

the search for the little place began. It was anxious and
arduous; the friendly settlement manager was consulted,
but could suggest nothing within Vance's means. Other en-
quiries failed; and at last it was Rebecca Stram who, oddly
enough, came to the rescue. She had an old Jewish mother
who lived out on the fringes of the Bronx, and a brother in
real estate who picked up unlikely bargains, and waited;
and among them they found a shaky bungalow containing
some rattan chairs, a divan and a kitchen range. It stood
alone on a bit of bedraggled farmland, in the remains of an
orchard, with a fragment of woodland screening it from
flathouses and chimneys. Not far off, the outskirts of the
metropolis whirled and rattled and smoked; but in this syl-
van hollow nature still worked her untroubled miracles, and
Vance had to walk through deep ruts, and past a duck pond
and an ancient pump, to pick up turnpike and trolley. Behind the house the land rose in a wooded ridge, and beyond that was real country, still untouched; it was heaven to
dwellers at Mrs. Hubbard's, and for the first weeks the mere
sense of peace and independence gave Vance the illusion
that all was well. He consolidated the divan, and bought a
stove, a couple of lamps, some linen, a jute rug; he managed
their simple marketing, and rigged up shelves and hooks;
and the house being made habitable, Laura Lou began the
struggle to keep it going. At first it did not much trouble
Vance. He took his fountain pen and his pad and wandered
off along the ridge, where there were still shady hollows in
which you could stretch out and dream, and watch the
clouds travel, and the birds; it was enough to be in this
green solitude, and he did not much care what food, or lack
of it, he came back to. But for a good many weeks he did little more than dream. The foundations of his being had been
shaken; he was full of warfare and alarms. What he wrote
he tore up, and he read more than he wrote; the few books
he had picked up at a cheap sale, as they were leaving New

York, were devoured before the summer was half over. But all the while he was rebuilding his soul; he found no other term for the return of the inner stability which was like a landing field for his wide-pinioned dreams. And then one day he looked out of the window and saw the apple bough, and his new book hanging on it. He held his breath and watched. . . .

He had no idea of reviving *Loot*. All desire to treat the New York spectacle was gone. The tale he saw shaping itself was simpler, nearer to his own experience. It was to be about a fellow like himself, about two or three people whose spiritual lives were as starved as his own had been. He sat for a long time penetrating his mind with the strange hard beauty created by that bit of crooked apple bough against a little square of sky. Such ordinary material to make magic out of—and that should be his theme. As he meditated, a thousand mysterious activities began to hum in him, his mind felt like that bit of rustling woodland above the cottage, so circumscribed yet so packed with the frail and complicated life of birds, insects, ferns, grasses, bursting buds, falling seeds, all the incessantly unfolding procession of the year. He had only to watch himself, to listen to himself, to try and set down the million glimmers and murmurs of the inner scene. "See here, Laura Lou," he cried out, pushing back his chair to go and tell her—and then remembered that nothing he could tell would be intelligible to her. He stood still, picturing the instant shock of thought if it had been Halo he had called, Halo who had hurried in from the kitchen. . . . He sat down at the desk and hid his face in his hands. "God," he thought. "When I was beginning to forget. . . ." He pulled his pen out, and wrote a few lines; then he was struck by Laura Lou's not having responded to his shout—she who always flew to him at the least pretext. A minute or two ago he had heard her busying herself with the preliminary assembling of food fragments which she called getting dinner. It was funny she hadn't answered; he thought he would go and see. . . .

She was in the kitchen, over the range. He thought he saw her push something into it—a white rag or paper, it seemed—and a moment later he caught the smoky acrid smell of burning linen. She turned with a face as white as the rag, and a smile which showed her teeth too much, as if her lips had shrunk away. "Yes . . . yes . . . coming . . ." she said nervously.

"Why, what's that queer smell? What are you burning?"

She gave the same death's-head smile. "I can't get the fire to draw—I just stuffed in anything. . . ."

"I should say you did. What a stench! I guess you've put it out now—"

She went and sat down on the chair by the kitchen table without making any answer.

"I don't see the joke," he grumbled, exasperated at being shaken out of his dream.

"I guess there's something wrong with the range—you'll have to get somebody to mend it," she brought out in a queer thin voice, as if she had been running. On the table was her untidy work basket, and near it were more white rags, or handkerchiefs or something, in a dirty heap. She crammed them into the basket, looking at him sideways. "Baby clothes?—" he thought, half dismayed, half exultant. He stood a moment irresolute, finding no words; but suddenly she spoke again, in the same breathless reedy voice. "You better go and find somebody to repair it. . . ."

"Oh, Lord. I'll see first if I can't do it myself," he grumbled, remembering the cost of the last repairs to the range.

"No, no, you can't. You better go out somewhere and get your dinner today," she added.

"What'll you eat then?"

She gave the same grin, which so unnaturally bared the

edges of her pale pink gums. "Oh, I'll take some milk. You better go out for your dinner. Then I'll lie down," she insisted breathlessly.

He stood doubtful, his book palpitating in him. The glorious blue air invited him—very likely she'd be glad to have a rest. He noticed the purplish rings about her eyes, and thought again: "It might be that," recalling the scenes in fiction in which blushing wives announce their coming motherhood. But Laura Lou did not seem to want to announce anything, and he was too shy to force her silence. "Want to get rid of me today, do you?" he joked; and she nodded, without other acquiescence than that of her queer fixed smile.

He rummaged in the cupboard for bread, and a piece of the cheese they had had for supper; with an apple from the magic tree it would be all he wanted. He would go on a long tramp, to a wonderful swampy wood he knew of, the first to catch fire from the autumn frosts. A sense of holiday freedom flamed through him. "Well, so long," he called out, nodding back from the door. Her fixed smile answered. "She looks sick," he thought—and then forgot her.

Magic—why not call the book that? The air was full of it today. All the poetry which the American imagination rejects seemed to have taken refuge in the American landscape, like a Daphne not fleeing from Apollo but awaiting his call to resume her human loveliness. Vance felt the dumb entreaty of that trembling beauty with arms outstretched to warmth and light from the slope of the descending year. As the mood grew on him the blood of the earth seemed to flow in his veins, his own to burn in red maple branch and golden shreds of traveller's joy. It was all part of that mysteriously interwoven texture of the universe, in the thought of which a man could lie down as in his bed. . . .

He tramped on and on, humming snatches of poetry, or meaningless singsongs of his own invention, feeling as happy as if he had been taken into the divine conspiracy and knew the solution of all the dissonances. It was as wonderful and secret as birth. . . . The word turned his mind to Laura Lou. How queer if she were going to have a child! He tried to imagine how life would arrange itself, with two people to feed, nurse, clothe, provide for—oh, curse that everlasting obstacle! He didn't even know how Laura Lou and he were going to face the winter alone. If she were to have a child he supposed they must humble their pride and accept his father's hospitality. But he did not want to dwell on that. Things were so right as they were. The bungalow in the apple orchard was just the place for him to dream and work in, and as for Laura Lou, she was happy, she was herself, for the first time since their marriage. Her domestic training had been rudimentary, and she was heedless and improvident, and sometimes—often—too tired to finish what she had begun. But now that she had her husband and her house to herself she atoned for every deficiency by a zeal that outran her strength and a good-humour that never flagged. In New York she used to sit for hours by the chilly radiator without speaking or moving, to listless to tidy up, leaving her clothes unmended, shelves and drawers in a litter; now she was always stirring about, sweeping, mending, washing. She even began to concern herself with the adornment of the rooms, wheedled out of Vance embroidered covers for their pillows and surprised him one evening by a bunch of wild flowers on the supper table. "I guess that was the way the table was fixed the day we lunched with the Tarrants," she said, with a reminiscent smile; and Vance laughed and declared: "Their flowers weren't anything like as pretty." Often now he heard her singing at her work, till her silence told him she had interrupted it to drop down in the kitchen rocker while the wave of weariness swept over

her. . . . Poor Laura Lou! These months in the bungalow
had made her intelligible to him, and turned his pity back to
tenderness. After all, perhaps she was the kind of wife an
artist ought to have. . . .

He reached the wood, climbed to a ledge from which
he could catch the distant blue of the Sound, and stretched
out in the sun with his bread and cheese and his dream.
. . . Certainly the book must be called *Magic*. . . .

The curtain went up on his inner stage—one by one his
characters came on, first faintly outlined, then more clearly,
at last in full illumination. The outer world vanished, love,
grief, poverty, sickness, debt, the long disappointments and
the little daily torments, even the consoling landscape which
enveloped him, all shrivelled up like the universe in the
Apocalypse, with nothing left in an unlit void but that one
small luminous space. The phenomenon was not new, but
he had never before been detached enough to observe it in
its mysterious acuity. Of all the myriad world nothing was
left but this tiny centre of concentrated activity, in which
creatures born without his will lived out their complicated
and passionate lives. At such moments his most vivid personal experiences paled with the rest of reality, and some
mysterious transfusion of spirit made him no longer himself
but the life element of these beings evoked from nowhere.
They were there, they were real, they were the sole reality,
and he who was the condition of their existence was yet
apart from them, and empowered to be their chronicler.
. . . Tramping back after dark, hungry and happy under
the sharp autumn stars, he stood still suddenly and thought:
"God, if I could tell her—" But even that pang was a passing one. These people were *his* people, he held the threads
of their lives, it was to him the vision had been given—for
the time that seemed enough, seemed all his straining consciousness could hold. . . .

From the bungalow a light winked through the apple

branch on which his book had hung. The gleam gave him a
feeling of homely reassurance. He saw the supper table in
the kitchen, his desk with the beckoning lamp. As soon as he
had eaten something he would get to work under that lamp,
with the great shadowy night looking on him. . . .

Under the apple tree he halted and listened. Perhaps he
would hear Laura Lou singing, and see her shadow moving
on the drawn-down blind. But the house was silent. He
walked up to the door and went in. The table was laid with
a box of sardines, potatoes, and pickles. All was orderly and
inviting; but Laura Lou was not there. The remembrance of
her pale face with that queer drawn smile returned disquiet-
ingly, and he pushed open the door of their room. It was
dark, and he went back for the lamp. Laura Lou lay on the
bed, the blankets drawn up. She was motionless; she did not
turn as he entered. Lamp in hand he bent over, half afraid;
but as the light struck her lids they lifted, and she looked at
him calmly, as she had on their wedding night when he had
come back with provisions from the farm and found her
sleeping. His anxiety fell from him. "Hullo—I guess I woke
you up," he said.

She smiled a little, not painfully but naturally. "Yes."

"You're not sick, child?"

"Oh, no, no," she assured him.

"Only a little bit tired?"

"Yes. A little bit."

He sat down on the edge of the bed. "I guess we'll have
to get a woman in to help you."

"Yes. Maybe just for the washing . . ."

"You think it was the washing that tired you?"

"Maybe." She shut her eyes peacefully and turned her
head away.

"All right. Have you had anything to eat?"

"Yes. I had some milk."

"And now you want to go to sleep again?"

Out of her sleep she murmured: "Yes," and he stooped
to kiss her and stole away.

As he sat down to his supper he reflected: "Certainly I
must get a woman in to wash for her." Then his thoughts
wandered away again to his book. After he had eaten he
heated a cup of coffee, and carried that and the lamp back
to his desk.

For the next few days Laura Lou was weak and languid, and he had to get a woman in daily to do the work.
But after that she was up and about, looking almost well,
and singing in the kitchen while he sat at his desk. The
golden October days followed each other without a break;
and when the housework was done he would drag one of
the rattan armchairs out under the apple tree, and Laura
Lou would sit in the sun, well wrapped up, and busy herself
with the mending, while every now and then he called out
through the window: "To hell with the damned book—it
won't go!" or: "Child—I believe I've found what I was
after!"

❧ XLIII ❦

THE GOLDEN days began to be tarnished with rain; but the air remained mild, and life at the bungalow followed its quiet course. Vance, plunged in his imaginary world, hardly noticed that in the real one the hours of daylight were rapidly shortening, and that in the mornings there was a white hoarfrost in the orchard.

Laura Lou seemed to have recovered; but she was still easily tired, and the woman who came for the washing had still to be summoned almost daily to help with the housework. Then the weather turned cold, and the coal bill went up with a rush. The bungalow was not meant for winter, and Vance had to buy a couple of stoves and have the stovepipes pushed up through the roof. But in spite of these cares he was still hardly conscious of the lapse of time, and might have drifted on unaware to the end of the year if the old familiar money problem had not faced him. What with the coal and the stoves and the hired woman, and buying more blankets and some warm clothes, the monthly expenses had already doubled; what would it be when winter set in? Still, they had the derelict place for a song, and it would perhaps cost less to stay on there than to move.

About a month after his grandmother's departure from New York a letter came from her. She reported the success of her lecture tour, and was loud in praise of "Storecraft's" management. She spoke enthusiastically of the way in which the publicity was organized, and said it was bringing

495

many souls to Jesus; and she reminded Vance affectionately
of her offer to provide him and Laura Lou with a home. She
would be ready to do so, she said, as soon as she paid off her
debt to Mr. Weston; and that would be before long, judging
from her present success. To justify her optimism she enclosed one of the advance circulars with which "Storecraft"
was flooding the country, together with laudatory articles
from local papers and a paean from her own special organ,
Spirit Life, (which was now serializing her religious experiences). She said ingenuously that she guessed she had a
right to be proud of such results, and added that anyhow
they would show Vance there were plenty of cultured centres in the United States where the spiritual temperature
was higher than in the Arctic circles of Park Avenue.

The letter touched Vance. It came at a moment when
the problem of the winter was upon him, and he might have
yielded to Mrs. Scrimser's suggestion—if only she had not
enclosed the newspaper articles. But there they were, in all
their undisguised blatancy, and her pride in them showed
her to have been completely unaffected by her grandson's
arguments and entreaties, or at any rate blind to their
meaning. And after all, that very blindness exonerated her.
If she really believed herself a heaven-sent teacher, why
should she not live on what she taught? Where there was no
fraud there was no dishonour. She was only giving these
people what they wanted, and what she sincerely believed
they ought to have.

Yes, but it was all based on the intellectual laziness that
he abhorred. It was because she was content with a shortcut to popularity, and her hearers with words that sounded
well and put no strain on their attention, that, as one paper
said, she could fill three-thousand-seat auditoriums all the
way from Maine to California. The system was detestable,
the results were pitiable. . . . But his grandmother had to

have the money, and her audiences had to have the particular blend of homemade religiosity that she knew how to brew. "Another form of bootlegging," Vance growled, and pitched the newspapers to the floor. The fraud was there, it was only farther back, in the national tolerance of ignorance, the sentimental plausibility, the rush for immediate results, the get-rich-quick system applied to the spiritual life. . . . The being he loved with all the tenacity of childish affection was exactly on a level with her dupes.

He did not answer the letter, and his grandmother did not write again.

Vance thought he had thrown all the "Storecraft" documents into the stove; but one day he came back and found Laura Lou with one of the advance circulars smoothed out before her on the kitchen table. She looked up with a smile.

"Oh, Vanny, why didn't you show me this before? Did your grandmother send it to you?"

He shrugged his acquiescence, and she sat gazing at the circular. "I guess it was Bunty who wrote it himself—don't you believe so?"

Vance's work had not gone well that day, and he gave an irritated laugh. "Shouldn't wonder. But you probably know his style better than I do."

The too-quick blood rushed to her cheeks, and ebbed again with the last word of his taunt. She looked at him perplexedly. "You don't like it, then—you don't think it makes enough of your grandmother?"

"Lord, yes! It makes too much—that's the trouble." He picked the leaflet up and read it slowly over, trying, out of idle curiosity, to see it from Laura Lou's point of view, which doubtless was exactly that of his grandmother. But every word nauseated him, and his sense of irony was blunted by the fact that the grotesque phrases were applied to a being whom he loved and admired. He threw the paper down contemptuously. "I suppose I could make a good living myself writing that kind of thing. . . ."

Laura Lou's face lit up responsively. "I'm sure you could, Vanny. I've always thought so. Bunty told me once that a good publicity writer could earn every bit as much as a best seller."

He laughed. "Pity I didn't choose that line, isn't it? Since I don't look much like being a best seller, anyhow."

She scented the sarcasm and drew back into herself, as her way was when he stung her with something unanswerable. Vance picked up the paper, tore it in bits, and walked away majestically to his desk. These women—! . . . Of course his work had been going badly of late—how could it be otherwise, with the endless interruptions and worries he was subjected to? A man who wanted to write ought to be free and unencumbered, or else in possession of an independent income and of a wife who could keep house without his perpetual intervention. Other fellows he knew . . . The thought of the other fellows woke a sudden craving in him, that craving for change, talk, variety, a general freshening-up of the point of view, which seizes upon the creative artist after a long unbroken stretch of work. He wanted the Cocoanut Tree again, and the "Loafers'," and a good talk with Frenside. . . . He wanted above all to get away from Laura Lou and the bungalow. . . .

"See here—I've got an appointment in town. I guess if I sprint for the elevated I can make it before one o'clock," he announced abruptly; and before she could question or protest he had got into his hat and overcoat, and was hurrying down the lane to the turnpike.

It was weeks since he had been to New York, and then he had stayed only long enough to persuade Dreck and Saltzer to give him a small advance on his royalties. Today, at the huge roar of the streets enveloped him, he felt his heart beating in time with it. He hadn't known how much he had missed the bracing air of the multitude. He avoided the *New Hour,* but turned in for lunch at the Cocoanut Tree, where it was bewildering and stimulating, after those endless weeks of country solitude and laborious routine, to find the old idlers and workers, the old jokes, the old wrangles, the old welcome again. Eric Rauch met him amicably, and seemed glad to hear that the novel was growing so fast. "Queer, though, if you were to get away the Pulsifer Novel Prize from the boss," he chuckled in Vance's ear. Vance stared, and had to be told, in deepest confidence, that Tarrant was also at work on a novel—his first—and that the few intimates who had seen it predicted that it would pull off the Pulsifer Prize, though perhaps not altogether on its merits.

"Luckily, though," Rauch ended, "it's a First Novel Prize, and that rules you out, because of *Instead.*" He seemed to derive intense amusement from the narrowly averted drama of a conflict between the editor of the *New Hour* and its most noted contributor.

When Vance left the Cocoanut Tree, rather later than he had meant to, he went to Frenside's lodgings, but found a card with "Away" above the latter's name in the vestibule. Then he recalled the real object of his trip: he must try to get another two or three hundred out of Dreck and Saltzer. His reluctance to ask for a second advance was manifest, and theirs to accord it no less so. The cashier reminded him affably that it wasn't so very long since his last application. That sort of thing was contrary to their rules; but if he'd look in after the first of the year, possibly Mr. Dreck would see what he could do. . . . Vance turned away, and walking back to Fifth Avenue stood for a while watching the stream of traffic pour by—the turbid flood which had never ceased to press its way through those perpetually congested arteries since he had first stood gazing at it, hungry and

light-headed, or the later day when, desperate with anxiety
for Laura Lou and the need for money, he had breasted the
tide to make his way to Mrs. Pulsifer's and beg for a loan.

He stood there idly on the curbstone, smiling at his past
illusions and at the similarity of his present plight. He was
as poor as ever, with the same wants to meet, the same burden to bear, and none of his illusions left. Nothing had
changed in his life except his easy faith in the generosity of
his fellows. There was his grandmother, indeed, whose generosity was no illusion—at a word she would shoulder all his
difficulties. But that word he could not speak. And in all the
rest of the world he knew of no one ready to take on the
burden of an unsuccessful novelist. . . .

He wandered up Fifth Avenue, letting the noise and
the tumult drug him to insensibility. The cold brief daylight
had vanished in a blaze of nocturnal illumination. Vance
crossed over to Broadway and tramped on aimlessly till a
call flamed out at him from among all the other flaming
calls. *Beethoven—The Fifth Symphony* . . . He had heard
it for the first and only time with Halo Tarrant, the previous
winter.

. . . Well, he was going to hear it again, to hear it by himself that very evening. He turned in at the concert hall, secured the last seat in the highest gallery, and wandered
away again to pick up a sandwich and a cup of coffee before the concert began. The night was cold, and the hot
coffee set all his veins singing. Music and heat and love
. . . they were what a fellow needed who was young and
hungry and a poet. . . .

From his corner of the upper heaven he could lean over
and catch sight of the orchestra stalls where he and Halo
had sat on that divine night. He remembered, vaguely, her
having said something about their being subscription seats
—about her husband's always having them for the Bee-

thoven cycle—and his heart began to beat at the thought
that she might actually be sitting there, far below him, that
he might presently discover her small dark head and white
shoulders standing out from the indifferent throng. But he
had come early; nearly all the orchestra seats were still
empty, and it was impossible to identify the two they had
occupied. With a painful fixity he sat watching as the great
auditorium gradually filled up. He had forgotten all about
the music in his agonized longing to see Mrs. Tarrant again.
He did not mean to try to speak to her—what was the use?
—but to see her would be a bitter ecstasy; and he was in
pursuit of all the ecstasies that night. . . .

And then, abruptly, the music began. Unperceived by
him the orchestra had noiselessly filed in, filling the stage
tier by tier; the conductor's gesture broken the hush, and in
the deep region of the soul the echo of the fateful chords
awoke.

Vance listened in the confused rapture of those to
whom the world of tone is an inexplicable heaven. When
Halo Tarrant had first introduced him to it he had resented
his inability to analyse this new emotion. It seemed as
though great poetry, the science of Number, should be the
clue of the mathematically definite laws underlying this kindred art; and when he found it was not so, that the ear most
acutely taunted to verbal harmonies may be dull in the dis-
section of pure sound, he felt baffled and humbled. But
gradually he came to see that for the creative artist two such
fields of emotion could hardly overlap without confusion.
He needed all his acuteness and precision of sensibility for
his own task; it was better that his particular domain should
lie surrounded by the great golden haze of the other arts,
like a tiny cultivated island in the vagueness of a sunset
ocean. . . . A sunset ocean: that was it! The inarticulate
depths in him woke to this surge of sound as they did to the

surge of the waves, or to that murmur of the blood which the lips of lovers send back to their satisfied hearts. . . . And that was enough.

When the first interval came he sat for a while with his eyes covered, as though the accumulated impress must escape if he opened them. Then he roused himself, and look down at the stalls. They were filling fast; he was able to distinguish definitely the two seats which he and Mrs. Tarrant had occupied. They were empty, and that seemed to establish their identity, and to put a seal on the memory of that other evening. But now he did not greatly care if she came or not—she was his in the plenitude of the music. He shut his eyes again and the multitudinous seas poured over him. . . .

THE SNOW lay so deep outside the bungalow that Vance had had to interrupt his work (he seemed to be always interrupting it nowadays) to clear a path from the door to the lane. The shovelling of heavy masses of frozen snow put a strain on muscles relaxed by long hours at his desk, and he stood still in the glittering winter sunshine, leaning on his shovel, while the cold and the hard exercise worked like a drug in his brain.

Weeks had gone by since his last visit to New York. He had not returned there since the evening of the Beethoven concert. His talk with his friends at the Cocoanut Tree and his long evening of musical intoxication had set his imagination working, and he had come home as from an adventure in far countries, laden with treasure to be transmuted into the flesh and blood of his creations. He had often noticed how small a spark of experience or emotion sufficed to provoke these explosions of activity, and with his booty in his breast he hurried back to his solitude as impatiently as he had left it.

But though he came home full of spiritual treasure, it was without material results. He had found no way of raising money, and he knew he must have some before the end of the month. For a fortnight past the woman who came to help Laura Lou had not shown herself. She lived some distance away, and when Vance went to hunt her up she excused herself on the plea of the cold weather and the long snowy walk down the lane from the trolley terminus. But Vance knew it was because he owed her several weeks' wages, and when she said: "I'd never have come all that way, anyhow, if it hadn't been I was sorry for your wife," he received the rebuke meekly, conscious that it was a way of reminding him of his debt.

With the coming of the dry cold Laura Lou seemed to revive, and for a while she and Vance managed to carry on the housekeeping between them, though the meals grew more and more sketchy, and it became clear even to Vance's inattentive eyes that the house was badly in need of cleaning. Carrying in the bags of coal (which he now had to fetch from the end of the lane) left on the floors a trail of black dust that Laura Lou had not the strength to scrub away, and the soil was frozen so hard that Vance could no longer bury the daily refuse at the foot of the orchard, but had to let it accumulate in an overflowing barrel. All that mattered little when she began to sing again about the house; but his nerves were set on edge by the continual interruptions to his work while he was still charged with creative energy, and often, when he got back to his desk, he would sit looking blankly at the blank page, frightened by the effort he knew his brain would refuse to make.

But today, after his labour in the snow, brain and nerves were quiescent. He would have liked to put more coal on the stove and then stretch out on the broken-down divan for a long sleep. But he knew he had to get the kitchen ready for Laura Lou, and after that . . . there was always an "after" to every job, he mused impatiently. He leaned the shovel against the door, stamped the snow off his feet, and went in.

Laura Lou was not in the kitchen. The fire was unlit, and no preparations had been made for their simple breakfast. He called out her name. She did not answer; and thinking somewhat resentfully of his hard work in the snow while she slept warm between the sheets, he opened the bedroom door. She lay where he had left her; her head was turned away, facing the wall, and the blankets and his old overcoat were drawn up to her chin.

"Laura Lou!" he called again. She stirred and slowly turned to him.

"What's the matter? Are you sick?" he exclaimed; for her face wore the same painful smile which had struck him on the day when he had found her pushing the mysterious rags into the kitchen fire.

"Time to get up?" she asked in a scarcely audible whisper.

He sat down on the bed and took her hand; it was dry and trembling. His heart began to beat with apprehension. "Do you feel as if you were too tired to get up?"

"Yes, I'm tired."

"See here, Laura Lou—" He slipped down on his knees, and slid his arm under her thin back. "Why is it you always feel so tired?" Her eyes, which were fixed on his, widened like a suspicious animal's, and he drew her closer to whisper: "Is it—it isn't because you're going to have a baby?"

She started in his arms, and drew back a little instead of yielding to his embrace. Her tongue ran furtively over her dry lips, as if to moisten them before she spoke. "A baby—?" she echoed. Vance pressed her tighter.

"I'd—we'll manage somehow; you'll see! I guess it would be great, wouldn't it? Wouldn't you be less lonely, sweet?" he hurried on, stringing random words together to hide the confused rush of his feelings.

She drew her head back, and her free hand, slipping from under the blankets, pushed the hair off his forehead. "Poor old Vanny," she whispered.

"Were you afraid I'd be bothered if you told me? Is that why—?" She made a faint negative motion.

"What was it then, dear? Why didn't you tell me?"

The painful smile drew up her lip again. "It's not that." She looked at him with an expression so strangely, lucidly maternal, that he felt as he sometimes had when, as a little boy, he brought his perplexities to his mother. It was the first time that Laura Lou had ever seemed to stoop to him from heights of superior understanding, and he was queerly awed by the mystery of her gaze. "Not that, darling?" he echoed.

Her hand was still moving in his hair. "Wouldn't you have liked it, dear?" he repeated.

"I might have—only I'm too tired." Her hand dropped back to her side. It was always the same old refrain: "I'm too tired." Yet she did not cough any longer, she ate with appetite, she had seemed lately to do her work with less fatigue.

"What makes you so tired, do you suppose?" But he felt the futility of the question. "I'll run down to the grocer's and call up the doctor," he said energetically, clutching at the idea of doing something definite. But Laura Lou sat up in bed and stretched her thin arms out to him. "No, no, no— Vanny, no!"

"But why not, darling?"

"Because I'm not sick—because I don't want him— because there'd be nothing to tell him . . ." He knew it was on her lips to add: "Because there'd be nothing to pay him with."

"Nonsense, Laura Lou. You must see a doctor."

"What would he say? He'd tell me to take a tonic. I'm all right, Vanny—I'll be up and have breakfast ready in half an hour. . . . Can't you give me till then?" she pleaded, sobbing; and full of contrition and perplexity he hurried back to the bed. "There, there, child; don't cry. . . ."

"You'll promise not?"

"I promise. . . ."

He left her to go and make up the kitchen fire, and get out the condensed milk and the tin of prepared coffee. In-

wardly he said to himself: "As soon as she's up I'll go to
New York and not come home till I've raised money enough
to get back the hired woman and pay the doctor. She's
probably right; it's nothing but worry and fatigue that's the
matter with her." He fastened his mind on this conviction
like a shipwrecked man clinging to a bit of wreckage. "She's
anaemic, that's what she is. . . . What she needs is good
food and rest, and a tonic." The more he repeated it to himself the stronger his conviction grew. He felt instinctively
that he could not get on with his work without reassurance,
and yet his work must be got on with to buy the reassurance. . . . The last gleam of inner light faded from his
brain as it struggled with this dilemma. For a moment a vision brushed his eyes of the long summer afternoons at the
Willows, with the sound of the bees in the last wistaria
flowers, and Halo Tarrant sitting silent on the other side of
the green velvet table, waiting for the pages as he passed
them over. . . . But he dragged his thoughts away from the
picture. . . . As soon as Laura Lou was up they break-
fasted together; then he hurried off to the trolley. . . .

At "Storecraft" they told him the manager was in his
office, and Vance flew up in the mirror-lined lift. He had not
been in the place since he had taken Laura Lou there to see
his bust at the "Tomorrowists'" exhibition. In the distorted
vista of his life all that seemed to be years away from him.
The lift shot him out on the manager's floor and he was
shown into an office where Bunty Hayes throned before a
vast desk of some rare highly polished wood. Vance was
half aware of the ultramodern fittings, the sharp high lights
and metallic glitter of the place; then he saw only Bunty
Hayes, stout and dominant behind a shining telephone receiver and a row of electric bells.

"I want to know if you've got a job for me," Vance
said.

Bunty Hayes rested both his short arms on the desk.

With a stout hairy hand he turned over a paperweight two or three times, and his round mouth framed the opening bar of an inaudible whistle.

"See here—take a seat." He leaned forward, fixing his attentive eyes on his visitor. "Fact is, I've been thinking we ought to start a publishing department of our own before long—if it was only to show the old fossils how literature ought to be handled. But I haven't had time to get round to it yet. Seems as if Providence had sent you round to help me get a move on. My idea is that we might begin with a series of translations of the snappiest foreign fiction, in connection with our Foreign Fashions' Department. . . ." He leaned forward eagerly, no longer aware of Vance except as a recipient intelligence. "Get my idea, do you? We say to the women: 'Read that last Geed or Morant novel in our "Storecraft" Series? Well, if you want to know the way the women those fellows write about are dressed, and the scents they use, and the facial treatment they take, all you got to do is to step round to our Paris Department'—you see my idea? Of course translations would be just a beginning; after we got on our legs we'd give 'em all the best in our own original fiction, and then I'd be glad to call on you for anything you wanted to dispose of. Fact is, I've got an idea already for a first 'Storecraft' novel—"

He stopped, and Vance once more became an individual for him. "Maybe you don't get my idea?" he said with a sudden shyness.

Vance felt the nausea in his throat. He began: "Oh, I don't believe it's any good—"

"What isn't?" Hayes interrupted.

"I mean, my coming here." His only thought now was how to get away; he could find no further words of explanation. But Hayes, still leaning across the desk, said mildly: "You haven't told me yet what you came for. But I guess there's hardly any case 'Storecraft' isn't ready to deal with."

Vance was silent. In a flash he pictured his plight if he let his disgust get the better of him and turned away from this man's coarse friendliness. After all, it was not Hayes the man who disgusted him any longer, but the point of view he represented; and what business had a fellow who didn't know where to turn for his next day's dinner to be squeamish about aesthetic differences? He swallowed quickly, and said: "Fact is, I thought perhaps you might be willing to take me on in your advertising department."

The whistle which had been lurking behind Hayes's lips broke forth in an astonished trill. "See here—" he exclaimed, and sat inarticulately contemplating his visitor.

His gaze was friendly and even reverential; Vance guessed that he was not beyond being impressed by the idea of a successful novelist offering his services to "Storecraft." "I suppose you've had some practice with book blurbs?" he began at last, hopefully.

Vance shook his head. "Not even."

"Oh, well—"

Vance had recovered his self-possession. He set forth, in as few words as possible, his business relations with the *New Hour* and Dreck and Saltzer, and his urgent need of raising money. He explained that he was debarred from selling his literary work to other bidders, and that he wanted to try his hand at publicity. It hardly seemed to be his own voice speaking—he felt more as if he were making a character talk in one of his books. When Hayes opened a parenthesis to ease his mind on the subject of Tarrant and the *New Hour,* Vance recalled the drunken row in the office— but that too had become far-off and inoffensive. The only thing that was actual and urgent was what this man on the other side of the desk was going to say in reply to his appeal for help. He stiffened himself inwardly and waited.

Hayes leaned back and drummed on the desk. "Cigarette?" he queried, pushing a box across the table. Vance shook his head, and there was another silence. Then: "How's your wife?" Hayes asked abruptly.

The blood rushed to Vance's temples. "She's fairly well," he said coldly.

"I see. Living at the same old stand?"

"No. We're out in the country now."

"Say—are you?" Hayes lit his cigarette, took a puff or two, and then stood up. "See here, Mr. Weston, I guess we can fix you up some way or other. Come round with me now to our Publicity Department—" He opened the glass door and led the way down a corridor to another glazed enclosure. . . .

When Vance got into the elevated to return home he had five hundred dollars in his pocket. He had spent an hour with "Storecraft's" publicity agent, and besides the money his pockets were bulging with models of advertisements—"blurbs" and puffs of every conceivable sort, from an advertisement of silk stockings or face cream, or "Storecraft's" insurance policies, to circulars and prospectuses featuring the lecture tours managed by "Storecraft's" Arts and Letters Department. In the bunch, as Vance glanced over them, he found his grandmother's advance circular, and thrust it disgustedly under the others; but the disgust was easily dominated. He had the money in his pocket, a retaining fee, Hayes had explained to him. It was worth the money to "Storecraft" to have a well-known novelist on their publicity list; and he'd soon pick up the hang of the thing sufficiently to earn his advance, and more too. Fellows who knew how to sling words were what they were after, Hayes continued; many of the literary people didn't seem to realize yet that writing a good advertisement was just as much of an art as turning out *Paradise Lost* or *Gentlemen Prefer Blondes*. Vance hardly noticed at the time that the pecuniary transaction did not take place in the Publicity Department, but in Hayes's private office, to which the manager invited him back for a cocktail and a final talk. He had the money in his pocket, and he was going to turn to and try to earn it, and as much more as he could. Compared with these monumental facts everything else seemed remote and negligible; and when Hayes, at the close of their talk, said a little awkwardly: "Well, so long. . . . Glad to hear your wife's all well again, anyhow," Vance felt a sudden compunction, as if he had been deliberately deceiving the first person who had really befriended him. "Well, she hasn't been very bright lately," he confessed with an effort at frankness.

"That so? Sorry to hear it." Hayes paused uncertainly, and shifted his weight from one foot to the other. "I don't believe I know just where your burg is. Maybe I could call round one day and see how she's getting on—bring her a little grapefruit and so on, eh?"

Vance hesitated. Since they had left New York he had given his address to no one; even Eric Rauch had not been able to wheedle it out of him. In reply to Hayes he mumbled that he was hard at work on his novel, and had to keep away from people as much as he could—and he saw Hayes redden at the rebuff, and was sorry, yet could not bring himself to say more. "Well, you'll be round again soon with something to show us, I suppose?"

Vance said yes, and after another awkward moment the hands of the two men met.

"You've done me a mighty good turn," Vance stammered, and the other replied: "Oh, well—call on me if there's any other way I can be of use." Then the lift received Vance, and he dropped down the long flights, dizzy with what he had achieved, and a little ashamed at the poor return he had made for it. But Hayes with his damned grapefruit spying out the misery of the bungalow—no.

On the way home he felt a sudden buoyancy, combined

with a new steadiness and composure of mind. He was even able to enjoy the humour of the situation as he ran over the list of subjects the publicity agent had given him to try his hand on. At a newstand he bought a handful of picture magazines, and plunged into the advertising pages, comparing, criticising, mentally touching them up. Evidently what "Storecraft" wanted was a combination of Sinclair Lewis, Kathleen Norris, and Mrs. Eddy. Well, he thought he could manage that, and even go them one better. . . . He longed for someone to share his laugh, and the thought of Halo Tarrant flashed out, as it always did when the human comedy or tragedy held up a new mask to him. Poor Laura Lou would not be able to see the joke. Her admiration for Bunty Hayes was based on his scholarship and eloquence—Vance remembered how much she had been impressed by the literary quality of Mrs. Scrimser's advance circular. Her simplicity had irritated him at the moment; now he saw it through a rosy gleam of amusement. After all, he decided he would tell Laura Lou about his visit to Hayes and their arrangement. It would please her to know that the two men were friends; and somehow he felt he owed it to her not to conceal Hayes's generosity. He had never forgotten the crumpled love letter he had picked up in her room, in the early days at Paul's Landing. He reached his journey's end, and swung down the lane whistling and singing through the night. . . .

He banged on the front door, but there was no answer. He tried the handle and it opened. How often he had told Laura Lou to lock up in his absence! Really, her carelessness . . . The room was pitch-dark and cold. He stumbled over something and fell to his knees. "Laura Lou—Laura Lou!" he cried out in deadly terror.

By the light of his electric torch he saw her lying almost across the threshold. She was quite still, her face ashy white under the faint yellow hair. At first in his horror he imagined an accident, a crime; but as he bent over, whispering and crying her name, and chafing her icy hands in his, her lids lifted and she gave him the comforted look of a tired child.

"Laura Lou! Darling! What's the matter?"

"Carry me back to bed, Vanny. I'll be all right." She spoke so quietly that he was half reassured.

Her head fell back on his shoulder as he lifted her to his breast. In the darkness he stumbled across the room, groped his way to the bed, and laid her down on it. Then he found a match and lit the lamp. His hands were shaking so that he could hardly carry it. He held the light over the bed and saw, on the floor beside it, a basin half full of blood, and a crumpled pile of rags, such as he had seen her push into the kitchen range.

"Laura Lou—you've had a hemorrhage?"

Her lids fluttered open again. "Ever since that day I caught cold—"

"It's not the first?"

Her lips shaped an inaudible: "Never mind."

"But, child, child—how could you hide it from me? In God's name, why didn't you get the doctor?"

The old terror returned to her eyes as she clutched his sleeve with her weak fingers. "No, no, no . . ." She lifted herself up haggardly, her eyes wide with fear, like a dead body raising itself out of its grave. "Never, Vanny, never! You've got to promise me. . . . They'd take me away from you to some strange place, with nurses and people, where I'd never see you. . . . I won't go, I won't . . . but if the doctor comes he'll make me . . . and I'd rather die here. . . . You promise me. . . ."

"Of course I promise. But you won't die—you won't, I tell you!" He held her tight, burning with her fever, straining to pour his warmth and strength into her poor shuddering body; and after a while her head drooped back on the pillow, and her lids fell over her quieted eyes.

⊀ XLV ⊱

THE DOCTOR said he was going to let Laura Lou stay just where she was. Evidently, then, Vance concluded, he didn't think it was so serious. What she wanted was feeding up, warmth, nursing. Vance could get a woman in to help? Oh, yes. . . . And sterilized ice? And fresh milk? . . .

Laura Lou lay back smiling, blissful, a little pink in the hollow of her cheekbones. She had emptied the glass of milk Vance had brought her, and the mild sun streamed in onto her bed. It was a day like April, the ground reeking with a sudden thaw.

Vance followed the doctor out onto the porch, and the two men stood there in silence. On the way Vance had handed to the doctor the sum that was owing him; and the doctor, who was a good fellow, and no doubt saw how things were, had said: "Oh, see here—there's no sort of hurry. . . ." After that they stood and looked for a while at his mud-spattered Ford, which had dug its way down the lane through the morass of the thaw.

"You'll be back soon?" Vance asked, wondering how to let the doctor know that there would be no trouble now about paying for his visits.

"Oh, sure—" said the doctor, who was young and not very articulate. He stamped his feet on the wooden step, and added: "Not that there's much else to do."

"You mean she'll pull round soon, with this tonic?" Vance held the prescription in his hand.

514

The doctor looked at his Ford, and then at Vance. He had a poor sort of face, not made for emotional emergencies, and seemed to know it. He laid his hand awkwardly on Vance's shoulder. "If I was sure she'd pull round, I'd have to take her away from here today. I'm not sure—that's why I'm going to let you keep her." He turned and went down the steps. From his seat in the car he called out to Vance, who had not moved: "Anyway, I'll look in tomorrow."

After the doctor had driven away Vance continued to stand in the same place in the porch. He was trying to piece together the meaning of the words: "That's why I'm letting you keep her." Laura Lou had doubtless known that if the doctor had been sent for sooner she would have been packed off to a sanitarium. Now it didn't matter—and that meant that she was dying, or at least that the doctor thought so. Vance tried to grasp the reality underlying the words, but it slipped out of his hold. He knew very little of the character of tuberculosis, except for its more melodramatic features: fever, hemorrhages and night sweats—the sort of consumption people had in sentimental novels. Of the real disease he had no experience. But he saw that Laura Lou was less ignorant; he had guessed instantly that in her terror of being taken from him she had concealed her condition as long as possible; and he wondered dully if she had understood that the doctor's permission to her to remain at the bungalow was her death warrant. But even that dark word conveyed little meaning. The doctor's phrase had acted like some strange corrosive, decomposing Vance's visible world. He stood in the porch repeating to himself: "Laura Lou, Laura Lou," as if the name were a magic formula against destruction. He tasted something salt on his lips, and found that the tears were running down his face. . . .

Well, after all, the doctor had to admit the next day

that his patient was a good deal better than he had expected. A wonderful rally, he said. . . . Vance, at the foot of the bed, caught a quick flit of fear in Laura Lou's eyes. The doctor must have caught it too, for he added with his clumsy laugh: "Anyway, I guess this air's as good as the Adirondacks . . ." and Laura Lou's head fell back contentedly. . . . After that she seemed to maintain her strength, though without making perceptible progress. The doctor did not come often; he said there was nothing to do beyond nursing and feeding, and Vance could always get hold of him by telephoning from the grocery. . . . The hired woman came regularly, but she could not be persuaded to stay at night, and Vance trembled to think of what might happen if anything went wrong and he had to leave Laura Lou while he rushed out for help. He tried to persuade her to let him get a trained nurse for the night, but the same looks of fear came into her eyes, and she asked if the doctor had said so, and if it meant that she was going to die right off. Vance laughed the question away, and dragged the divan mattress into a corner of the bedroom. That frightened her too, and finally he had to go back to his previous arrangement of sleeping in the living room, and trying to wake himself up at intervals to creep in for a look. But youth and health made him a heavy sleeper; and after vainly trying to force himself to wake at regular intervals he got the hired woman to brew a pot of strong coffee every night before she left, and kept himself awake on that.

As the doctor said, there was really very little to do; and after a few days Vance tried to get back to work. As soon as he sat down at his desk he was overwhelmed by an uncontrollable longing to plunge again into his novel. Once before—after seeing his grandfather by the river with Floss Delaney—he had been dragged back to life by the need to work his anguish out in words. Now, at this direr turn of his life, he found himself possessed by the same craving, as if his art must be fed by suffering, like some exquisite insatiable animal. . . . But what did all that matter, when the job before him was not novel-writing but inventing blurbs for "Storecraft"? He had already spent a good part of Hayes's cheque, and he would need more money soon; his business now was to earn it. He clenched his fists and sat brooding over the model "ads" till it was time to carry in the iced milk to Laura Lou. But he had not measured the strength of the force that propelled him. In his nights of unnatural vigil his imagination had acquired a fierce impetus that would not let him rest. Words sang to him like the sirens of Ulysses; sometimes the remembering of a single phrase was like entering into a mighty temple. He knew, as never before, the rapture of great comet flights of thought across the heaven of human conjecture, and the bracing contact of subjects minutely studied, without so much as a glance beyond their borders. Now and then he would stop writing and let his visions sweep him away; then he would return with renewed fervour to the minute scrutiny of his imaginary characters. There was something supernatural and compulsory in this strange alternation between creating and dreaming. Sometimes the fatigue of his nights would overcome him in full activity, and he would drop into a leaden sleep at his desk; and once, when he roused himself, he found his brain echoing with words read long ago, in his early days of study and starvation: "I was swept around all the elements and back again; I saw the sun shining at midnight in purest radiance; *gods of heaven and gods of hell I saw face to face and adored them* . . ." Yes, that was it; gods of heaven and gods of hell . . . and they had mastered him. . . . He got the milk out of the icebox, and carried it in to Laura Lou. . . .

He had forgotten all about Bunty Hayes and the "Storecraft" job. Every moment that he could spare from his wife was given up to his book. And Laura Lou really needed so little nursing. . . . One day the doctor, as he was leaving, stopped in the porch to say: "Isn't there anybody who could come over and help you? Hasn't your wife got any family?" The question roused Vance from his heavy dream. He had not yet let Mrs. Tracy know of her daughter's illness. He explained to the doctor that Laura Lou had a mother and brother out in California, but that he hadn't sent them word because if he did the mother would be sure to come, and Laura Lou would know that only an alarming report would make her undertake such a journey—and he feared the effect on his wife.

The doctor considered this in his friendly inarticulate way. "Well, I don't know but what you're right. I suppose you're willing to take the responsibility of not letting them know?" he said at length; and on Vance's saying yes, he drove off without further comment.

The days succeeded each other with a sort of deceptive rapidity: they had the smooth monotonous glide of water before it breaks into a fall. Every hour was alike in its slow passage, yet there did not seem to be enough of them to eke out an ordinary day. After an interval of cold and rain the weather became fine and springlike again, and on the finest days Vance carried Laura Lou into the living room, and she sat there in the sun, wrapped in blankets, and watched him while he wrote.

"Soon I'll be copying for you again," she said, with the little smile which showed the line of her pale gums; and he smiled back at her and nodded.

"I guess I'll do it better than I used to . . . I won't have to stoop over so," she continued. He nodded again and put his fingers on his lip; for the doctor had told her not to talk. Then he went on with his writing, and when he turned to look at her again her head had fallen back and she was sleeping, the sun in her hair.

One day she persuaded him to let her stay up longer than usual. She liked to see him writing, she said; and what harm was there, if she sat as still as a mouse and didn't talk? He could tell the doctor that she didn't talk. . . . Vance, deep in his work, absently acquiesced. He liked to have her near him while he wrote—he felt as if nothing could go really wrong while he was close to her, and he knew that she felt so too. He no longer believed she was going to die, and he had an idea that she did not believe so either; but neither of them dared to say a word to the other. It was as if they must just sit and hold their breath while the footsteps of the enemy hesitated outside on the threshold.

Vance wrote on as long as the daylight lasted; then he got up to fetch the lamp. The fire had gone out, and he noticed with dismay how cold the room had grown. He called to the woman in the kitchen to bring in some coal. He stood the lamp on the desk, and as the unshaded light fell on Laura Lou's face he felt a return of fear. She was sleeping quietly, but her face was so bloodless that there seemed to be nothing alive about her but the hair bubbling up with unnatural brilliance from her drawn forehead. "I wonder if it's true that the hair dies last?" he thought.

When the fire was made up he said: "We'd better get her back to bed," and while the woman went in to prepare the bed he stooped over Laura Lou and gathered her up. Her eyes opened and rested on his, but with a look of terror and bewilderment. "Who is it?" she exclaimed, and began to struggle in his arms; and as he lowered her to the bed the hemorrhage came. . . . He hurried the woman off to telephone for the doctor, adjuring her to come back as quickly as she could; and when she had gone he tried to remember what he had been told to do if "it" happened, and to stumble through the doing as best he could. By and by the bleeding stopped and he sat down by the bed and waited. The night was so still that he could hear every sound a long way off; but no one came, and as he sat there remembered the frightened fugitive look in the woman's eyes, and said to himself that she probably did not mean to return. . . . The time dragged on—hours and hours, days and nights, it might have been—and finally he heard the doctor's motor-horn down the lane. He looked at his watch and saw that it was hardly an hour since the woman had gone for him.

The doctor said there was nothing to do—never had been, anyhow, from the first. In those cases he never bothered people—just let them stay where they wanted to . . . No, there wouldn't have been anything to do last winter, even. Of course, if they'd known long ago . . . but it was the quick kind, that had probably been only a few months developing, and in those cases there wasn't any earthly good in sending people off. . . .

He agreed with Vance that the woman probably wouldn't come back; hemorrhages always scared that kind of people out of their senses; but he promised to try and get a nurse the first thing in the morning. There was a bad epidemic of grippe, and nurses were scarce in the district; but he'd do what he could . . . and for the time being he thought everything would be comfortable. When he had gone Vance looked at his watch again and saw that it was not yet ten o'clock. He sat down by the bed, where Laura Lou was sleeping with a quiet look on her face.

Before daylight Vance crept out to put coal on the fire and start up the range. He opened the front door and looked out into the thinning darkness. All his actions were mechanical; his mind refused to work. He felt a lethargic heaviness stealing over him, and finding a pot of cold coffee in the kitchen he put it on the range to warm. Then he crept back to Laura Lou, sat down by the bed, and fell asleep . . . When he woke it was broad daylight, but she was still sleeping. He shook himself, got the hot coffee, and swal-

lowed it at a gulp. Then he began to set about such rudimentary housework as he was capable of, while he waited
for Laura Lou to wake.

After a while he heard a motor horn. It was not the
doctor's hoot; but perhaps it might be the nurse? He interrupted the cleaning of the kitchen dishes, and when he got
to the front door he saw that a big motor had stopped halfway down the lane, and that a man was advancing on foot
under the apple trees. He and Vance stared at each other. It
was Bunty Hayes.

"Say—this is country life all right!" Hayes exclaimed,
coming forward with outstretched hand. "It takes a sleuth to
run you folks down."

Vance stood motionless on the porch. The shock of
Hayes's sudden appearance acted stupefyingly on his un-
strung nerves. For a moment he could not adjust himself to
this abrupt intrusion of a world that had passed out of his
thoughts. Then anger seized him.

"It was no earthly use running us down," he said.

"No use?"

"I haven't got anything for you. I haven't done a stroke
of work, and I've spent every cent of the money you gave
me."

Hayes received this with a look of embarrassment, as
though the words offended not his pride but a sense of delicacy which Vance had never suspected in him. He stood in
the grass below the doorstep and looked up at Vance, and
Vance looked down on him without making any motion to
invite him in.

"Why, I didn't come on business—" Hayes began.

Vance continued to stand squarely on the upper step.
"What did you come for?" he asked; and he saw the blood
purple the other's ruddy face. "I presume you think it's
rather too early in the day for a call?" Hayes continued. He
was evidently trying for a tone of conciliatory ease. "Fact is,

I heard by accident you were living out in these parts, and as I was running up to the Hudson to spend Sunday I thought you and Mrs. Weston would excuse me if I dropped in on the way. . . ."

Vance continued to stare at him. "Is this Sunday?" he asked.

"Why, yes." Hayes hesitated a moment. "I'm sorry if I butted in. But see here, Weston—you look sick. Can I do anything? Is there anything wrong?"

Vance pushed his hair back from his forehead. He realized for the first time that he was unshaved, unwashed, with the fever of his wakeful nights in his eyes. He looked again at Hayes, with a last impulse of contempt and futile anger. A trivial retort rose to his lips; but his voice caught in his throat, he felt the muscles of his face working, and suddenly he broke into sobs. In a moment Hayes was by his side. Vance pressed his fists against his eyes; then he turned and the two men looked at each other.

"Laura Lou?"

Vance nodded. He walked back into the house and Hayes followed him.

"Christ, it's cold in here!" Hayes exclaimed below his breath.

"Yes. I know. I made the fire, but it's gone out again. The woman didn't come back. . . ."

"The woman?"

"The hired woman. When she saw the hemorrhage last night she bolted. The doctor's trying to find a nurse." The two spoke to each other in whispers. Hayes's flush had faded at Vance's last words, and his face had the ghastly sallowness of full-blooded men when their colour goes.

"Damn the nurse. Here, I guess I'll do as good as any nurse." He lowered his voice still more to add: "Is it warmer in where she is?" Vance nodded. "Then I'll get this fire started first off." He pulled off his coat and looked about him. "You go back to her—I'll see to things. I'm used to camping. Don't you mind about me. . . ."

Vance, as if compelled by a stronger will, turned obediently toward the bedroom. He had not known till Hayes entered the house how desperately his solitude had weighed on him. He felt as if life had recovered its normal measure, as if time were re-established and chaos banished. He understood that he was dizzy with hunger and sleeplessness and fear. He crept back to Laura Lou's bed and sat down beside her.

She was still asleep; in the half darkness he could just see the faint stir of her breathing. He longed to feel her pulse, but was afraid of disturbing her, and sat there, holding his breath, his body stiffened into immobility. Outside he heard Hayes moving about with a strangely light tread for so heavy a man. "He must have taken off his shoes so as to make less noise," he thought, with a little twinge of gratitude. It helped him to hear Hayes padding softly about, and to wonder what he was doing. After the ghastly stillness of the night, it made everything less dreadful and unreal to listen to those familiar household sounds.

Presently he thought he would go and get Laura Lou's milk, to have it within reach when she woke. But the truth was that he could not stay still any longer—he felt a sudden need to see Hayes again, and hear his voice.

He stretched out one foot after another, trying to get stealthily to his legs without her hearing him. But as he got up the chair slipped back and knocked against the side of the bed. He stopped in terror, and Laura Lou stirred, and seemed to struggle to raise her head from the pillow. He ran to the window to pull up the blind, and when he got back to the bed she lifted herself up to him with outstretched arms, and the unbearable look of terror in her face. "Vanny, I'm—" She dropped back and lay still. He knelt down beside the bed and took her hand; but presently she began to breathe in short racking gasps. A mortal chill stole over him. Those gasps were like the sound of something being wrenched out of its socket. Her eyes were shut and she did not seem to know that he was there.

He got up and went to the door. Through the crack he saw Hayes in his shirtsleeves putting a coffee pot and something steaming in a dish on the table. He beckoned to him and said: "The doctor—you'd better go for him quick." Then he thought he heard a sound in the bedroom and turned back, trembling. As he moved away Hayes caught his arm. "Is she worse? Can I see her a minute first?" he whispered.

Vance suddenly felt that it would be a relief to have someone else look at that far-off face on the pillow. Perhaps Hayes would know . . . He sighed "Yes," and Hayes crept into the room after him. They went up to the bed, and Hayes bent over Laura Lou. Her eyes were open now. They looked straight up at the two men, and beyond them, into the unknown. Her hand twitched on the sheet. Suddenly she drew a short breath and then was quiet again. Vance and Hayes stood side by side without speaking. Her hand stopped twitching—it lay still on the sheet, dry and frail as a dead leaf. Hayes suddenly stooped lower, bringing his round close-cropped head close to her lips; then he slowly straightened himself again. "She's dead," he said.

Vance stood motionless, uncomprehending. He saw Hayes put out one of his short thick hands and draw down the lids over Laura Lou's eyes. Then he saw him walk out of the room, very stiffly, with short uneven steps.

The hours passed. Hayes went off to telephone; when he came back the doctor was driving up with a nurse. The two went into the bedroom together, and Vance sat outside on the porch. He felt like an indifferent spectator. After a while Hayes came out and said: "Here, you ought to have something to eat—there's some eggs and hot coffee in the kitchen." Vance shook his head and the other disappeared again. The doctor drove off; he told Vance that Mr. Hayes would take the nurse back when she had finished. The word "finished" had a dreadful sound; but Vance did not stir from his place. He felt that whatever was happening within was something with which he had no concern. At last the nurse came out, and Hayes drove her down the road to the trolley. When he came back Vance was still sitting in the same place.

"Won't you go in and see her now?" Hayes asked hesitatingly.

Without answering, Vance got up and followed him into the house. Hayes paused in the living room, and Vance went up to the closed door of the bedroom. Then he stopped and turned back. "You come too," he said to Hayes.

The other shook his head. "No, no."

But Vance felt an indescribable dread of going alone into the utter silence of that room. "You come too," he repeated, in the tone of an obstinate child. Hayes flushed up, and followed him into the room.

The bed was all white; as he approached, Vance saw that it was covered with white roses and Easter lilies. Hayes must have brought them back in the big box he had lugged in from the motor. Emerging from the coverlet of flowers was a small waxen image with the lineaments of Laura Lou. Her eyes were shut, her pale lips smiled. She seemed to have been modelled by a sculptor who had no power of conveying the deeper emotions—or to have reached a region where they drop from the soul like a worn garment.

Vance had forgotten that Hayes was in the room. For a long while he stood gazing at the empty shell of Laura Lou. He dreaded to touch her, to feel the cold smoothness of her quieted flesh; but he felt that she might know he was there, and perhaps in a dim way resent his indifference. With an effort he bent over her, and laid his hand on her cold hands and his lips on her cold forehead.

Behind him he heard Hayes moving. He turned and saw that the heavy man had got down on his knees, a little way from the bed. He lifted his clasped hands and said in a queer artificial voice: "Shall we pray . . . ?" Vance said nothing, and Hayes went on: "Our Father Who art in Heaven, hallowed be Thy Name . . ." He hesitated, as if he were not sure of the next words. . . . "Forgive us our trespasses against you . . ." he went on ". . . as I forgive Laura Lou. . . . Oh, God, yes, I do forgive her!" He burst into miserable helpless sobs, burying his face in his hands.

Vance had remained standing beside the bed. He went up to Hayes and put a hand on his shoulder. The other got awkwardly to his feet, fumbling for a handkerchief. Vance took him by the hand, and the two men walked side by side out of the quiet room.

❧ XLVI ❧

It was Vance's last day but one. He was going back to his family at Euphoria.

He had lingered on at the bungalow to try to sleep off his lethargy before seeing people again, and taking up the daily round. He would have liked to go on living there alone, watching the approach of spring, tramping in the woods, writing, dreaming, trying to adjust himself to life again. The solitude of the place, so dreadful to him during the last days of Laura Lou's illness, had become soothing now that he was alone. But practical reasons made it impossible to remain; and for the present the simplest thing was to return to his parents.

He was beginning to shake off the state of apathy which had overcome him as soon as the strain was over; but even now he could not have said how the days had passed since Laura Lou's death. All he was certain of was that, after all, no great inner change had befallen him. He remembered how once before, after he had carried her off to New York, reconquering her from her mother and Bunty Hayes, he had expected that everything in their lives would be new and different and how he had gradually come to see that nothing was changed. And it was the same now: life could not change Laura Lou, and neither had death changed her. At first he had imagined that death, the great renewer, would renew his blurred vision of her, set her before him in a completeness he had somehow always missed.

527

But death did nothing of the kind. It left him only that larval image among the white roses, with which his imagination could do nothing. Behind that uncommunicative mask the face of the real Laura Lou was as he had always known it. How could death give people anything they had not had in life, except the pathos of the thwarted destiny? And that he had always felt in Laura Lou. He had always thought of her as someone thwarted and unfulfilled; had often imagined her life with another man—with Bunty Hayes even—as more likely to have given her the chance to express what was in her. But fate had made her choose him instead; and in spite of the incompleteness of their life together he knew, to the very last, that it was what she wanted. It had not needed death to show him that. It was because he knew that he was her choice, and that she would certainly have chosen rather to be unhappy with him than comfortable and contented with anyone else, that the tie between them was sacred. Death had altered nothing in his vision of her, and added nothing to it. Death had simply closed the book in which he had long ago read the last word. . . .

When these thoughts first came they frightened him. It seemed as though he could never have loved Laura Lou; yet this was not so. And she had never been so dear to him as during their last months together. But since he had honestly tried to give her all that she was capable of receiving from him, how was he to blame if her going had left the live forces in him untouched? It was as if a door had quietly opened and shut in a room in which he was working—and when he looked up from his work he saw no change. Someone had gone out, but the room was not more empty. . . .

He had not seen a human being for the last three or four days. The hired woman, ashamed of her desertion, had offered to come back and help him, but he had refused; the doctor had made him promise to telephone if he needed anything; Hayes had wanted him to come and stay in his flat in town. Vance felt a great kindness toward them all— even toward the frightened hired woman he had no resentment. But what they could not any of them understand was how much he wanted to be alone. . . . He had broken into a laugh when, the day after the funeral, he had surprised Hayes and the doctor furtively hunting for his revolver when they thought he was out of sight. . . .

Now that the time to leave had come, he was sorry he had not decided to go on camping alone in the bungalow. It was a soft day at the end of March; the air was full of the smell of wet earth and new grass; and he sat on the porch and smoked his pipe, and thought of what that swampy wood of his would be in a week or two. He had grown into harmony with his solitary life; the thought of his book was reviving, the characters were emerging again, gathering about him unhindered, like friends banished by some intimate preoccupation and now stealing back to their familiar places. . . .

He was disturbed by the sound of a motor horn, and got to his feet impatiently. Whoever his visitors were, they were unwanted. He turned to slip out at the back of the house, and scramble over a fence into the wood lot. But the sound was not repeated—probably it came from a passing car on the turnpike. He sat down, leaning his head contentedly against the post of the porch, and gazing up at the pools of spring sky between the crooked arms of the apple tree. Lost in those ethereal depths, he was aware of nothing nearer earth till he heard his name; then he started up and saw Halo Tarrant a little way off, under the apple-tree. She looked very pale, but his eyes, full of the sunlit sky, seemed to see her through a mist of gold.

"Vance—I've found you!" She came toward him with her quick impetuous step, and as she drew near he saw that the radiance was not caused by the sun dazzle in his eyes but by some inner light in hers. He thought: "It's funny I was thinking about that wood—I'd like to show it to her. . . ." Then the reality of things rushed back on him, and he stood tongue-tied.

She glanced past him at the dilapidated bungalow. "This is where you've been living all these months?"

"All these months—yes."

Her eyes had travelled on to the background of bare woodland on the ridge. She screwed her lips up in her short-sighted way, and the little lines about her eyes made her seem nearer to him, and more real. "It must be lovely over there," she said.

"Oh, there's a wood beyond, with a gold and purple swamp in the middle—I wish I could take you there!"

"Well, why not?" She smiled. "I have so much to say to you. . . . We might go there now, if it's not too far. . . ."

He said thoughtfully: "It's too far for this afternoon. We'd have to make a long day of it."

"Oh, that would be glorious!" She glanced about her again. "But I like it here too. . . ." She looked at him hesitatingly: "Are you living here all alone?"

"Yes."

She still seemed to hesitate. "May I come in and see what it's like?"

Vance felt his colour rise. He did not want her to see the shabbiness of the dismantled bungalow, with his few possessions stacked up for departure, and the untidy divan on which he had slept since Laura Lou's death. "Oh, it's a poor sort of place. It's a good deal pleasanter out here in the sun."

"I daresay. It's lovely here," she agreed. "But everything's lovely to me . . . I'm a little drunk with the spring —and finding you. . . . Shall I sit down here beside you? You mustn't smuggle away your pipe—please don't!"

He pulled out his pipe and relit it. "Wait till I get you a cushion or something. He fetched a blanket off the divan and laid it on the upper step, and they sat down side by side. "It's good here in the sun," he said, his voice trembling.

"Yes, it's good."

They sat silent for a minute or two, and he could feel that she was penetrated by the deep well-being that steeped his soul.

"You said you had a great deal to tell me," he began at last, half reluctant to break the silence.

"Yes, a great deal." She paused again, and met his eyes with another little smile, half shy, half challenging. "But it's a long story—and perhaps you won't understand after all."

He was silent, not knowing what to say, and wondering why they needed to tell each other anything, instead of just basking in the fulness of their mutual intelligence. But he saw that she expected an answer. "What makes you think I won't understand?"

She laughed nervously. "Because I want you to so much."

"Well—try."

She stood up, walked away under the apple trees, and came back and sat down beside him. "Vance—you remember that night when you brought me the first chapters of *Loot* to read?" He nodded.

"And you remember what you said afterward—and what I said?" He nodded again.

"That night when I saw you go I thought I couldn't bear it."

"No—"

She turned and looked at him. "You too—?"

"Yes."

"Oh, then—then I can tell you." He noticed, with that odd detachment which sometimes came to him in emotional moments, that her eyelids trembled slightly, as people's lips tremble when they are agitated. She seemed conscious of it, for she turned her head away without speaking.

"You were going to tell me," he reminded her.

She looked at him again, gently, attentively, as if her eyes were feeling the way for her words. "It begins so far back—the day we went up Thundertop. That day I made up my mind I must marry Lewis." She stopped. It was the first time Vance had ever heard her allude to her marriage. He had poured out all his secret misery to her on the night when he had sought her out to reproach her for having forced her way into Laura Lou's room. She knew the whole history of his married life, but no allusion to hers had ever escaped her, and he had imagined that she avoided the subject lest her confidences should complicate Vance's relations with her husband.

After a moment she continued: "But what's the use? People do what they must—what they think they must. It's all bound up with my family history—it's too long to tell. But Lewis was generous to them at a time when I couldn't be, and that held me fast. . . . You understand?"

Vance understood. He thought of the generosity of Laura Lou, who had lavished her all on him, and had held him fast.

"Life's such a perplexity and a waste," she pursued—"or at the time it seems so. There were so many times when I knew I was utterly useless to Lewis, and when I imagined I could have helped you if I'd been free. And now, all of a sudden, everything's changed. . . ." She put her hand on his. "Could I help you still—?"

"Yes."

"Vance!" She sat silent, and he laid his other hand on hers. At length she began to speak more connectedly, to tell him of two almost simultaneous events in her life—the sudden death of the old Miss Lorburn of Stuyvesant Square,

who had left her the Willows, with more money than she
could have hoped for, and the discovery that the tie between Tarrant and herself had become as irksome to her
husband as to her. The latter announcement was no surprise
to Vance, for at the *New Hour* office the jokes about the
Pulsifer First Novel Prize had been coupled with a good
deal of gossip about the donor and Tarrant. Vance recalled
his own experience with Mrs. Pulsifer, and felt a recoil of
disgust.

"And you see I had to tell you first of all—you do see
that, Vance? Because it seemed to me that life had slipped
back again to that night when you said—oh, Vance, I could
repeat to you every word you said! And I knew how you
loved me and hated me while you said them—yet I was
held fast. But now it's all over, and I'm free, free, free!" She
sprang to her feet again. "What a child I must seem to you!
And I'm older than you—and you let me go on talking all
this nonsense. . . ."

He had tried his best to listen attentively to what she
was saying; but it was drowned under a surge of joy. It was
curious, how hard it was for him to follow the words of anyone too close to his soul for words to be needed. He wondered she did not feel that too—feel that the spring sunshine, and their sitting in it together, was enough for her as
it was for him. He caught himself speculating whether, after
all, they might not have made a dash for that bit of woodland—and then fixing his thoughts curiously on the long
slender hands on her knee. He thought perhaps it was because, for so long, his mind had been all darkness and confusion, that the sudden clarity blinded him, made him want
more time before he groped his way back to her. But no—
the real trouble, he thought, was that most people took so
long to discover the essential; wasted such precious moments clearing away rubbish before they got to the heart of
a thing. All women were like that, he supposed—but what

did it matter? Presently she would understand—would stop talking, and just let her hand lie in his. "It's so good, sitting here with you," he said. "I never thought we should."

"Oh, Vance . . ."

By and by, he reflected, there would be a thousand things to tell her; now he could only think of that spring wood, and the Fifth Symphony, and dawn over Thundertop. . . .

She seemed to understand; she sat down beside him again and gave him back her hand. But after a while the sun waned from the porch, and the chill of the afternoon air fell on them. She gave a shiver and stood up. "It will be dark soon—I must be going."

He looked at her in surprise; it was bewildering to him that the passing hour should still have rights over them. "Why can't you stay with me?" he said.

"Stay—now?" She drew back a step, and looked at him, and then over his shoulder at the little house. "Oh, Vance—you must know what I want. If only we could be back together at the Willows. I should be so content if I could help you as I used to. You remember the things we found together when you were doing *Instead*—the ideas you said might not have come to you if we hadn't talked it all over? Well, that's what I want . . . that you should come back to the Willows, now it's mine, and let me help you. Oh, Vance, say yes—say we can go back and begin again. . . ." She leaned toward him with a gesture of entreaty. "Don't you understand that what I want is all you can give me without having to hurt anybody else?"

He was silent, trying to take in her words. But the old difficulty persisted—she was too near, he was too much submerged by her nearness. "You don't see—" he began.

She interrupted passionately: "But I do—I do. How can you think I don't. Can't you see that I know it's different with you—perhaps always must be? All I want is that we should try to renew our friendship . . . that you should let me help you as I used to. . . . Don't you think I could make Laura Lou understand that?"

The sound of the name shook him abruptly out of his trance. "Laura Lou? She's dead," he said.

Halo Tarrant moved back a step and stood staring at him in dumb bewilderment. Then she began to tremble. Her face twitched, and she lifted her hands to hide it. Vance saw that she was crying; and presently her tears broke into sobs. She was suffering terribly; he saw that she was horrified and did not know how to express her dismay. He supposed that she thought him to blame for not telling her at once—perhaps regarded him as brutal, unfeeling. But he could not imagine why. All that belonged to another plane, to another life, almost . . . his mind refused to relate it to what he and she had in common. But how explain this to her, if she could not feel for herself the difference between that shadow and this burning reality?

"Vance—Vance—you ought to have told me," she sobbed reproachfully.

"I know," he said. "I was going to. . . ."

"What must you think of me? How could you let me go on talking like that?"

"I liked just to listen to your voice. . . ."

"Don't—don't say such things to me now!" She broke off to ask in a whisper. "How long ago was it?"

He had to make an effort of the memory. "It was a week ago yesterday."

"Only a week ago—oh, what must you think of me?"

"I wish you wouldn't cry," he pleaded.

"Oh, Vance—can you ever forgive me?"

"Yes."

"It seems so dreadful—but how was I to know?"

"You couldn't have known."

"Oh, poor little Laura Lou! I shall never forgive myself —but you must say that you forgive me!"

It was curious: he had to reason with her as if she were a child. It was almost as if he were reasoning with Laura Lou. He felt himself calling upon the same sort of patience —as if he were sitting down on the floor to comfort a child that had hurt itself. . . . And when at last he drew her arm through his and walked beside her in the darkness to the corner where she had left her motor, he wondered if at crucial moments the same veil of unreality would always fall between himself and the soul nearest him, if the creator of imaginary beings must always feel alone among the real ones.

❧ AFTERWORD ❦

Literature contains many portraits of the artist as a young person, depictions of the development of a creature endowed with unusual sensibility, talent, and ambition in an environment always shown to be hostile to art and the sensitive soul. The main conflict of such novels is usually the young artist's attempt to free himself from society's encompassing nets and nooses (as in Joyce's Dublin, in *A Portrait of the Artist as a Young Man*) that restrain him from full individuality; or the stronger—and different—pressures placed on young women, constraining them within lives limited to biological and at most, social fulfilment.

Portrayals of artists as young men differ from those of young women in other ways as well. While young people of both sexes have only shaky confidence in their abilities and feel in some way like aliens in their worlds, women—to speak in simple, general terms—tend to feel wrong and guilty about their alienation, while men tend to feel right, justified. Artistic young women (consider the work of Antonia White, Rosamond Lehmann, or Janet Frame, for example) usually feel themselves anomalous, deviants, and lacking in femininity and social grace. Artistic young men may feel similar lacks (of manliness and social polish), but they tend to present themselves, in literature at least, as arrogant, selfish and scornful. Writers who would handle such characters ironically if they were not artists, accept unthinkingly the male artist's prerogative to behave egotistically. Even when an author creates ironic distance between his male artist figure and the narrative line—as Joyce does, for example—he seems to accept the self-boundedness and egotism of the figures as necessary to his vocation. Without such qualities, it is implied, the character would not be able to maintain himself in a hostile and undermining environment.

Edith Wharton's novel, *Hudson River Bracketed*, is a portrait of the artist as a young man. What is unusual about it is that it depicts the development of a young male writer, but is written by a woman. Although it is not uncommon for writers to portray protagonists of the opposite sex movingly and believably, it is extremely unusual for a writer to portray a member of the opposite sex as a writer— that is, to describe the author's own occupation and experience, but *as* experienced by someone subject to very different pressures. To do so requires not only an understanding of what those pressures are, but also of how such pressures feel to someone of extraordinary sensitivity and ambition.

Wharton's portrait of a young male artist is totally believable; she is acutely aware of her hero's situation, although in most respects it is the opposite of her own life situation when young. Vance Weston is male; he has received an education that has left him ignorant of most literature (Wharton, who received no formal education to speak of, educated herself, like Virginia Woolf, in her father's excellent library). Vance is culturally unsophisticated, and once he leaves home, is without financial means. Perhaps her most profound insight into the character is his need for love and intimacy—a need which he (like so many men, young artists or not), does not really credit and which he does not respect. Wharton could not have learned much about this need from the work of male authors, since most of them have been equally blind about male emotional dependency (as opposed to sexual need); she must have observed it in life. Wharton also grants her male artist his male prerogatives—arrogance, thoughtlessness, selfishness, wilfulness. But she cannot refrain from also, on occasion, showing the effect of his behaviour on the women around him. Unfortunately, this added focus does not enrich the portrayal, but dissipates it.

It is not possible to know precisely what Wharton intended in her portrait of the young artist. For the most part, the narrator seems to identify with Vance's suffering and struggles to find his own vision and voice, to survive physically and emotionally, and to free himself from the moral and literary conventions of his time. The narrator views his labours and his poverty sympathetically; and comprehends his uncertainty about direction, and usually supports his feeling that he must insist upon his own will. But because the reader often enough sees Vance as heartless, the point of view encompassing him and his world seems ambivalent. If that ambivalence were conscious and intentional, Wharton would have built upon it, creating an ironic distance between the narrative line and the character of Vance—something she did brilliantly in other novels, *The Age of Innocence*, for instance, or *The Custom of the Country*. She does not do this. Throughout this novel, Vance is presented as a hero: muddled, ambivalent himself, unsure of his abilities and direction, yet admirable and *sympathique*. Since the reader who has picked up her hints about his careless cruelty to people who love him cannot offer him wholehearted admiration or sympathy and since he is the centre of the novel, the core is soft, weak, and the novel less compelling than it might be.

This flaw—for I believe it is one—is not a result of Wharton's writing from the point of view of a male protagonist, even to including male slang and many misogynistic remarks; she wrote with depth and sympathy for the male protagonists of *The Age of Innocence* and *The Children*. Nor is it a consequence of her writing about a character from a different class from her own: she wrote beautifully and movingly about poor people in the early *Bunner Sisters*, in *Summer*, and in *Ethan Frome*. The weakness arises, I believe, from an unconscious split in her own sensibility. She wanted to write about an artist's development, about the nature of art and artistic process, and about the weight of the pressures impeding any artist from working at all, and even more, from doing genuine work. These are subjects she knew intimately and felt deeply about, and the sections of the novel devoted to these subjects are often infused with passion. But she did not feel she could model her artist on herself, on her own experience.

For she was a woman, and the internal and external pressures a woman faces when she tries to be anything more or other than a functionary in male life—daughter, wife, lover, mother—were not legitimate subject matter for literature in 1929, nor even much later. Wharton was not alone in feeling she could not break the convention which accords importance to women's experience only when that experience centres around a man, or men. Not only was the desire of a woman for anything more than romance, marriage, love, financial security, her children's well-being, or status, considered illegitimate in literature *and* in life, but most female authors felt they could not create a heroine who was able to balance creative work, a fulfilling emotional-sexual life, and community, a set of good friends—even though many of them had managed to forge such integrated lives themselves. Although we cannot be sure of the reasons why they did not create such heroines, we can surmise they felt such a character would not be believable.

It is certainly understandable that Wharton might feel she could not believably present a young woman from the American Middle West who in the early twentieth century had attended college (albeit a poor college), and who, with her bit of education, but without cultural or social polish, without enough money to support herself, could nevertheless survive alone in New York City, and even manage to become a writer who was taken seriously by the New York literary establishment. Such a feat would be extremely difficult for a woman even in our own time. Even if she could have made such a figure believable, could she, in 1929, create a heroine who lived in considerable emotional freedom, who marries the wrong man out of lust and does not suffer incredibly for it? The heroine of *Summer* violates the mores of society, but she does it out of desire that includes love. The heroine of *A Mother's Recompense* has made mistakes, but they are in her past, and she has suffered greatly for them, and continues to suffer for them throughout the novel. Out of desire and the knowledge that he will always be able to dominate her, Vance marries a woman who is not intellectually compatible with him. He does suffer, but not terribly, and in the end, he is given another chance. In short, it is likely that Wharton felt that no woman could overcome the obstacles she wished to consider—ordinary obstacles in the lives of artists—and still manage to become a writer, the pressures on women being in all societies so much greater than those on men.

Instead she created a male hero, endowing him with dreams and doubts similar to those she had experienced as a young writer, but substituting others for constrictions particular to her sex and class. It was legitimate for a male to feel impelled to create literature of the beauty and weight of Coleridge's *Kubla Khan* (the poem that first really inspires Vance); whereas the young Edith Wharton, speaking of her need to write and to live differently from others of her class, could only say "I could not breathe." Still, it is one thing to place one's own desires in the heart of a character of the opposite sex, and another to create the man. Perhaps Wharton modelled Vance on young male authors of her acquaintance—by the time she wrote this novel, she knew a great many, among them Scott Fitzgerald and Sinclair Lewis. And perhaps she modelled him partly on young male writers in fiction.

In any case, she seems unthinkingly to have accepted arrogance and selfishness as characteristics of such a figure, and bestowed them upon her "young genius" (although whether he is indeed a genius is unclear in this novel). This is not matter for wonder: male authors, past and present, have endowed their young artists with such qualities, and to this day real people willingly tolerate arrogance and egotism in "superior" men. But, unfortunately for her novel, fortunately for us, Edith Wharton's honest eye forced her to see and to include description of such behaviour. She does not lavish attention on the effects of Vance's behaviour; she merely points it out. She makes no comment about Vance's failure to answer a loving letter from the grandmother who adores him and has offered to help him; or when he ignores signals from his martyred wife, Laura Lou, that she is extremely sick; or on the frequent occasions when he considers her needs and desires, feels guilty about his failure to meet them, but dismisses them from his mind as intrinsically less important than the demands of his work. No explanation is provided when Vance is offered an opportunity to be rid of the wife he finds a burden, in a way that would in fact benefit her, but rejects it because of his own emotional need. No judgement is made on him when he subsequently fails to take responsibility for that need and that decision. No comment is necessary; the narrator has simply told us what Vance does—we make our own judgements, provide our own understanding. But we must realise that even the mere statements that these things occur do not appear in similar novels by men.

Henry James suggested that artistic works which were flawed were more interesting than those which were perfect, that one could learn from and discuss, analyse, flawed works in a way perfection does not allow. Perfection demands silence. I'm not sure any human product can be called perfect, or that perfection demands silence. But I do agree that flawed works offer wonderful grounds for discussion. *Hudson River Bracketed* is a fascinating example of an author working unconsciously against herself: consciously portraying a hero who is admirable and *sympathique*, while unconsciously subverting the portrait by showing the cruelty of arrogance and irresponsibility. Vance Weston can be an admirable hero only to readers who, like the character himself, overlook as unimportant his treatment of people he considers inferior to himself.

Those of us who do not consider the profession of artist to be a licence for egotism will read the book as if it were a running commentary on itself. On the one hand we have the artist as a young man; on the other, those unfortunates who love him. On one side are aspiration and ambition, uncertainty and labour; on the other, support and nourishment, recognition of dependency and interconnection. On the one side is the young male hero; on the other, three major female characters: Laura Lou, the simple, passive, dependent woman he marries and is dependent upon, and who resents him for his contempt for her and indifference to her needs, while he resents her for her dependency; Grandma Scrimser, a marvellous character who becomes famous as an evangelist in her older years, and who offers the fruits of her triumph to a grandson who has contempt for her work if not for her; and the most complex, Halo Spear, later Tarrant, who is Vance's early mentor and who remains the nourisher of his intellectual life. None of these characters is idealised or sentimentalised; all are seen as they impinge upon Vance. But the feelings of all of the women are expendable to him in his single-minded pursuit of making art. Indeed, all relations are expendable to him. In a manner reminiscent of novels by male authors, Vance leaves behind him, dismisses, disconnects himself from all communities, of family, in-laws, friends, and acquaintances. His eventual isolation is not a subject of narrational commentary—it is seen as natural, inevitable, as it is in many novels, but rarely in life.

The background of the novel, however, is important. The book was written in the last years of the twenties, a time when artistic Americans were still abandoning their homeland for a more supportive cultural climate in Europe, and the United States was still felt by many writers to offer a harsh, philistine environment concerned only with money and status. Wharton's descriptions of the American scene are based on such a perception of it, but because she had spent little time in the States in the previous decade, and had little knowledge of the Middle West, they lack the detail that informs the work of Ellen Glasgow, Willa Cather, or Sinclair Lewis. What Wharton's descriptions of the American scene offer, however, is humour.

The title of the novel, *Hudson River Bracketed*, refers to a style of architecture popular in the nineteenth century in New York State, along the Hudson River. In an 1842 book on landscape gardening, A. J. Downing described this style and distinguished it from other major architectural styles—Grecian, Chinese, Gothic, and Tuscan. There is, thus, an irony in the title, for Hudson River

Bracketed is not an enduring style, nor has it the classical beauty of the styles with which Downing compared it.

The culture Wharton describes in America is as quirky and oddly ornamented as Hudson River Bracketed; and as transient. Vance's real name is Advance; he was named for the town where he was born and where his father made a fortune in real estate. His family, and the entire society in which he grows, are devoted to progress, to what is new, and to making money, "getting ahead". Life is seen as an infinite track in which people get richer and richer and acquire more and more modern devices, like gramophones. The character of that society is suggested by the names of the towns where the Westons have lived—Pruneville, Nebraska; Hallelujah, Missouri; Advance; and Euphoria, Illinois, where the family finally settles and where Vance goes to college. Wharton depicts the American Middle West as rootless, foolishly and shallowly religious, valuing novelty for its own sake, and entertaining a spurious sense of superiority. (There are contemptuous references to "Poles and Dagoes", for instance.) It is a culture without any sense of history or value for continuity. Inevitably there is no respect or knowledge for the culture of the past, for art, literature, or music; and Vance manages to finish college at nineteen without knowing more of Coleridge than *The Rime of the Ancient Mariner*.

In an effort to reach New York, where he intends to try to become a journalist, Vance stays for a time with some family friends at Paul's Landing, a small town along the Hudson. Here he discovers The Willows, the first fine *old* house he has ever seen, and which is built in the Hudson River Bracketed style. The Willows has a library, as well as fine old furniture and paintings, and it is empty. The library becomes his schoolroom for a time, under the tutelage of Heloise (Halo) Spear, daughter of an old prestigious but impoverished New York family.

In time, Vance goes to Manhattan itself, and is welcomed by the New York literary establishment of his day. This establishment is no less sharply satirised than the Middle West. Wharton describes an important literary prize called the Pulsifer, and its bestowal according to the whims of an elegant, lecherous widow. Using disguised names, and titles like *Voodoo, Price of Meat*, and *Egg Omelette* she mocks the work of her contemporaries. (The last title refers to Joyce's *Ulysses*.) The element she most selects for reproach is lack of a sense of the past, a craving for novelty for its own sake. This longing for the new still to some degree characterises American cultural institutions, and may even be said to have come to dominate them. Wharton saw it long ago, and however mistaken we may now find her opinion of Joyce, she was seeing something true about the American scene. She believed in continuity, in culture as an organic unity, rooted in earth and the needs of the body, in the human past as well as in the present.

So, Wharton never forgets or slights Vance's financial difficulties, even though she had never experienced any such thing; and the pressure they place upon him to do shoddy work, or give up writing entirely. The body must be fed, and artists cannot do their best work if they are starving romantically in a garret. She never forgets the needs of the heart, the craving all people— whatever their sex—feel for intimacy, shared life, and a community of equals. She is also eloquent on the loneliness inherent in writing, and the writer's longing to share her/his perceptions with a loved other, and the despair that arises when no such communication is possible. But neither does she forget the needs of the imagination, the psyche, or whatever we may call the part of the self from which art emerges, and she sprinkles descriptions of the creative process itself throughout the book:

> Just outside the cottage window an apple branch crossed the pane. For a long time Vance had sat there, seeing neither it nor anything else, in the kind of bodily and spiritual blindness lately frequent with him; and now suddenly, in the teeming autumn sunlight, there the branch was, the centre of his vision.
>
> It was a warped unsightly branch on a neglected tree, but so charged with life, so glittering with fruit, that it looked like a

dead stick set with rubies. The sky behind was of the densest autumnal blue, a solid fact of a sky. Against it the shrunken rusty leaves lay like gilt bronze, each fruit carved in some hard rare substance . . .

Whatever happened to Vance on the plane of practical living, in the muddled world where bills must be paid, food provided, sick or helpless people looked after, there still came to him this mute swinging wide of the secret doors. He never knew when or how it would happen: it sometimes seemed that he was no more than the latch which an unseen hand raised to throw open the gates of Heaven . . .

And here he was, inside! No mere latch, after all, but the very king for whom the gates had been lifted up . . . It was utterly improbable, inexplicable, yet the deepest part of him always took it for granted, and troubled no more over the how and why than a child let loose in an unknown garden. In truth it was the only human experience that was perfectly intelligible to him, though he was so powerless to account for it . . .

As usual with him now, the sudden seeing of the apple branch coincided with the intensely detailed inner vision of a new book. In the early days that flash of mysterious light used to blot out everything else; but with the growing mastery of his craft he noticed, on the contrary, that when the gates swung open the illumination fell on his daily foreground as well as on the heavenly distances. Mental confusion ceased for him from the moment when the inner lucidity declared itself, and this sense of developing power gave him a feeling of security, of an inviolable calm in the heart of turmoil . . .

I find moving this image of art as a vivid living fruit born out of ruin and decay, the apple of knowledge that blooms and gives life beauty when life itself seems dead; and it is appropriate for Vance at this moment when his life lies in ruin in his hands. There is, then, much of interest in this novel, not least the nature of its sometimes cruel hero. It is clear that Wharton intended Vance to be the insensitive, thoughtless man he is, that, like male authors, she found such egotism essential to the development of an artist. The novel is a true portrait of a certain kind of man, truer than most such portraits because it includes mention of how he treated others, and suggests the effects of his behaviour upon them. And perhaps Vance's long stretches of failure as a writer constitute a comment on his blindness about human nature, including his own.

Beyond that, there is fun in the satire; vividness in the characters—especially the Scrimsers, Grandma the evangelist and Grandpa the lecher; the brilliant Halo and her husband, Lewis Tarrant, a cultivated but pampered dilettante; George Frenside, the intelligent, perceptive writer who could not succeed in America; and most important, Laura Lou, the ignorant, simple girl who loves Vance but cannot exist in his world, who tries to subordinate herself totally and cannot quite manage it, but destroys herself in the process. There is a host of wonderfully drawn lesser characters—the upwardly mobile Bunty Hayes, who would be at home in *The Custom of the Country*; Lorry Spear, Halo's brother, a cadger in evening dress; the Spear parents, faded sophisticates and political idealists whose real values are comfort and leisure, and who are willing to ''sell'' their daughter to obtain them. There is also a special fascination in the passages on creative process, because they must reflect Wharton's own experience. We may hope that before too long, the sequel to *Hudson River Bracketed*, *The Gods Arrive*, will also be reprinted.

Marilyn French, New York, 1985

VIRAGO MODERN CLASSICS
&
CLASSIC NON-FICTION

The first Virago Modern Classic, *Frost in May* by Antonia White, was published in 1978. It launched a list dedicated to the celebration of women writers and to the rediscovery and reprinting of their works. Its aim was, and is, to demonstrate the existence of a female tradition in fiction, and to broaden the sometimes narrow definition of a 'classic' which has often led to the neglect of interesting novels and short stories. Published with new introductions by some of today's best writers, the books are chosen for many reasons: they may be great works of fiction; they may be wonderful period pieces; they may reveal particular aspects of women's lives; they may be classics of comedy or storytelling.

The companion series, Virago Classic Non-Fiction, includes diaries, letters, literary criticism, and biographies – often by and about authors published in the Virago Modern Classics series.

'Good news for everyone writing and reading today' – *Hilary Mantel*

'A continuingly magnificent imprint' – *Joanna Trollope*

'The Virago Modern Classics have reshaped literary history and enriched the reading of us all. No library is complete without them' – *Margaret Drabble*

VIRAGO MODERN CLASSICS
&
CLASSIC NON-FICTION

Some of the authors included in these two series –

Elizabeth von Arnim, Dorothy Baker, Pat Barker, Nina Bawden,
Nicola Beauman, Sybille Bedford, Jane Bowles, Kay Boyle,
Vera Brittain, Leonora Carrington, Angela Carter, Willa Cather,
Colette, Ivy Compton-Burnett, E.M. Delafield, Maureen Duffy,
Elaine Dundy, Nell Dunn, Emily Eden, George Egerton,
George Eliot, Miles Franklin, Mrs Gaskell,
Charlotte Perkins Gilman, George Gissing,
Victoria Glendinning, Radclyffe Hall, Shirley Hazzard,
Dorothy Hewett, Mary Hocking, Alice Hoffman,
Winifred Holtby, Janette Turner Hospital, Zora Neale Hurston,
Elizabeth Jenkins, F. Tennyson Jesse, Molly Keane,
Margaret Laurence, Maura Laverty, Rosamond Lehmann,
Rose Macaulay, Shena Mackay, Olivia Manning, Paule Marshall,
F.M. Mayor, Anaïs Nin, Kate O'Brien, Olivia, Grace Paley,
Mollie Panter-Downes, Dawn Powell, Dorothy Richardson,
E. Arnot Robertson, Jacqueline Rose, Vita Sackville-West,
Elaine Showalter, May Sinclair, Agnes Smedley, Dodie Smith,
Stevie Smith, Nancy Spain, Christina Stead, Carolyn Steedman,
Gertrude Stein, Jan Struther, Han Suyin, Elizabeth Taylor,
Sylvia Townsend Warner, Mary Webb, Eudora Welty,
Mae West, Rebecca West, Edith Wharton, Antonia White,
Christa Wolf, Virginia Woolf, E.H. Young.

Also by Edith Wharton

THE GODS ARRIVE

Afterword by Marilyn French

'The most accomplished novelist of her generation'
– Raymond Mortimer

Halo Tarrant sets sail for Europe with the young writer Vance Weston 'like someone stepping into hot sunlight from a darkened room'. They are leaving behind the literary life of New York so brilliantly evoked in *Hudson River Bracketed*, to which this novel is a companion volume. Temperamental Vance thinks of Halo as his mentor and guide, but the pressures of their relationship and of his literary ambitions drive him into a restless search for stimulus from which Halo is increasingly excluded. First published in 1932, this is a convincing account of a writer's struggle to be true to his vision and of the strain on two lovers, dependent yet determined on a lofty ideal of individual freedom.

MADAME DE TREYMES

New Introduction by Janet Beer Goodwyn

'[Her novels] ensure her a place amongst the greatest of writers in English in the twentieth century' – *Observer*

Is Madame de Treymes friend or foe to the Marquis de Malrive and the upright American who loves her? In 'The Touchstone', is impecunious Glennard justified in selling the private letters of a famous writer to fund his own happiness? Has Kate's son inherited his father's moral blindness, and can Kate protect him? And is sisterly self-sacrifice the right choice for Ann Eliza? Secrets, temptations and profound moral choices pervade each of these four superb novellas. Edith Wharton demonstrates her astonishing range, from Parisian high society in the title story to the drabbest poverty in downtown New York, in this volume – the only edition in print.

Books by post

Virago Books are available through mail order or from your local bookshop. Other books which might be of interest include:–

☐ The Age of Innocence	Edith Wharton	£5.99
☐ Custom of the Country	Edith Wharton	£6.99
☐ Ghost Stories	Edith Wharton	£6.99
☐ The Glimpses of the Moon	Edith Wharton	£6.99
☐ The Gods Arrive	Edith Wharton	£6.99
☐ Madame de Treymes	Edith Wharton	£6.99
☐ The Mother's Recompense	Edith Wharton	£6.99
☐ Old New York	Edith Wharton	£6.99
☐ Twilight Sleep	Edith Wharton	£6.99

Please send Cheque/Eurocheque/Postal Order (sterling only), Access, Visa or Mastercard:

☐☐☐☐☐☐☐☐☐☐☐☐☐☐☐☐

Expiry Date: _____ *Signature:* _____

Please allow 75 pence per book for post and packing in U.K.
Overseas customers please allow £1.00 per copy for post and packing.

All orders to:
Virago Press, Book Service by Post, P.O. Box 29, Douglas,
Isle of Man, IM99 1BQ. Tel: 01624 675137. Fax: 01624 670923.

Name: _____

Address: _____

_____

Please allow 20 days for delivery.
Please tick box if you would like to receive a free stock list ☐
Please tick box if you do not wish to receive any additional information ☐

Prices and availability subject to change without notice.